Praise for Tea Cooper

"Refreshing and unique, *The Woman in the Green Dress* sweeps you across the wild lands of Australia in a thrilling whirl of mystery, romance, and danger. This magical tale weaves together two storylines with a heart-pounding finish that is drop-dead gorgeous."

J'NELL CIESIELSKI, AUTHOR OF *THE SOCIALITE*

"Readers of Kate Morton and Beatriz Williams will be dazzled. *The Woman in the Green Dress* spins readers into an evocative world of mystery and romance in this deeply researched book by Tea Cooper. There is a Dickensian flair to Cooper's carefully constructed world of lost inheritances and found treasures as two indomitable women stretched across centuries work to reconcile their pasts while reclaiming love, identity, and belonging against two richly moving historical settings. As soon as you turn the last page you will want to start again just to see how every last thread is sewn in anticipation of its thrilling conclusion. One of the most intelligent, visceral, and vibrant historical reads I have had the privilege of visiting in an age."

RACHEL MCMILLAN, AUTHOR OF *THE LONDON RESTORATION*

"Boast[s] strong female protagonists, an infectious fascination with the past, and the narrative skill to weave multiple timelines into a satisfying whole . . . fast paced and involving storytelling . . . smartly edited, cleanly written . . . easy to devour."

THE SYDNEY MORNING HERALD, AUSTRALIA

"A freshly drawn, bittersweet saga that draws nuggets of 'truth' with timeless magic and might-have-beens."

NORTH & SOUTH MAGAZINE, NEW ZEALAND

"A rich historical fiction novel about the choices we make and the unimaginable consequences that can unravel for us and for those who come after us . . . a gripping historical gem . . . strong and interesting female characters [who] showcase the enduring strength of the female spirit. With its intriguing plot, rich historical detail, and great characters . . . *The Woman in the Green Dress* is a fine read, sure to be devoured by . . . all fans of quality fiction. An utterly engrossing story about Australia's first opal and a mysterious woman in a green dress."

BETTER READING, SYDNEY

"*The Woman in the Green Dress* is a stunning historical fiction showpiece, with some wonderful elements of mystery . . . a prime example of Cooper's prowess in the area of carefully considered historical fiction . . . with a rich and pervading sense of place, accompanying a rich character set."

MRS B'S BOOK REVIEWS, AUSTRALIA

"A mesmerising read . . . just the right amount of adventure, romance, and mystery."

STARTS AT 60, AUSTRALIA

"Australian historical fiction writer, Tea Cooper, has produced another engaging, dual-period novel in the style of *The Naturalist's Daughter.* Cooper's mastery is to produce these seemingly unconnected characters with their own personal challenges and quests, gradually revealing a series of geographical and familial connections that culminate in the solving of a sixty-six-year-old mystery. Cooper weaves historical fact and creative fiction through the two periods with success. Her primary and additional characters are interesting and well developed. The plot of *The Woman in the Green Dress* contains Cooper's signature mix of colonial and indigenous social history, scientific discovery, mystery, and a hint of romance. The colour green appears throughout the novel as a fascinating visual symbol, adding an extra layer of intrigue."

HISTORICAL NOVEL SOCIETY AUSTRALASIA

"I was captivated by not only the strength and determination of the two women, but also the cast of secondary characters . . . A masterfully crafted tale of mystery and intrigue."

GREAT READS AND TEA LEAVES

"A breathtakingly beautiful novel . . . well written and cleverly structured."

Chapter Ichi

"I'd recommend this to lovers of: Australian history, the voices of unsung women, the natural environment, and those who are curious about the lifestyles of all manner of people from the past."

Jay Hicks

The WOMAN *in the* GREEN DRESS

Also by Tea Cooper

The Horse Thief
The Cedar Cutter
The Currency Lass
The Naturalist's Daughter
Matilda's Freedom
Lily's Leap
Forgotten Fragrance

The WOMAN *in the* GREEN DRESS

TEA COOPER

THOMAS NELSON
Since 1798

The Woman in the Green Dress

Original edition of this book published in Australia in 2019 by Tea Cooper

Published in Nashville, Tennessee, by Thomas Nelson. Thomas Nelson is a registered trademark of HarperCollins Christian Publishing, Inc.

Interior design by Phoebe Wetherbee

Thomas Nelson titles may be purchased in bulk for educational, business, fund-raising, or sales promotional use. For information, please email SpecialMarkets@ThomasNelson.com.

Publisher's Note: This novel is a work of fiction. Names, characters, places, and incidents are either products of the author's imagination or used fictitiously. All characters are fictional, and any similarity to people living or dead is purely coincidental.

ISBN 978-0-7852-3516-3 (e-book)
ISBN 978-0-7852-3518-7 (audio download)

Library of Congress Cataloging-in-Publication Data

Names: Cooper, Tea, author.
Title: The woman in the green dress / Tea Cooper.
Description: Nashville, Tennessee : Thomas Nelson, [2020] | Originally published in Australia. | Summary: "A mystery surrounding an opal and a green dress links two women-one in the mid-1800s and the other at the close of World War I"-- Provided by publisher.
Identifiers: LCCN 2019055344 (print) | LCCN 2019055345 (ebook) | ISBN 9780785235125 (trade paperback) | ISBN 9780785235163 (epub) | ISBN 9780785235187 (audio download)
Classification: LCC PR9619.4.C659 W66 2020 (print) | LCC PR9619.4.C659 (ebook) | DDC 823/.92--dc23
LC record available at https://lccn.loc.gov/2019055344
LC ebook record available at https://lccn.loc.gov/2019055345

Printed in the United States of America

20 21 22 23 24 LSC 5 4 3 2 1

For Cooper and Violet

Chapter 1

London
November 11, 1918

An unexpected morning off. With pay! All because Mrs. Black reckoned the Allied forces had driven back the Huns, the paperwork had finally been signed, and the Armistice was a done deal. The whole idea of this nightmare coming to an end had Fleur Richards's heart pounding fit to bust.

It wasn't until she reached the end of the Strand and walked around the corner that she was finally convinced Mrs. Black knew what she was talking about. Hundreds of thousands of people crowded into Trafalgar Square, though they were strangely quiet.

A huge rumble shook the pavement. The sound of cannons being fired, followed by a blinding flash of light, filled the air. Smoke billowed into the air.

In the stillness of the moment she fancied Hugh stood beside her.

The sky is higher in Australia. Truly?

The stars are brighter and the sun always shines.

I don't believe you.

You will. Not long now. I promise.

A flurry of bugles sounded the all clear, drowning out his voice in her head, and the streets erupted. The whole of London must have dropped their tools. Everyone was hugging each other, cheering wildly, throwing their hats in the air, a swirling whirlpool of happiness;

strangers with tears streaming down their faces, embracing one another, and the bells, bells that hadn't rung for four years, pealing like it was Christmas, Easter, and the King's birthday all rolled into one.

Not long now, my love. Not long now. We're going home.

Without thinking she threw her arms around the nearest person. He picked her up, twirled her around, and deposited her back on the pavement with a thump. Before she could move, the tall, lanky soldier grabbed her hand and towed her toward one of the packed buses circling the square.

If she closed her eyes she could almost imagine it was Hugh's hand she held.

She hadn't known love could be like that. One look at each other and it was as though their souls had merged. The image of his face always before her eyes and his voice drowning out her fears.

I'll be back before you know it!

Hands reached out and grabbed her. Her feet took on a life of their own, and she was hauled aboard the bus, dizzy with excitement, her head swimming.

A number 13. Her dad's bus.

"Oi! Fleur. Hold tight." The clippie handed her a ticket, bringing her back to reality. "Your dad can't be here, nor your mum neither, but you are. I'll bet me boots they'll be watching and cheering up there, waving the old flag."

Blowing the clippie a kiss she swung up the steps, squeezing past the people hanging on by their fingernails, and eased onto the platform. The soldier threw her a cheeky salute and blended into the crowd.

Fleur studied the crowd of smiling passengers. "Is it really over?"

A young boy, hardly old enough to shave, never mind wear his tattered uniform, grinned at her. "Armistice was signed at five this morning. 'Ostilities to cease on all fronts at 11:00 a.m. on the knocker. That's what they said."

Mrs. Black was right!

The driver—she couldn't remember his name, but she'd met him at Mum and Dad's memorial—patted the small space on the edge of the seat. "Sit yourself down. We're off to see the King." The bus slewed to one side, throwing her against his broad shoulders as they turned into the Strand. "Never thought we'd see the day."

She'd had serious doubts herself, but thankfully she'd been proven wrong. "I'm meant to be going to work this afternoon."

"Nah, you're not. No work today. Not for you. Not for anyone."

She didn't mind work. It gave her a sense of purpose, and at least she didn't have to worry about a decent meal and queueing for hours for a pound of tea and some canned meat. Her feet might ache at the end of the day, but her stomach didn't rumble.

The man heaved himself to his feet. "Ladies and gents. This 'ere young lady's worried about missing work. Do we think she should go?"

A resounding roar filled the bus and she was snatched from her seat and swirled around, landing on the lap of an American with big white teeth and a smile to match. "No work for you today, doll. And I'll be taking on anyone who tries to tell you otherwise." That was something she'd like to see. This man might be all big and brash, but Mrs. Black would make mincemeat of him, then slap him between two pieces of pastry.

The bus lurched around the corner and trundled off, but didn't get far. A procession of cheering civilians and fighting men all decked out with flags filled the Mall, bent on reaching the gates of Buckingham Palace, every one of them shouting, "We want the King! We want the King!"

The American grabbed her hand. "Come on! We're not missing this."

They jumped off the bus and joined the throng, pushing forward as though their lives depended on it.

They didn't have to wait long.

A thunderous cheer echoed and the King, all dressed up in a posh uniform with enough gold braid to rival the crown jewels, appeared on the palace balcony.

The Yank's eyes glowed in awe. "Is that the Queen next to him?"

"She's the one in the dreadful hat, and that's her daughter, Princess Mary. I'm not sure who . . ." Fleur clamped her mouth closed, realizing an all-encompassing hush had descended on the crowd. So quiet even the Queen up on the balcony could have heard her.

The King stepped forward and Fleur craned to hear his words. "With you I rejoice and thank God for the victories which the Allied arms have won, bringing hostilities to an end and peace within sight."

And that was all. The Queen waved a Union Jack and a massive roar rocked the air, the force of it shaking the ground.

Somewhere behind her a band struck up and she found herself yelling—not singing, no one could call it singing—"God Save the King," "Tipperary," "The Old Hundredth." With her heart fit to burst, she sucked in enough air to join in "Auld Lang Syne."

Then the King waved his hat to the crowd and trooped off with all the other overdressed dignitaries.

Four years, fourteen weeks, and two days of hell. And it was over. Just like that.

Not long now, my love!

Several hours later Fleur floated home dizzy with delight, with bubbles of happiness fighting for space in her chest.

I'll take you home. As soon as it's over, I'll take you home.

She was going to Australia, with Hugh. Soon, so soon.

By the time she'd reached Kings Cross, rain had seeped under her collar and trickled down the back of her blouse, but nothing could dampen her euphoria. Not even the familiar stench of stale sweat and old cabbage that greeted her when she threw open the front door. She could cope with anything. All she had to do was wait for Hugh.

She tripped up the stairs, slipped her key into the lock, and went straight across the room to fling open the window.

So much had changed since she'd stood on Waterloo station waving a soggy handkerchief, watching the train pull out taking Hugh away and leaving her with nothing but dreams and a carefully folded marriage certificate in her pocket, convinced she'd never see an end to the war. Now hundreds of bonfires had consumed the blackout and the acrid smell of the fireworks dispersed more than the stench of her room. Her fear, too, was gone.

A group of crazy Tommies called up a greeting as they staggered down the street brandishing trophies and souvenirs from different uniforms. Hugh always looked so smart. Slouch hat, turned up at the side; puttees and belt always worn. Not like these disheveled revelers bundling their friends into flag-strewn motor cars. She grinned down at them and waved as they disappeared into the clamoring crowd amidst a flurry of bunting and shaking rattles.

There was no need to waste her money on lighting tonight; the glow from the streets and the joy in her heart could illuminate the whole of London. The bloody slog was over.

With a delicious yawn, she collapsed onto the bed and pulled off her shoes, wriggling her toes in relief, tasting the remnants of brandy from the hip flask the American had kept pressing on her.

Rummaging in her pocket for sixpence for the gas, she came up blank. There had to be one somewhere. She reefed open the drawer of her bedside table and shot the contents all over the floor.

Bending down, she scooped up the odds and ends and frowned at the white envelope staring up at her.

Ministry of Information was printed in the top left-hand corner and slap bang in the middle *Mrs. Hugh Richards*.

There must be a mistake. She didn't use her married name, hadn't told more than a handful of people about her marriage. The letter must have been meant for someone else, another Mrs. Hugh Richards.

It couldn't be bad news. Bad news came in a telegram.

"Fleur. Fleur. Are you there?"

No, she wasn't. At least she didn't feel as though she was. The door inched open. She slid to her knees, started to edge beneath the bed, overtaken by some childish craving to become invisible. "Oh, Fleur. I'm sorry. I'd hoped to catch you before you came upstairs."

Fleur forced down the overwhelming need to hide and eyed her landlady with suspicion. What was she doing here? What did she want? The rent was paid.

"You found the letter?"

Oh no! So it wasn't her imagination. She bent over and picked up the envelope.

"You're going to have to open it, you know." Mrs. Tenney took two steps into the room.

Fleur cradled the envelope against her chest. "There's been a mistake."

"No, dearie, I don't think so."

Why was the battle-ax calling her dearie? She'd never heard any form of endearment slip out from between her nasty, narrow lips.

"You're going to have to open it. Here, let me." The woman stretched out her hand and tugged at the envelope.

Fleur grasped it tight in her fingers and sank down onto the bed.

"Come on, dearie. Best to know." The interfering busybody eased down beside her.

Fleur jumped to her feet. "Go away. Leave me alone."

"I was only trying to be helpful. Have it your own way." Huffing and puffing, the woman stomped off, shutting the door with an irritated clunk.

It couldn't have anything to do with Hugh. It said *Ministry of Information*. He was a soldier, just an ordinary Australian soldier, a tunneler. And if anything had happened to him she would learn of it from a telegram.

She shot the bolt on the door. No audience, no snooping onlookers, no meddlesome landlady. Just her and an envelope.

The words *The war is over* shrieked through her head like the six o'clock steam train out of Waterloo station, all noise and belching clouds of smoke. She'd trailed down there often enough, stood in the shadows watching, waiting, hoping Hugh would step onto the platform, his face creased with the lopsided smile he saved for her and his blue eyes sparkling, and now there was this. A nasty envelope with her name—his name—smudged on the front. A name she'd barely become used to wearing. A surname she didn't deserve to have. It belonged to his mother, his sister, someone whose arms had held him far more often than hers had.

The typewriter's *s* key had blurred from overuse: all the wives and mothers who'd received frightful news. News she wasn't going to receive.

The folded paper crackled as it fluttered in her fingers. She glanced down at the precise writing:

Dear Mrs. Richards,

I have information regarding your husband, Corporal Hugh Richards.

What did that mean? Perhaps he was coming home; maybe he'd been injured. Was he missing in action? She forced her eyes back down to the paper.

I would appreciate it if you could call at Wellington House, Buckingham Gate, at ten on the morning of Tuesday 12th.

Yours most sincerely,

Archer Waterstone

What was going on?

Hugh couldn't be dead. She would have received a telegram, not a handwritten letter on expensive writing paper. Besides, she'd have known if he was dead, felt it in the special part of her heart reserved for Hugh and Hugh alone.

We've got our whole future ahead of us.

She twisted the thin silver band on her finger.

No one's going to take me away. Not now that I've found you.

He made her heart sing, and now she doubted she could even manage a half-hearted whistle, never mind a sob. She was cold, so very cold.

"Fleur? Open the door. Fleur! I've got a cup of tea for you." Was it too much to ask for a few minutes' peace? The doorknob rattled.

"Fleur, I know you're in there. Is it bad news?" It wasn't a telegram. It wasn't bad news.

"I'll leave the tea outside." Footsteps retreated and then silence, blissful silence.

Shivering, Fleur teetered to the door and slid the lock. What she wouldn't give for a bath. Hugh said that in Australia they had the bathrooms out the back and in summer they would take a bath under the stars.

No need to worry about anyone watching, not when you've got acres and acres to call your own.

She'd go mad if she didn't pull herself together. She picked up the tray and kicked the door shut behind her.

Wearing Mum's trousers under her dressing gown and Dad's old cardigan over the top, she curled up in the chair.

Why hadn't she heard from Hugh? She'd longed for letters. *Billet-doux* he called them. Billet-don't, more like. He'd written a few, then they'd dried up quick enough to make her wonder if he'd changed his mind, regretted their madcap race to the registry office.

She eyed the expansive handwriting sprawling across the immaculate envelope. Those words had to have been written by someone with elegant hands, like Hugh's. Long fingers and pale nails—a pianist's hands.

Concentrate. She had to concentrate. Buckingham Gate! Ten o'clock.

How could she be there then? It was halfway through her shift. Right at the busiest part of the morning. No chance. Not after today. Mrs. Black would have a fit. Didn't the man understand women had responsibilities? And she certainly couldn't do without her job. Not if . . . A groan slipped between her lips and she swallowed it down with a mouthful of tea, choking in the process.

She couldn't miss work. Couldn't ask for any time off. Not after she'd missed today. She was tired, so tired. Her eyes kept closing of their own accord. She'd write a note, get Mrs. Black's boy to deliver it when she started her shift. That was the answer. Tell Mr. Archer Waterstone she'd make it another time.

She slipped underneath the blankets and curled into a tight ball, hugging her memories close, waiting for the dream to come, the same dream she'd had every night since the first zeppelin raid, the ominous shadow dampening the gray morning light. She groaned and covered her ears, knowing the whine of the bombs would come next. Then the sudden silence as the world held its breath to see what devastation the bloody Huns had wrought, waiting to see whose turn it was to die.

Strangely, she couldn't see Dad's hands clutched, knuckles white on the steering wheel as though, even in death, it was his responsibility to drive his passengers away from danger. No clouds of smoke, no wreckage full of screaming, twisted agony. Instead she dreamed of Hugh.

She lifted her eyes, past the dome of St. Paul's to the hill where St. Martin's stood, and he was there, bathed in sunlight on a patch of grass, holding out his hand, and she ran, ran through the tattered streets, sliding on the rain-soaked cobbles, and she reached out to him . . .

He'd filled her head and her heart with dreams and promises of clear skies and pure white birds.

Doves?

No, cockatoos with crests as golden as the midday sun.

Chapter 2

SYDNEY, NEW SOUTH WALES
1853

After 265 days aboard ship Stefan von Richter stepped off the gangplank and onto Australian soil, leaving behind the misery that had haunted him since he'd fled Vienna.

Chickens clucked underfoot, and pigs snuffled through the refuse where vendors stood and shouted their wares. A ripe stench caught in the back of his throat, making his eyes water and his lungs snatch.

A series of dilapidated sandstone steps led away from the gin dives and warehouses fringing the quay, but with his large traveling trunk, botanizing box, and specimen case, he'd need the services of a barrow boy.

An assortment of folk dressed in drab and tattered garments milled between overfilled carts, carriages, horse dung, and noise. A mangy tortoiseshell cat and a three-legged dog rummaged in blood-soaked dirt beneath a butcher's stall. And beyond, a skinny, freckle-faced urchin balanced on one leg, clinging to a lamppost, eyeing him with dubious curiosity. Shading his eyes from the midday sun, Stefan raised his hand, and before he'd even framed the words the lad sidled up to him.

"Need some help wiv that lot, Guv?" The lad inclined his head toward Stefan's luggage. "Where you headin'?" The boy's face looked as if it hadn't been washed in weeks, and a line of gray dirt traced the back of his neck. Nevertheless, his eyes shone bright, reminding Stefan of someone he'd long forgotten.

"The Berkeley Hotel, Bent Street."

"Opposite the public fountain."

Stefan glanced down at the crumpled notes in his hand. "Quite right."

"Be back in a tick. Gotta get me barrow. Good job I spotted you."

"A bit of extra height gives a man an advantage."

Avoiding a goat tethered to a lopsided cart, the lad darted away over a series of festering rubbish heaps with the speed of one of the famed marsupial rats and vanished into the seething mass of humanity.

Within moments a tattered barrow nudged against his thigh and in a flash the boy had Stefan's belongings neatly stacked. "Can't take this lot up the steps. Doubt you'd make it either with that limp. We'll 'ave to go round the back of the warehouses and cut across in front of the fort. Stick wiv me and you won't get those boots wet." He set off at a gallop without waiting for an answer.

Fifteen minutes later Stefan stood outside an impressive three-story sandstone hotel inhaling his first dose of fresh air since the ship docked. If his walk from the quay was anything to go by, the Berkeley Hotel must be one of the finest buildings in the colony. He pushed open the door and made his way to the desk. He didn't miss the flicker of recognition when the clerk's eyes lit on his uniform.

"Captain, may I say how happy we are to see you gracing our humble establishment. I cherish my memories of the baron's visit."

Stefan brought himself to his full height and clicked his heels. When the barrow boy's face broke into a wide grin, he realized his mistake; he was in Australia, not rubbing shoulders with a bunch of aging European diplomats. He removed his shako and ran his fingers through his damp hair. "I take it you received my instructions, Herr Sladdin?"

The clerk interlaced his long white fingers and bowed his head. "Indeed, indeed, and we have set aside the baron's suite."

"Gut."

"And should you be interested, our gaming tables are in operation tonight if you have a mind to try your hand."

"Not tonight. I have an invitation." In fact, he had a raft of them and letters of introduction that would have to be attended to before he could settle the matter closest to his heart.

"And you will be traveling, as the baron did?"

"I will. I have been assigned the privilege of transcribing his *New Holland Journal* and preparing his notebooks for publication." As a sop to compensate for the musket ball in his leg that rendered him less than useless.

Sladdin gave an obsequious bow and dangled a long shanked key between his thumb and forefinger. "May I escort you to your rooms?"

Scrawny but determined, the lad elbowed his way between them and, with a flash of cheek in his coal-black eyes, stood on tiptoes and grabbed the key.

"Watch it." Sladdin shot him a look that would have curdled cream and darted around the desk, pushing the lad aside. "I'll see to it." He bent to lift one end of the collector chest, and it landed with a resounding crash, just missing his toes.

With a grin of triumph, which lasted only until Sladdin landed a well-aimed boot on his backside, the boy hefted the chest onto his shoulder and went scuttling up the stairs.

"Follow me, Captain. The baron's suite, on the second floor, has a delightful view. I trust it will be to your liking."

As long as it was clean it would do, although Stefan was certain the harbor miasma would taint the air if the wind was blowing from the northeast.

Once they reached the top of the stairs, Sladdin slithered around the boy and threw open the door with a theatrical flourish. He crossed the room and drew back the heavy velvet curtains, letting the light stream in. "Through here we have the bedchamber." A connecting door revealed a well-sprung bed with snowy linen.

"Gut. Danke schön."

"I can arrange accommodation for your manservant on the third floor . . ."

"I am traveling alone."

"Don't leave the trunks unattended, boy. Bring them here." The chest clattered onto the floor at the end of the bed and the lad skittered out of the room. "Would you like me to arrange a reputable manservant?"

"I have no need of one. What you can do, however, is have hot water sent up along with some black coffee, and make some inquiries for me regarding a decent mount and a packhorse. I intend to travel to Wisemans Ferry and explore the Hawkesbury district. I hope to see something of your remarkable flora and fauna."

"Will the baron be joining you?"

"Sadly, no. He now holds a diplomatic position at the court of Tuscany."

"Delightful. I could perhaps be of some service to you." Like a magician Sladdin produced a flyer from his inside pocket and dropped it onto the table. "May I suggest the Curio Shop in Hunter Street?"

The man's oily subservience made his flesh creep. "Would you excuse me? It took an eternity to disembark and I am late for an engagement." Stefan pointedly held the door wide, and Sladdin bowed and scraped his way out. Before Stefan had the opportunity to turn, the urchin reappeared bent double, lugging his trunk.

"Where'd you want this?"

"Under the window will do just fine." Stefan rummaged in his pocket and pulled out a coin and flicked it high in the air. It disappeared into the lad's pocket before it had finished spinning.

"Anyfing else, Capt'n?"

"That'll be all for the time being. I might have something for you tomorrow. Where will I find you?"

"Just ask him downstairs." He made a fine imitation of Sladdin's wringing hands and winked. "Hang around the public fountain most days—tips are good. Lotsa gents use this place."

"Off you go then." A guttersnipe this boy might be, but he had a brain by the sound of it. There was something about the lad that made Stefan smile.

As he was about to toss out the flyer Sladdin had left on the table, the headline caught his eye.

Visitors to Sydney should not leave without calling upon the Curio Shop of Wonders at 84 Hunter Street.

What in heaven's name was the clerk up to? He smoothed out the paper and moved to the window where the light was better.

Skins of native birds, beasts, and reptiles well-preserved and ready for setting up. Fur and feather rugs made up or made to order. Entomological specimens and requisites, carved emu eggs, and other beautiful souvenirs. All kinds of taxidermical work executed in the finest style.

Fascinating. Truly fascinating. He very much wanted to see these strange animals in their natural habitat, and enhancing the baron's journal with a display of taxidermied specimens when it was published would appeal to the population of Vienna who continued to be besotted by all matters New Holland.

He folded the flyer and tucked it into his uniform pocket. There would be plenty of time the next day to take a walk around town; meanwhile, he had several weeks of shipboard grime to dispense with and a ball to attend.

By the time Stefan had availed himself of the hot water and changed into his dress uniform, the sun had dipped below the buildings. Having locked the door behind him, he made his way to the ground floor. Sladdin was nowhere to be seen and there was not a carriage in sight.

True to his word, however, the young lad lurked near the fountain, picking at the patchwork of scabs on his knees. He shot to his feet. "Do anything for you, Captain von Richter?"

The use of his name took him by surprise; Sladdin had simply addressed him by rank. He raised an eyebrow.

"Gotta know who you're dealing wiv."

He'd discerned the intelligence in the lad's eyes right enough, even though the boy reeked of stale fish and a few other odors Stefan would rather not dwell on. "And who am I dealing with?"

"Albert Peregrine Burless, at your service." He executed a bow that would have stood him in good stead in Prince Metternich's circles and clicked his bare, blistered heels together.

"Very well, Herr Burless. Make sure you are available tomorrow morning."

"Bert'll do, Captain. Can't 'ave people finkin' I got ideas above me station."

Until he had a decent bath and found a pair of boots, that was highly unlikely to happen. Still, Stefan couldn't fault him for trying.

"*Guten Abend*, Bert." Stefan turned, searching for a carriage. If he didn't get a move on he'd be making a spectacle of himself arriving late at Government House.

"If you cut through the park you'll get to the governor's quick smart."

How did Bert know where he was heading? "What makes you think . . ."

"The scrambled egg gives it away." He gestured to Stefan's epaulettes and the surplus of braid adorning his redundant uniform. "Lights have been blazing for hours and there's a stream of carriages. Better off on foot."

Stefan struck out down the street in Bert's wake where, unless he was very much mistaken, there was a distinct improvement in the night air, nowhere near as odorous as down near the docks. His lips twitched at the memory of the baron's observation that the Antipodes housed some of the worst smells in the universe.

To their right the fort loomed, a useless cardboard-like edifice more suited to a child's toy box than any real defense. As they rounded the corner, a castellated, turreted gothic edifice appeared. Bert skirted the vehicles crowding the carriageway and surrounding access road.

"What's the escort worth?"

"Nowt." Bert disappeared into the shadows without waiting for another tip, a further point in his favor.

By the time Stefan reached the doorway, the reception line stretched the length of the hallway, but fortunately the governor, Sir Charles FitzRoy, spotted him and waved him to his side. "My pleasure to welcome you to our shores, Captain von Richter."

"The pleasure is entirely mine."

"It must be nigh on twenty years since the baron was here. I trust we will have the opportunity for further conversation."

"I have no doubt of that." He took his leave and made his way into the ballroom where beribboned girls and powdered matrons glided across the floor, eyelashes batting against flushed cheeks like large moths seeking entry to a candlelit soirée. Whatever had possessed him to attend? Weeks aboard ship starved of female company, no doubt. Would he ever learn?

Unable to catch one of the waiters circulating between the variegated lamps and wreath-encircled columns, he crossed to the tall doors standing open onto a terrace framing the view of the gardens. The moon cast a silvery sheen over the plants, giving them a ghostly, almost incandescent glow, and the balmy night air carried a hint of eucalyptus and salt from the harbor.

"Captain." Sir Charles's hand rested on his arm. "I have managed to escape for a few moments. I'd very much like to hear the news." He led Stefan outside and down some steps to a sandstone bench overlooking the harbor.

"Letters and dispatches and six-month-old newspapers leave much to be desired. I believe you were with the prince when the chaos erupted in Vienna."

Stefan had hoped to leave the memories of the March Revolution and Prince Metternich's subsequent escape behind. As chief minister, Prince Metternich bore the brunt of the hostility to the Hapsburg's oppressive rule. Deserted by his friends and unwell, he turned to the baron for assistance. "We escorted him, and the princess, through the mobs in Vienna, then to Holland, and on to England. It took us almost a month to make our way to London. Fortunately no one suffered any lasting injuries." His leg gave a sympathetic twinge and he rubbed at his thigh.

"You are being modest. I am well aware of the part you played. Your wounds have healed satisfactorily?"

"Indeed they have. I have simply acquired a little extra baggage."

"They couldn't remove the musket ball?"

"No. It's left me with a slight limp, nothing more."

"And the prince has now returned to court after his exile and the baron is firmly ensconced in Florence."

Sir Charles appeared to have a very up-to-date knowledge of the circumstances despite his request for news. "As Austrian Envoy Extraordinary, ambassador to the Grand Duchy of Tuscany. And he finally married, so his traveling days are over. I am acting as his amanuensis, charged with the task of reworking his diaries and copious notes of his travels here in Australia and preparing them for publication." He glanced over his shoulder at the sweep of gardens surrounding the residence. The fresh scent of the eucalyptus trees hung in the breeze. "I also have another reason for gracing your shores, a more private matter."

"And you require my assistance?"

He inclined his head. "The baron received a letter from an old acquaintance, a mineralogist by the name of Professor Johann Menge, who found what he believed to be a precious stone."

"In the colony?" Sir Charles groaned. "What sort of precious stone?"

"An opal."

"For goodness' sake. The country is currently in the grips of gold fever, inundated with an increasing stream of fortune hunters. At this precise moment in time I would prefer to keep the matter quiet."

"And so would the baron. Unfortunately, Professor Menge passed away and the stone has yet to be authenticated. He believed it to be the first found in Australia."

Sir Charles shook his head. "Where is this opal?"

"That is where I hope you can help. Before Professor Menge died he sent it to an acquaintance of his, one Thomas Bishop. Perhaps you know of him? I believe he resides in Sydney. I have been asked to collect it."

"Thomas Bishop. Indeed I do, poor man."

His stomach sank. If Sir Charles was going to tell him some misfortune had befallen Bishop, their entire plan would be shot. "Poor man?"

"Such a sad story. His wife died most unexpectedly in a tragic house fire. Only days after my own wife."

"Please accept my condolences."

"I miss her very much." Sir Charles stared out across the water at the rising moon for a few moments before turning back to him. "Mrs. Bishop was a charming woman. Mr. Bishop has removed himself from the city, something I quite understand, upped sticks and bought land in the Hawkesbury district, not far from St. Albans." The governor slapped his hands together as though dismissing the whole affair. "Now, if you'll excuse me, I must attend to my other guests. But I'd very much like an opportunity to speak at greater length." He stood. "Don't get up." Sir Charles took the steps two at a time and disappeared into the throng of dancers.

Chapter 3

Mogo Creek, Hawkesbury, NSW
1853

"Della, get back here."

Perhaps one day Charity would accept that she was no longer a child and was capable of looking after herself, but today wasn't the day and Della doubted it would ever come.

"There's another storm brewing and you've got chores."

"I won't be long." The never-ending round of jobs could wait.

Tidda was more important. Della hadn't seen her for days. "There's a pile to finish before Gus and Dobbin arrive."

Ignoring Charity's carryings-on, Della continued along the meandering path she'd created to the spot where the creek billowed into a swimming hole. High in the spreading branches of the whispering she-oaks, red-tailed black cockatoos perched cracking the cones and sending their aromatic shells showering onto the ground below. Nothing else broke the deep, timeless tranquility. Here she found the solitude she craved.

No sun shone on the creek, and the clouds had begun to mass into tall thunderheads beyond the hills. The atmosphere, heavy with the peppery scent of the native flowers and eucalyptus blossoms, made Della's head pound and her muscles tense. That and the fuss Charity was kicking up because Gus and Dobbin were due. Della picked her way across the rocks, careful not to slip on the velvety moss.

Earlier in the day she'd spotted a mass of appleberries on the twining vines. She hadn't seen the Darkinjung women for weeks, and they always came for the berries on their way to the birthing sites up in the hills beyond the ridge. She hadn't seen Jarro either, or any of the boys.

A neat little pile of droppings on top of one of the rocks and the waft of Tidda's sweet grassy smell meant her friend was close at hand. Della picked up her pace, then stopped as a pitiful cry of a young child broke the silence, followed by a flurry of movement and some hushed words.

She rounded the bend and there, in the clearing, saw a huddle of women and children, their dark faces fearful, their eyes wide and staring.

A woman stepped away from the group, her hand outstretched.

Della clasped her rough, warm hand. "Yalana, I've missed you."

They sat down on the bank, and Della hooped her arms around her knees, waiting for the older women to settle.

"I haven't seen Jarro or the other boys for ages."

"Not boys. Men."

Della didn't have to ask; she knew what Yalana's words meant. Jarro and the others had left the women for their learning and initiation. Next time she saw him, if there was a next time, he would be deemed an adult and would have learned the sacred songs, dances, and stories of his people. "Where are you going?"

She pointed up over the ridge.

Della nodded. Their walking tracks crisscrossed the local countryside. She and Pa had traveled them, shortcuts that saved time and followed a simpler route than the convict-built Great North Road. "Maybe you'll stay around here for a while. The appleberries are ready."

Yalana shook her head. "Hunters."

"Hunters? What hunters?"

"Yarramalong and Wollombi way." Yalana's lips pouted and her forehead creased in anger.

Charity said there'd been raids, settlers banding together to protect their land and livestock, but Della had heard nothing of hunters. The old woman pushed herself to her feet and the others followed suit, taking the track through the trees and fading into the distance.

Della sank down beside the creek, waiting for the flash of white fur that would herald Tidda's arrival. The first time she'd come across Tidda she'd been no more than a joey hardly big enough to be out of her mother's pouch. Perhaps because she was different, with her strange lack of color and red eyes, the mob had rejected her. Charity reckoned it was the sign of the devil, a punishment or a curse from the Darkinjung ancestral spirits. That was nothing but a load of rubbish. Tidda was more beautiful than most because of the strange trick nature had played upon her.

Fingers sore from hours of sewing, Della flexed her hands and picked at the calluses on her palm, missing the company of the women. Once she'd enjoyed her work, but the pleasure had leached out of it, along with pretty much everything now that Ma and Pa were gone. No one ever came, no one except Gus and Dobbin with the monthly supplies and yet another pile of skins for her to stitch. Charity tried to help, but she hadn't an eye for the intricate work. And besides, she'd changed. She never laughed or joked as she had in Sydney, her face had grown wary, and she jumped every time she heard an unexpected sound.

"Tidda! Tidda!" Della's voice bounced back, resounding on the sandstone rocks framing the gully. In the silence before the next rumble of thunder, leaves rustled in the undergrowth. She plucked at a patch of new green grass shoots as the watery sun broke through the massing clouds.

Dried leaves crackled and Tidda's sweet grassy scent filled the air. She was here, somewhere close. Della turned her head and there, still as a statue, stood the pure white kangaroo, her head tipped to one side in greeting, her front paws held out waiting for her evening treat. Careful not to make any sudden movement, Della shuffled forward and rested her face against Tidda's soft fur, breathing in her warm comfort. A zigzag of lightning flickered behind the hills and she flinched as it crackled. Tidda held firm, just as she had that first day, the day they'd arrived after burying Ma and Pa.

Della had been stunned to stillness by Tidda's brilliant white fur, and when they'd locked eyes it was as though they'd recognized each other's loneliness. Tidda had turned and bounded away, but the next day she was back, and the next, every evening. It was fanciful, but Della liked to believe that Ma and Pa had sent the kangaroo to watch over her.

A mighty crash made the rocks shudder, and huge drops of rain pitted the surface of the creek. Tidda shot her a look of regret before she bounded up to the ridge and disappeared into the scrub. Della stared after the kangaroo, the rain drenching her hair, plastering it to her head. Throwing the last of the handful of grass across the clearing, she pulled off her heavy leather apron and draped it over her head before bolting along the path.

By the time she reached the workshop, she was drenched to the skin and could barely see her hand in front of her face. Muscles screaming, she pulled open one of the heavy doors and slipped inside, fighting to fasten it tight. The wind lashed the shutters, sending flurries of rain inside and dampening all her finished specimens.

One by one she dragged them into the center of the room and threw a series of burlap sacks over the top of the massed collection. Gus and Dobbin would be less than impressed with a wasted journey.

Satisfied everything was out of harm's way, she wiped aside the trailing creeper that liked to snatch at her face with every gust of wind and slipped through the walkway to the place she and Charity called home. Two small buildings and a washhouse, all built facing the creek. Alongside the kitchen, herb and vegetable gardens and an orchard, and in the slab hut two small bedrooms and the big room with the fireplace. One room for her and the other for Ma and Pa; now Charity had that room because Della couldn't bring herself to use it. When it was cold they ate at the table in front of the fire, and in summer they sat on the veranda where the cool breeze swung up from the creek.

The main room was empty, a pile of dying embers wallowing in the grate. She knew where Charity would be—tucked under the blankets in her bed sheltering from the storm, quaking. Della stoked the fire, put the billy on the hob, then pulled down the tea caddy and peered inside. There wasn't much left, just enough for two or three more brews. Gus and Dobbin had better not be late.

"I'm home." Della pushed open the door to the bedroom. The pile under the blankets moved and a pair of panicked brown eyes set in a small plump face appeared.

"The storm's moving through. There'll be more rain, though not much more banging and crashing."

Charity pushed back the blankets and struggled off the straw pallet, tossing her long black plait over her shoulders.

"Kettle's on.. Come and have a cuppa."

"If this keeps up we'll be flooded in and Gus and Dobbin won't make it across the creek."

"We'll worry about that when the time comes." Della turned to leave the cramped room when another crash sounded, sending Charity scuttling back under the blankets.

"Come on. It's not that bad." She held out her hand.

"They can transport me thousands of miles to this godforsaken colony, but I'll never get used to being out here in the wilderness. Ain't right, out in the middle of nowhere."

"Sydney has thunderstorms, and London."

"Not like this they don't." Her mouth pulled down at the corners. "I want to go back to Sydney."

When Della awoke, tiny bright stars still glittered through the barred window but the first fingers of light ruffled the horizon. Charity wouldn't have dragged herself from her bed or stoked the fire yet. Far too cold for her to get up. The early signs of winter had taken hold, and before long the first dusting of frost would ice the valley.

A possum eyed her from the tree outside, its eyes wide and glinting in the half light. The wind howled and rattled the loose-fitting slabs, failing to thaw the cold seeping through the jagged gaps. Della hugged her shawl around her shoulders, shivered, and stretched her stiff fingers, forcing the blood to flow while she stared blankly around the room. She didn't need the full light to show the details. She knew every inch of the small holding as well as the palm of her own hand.

At night she might mourn Ma and Pa, but with the morning light her tears dried and she'd put herself to the task at hand. But to go back to Sydney and face all the people, the shop, the incessant noise, was another matter. She let out a big sigh and the kookaburras cackled at her nonsense.

It had broken her heart when Gus had trapped and wrung the necks of the two adult kookaburras. They had kept her company while she worked. As a tribute, she'd spent hours creating an intricate mount with a dead branch. When it was complete it looked so lifelike the remaining kookaburra had attacked, thinking his territory had been invaded. That was the last time she'd had a note from Aunt Cordelia, telling her the kookaburras had pride of place in the front window of the shop.

She loved the bright sapphire flash of color on their wings and their knowing gaze. They reminded her of the gentlemen she'd see making their way to Macquarie Street while she sat in the shop window dreaming that one day a handsome man would walk through the door and whisk her away. That was about as far-fetched as Charity's ideas about upping sticks and returning to Sydney.

Pa had great dreams about building up the farm—the water was plentiful, the land down by the creek rich and fertile—but nothing had come of that because the sickness had struck. Asiatic cholera, the doctor had said, though he'd been surprised neither she nor Cordelia nor Charity had suffered even a moment's sickness. Ma and Pa had withered before her, eyes bloodshot, faces as gaunt as skinned carcasses. They'd died shrunken skeletons, every ounce of flesh stripped by the relentless disease. And nothing she had done had helped to stem the tide.

Charity sashayed in, disrupting her morbid memories, and sat down in front of the fire, hiking her skirt above her knees and rubbing her hands together in front of the flames. "I want to go back to Sydney. It's not for Cordelia to decide. She's your father's sister, not your keeper, and she's certainly not mine. You own the shop now your pa's gone. She shouldn't be there running the show, putting on airs and graces as though she's forgotten her roots."

Della was more than happy to let Cordelia run the Taxidermy Shop. Della's interest lay in her job—her "art," as Pa called it. *Art* seemed far too highfalutin a word for sewing; after all, that's all she did, that and creating the straw models that held the skins' capes in place.

She enjoyed her work, though, took pride and pleasure in the tableaux she created. But she didn't see herself as an artist—not the same as those people who painted huge canvases or portraits to hang in the new mansions in Sydney.

Chapter 4

London
1918

"I've told you before, Fleur, I don't hold with fancy men coming here, 'specially not when you're working. You do that on your own time."

Would the woman never let up? Just because Hugh had sneaked into the shop most afternoons and sat nursing a cup of her precious black coffee. "No fancy man, Mrs. Black. He is my husband, and for the record he's still out there somewhere so he won't be bothering you for a while."

Mrs. Black's already rumpled face sagged even more. "No need to speak to me like that, missy. How was I supposed to know?"

Good question, really. Fleur hadn't told anyone she was married. What was there to tell? She'd fallen in love, married the man on a whim, and now what was she left with? A heart in danger of breaking and a letter from the Ministry of Information. Not even that—she'd torn it into a thousand pieces and thrown it out.

"Well, you better get over there and tell him you're not interested, 'cos he can't take his eyes off you."

"I'm sorry?"

"Can't you listen to anything I say? No more fancy men. Get over there and find out what's 'is problem." She tipped her head like an irate sparrow in the direction of the window. Hugh's seat. Fleur's stomach flipped.

When the man raised his head, she saw her mistake. In his black cashmere coat and trilby, with shading heavy brows and an imposing nose, he was no more Hugh than the Duke of Wellington. Nothing like Hugh.

Why wasn't the man in uniform? More to the point, why was he sitting there and Hugh was . . . She swallowed the threatening sob. This had to stop.

"Asked to speak to you, he did. *Mrs. Fleur Richards*, if you please. Giving yourself airs and graces won't make you belong." She gave a tedious, long-drawn-out tut. "And straighten your pinny. This one's upper crust, not like that last one with his funny accent and cheek."

Fleur pulled down her apron and walked across the crowded restaurant, squeezing between the chairs and tables, careful not to jog a gesticulating arm or knock a precariously balanced teapot.

"Fleur Richards?" The lanky man with his expensive overcoat half rose, steadying himself on the back of the chair, and took off his hat.

She nodded. "Can I get you something?"

"Just a moment or two of your time. My name's Waterstone. Archer Waterstone."

Fleur threw a look over her shoulder at Mrs. Black standing with her arms folded, her face a perfect match for her name.

"You are Fleur Richards, aren't you? Pretty name. French heritage?"

Just a mother who dared to dream. She was no more French than this man was a soldier. How had he managed to escape the war? "Yes. I mean, no."

His eyebrows rose, wrinkling his brow.

"I'm Fleur Richards, but I'm not French. My parents were both English, born and bred in Islington. Dad was a bus driver, Mum a clippie."

"Were?"

"The first zeppelin raid."

"I'm sorry. So you're alone. No family?"

"I've been on my own since then." Until Hugh came along and whisked away her loneliness. A sob caught at the back of her throat and she forced it down. "I'm sorry, Mr. Waterstone. I received your letter. We've been rushed off our feet. I haven't been able to take time off. When it rains . . . you know." She gestured at the torrent of water streaming down the steamy window. The man must think her a total fool.

"Sit down." He gestured to the chair. She couldn't sit down. Mrs. Black would have a fit. "I regret it's my duty to inform you Hugh has made the great sacrifice for King and country."

Great sacrifice? What did that mean? All the men had made the great sacrifice, left home to go and fight in nasty, muddy, rat-infested trenches against a bunch of greedy, land-grabbing Huns.

"Hugh died on November the fourth, killed by a German shell. The tunnelers were brought in to put a bridge over a heavily defended canal."

Hugh was dead? He couldn't be.

No one's going to take me away. Not now I've found you.

She was supposed to get a telegram. November the fourth was days ago, over a week. A howl built and she swallowed it down. She'd clung to the hope that the letter was all some horrible mistake.

Her stomach gave some sort of disgusting lurch and she had an overwhelming need to rush out the back. She glanced over her shoulder again. Mrs. Black was still in the same place, hands on hips, watching her like a carrion hawk. Fleur would have to push past her to even make the outhouse. She dragged in a breath and swallowed.

"I'm sorry to be so blunt. The matter is somewhat convoluted, which is why I asked you in my letter to come to the offices; however, I need to hurry things along."

What on earth would he and his newfangled government department want with her? "I'm sorry, you'll have to forgive me. I must get back to work."

He narrowed his eyes and tipped his head to one side as though waiting for something more.

Mr. Waterstone's cool hand reached across the table and covered hers. She reared back. "I understand this is something of a shock. Shall I order some tea?"

That was her line. "No. No tea."

"Please, let me explain as quickly as I can and then when you've had time to . . ." He cleared his throat. "I'm dreadfully sorry for your loss; however, I need an answer today."

An answer? To what? What else was there?

"What do you know of Hugh's life?"

"He is an Australian and his family are miners. He said when the war was over we'd go to Australia. The sun shines there." Her voice hitched on a pathetically high note and she blinked the memory away. "I believed him." She sank into the chair and dropped her head into her hands. "I don't see what this has to do with me, Mr. Waterstone. If a German ended Hugh's life, whether he was a miner or a soldier makes no difference now." There, she'd said it. She couldn't summon a single tear. All she wanted to do was curl up in a ball like a dying animal and be left alone.

The massive water urn billowed and sent out a hiss of boiling hot steam. The clanking of teacups stopped and a thundering took over, forcing her to squeeze her eyes closed.

"That's where you are wrong. As Hugh's next of kin, you are his heir."

The silence shifted and she snapped open her eyes and gazed into Mr. Waterstone's dark eyes. His eyelashes, still damp from the rain, clung together, and there was a small scar running through his right eyebrow.

"I have managed to secure you a berth on a ship leaving for Sydney, hence my need to speak to you immediately. I'd like you to come to the office so we can go over the details, as I know them. Of course, Hugh's solicitors in Sydney will be able to give you more information once you arrive. If you choose not to take this opportunity, I'm not sure when another passage will become available. With the repatriation of thousands of troops, it will be particularly difficult."

"I can't go to Australia!" A wave of heat flushed through her body, making her pulse hammer. Not without Hugh. "What about my job? My rent's overdue. I . . . What if Hugh comes back looking for me?"

His cold fingers clasped her hand again. "Hugh's not coming back, my dear. And you have responsibilities."

The drumming noise in her ears was too much. She dropped her head onto the table.

"Let me get you a cup of tea and have a word with Mrs. Black."

Quite honestly she didn't care what he did. It was all too much for her addled brain to absorb. Responsibilities? What responsibilities? What was the man talking about? She might as well be standing on a precipice peering into the unknown. It made her all jittery and weak-kneed.

"Drink this."

Her head weighed a ton. She propped her chin in her hand, blinked to bring Mr. Waterstone's concerned face into focus.

"Plenty of sugar." He ladled a week's ration into the cup. Mrs. Black would have a fit. "Drink up. Come on, now." He pushed the cup closer. "I've spoken to Mrs. Black. She's quite happy for you to leave early."

"I can't leave. What will I do for a job?"

"My dear, you have more important matters to attend to."

The scalding tea burnt its way down her throat. She licked her lips and placed the cup carefully back in the saucer. "I don't understand."

"You will. Come along now. Go and get your hat and coat. We'll take a cab to my office."

Fleur pushed down hard on the table, making the saucers clatter. It was such an effort to move. Tears streamed down her face, blinding her as she walked toward the till and Mrs. Black.

Stale smoke, biscuits, and steam seeped into her consciousness and she licked away the salt on her lip.

"Not like you to cry." Mrs. Black pressed a rumpled handkerchief into her hand. "Clean yourself up and tell me all about it."

"Nothing to tell really." She sniffed loudly and offered a half-hearted smile, more a grimace really. "Mr. Waterstone says my husband is dead and I have an inheritance."

"An inheritance? That's nothing to cry over."

"Oh, but it is. I don't know what to do." She stuffed the corner of the handkerchief into her mouth to trap the wail. "Hugh can't be dead."

"Come with me." Mrs. Black grasped her elbow and frog-marched her into the kitchen. "I'm sorry for your loss, but you have to stop this caterwauling. The customers," she hissed.

"I don't want to go to Australia, not without Hugh. And I don't want his money."

Her mouth sagged open, then snapped shut. "What's the matter with you, girl? Most people I know would take the money and run."

Whatever had possessed her to imagine Mrs. Black would understand?

Fleur's mind flooded with memories. The heady rush of euphoria. She'd been so sure it was love. And before she knew it they were standing outside the registry office. He'd handed her a bunch of violets and lifted her face to his lips.

I love you, Mrs. Richards. With every fragment of my tattered heart, I love you.

And she'd known he'd spoken the truth. "He died fighting for you,

Mrs. Black, for a country he didn't even call home. Remember that!" Fleur snatched her coat and hat from the peg behind the till and followed Mr. Waterstone out into the street.

"Mr. Waterstone, I don't think I've made myself clear. I have no intention of taking one penny of Hugh's money. There must be someone more deserving or entitled."

"Mrs. Richards, Fleur, I'm sure this is what Hugh wanted. Why else would he have contacted his solicitor in Sydney and told them of your marriage?"

She had no idea he had. No idea she stood to inherit anything. She lifted her shoulders; if she tried to speak she'd simply break down again.

Like magic a cab slithered to a halt beside them, spraying her shoes with water. She shot a puffy-eyed look over her shoulder, thought about running, hesitated too long. Mr. Waterstone ushered her inside and slammed the door closed.

"Wellington House, please." He turned to look at her. "I'll give you a few moments to gather your thoughts. We'll continue the conversation in my office."

Left with no alternative, she sat back, watching the incessant rain flooding along the gutters. When she lifted her head, Buckingham Palace loomed large. Twice in a matter of days. What she would give for it to be the last time she'd seen Buckingham Palace. Before the nasty envelope, when she still had dreams. She wanted to crawl away and hide.

The taxi turned another corner into the Mews and slowed. "This shouldn't take long." Mr. Waterstone wound down the window and nodded to a soldier standing inside a sentry box. "Almost there."

Five minutes later she was sitting with her hands in her lap like an errant schoolgirl facing Mr. Waterstone across the biggest desk she'd ever seen in her life. "Hugh can't be dead. I haven't received a telegram. I can't go to Australia without him."

He pulled out a large buff-colored file and opened it. "It's most unusual, but Hugh's commanding officer wasn't aware of your marriage; that's why you haven't received a telegram. He will forward Hugh's personal possessions to his solicitor in Sydney as Hugh requested. When you arrive they will be waiting for you. I'm sure once you are there you will see matters in a different light. I appreciate this has come as something of a shock, but I feel it is my duty to encourage you to do what is best. You said you have no family commitments. As I mentioned, if you don't take the opportunity of this passage, there's no knowing when I might be able to find you another berth. You loved Hugh, didn't you?"

His name thrummed through her veins. Yes, she loved him . . . From the very first moment his eyes had locked with hers, something soft and wordless had passed between them. He'd drawn her hand toward him, pushed up the edge of her cuff with his thumb, and pressed his warm lips against her wrist.

She'd felt her heart open and her spirit settle. Her eyes burned but she couldn't cry. She had no more tears.

"It's most important that you take this opportunity."

She stared into Mr. Waterstone's pale eyes, willing him to tell her it was all a dreadful mistake.

"I can't just up and traipse halfway across the world." Her words ended in a high-pitched squeak.

"If you are absolutely positive you don't want to fulfill Hugh's wishes, then I can contact his solicitors for you and they can arrange for the properties to be sold and the money deposited in your account."

That was the final straw. "No!" Suddenly she was standing. "You don't understand. I don't want it. Tell them that." There had been a mistake. She knew there had. Hugh was still alive, lying injured somewhere, unable to contact her, or worse still, unable to remember her. Who was to say he wasn't in some hospital, his memory shot to pieces, deaf or blind from the gas? Mr. Waterstone didn't have Hugh's personal possessions, nothing to prove he'd died. No one had told her where he was buried.

Hugh was alive. Hope blossomed and her heart gave a sudden hitch.

"What better way to fulfill Hugh's wishes? Leave all these wartime restrictions and the ghastly influenza epidemic behind. What have you to lose? It'll be summer when you get to Australia. It's what Hugh wanted."

In Australia the sun always shines. We'll be together. You'll see.

Chapter 5

Sydney, NSW
1853

"Captain von Richter, allow me to introduce Mrs. Cordelia Atterton."

Stefan stifled a groan and schooled his face. He'd been introduced to the diminutive woman in the introduction line but had failed to take note of her name. "May I introduce Mrs. Cordelia Atterton," she repeated, clapping her fleshy hands as though she'd conjured an apparition from the heavens.

A tall woman stepped forward. Her slender fingers hovered for a moment and he bowed sharply, his lips a mere inch above the lace of her glove. She extracted her hand before he had the opportunity to stand upright. When he came to attention he found himself level with an icy, appraising stare. "Mrs. Atterton, my pleasure." Her ivory skin was drawn smooth across sculpted cheekbones and her lips brushed with carmine. She might have been one of the statues supporting the Parthenon. Tall, straight, and exquisite, she gave the impression of being capable of shouldering whatever burdens life might throw at her.

"Could I beg a moment of your time?" Unabashed, she rested her thin, bird-like hand on his forearm, staring boldly into his face instead of modestly lowering her eyes. Had she been any of the moths flitting their way around the ballroom he would have made some excuse, but her fixed gaze intrigued him.

"Shall we move to the veranda? The music is very loud."

He bowed his head in agreement, offered his arm, and escorted her outside, then came to an abrupt halt, ensuring they were in full view of the entire assembly. The baron had drilled the conventions of this strange society into him. There was also a large possibility Herr Atterton might be lurking somewhere in the shadows, and he had no intention of beginning his stay by offending anyone. He dropped his hand. "How may I assist you?"

"I believe *I* may be able to assist you."

Did she indeed. He doubted that, unless she owned a stable of fine horses and was prepared to offer him the use of several for the remainder of his visit.

"I would like to extend an invitation."

He muffled a sigh. Invitations weren't in short supply, and after six months confined aboard ship he yearned for the peace and solitude of the countryside and the opportunity to sample some of the delights of New Holland the baron so eloquently described. Magnificent stands of eucalyptus trees and all manner of strange and beguiling plants and flowers, the invigorating scents of the wildflowers so prolific after rain. It had rained only the night before while they were moored inside the Heads, though one could hardly believe it as the moon threw its showy beams across the harbor.

"I have an establishment that might be of some interest to you. I own the Curio Shop of Wonders."

No husband then. A whore? Surely not. His gaze raked over her thin body, noticing the bony flare of her shoulder blades masked by ripples of green silk, as though she hadn't quite recovered from some debilitating sickness. She was not as young as he'd first imagined. "Thank you, but I intend to leave Sydney tomorrow."

"I am aware of that. I understand you are interested in the flora and fauna of the Antipodes."

"Indeed I am." There was only one person he'd told that tale to:

Sladdin. News traveled fast. Perhaps it was just as well his ruse had worked. He had no intention of making his search for Menge's opal public.

"You have me at a disadvantage, Mrs. Atterton. Our introduction was brief." He turned in search of the tiny woman with the bulbous eyes but she had disappeared into the swirling throng. In fact, he and Mrs. Atterton stood isolated like the tiny island of Pinchgut in the center of the vast harbor, patrolled only by the matronly sharks encircling the ballroom.

Her curious gaze scanned his face and he struggled to remain impassive. "Despite our ever-increasing population, Sydney Town is nothing but a small village. Word gets around. So, shall I show you the shop?"

He stifled a laugh. "As I said, I intend to leave Sydney forthwith." Not quite the truth unless Sladdin had managed to find him some horses in double-quick time.

"Then we have no time to waste." She pulled a long ribbon from a hidden pocket and dangled an intricate key tantalizingly between her fingers. "Unless, of course, you have a mind to indulge in some dancing, now would be the perfect time."

How could he refuse? She had him at his weakest point. His dancing days were long gone, cut short by the musket ball intended for Prince Metternich, and besides, the flyer had caught his interest. "Shall I call a carriage?"

"There's no need. The walk will take only a few minutes." She tilted her chin as though in challenge.

Like a waiting wraith, the tiny woman appeared at her side and handed her a green cloak. With a practiced flick, Mrs. Atterton tossed it across her shoulders and drew the furred hood over her head before he had the opportunity to assist her. "Shall we?" She lifted one dark eyebrow in question, then disappeared into the shadows.

Before she'd reached the steps leading to the garden he was at her side, the thrill of the unexpected invigorating him more than any of the oversweet wine being served. The small stones on the carriageway crunched beneath his boots as they walked into the velvety darkness.

"I believe you came directly from London."

"You continue to have me at a disadvantage, Mrs. Atterton."

Her laugh surprised him. Deep, rich, and throaty, it echoed in the night air. "As I said, Sydney Town is nothing but a small village."

"This establishment of yours . . ." He let the words dangle, wanting her to fill the void.

"Let's wait until we get there. A viewing will save so many words." She lifted the pace, her strides almost matching his. He had the strangest impression she'd like to lift her skirts and run. There was an undercurrent of tension, perhaps excitement or anticipation, about her movements.

They made their way up Macquarie Street through the yellow glow cast by the gas lamps, then she slowed her pace and slid into an inky alleyway. His right hand moved to the scabbard of his dress sword.

Again, the throaty laugh. "Fear not, Captain von Richter. You are quite safe with me."

A mere ten yards later she came to an abrupt halt in front of a shiny black gate tucked between other premises. "This is the back entrance. Rather than leave you standing alone in the street I thought we'd come this way." She slipped inside and along a short path to the back of a terrace building. She led him up a short flight of stairs to a door that opened to reveal a large room lit by a series of wall lamps. Ushering him inside she closed the door behind him, and he tasted the faintest odor of something earthy and strangely sweet.

"Straight ahead."

Stefan's heels clicked on the honey-dark timber floor and he inhaled the strange fragrance; the chemical taint reminded him of field hospitals and injuries he'd rather forget.

Light from the street puddled on the floor, and as his eyes began to adjust, he picked out a large window fronting the street. His breath caught and he froze. Three giant blackbirds, their wings spread, showing red-tipped feathers and sharp curved beaks, perched on a branch, prepared to take flight. He lifted his hand to fend them off. A lamp flared behind him and he lowered his arm, feeling his cheeks redden, his mistake obvious. "I thought for a moment they were alive."

He took several steps closer, marveling at the tableau the birds presented as the words on the flyer came back to him. *All kinds of taxidermic work executed in first-class style*. It was no exaggeration. It was impossible to know where to look first. The room spanned only fifteen feet and the tableau was but one of three. Another set of birds graced the corner of a display cabinet—this time owl-like birds with ruffled feathers and a quizzical gaze—and in the corner a water mole resting on a log, its leathery beak slightly open, as if in greeting. Exquisite as the finest detailed drawings, yet perfect specimens.

He stepped forward and ran the tip of his finger down the shiny black feathers of one of the birds while their beady eyes watched his every move. He gazed around the room, taking in the large glass cases filled with stuffed animals and birds, each telling a story of this wonderful land. Shells, emu eggs, birds of paradise with their plumage smooth and glossy, piles of skins, some uncured and others made into rugs and blankets. All as bizarre and unusual as the woman herself.

"They are authentic specimens."

"I don't doubt it."

"But you had to make sure?"

He lifted his head to look at the strangely alluring woman who had whisked him away from the ball into this fairyland of glass-fronted cabinets, botanical oddities, and preserved specimens.

She'd shed her cloak and gloves, the light of the lamps reflecting her smooth skin, alabaster white against the virulent green of her dress; Scheele's Green, unless he was very much mistaken. A good choice. It brought out the golden lights in her luminous eyes. Her hair was pulled back from her high forehead into an unusual arrangement at the base of her head, from which protruded two long, slender curved feathers he hadn't noticed before. He took a step to one side to get a better view, and she pulled one free and held it out.

"*Menura superba*, better known as the superb lyrebird because of its wonderful tail feathers"—she waved the curled feather beneath his nose, making his nostrils twitch with the faint cloud of powder—"which of course were not portrayed accurately in the first instance. I have attempted to remedy the situation." She gestured to a pair of mating birds, the male's ornate tail fanned out, completely covering his head, his back, and that of the female.

"Fascinating. You are very talented." She inclined her head, the first sign of color staining her cheeks. "And quite right when you said I would be interested in your enterprise." More than interested. He could spend hours roaming this very room. "Where do you source the specimens?"

"Largely from the Hawkesbury region. I have a property there." She extended her arm and indicated the other side of the room. "I also have a large collection of native artifacts that may interest you." The silk of her dress whispered as she led him around the room.

For one heart-stopping moment, his breath stilled as he prepared to safeguard her from a lurking warrior, then she lifted the lamp high to illuminate an ancient grasstree, its flower spike intact, and a relieved gasp slipped through his lips. The long, narrow shape was nothing more than the burnt trunk supporting a collection of native spears and other implements, weapons, ornaments, and curiosities.

"And you have established a relationship with the local tribes? I would be very interested . . ." His words tapered off as his thoughts tumbled to catch up. Mrs. Atterton and her curio shop had his imagination racing. What he wouldn't give to explore the area she spoke of. "Would it be possible to visit?"

A frown danced across her forehead and she gave a slight shake of her head. "Unfortunately, I have commitments in Sydney."

It had never crossed his mind that *she* would make the journey. "I'm planning a trip to the Hawkesbury. I have an acquaintance I must visit just outside St. Albans and I intend to travel by road, which I believe is more than adequate and leads directly to the Hawkesbury."

"Ah. The Great North Road." She chewed on her lower lip, her gaze resting on the birds in the window. "Something could perhaps be arranged."

Would he ever get used to this strange land? Everything was unexpected, not least a woman running her own business. She was offering a proposition, dangling a bait in front of his nose to ensure a series of sales. Sales she had already made, though he had no intention of admitting it.

His mind tumbled as he imagined a series of rooms housing specimens such as these. The fashion for the art of taxidermy had gathered momentum in the last few years, and these were so very different from the myriad hummingbirds and butterflies in glass domes that graced most drawing rooms in Vienna and London. "I should very much like to discuss this further, perhaps tomorrow before I leave?" He pulled his watch from his pocket. "We should return to the ball. Supper will be served shortly."

"I look forward to tomorrow. Would nine o'clock suit you?"

"Indeed it would."

"Let us make haste."

He reached for her cloak, which lay drooped across a glass-fronted wooden display case housing an intricate skeleton of a huge snake.

"I won't be returning to Government House. I somewhat overstepped the mark in attending in the first place. I will not deceive you. I am an emancipist, and as such I'm not welcome in polite society." Her lip curled in a dismissive smile and her strange eyes flared. "I was, however, keen to make your acquaintance and it seemed the easiest way."

A reply stuck in his throat. She'd come to Australia as a convict, her sentence served, otherwise she wouldn't be running a business. A spike of anger raced through him. "In that case neither will I." The baron was right. There was much about this country to infuriate a man with a conscience. "Perhaps I can offer you supper at my hotel. I'm staying at the Berkeley in Bent Street, not a stone's throw from here. Sladdin, the clerk, is an admirer of your enterprise."

A smile tipped the corner of her lips and she toyed with one of the wrapped lozenges filling a shallow wooden bowl on the desk. "Let's leave it until tomorrow morning. I have work to complete, and if you are serious about visiting the Hawkesbury, logistics to contemplate." She walked across the room and unbolted the front door.

His dismissal.

He cast one last, long look around the room and with a deal of regret pulled his heels together and bowed sharply. "Thank you, Mrs. Atterton, for a most interesting evening. I look forward to tomorrow. *Guten Abend*."

In a matter of seconds the front door closed, leaving him standing in the street while Mrs. Atterton's shadow doused the lights of the Curio Shop of Wonders.

Chapter 6

Mogo Creek, Hawkesbury, NSW
1853

"Charity, there isn't any tea left."

"I know. Have to make do with warm milk or water. There are some lemons on the tree and dried chamomile somewhere."

"When were Gus and Dobbin supposed to get here?"

"Yesterday if the tea caddy's empty."

Pulling the catgut tight, Della completed the neat row of stitching with a knot. "I didn't think I'd get this finished in time." She lifted the bird gently from her lap and laid it on the bench, smoothing the bright feathers, then turned to clear the table of her tools. The earthenware bowl still held the remains of the water and arsenical soap, and at her feet lay the strips of cloth she'd used to hold the limbs in place.

In only two days she'd created another display. The birds were easy and, more often than not, she'd find them herself. Not so the larger animals. Thankfully Gus and Dobbin cleaned the skins and boned the animals, leaving her with the task of building the frames and reassembling them before the skins became too brittle. She flexed her fingers and threw open the door.

Charity scooped up the detritus and threw it into a bucket. "I'll get this. You sort out your tools. You know where you want them." Della picked up the scalpel and wiped the razor-sharp blade and ivory handle clean before placing it in the pocket of the leather pouch next to the stiletto. These tools would last a lifetime—had lasted Pa's lifetime, and now they were hers.

He'd passed his trade on to her, not just the stuffing and molding Ma had done, but the careful recreation of each creature, a second life, he used to say, immortal. And so she captured their favorite pose, poised in flight or ready to pounce, as though at any moment they would leap back to life and take to the wing. The pliers and file slipped into the pouches, and she rolled up the soft leather and tied the cord tight before placing it in the drawer. "I hope Gus remembered the wire." Without it she wouldn't be able to mount these latest specimens.

The rain had cleared, and a watery sunshine puddled on the dirt floor as she threw open the shutters and extinguished the candles, letting the sweet air blow through and clear the dust and the overlaying coppery scent of blood.

Charity picked up a single green tail feather and picked her teeth, scrutinizing the three king parrots perched on a dead gum tree. "That's come up real well, it has." She wandered toward the window. "Looks like we're in for another dump." As the words left Charity's mouth a crash of thunder echoed, shaking the walls. She let out a shrill squawk and peered through her fingers. "Bloody brilliant timing. Here's Gus and Dobbin. I'd kill for a cup of tea."

With a resounding rumble the heavens opened and Della yanked the shutters closed. "I'll get my cloak. You stay here. They'll need a hand with the supplies, otherwise they'll be ruined."

Della grasped the door handle, tugging against the wind. Heads down, collars up, Gus and Dobbin battled against the storm to free the horses and settle them in the barn. A large gust lifted the canvas tarpaulin covering the wagon and it flew up into the tree, flapping like a demented emu.

She reefed her cloak from the hook, threw it over her shoulders, and battled toward the wagon. The stores would be ruined if the water got into the flour and tea, and the thought of soggy skins didn't bear thinking about. She and Charity would have weeks on starvation rations, just the way it had been when they'd first arrived.

"You're late."

"Only a day or two. Important business that couldn't wait." Gus threw the words over his shoulder and lowered the backboard, dragging the first of the burlap sacks off the bed of the wagon. She hefted it onto her shoulder and staggered across the yard. The moment she reached the workshop the door flew open.

"Dump it all in 'ere for the time being. We'll sort it out later."

Without bothering to reply to Charity she threw the sack of supplies onto the ground and returned to the wagon for another, ducking as a forked slash of lightning illuminated the yard. Dobbin elbowed her to one side and heaved three sacks into his arms.

"Where are the skins?"

"Stacked under the seats. Huge pile. Cordelia says she's got a big order. You worry about the supplies. Gus'll get those."

A roll of wire and several boxes neatly labeled. She checked them off in her mind as she picked them up. White arsenic, carbonate of potash, and camphor. She'd need some citrus for the arsenical soap. Thankfully the trees out back were laden, and wood ash and animal fat were not in short supply. Hessian bags stuffed with skins lay in a puddle and she tugged them out, slipping and sliding in the quagmire the yard had become.

The rain fell in great vertical slashes slapping her skin, the yard claggy with mud and rutted from the downpour. Dobbin's reek of unwashed flesh snatched at her breath. Sensing her distaste, he threw her a morose stare and lumbered off.

The filthy hem of her dress clutched at her legs, and her boots, weighed down by the mud clinging to the soles, made each step a struggle.

"Got the rest. You get inside."

She grunted at Gus and, grabbing the boxes in both hands, staggered toward the workshop, not daring to run. Without the arsenic, Charity wouldn't be able to make the soap she needed to preserve the skins or dust the feathers of her recent efforts.

By the time they'd emptied the wagon, Della was exhausted. She slumped against the wall and slid down onto her haunches, her stomach churning from the overpowering reek of tobacco, dung, and damp wool.

Charity rummaged in the pile of goods and pulled out a small sack of tea and one of sugar. "I'll make us all a brew, chase away the shivers, and I'll knock up a fresh loaf."

"There's a jar of honey in there somewhere. Go down a treat, 'specially with this." Gus produced a flagon of rum from under his coat and thrust it into Charity's hands. "Lace the tea with that."

It wasn't until Della had her hands clasped around a mug of tea that sensation began to come back to her fingers. "Why so many skins this time?"

"Cordelia reckons she's snaffled a really big order, friend of the governor." Dobbin scratched at his overhanging belly. "She's out to impress him. That's why we're late. Got us all lined up to meet with this big nob at St. Albans tomorrow. Take him up into the hills for a spot of 'unting."

"Why are you going up there?" Hopefully the Darkinjung women had moved on; they wouldn't want the likes of Gus and Dobbin hanging around their sacred sites. Gus and Dobbin hadn't any time for them. Worse than Charity, in fact. But she was just scared, though Della had no idea why. The Darkinjung never caused trouble, were more a help than a hindrance. But for Jarro and his friends, she and Pa would never have seen the animals in their natural habitat.

The atmosphere in the workshop shifted. She didn't miss the whack Gus landed on Dobbin's thigh as he leaned forward and tried to slop some more rum into his tea. "What's your problem?"

"Nuffink. Drink your tea and shut up. We'll camp in here tonight. Too wet outside and we've got to be off early if we're going to meet up with the nob."

"The captain." Dobbin waggled his head backward and forward and stuck out his burly chest. He received another belt from Gus, this time around his thick head. He shook Gus's hand away as if it were a persistent fly and lumbered to his feet. "I know. I know. Keep me trap shut." He knocked back the rest of the tea and crammed a lump of dried meat he'd pulled from his pocket into his mouth before wiping the back of his hand across his flaccid lips.

Della shuddered. Dobbin was almost childlike in his simplicity, except for the nasty, shifty glint in his eye. He was twice the size of Gus and had about half the manners, and that wasn't saying much. Nothing more than a guard dog. And he smelled like a rancid dingo, all sweaty and meaty in his filthy Crimean shirt and festering moleskins.

Della's fingers tightened around the door. She wanted to be away from them, away from their stench and their belligerence. Without another word, she left the workshop, relieved as the last echoes of their voices died and they banged the barn door shut behind her. Why did Cordelia employ them? Surely there were other men who could do the job, men less aggressive and, heaven forbid, better smelling. The stench of their hunting hung over them like a shroud. Disgusting.

She slumped down in the chair by the fire, eyeing her filthy brown homespun dress with distaste. She hadn't worn anything with any color since Ma and Pa died. Not even mourning black, just brown homespun. What did it matter out at Mogo Creek when there was no one to see? At least she didn't smell, or did she? She shivered and hunched close to the fire.

"What you need is a bath. Warm you up. Wet through you are." Charity dragged the old hipbath out from the corner, manhandled it in front of the fire, and filled up the big copper kettle over the fire. "Don't want you catching a chill."

"I'm not bathing with Gus and Dobbin out there."

Charity heaved a plank of timber across the door, then moved around the room checking the shutters. "Good enough to keep the blacks out, so it'll do for those two."

Once Della was settled up to her neck in warm water, she turned to Charity. "You don't think they'd hurt the Darkinjung people, do you?" She lay back, her hands behind her head, staring at the rafters and the patterns the flickering firelight threw.

"They'd get Gus and Dobbin long before they had the chance to do any damage. Creeping around on them bare feet, quieter than bloody diamond pythons and just as dangerous."

"Pythons aren't poisonous, Charity. I've told you that a million times."

"It ain't natural keeping one of them up in the ceiling."

"He keeps the rats and mice away."

"Now, rats I understand. They've got sense."

Maybe, maybe not. She'd rather have a shed full of diamond pythons than rats. Especially not the Sydney rats, the ones that came off the ships. At first the physician thought Ma and Pa had contracted their illness from the rats, then he'd changed his mind, blamed the Asiatic cholera that had swept the world.

She picked up the lump of soap and scrubbed at her skin. Her arms were brown to the elbows but above that her skin was as white as Tidda's fur and her legs looked as though they were striped. Brown feet and ankles from walking barefoot with her skirts tucked up, then white again all the way up to her thighs. She slid down in the water and let the warmth slip through her hair.

When she surfaced, Charity was standing behind her, soap in hand. "Sit still and I'll wash your hair for you. If you were living in Sydney, you wouldn't be getting around like some drudge. Can't remember when either of us had a new dress. It's time we went back."

She was no beauty, she knew that. Charity was just being kind. There were no mirrors in the house, no glass in the windows, but when the sun was right she could see her reflection in the swimming hole. Not a sign of Cordelia's high cheekbones and smooth, pale skin. The only thing they had in common was the strange copper-colored hair, although hers didn't glow like Cordelia's; it hung in shanks around her sun-blemished cheeks.

"When I was a girl me hair reached down to me waist. Black as coal it was, until the bloody soldier shaved it all off just 'cos I wouldn't go belowdecks with him." Charity ran her hand over her head. "Grew back all right though. Cordelia now, she was a different matter."

Curiosity aroused, Della rested her shoulders back on the top of the bath and let Charity's fingers work their magic. Charity hardly ever mentioned the past, but tonight, with the house shuttered and warm and Gus and Dobbin camped in the workshop, she seemed more at ease. Maybe it was the slug of rum Gus had thrown in the tea that made Charity talkative.

"She had every one of those sailors on their toes, moment we set foot on the bloody ship. And then of course soon as we landed in Sydney Town, your pa was there to meet her. Had no problem getting her assigned to him. Me, I got stuck in the Female Factory for bloody ages."

"But Pa got you out in the end, didn't he?"

"That he did. Trouble was, Madam had her foot well and truly in the door with her high-and-mighty nose-in-the-air behavior, and I was packed off to the kitchen. Never worked in the kitchen before in me life, always in the shop. Good man, your pa. Not many who'd pack up their life for their little sister, but she always called the shots. He just couldn't say no."

She knew that part of the story well enough, but she hadn't known Charity bore such a grudge. Ma often talked about their first few years in Sydney, setting up the shop, making the place their home. She'd brought all her fine linens and precious china and never had the chance to use them. Free or not, they were trade, and trade didn't mix with the new settlers who saw Sydney as their opportunity to lord it over their fellow man. Half of them probably had a history far worse than Cordelia and Charity's. "If Pa was so certain Cordelia was innocent, why didn't he make a stand in London? Get her set free?"

"He tried, tried hard enough. Didn't get far. That fancy man of hers dropped her right in it, he did, took off, leaving us to take the blame."

Childhood memories drifted through Della's mind, but as always they disappeared like smoke, leaving just the faint feeling that all was not as she remembered.

"'Nuff of this nonsense. Out you come, the water's cold."

Della wrapped herself in the sheet Charity offered and scrubbed herself dry. "Did you see the pile of skins Gus brought from Cordelia? I'm going to have my work cut out."

"There's a letter from her somewhere." Charity delved into the pocket of her skirt and brought out a piece of paper. "No, don't touch it until you're dry. It'll smudge."

Della pulled her nightgown over her head, tucked the shawl over her shoulders, and hunkered down next to the fire.

"Here you are. You have a read of that while I sort out this mess." Charity scurried around emptying the water from the tub.

"Aren't you going to have a bath?"

"What, me? No chance, not with them ne'er-do-wells in the shed." She lifted her arm and gave a sniff. "Nah, I'm fine. Tell me what Cordelia says."

Della shrugged and tried to focus on Cordelia's spidery handwriting. "Just the usual. The shop's doing well and she has an order for some larger specimens. No more birds."

A great yawn rolled its way through her body. She was tired, very tired. "I'll think about it tomorrow."

Chapter 7

Sydney, NSW
1919

Fleur stepped closer to the handrail and smiled at the soldier hanging over the rail. He dragged in a great lungful of air. "Can you smell it?"

She sniffed, although she had no idea what she was supposed to be smelling. It was unlikely she'd ever smell anything again. From the moment she'd stepped aboard, the acrid stink of coal smoke from the funnel had coated her nostrils, blocking out everything.

"You can, it's there. Never thought I'd long for the smell of eucalyptus. My mum used to rub it on me chest when I was a nipper."

She sniffed again, mostly to cover her smile in case he thought she was teasing him. She could smell something other than coal smoke, something vaguely medicinal. His description made her think of Vicks salve, but it was his voice that made her smile. He sounded so much like Hugh, the way he put his words together, the lilt at the end of the sentences, as though he were always asking a question.

"It's the gum trees. I dreamed of the sound of the wind rustling the leaves in the trenches. Never thought I'd make it back." His broad nasal twang did sound a little as though his nose were stuffed. The poor man—the ship was packed with soldiers who'd suffered appalling injuries in the trenches, far worse than anything she'd seen in London.

If she had her way she'd have every one of the German soldiers and their masters hung, drawn, and quartered at Tower Hill. "Do the trees cause a problem?"

"What?" He frowned at her, then laughed. "No. It's the smell of Australia. We'll lose it as soon as we see land. It's the way the wind's blowing, a good westerly. Off the Blue Mountains." He let out the longest sigh and rocked back on his heels. "It'll be good to be home." Whereas this was the farthest she'd ever been from home.

The only time she'd left London was for a day trip to Brighton with Mum and Dad. They'd huddled under the pier and eaten ice cream in the pouring rain.

Six weeks had gone some way to ease the confusion Mr. Waterstone's announcement caused. She'd been carried along in his wake. He'd taken over and organized her passage, though how he'd managed she had no idea. She felt guilty taking up space that belonged to some poor soldier returning home, but she'd shared the cabin with three of the nurses who were on board to care for the wounded and she spent much of her time trying to help in some small way, reading, writing letters, talking to pass the time. Some of the injured needed all the help they could get. She had no idea how they would manage once they got home.

"There's the Heads." The soldier almost threw himself overboard in his attempt to reach the deep indigo ribbon of the horizon. "We made it!"

She rubbed her eyes, still couldn't see anything but a vast expanse of water slipping by below the ship and the distant horizon, pretty much the same as it had been since they left England.

"Give it another six hours and we'll be heading up the harbor." He threw her a wink and limped off, no doubt to share his excitement with his mates.

In six hours she'd be on dry land. She'd read Mr. Waterstone's instructions so many times she knew them by heart. Collect her baggage, then ask someone to point her in the right direction. As long as it was before six o'clock, go to Hunter Street, Number 50, to the new premises of Lyttleton & Sons. They were expecting her and would have all the details. If there was a problem, check into the Berkeley Hotel on the corner of Bent Street—a reservation had been made in her name—and go to the solicitors the following morning.

Despite Mr. Waterstone's assurances, the cost still worried her. He'd given her a horribly large amount to tide her over. Emergency funds, he'd called it. More like more-cash-than-she'd-ever-seen-in-her-life funds. No matter how much she complained about not using Hugh's money, Mr. Waterstone had insisted. Kept saying it was her money now. It couldn't be. She knew with a deep, abiding certainty Hugh was still alive. That's why she'd made up her mind to come, convinced there was some sort of error.

When she got off the ship Hugh would be there waiting and, just as he'd promised on that windy day at Westminster Registry Office, their new life would begin.

As the weeks passed there'd been days when her conviction had faltered, seeing all the poor men on the ship, some of them with no idea who they were or where they had come from. Suppose Hugh was on another ship. Suffering from shell shock. Not knowing who he was or where he was going.

If Hugh had told his solicitors they'd married, why wouldn't he have told the army? Where were all his belongings? Something just didn't add up. And until it did she would search for Hugh.

The ship's horn sounded and there was a sudden rush of people to the rail, all pointing and laughing, the words *home*, *ripper*, and *bloody bewdy* on everyone's lips. She could pick out the shadow on the horizon now, growing clearer with every passing moment.

When they finally steamed between the two huge cliffs standing sentinel to the harbor, the panorama took her breath away. A clear blue sky mirrored in the crystal water, boats gliding in and out of the moorings, halyards chinking against the masts, gulls swooping and circling, more beautiful than anything she'd ever imagined. Golden stretches of sand fringed with green vegetation nestled at the end of the bay, and the neatest town she'd ever seen spread inland from the water's edge. They said it was a city, but it seemed no bigger than Brighton, although there wasn't a pebbly beach or a gray cloud in sight. Everything in Australia sparkled golden and bright against the azure backdrop of the towering sky.

After an unexpected seven days in quarantine on North Head, the wave of soldiers scrambling away from the wharf brought a smile to Fleur's face. They were as impatient as she was. The case of smallpox, which had held them up in Alexandria, and the threat of the influenza epidemic had put the fear of God into the authorities. Even the nurses said they'd all be wearing masks in the streets before long. However, nothing had eventuated and everyone had received a clean bill of health and been sent on their way.

"Number 50 Hunter Street, please." Fleur bent to pick up her suitcase, but the cabdriver beat her to it. He deposited it on the leather seat and handed her up as though she were a frail nineteenth-century miss.

"Have you there in no time, once we get through this lot. Come from London, have you?"

"Yes." She struggled out of her coat and draped it over her arm. The sun beat down like a great ball of fire. Mr. Waterstone had told her it would be warm, but it was sweltering, the hottest day she'd ever experienced. "Is it always this hot?"

"Should've been 'ere last week. Had one of those spells just to remind us what summer's all about. Cooled down a bit now with the southerly buster." He climbed up and flicked a whip across the horses' flanks.

Fleur did a quick recap of the contents of her suitcase. She only had one cotton dress, her best, and she'd given that a good flogging during the voyage. She couldn't bring herself to spend the money Mr. Waterstone had given her to buy another. She'd thrown in Mum's clippie boots and jacket, and for some reason she couldn't quite fathom, a pair of trousers. She'd suffocate in that lot. One skirt and a couple of blouses would have to see her through. She shucked off her gloves and tucked them into her pocket, then thought twice about her hat as they turned into a very smart street lined with large sandstone buildings that wouldn't have looked amiss in London.

"Got family here, have you?"

Fleur craned her neck to get a better look at the buildings. "No. Well, yes. Maybe."

The driver tossed her a quizzical frown and shook his head. She wasn't about to get into a discussion with him, especially when she couldn't explain it to herself.

"Macquarie Street." He gave an expansive wave of his hand, almost as though he'd single-handedly built every one of the large solemn-looking buildings. "Where all the nobs hang out. Parliament House and the like. 'Unter Street's just around the corner." He pulled out into the traffic, narrowly avoiding a clanging tram, and threw a turn that had the cab tipping on its wheels before it slewed to a halt. "Here you go. Number 50 'Unter Street. Lyttleton & Sons. Got some business to sort, 'ave you?"

She swallowed the inclination to tell the man to mind his own and rummaged in her bag for some money. When she pulled out one of Mr. Waterstone's pound notes, the cabbie's eyebrows disappeared under his cloth cap. "Ain't you got nothing smaller?"

"No, I'm sorry. I haven't."

"Well, duck inside and get them to break it."

She very nearly told him to keep the change but then sanity prevailed. It wasn't her money. She was just a caretaker. Hugh might well need every penny. "I won't be a moment." Leaving her suitcase on the pavement she ran up the steps. A big brass knocker hung dead center, and when she lifted it the door swung open, revealing a long, carpeted corridor. It was dreadfully smart. "Is there anybody home?"

Waiting for her eyes to adjust to the dimness of the interior, she stood like a fool on the doorstep while the cabbie dumped her case at her feet.

A rail-thin woman dressed in brown leather brogues and a high-necked blouse and dark skirt appeared at the end of the corridor. "Hello. Can I help you?"

"My name's Fleur. Fleur Richards." She smiled at the somewhat flustered-looking woman with a profusion of escaping hair.

"Oh my goodness." Her face flushed a little. "I'm Vera Lyttleton. We weren't expecting you quite so soon."

Fleur's stomach sank. She stood on the doorstep fidgeting while Mrs. Lyttleton shook her head and looked her up and down. "I can come back tomorrow."

"No. Come in. Please, come in."

"I must pay the cabbie and I don't have any change. I wonder if you could . . ." She waved the pound note in the air.

"I'll sort him out." Mrs. Lyttleton took the money and held back the door for Fleur to enter. "Kip, can you come and deal with Mrs. Richards' luggage, please? Go ahead. On the left. I won't be a moment."

Fleur pushed open the door. A large desk filled the space in front of the open window and a lovely bunch of cottage roses stood in a vase on the mantelpiece, perfuming the air. Not knowing quite what to do next, she hovered in the middle of the room.

"Just leave it in the hallway, Kip. We'd like some tea, if you don't mind, and there's oatmeal biscuits in the tin if you can find them." Mrs. Lyttleton came in and offered a half-hearted smile. "Welcome to Australia." She held out her hand. "This is the only respectable room, I'm afraid. We're in the throes of moving into the premises."

Fleur shifted her coat to the other arm, took Mrs. Lyttleton's hand, and gave it a brief shake with her damp and sweaty palm, worry fluttering in her stomach. "I'm pleased to meet you."

"Come and sit down. Let me take your coat." Mrs. Lyttleton hung it on a hat stand in the corner, and Fleur took one of the two chairs drawn up in front of the empty fireplace. "Mr. Waterstone's letter said not to expect you for another two weeks. When did your ship dock?"

"A week ago. We had to spend seven days in quarantine because there was a case of smallpox on board."

"And this threatening influenza, no doubt. I do hope no one is suffering."

"No, not a single person."

A young man in shirtsleeves, his overlong hair masking the pencil tucked behind his ear, brought in a rattling tray and thumped it down on the desk.

"Thank you, Kip. Fleur, this is Kip Cassidy—he helps me out."

The boy's ears turned bright pink as he mumbled something indecipherable, then made to leave.

"Just a moment, Kip. Could you please ring the Berkeley Hotel and inform them Mrs. Richards has arrived and will be requiring her room earlier than we anticipated?" Mrs. Lyttleton sighed. "I'm afraid you've caught me at a really bad time. As I said, we're moving in. All our paperwork is still boxed so I'm not able to deal with the formalities of your case. My husband, Mr. Lyttleton, was called away to assist with the repatriation board."

"Mrs. Lyttleton, I . . ." Fleur sucked in a deep breath and waited for the young man to leave. She didn't need any formalities; she needed to pin this woman down and tell her that she wasn't intending to accept anything of Hugh's. "I have to explain my reasons for coming to Australia."

"I'm thrilled you were able to. It will make matters so much easier. From what Mr. Waterstone said in his telegram, the inheritance has come as something of a shock."

More than a shock. "Hugh and I only knew each other for a matter of days." A blush rose to her cheeks.

"I'm so sorry. I've been remiss." She poured out a cup of tea, added some milk, and put it on the small table between them. "Please let me offer you our sincere condolences. Mr. Lyttleton told me Hugh was a delightful young man."

Fleur let out a long, slow breath and pulled back her shoulders. It had to be said, and now. She felt like a fraud. "I don't believe that I am entitled to benefit from Hugh's will." There, it hadn't been too difficult. Now for the rest. She had to give voice to her belief. "And to be honest, I'm not convinced Hugh's dead."

Chapter 8

Sydney, NSW
1853

After his preferred breakfast of black coffee, *Wurst*, and *Käse*, which Sladdin had managed to conjure up, Stefan peered out the window into the swirling confusion of the street below. An uncontrolled buggy skirted a barrow laden with fresh vegetables, forcing a group of overdressed gentlemen into the center of the street. They scattered, making way for three high-stepping, polished bays who would have done the Viennese school proud. He narrowed his eyes, squinting into the early-morning sunshine, then let out a crack of laughter.

Atop the huge stallion sat a small, scrawny figure, legs almost horizontal, barely spanning the back of the enormous steed. By the look of things young Herr Burless must have overheard his comments to Sladdin, and not wanting to miss an opportunity had found not two, but three excellent animals.

He threw up the window and raised his hand. Doffing his cap, Bert acknowledged his salute, then shimmied down and led the three horses across the crowded street, giving the overdressed gentlemen a wide berth.

"*Guter Mann*," he called, then slammed the window closed and bolted down the stairs in his shirtsleeves and braces.

"Can I be of any assistance, Captain?" Sladdin, all skinny black-suited arms and legs, blocked his path to the outside.

"None at all, none at all."

"A word, Captain von Richter."

Stifling a groan, he turned to Sladdin with raised eyebrows. "I trust you enjoyed your visit to the Curio Shop."

It was as well he wasn't conducting an illicit relationship—the man seemed to scrutinize his every move. "I did."

"Would you like me to procure some horses for you?"

"That won't be necessary." He pushed through the door and bounded into the street. He'd rather rely on the young lad than the all-knowing, sycophantic Sladdin.

"And the top of the morning to you."

Stefan's laughter echoed along Bent Street. "Irish today are you, lad?"

"Like to ring the changes. Found you some horses, if'n you're interested." Bert's grin stretched from ear to ear, cracking his dirt-encrusted face.

"And who might you have here?"

Bert made no reply as he walked around the three horses checking them from every angle. "Well?" he asked as he reached the horses' heads, his voice gruffer than he intended. The animals were excellent. Who had he stolen them from?

Bert lifted his chin, his eyes narrowing. "Thought you wanted to hire good horses. If that's not the case, I'll be on me way." He clicked his tongue and the animals turned neatly to follow him.

Three, not two as he'd asked. Why he was giving the lad such a hard time, he had no idea. The animals were just what he wanted, oozing stamina and reeking of good health. Out of the corner of his eye he could see Sladdin standing in the doorway of the hotel, his beady eyes capturing every moment. More than likely regretting the loss of business. "Wait a minute." Stefan ran his eye over the animals' perfect conformation. All three were magnificent, good strong bones, deep across the chest, bright eyes. "Where did you get them?"

Bert sniffed loudly and wiped the back of his spare hand under his filthy nose. "Man don't give away his sources."

"Man better if he wants to make a quid or two."

The lad rolled his eyes and looked heavenward. "I ain't nicked 'em, if that's what you think. You said you wanted two good strong horses."

"And you brought three."

"Thought maybe you'd need one for your manservant."

"I haven't got a manservant, as you very well know." He stopped in his tracks and studied the skinny, carrot-topped bunch of bones jiggling from one foot to another. "But I'm interested, and if you have a mind to accompany me I can offer you a decent wage." Now where had that come from?

Two bright eyes shone up at him and a wide grin split the grubby face.

"You can handle a horse on the open road, can't you?"

"'Course I can."

Stefan delved into his pocket and produced a handful of coins and notes. "Go and get yourself a decent set of warm clothes and good boots, arrange for the hire of the horses, and meet me back here in an hour. I've got some business to attend to."

"You for real?"

It was a bit of a gamble, but from what he'd heard, most men for hire hid their limited good qualities beneath a preference for copious amounts of rum that tended to render them useless. This lad amused him. "And get yourself scrubbed clean too." Bert seemed to have a good head on his shoulders and he liked his spirit.

"Yes, Capt'n." Bert gathered the reins and took off as though the hounds of hell were after him.

Whistling some waltz caught in his mind from the governor's soirée, Stefan turned onto O'Connell Street and then onto Hunter. The door of the Curio Shop stood wide open and he stepped inside, inhaling the strange medley of odors he remembered. The sinister overtones of the night before had vanished in the beam of sunlight that illuminated the polished timber floor.

Sitting, head bent, at her desk, a quill in hand, Mrs. Atterton made a pretty picture. "Good morning."

"Good morning, Captain." When she glanced up, the strange amber flecks in her cool green eyes caught the light. "I was in the throes of writing you some instructions." She leaned forward and he caught a faint breath of something metallic, not unpleasant, but unexpected. "Unfortunately my men have already left for the Hawkesbury. They won't be returning for another two weeks at least."

That was a pity. He'd set his heart on leaving as soon as possible to track down Bishop. He'd wanted to combine the trips. "Instructions for what?"

"Why, instructions to meet up with my men in the area where I source my artifacts. I presumed you wanted to visit since you have procured horses."

Was nothing a secret in this town? "That is my intention. I have an invitation to visit the Wisemans' family properties."

Her eyebrows rose. "Indeed! I am impressed by your unprejudiced interest in our society. Government House one day, an emancipist's family the next." The corner of her mouth twitched, robbing her words of offense. "My suggestion is that you should take the steamer up the Hawkesbury River to Wisemans Ferry. Once there . . ." She pulled a map from the desk drawer, laid it on the table, and stabbed at a spot north and inland of Sydney. "Once there you could easily travel to St. Albans. There is a remarkably good hotel called the Settlers Arms. My men will meet you there."

"I intend to call on someone on the Macdonald River. A Mr. Bishop. I don't have a mind to take the steamer." And what of the horses? He'd taken rather a fancy to them, and the boy. The trip from England had more than used up his interest in shipboard travel; he'd rather see something of the countryside and travel the paths the baron had taken.

"Then it is the perfect answer. My men will be in St. Albans in three days and will meet you and your manservant."

"I don't have a—"

"Young Bert."

Three days later, Stefan and a much-scrubbed and smartly attired Bert took the road out of Wisemans heading for St. Albans. Bert tipped his hat back from his face and leaned forward in the saddle to remove a speck of dust from his highly polished boots. "How d'you know this Mr. Bishop?"

"I don't. He has an item in safekeeping and I intend to retrieve it."

"How did he get it?"

"It's a long story. A mineralogist—"

"A what?"

"Someone who is interested in metals and minerals."

"Aw, you mean like them gold diggers."

"Exactly like that, Bert. Yes, a far easier way to explain."

"He's got some gold for you?" An almost fanatical fervor lit Bert's eyes.

"No, not gold, but something possibly quite valuable. An uncut gemstone, perhaps an opal." Hopefully the man still had the specimen and would be prepared to part with it. The offer of money would surely be far more tempting than a dubious rock sample.

"And you've come all the way just to get it?"

"Not just to get it. I'm also completing the baron's travel diaries."

"And you want some of them stuffed animals too."

The lad would make an excellent diplomat with the nose he had for intrigue and gossip. Perhaps he shouldn't have mentioned the opal. He would have to ensure that Bert understood the importance of discretion; until it was authenticated it was better kept quiet. "Australian flora and fauna are unique."

"Flora?"

"Plants."

"Then fawns'd be the animals. We call 'em little 'roos joeys, you know. Why not just get 'em from the Curio Shop?"

Why not indeed? Because of some insatiable need he had to see everything in its natural habitat. The baron's enthusiasm had first sparked his interest and now, as they rode through the landscape, he'd come to understand his fascination with this strange land. "According to the instructions Sladdin gave me, Mr. Bishop's property should be a little farther along here. There's a horseshoe bend in the river, and we should see the house from the road."

"If Sladdin says so, it'll be there."

They rode on for a few more minutes along the track, the verges full of daisies, yellow buttons, clematis, and a wonderful purple creeper.

"There it is. Over there." Bert stood tall in his stirrups, pointing his finger toward the wide sweep of the fast-flowing river. Surrounded on three sides, the house stood tall amid a vast patch of grass, greener than he'd seen anywhere else in this dry country. There was a complete lack of any adornment to the grounds, just a winding dirt track that led to the large two-story sandstone house, which would have been more suited to Macquarie Street.

"Take the horses down to the river and get them watered, let them graze for a bit. I'll walk the rest of the way. I don't intend to be long." He dismounted and threw the reins to Bert. Not only were the horses excellent specimens, they appeared very well trained and happy to stand and wait.

He made his way up the track, imagining an avenue of stately eucalypts delineating the edges. Two massive urns marked the steps leading to the front doors, which were shut tight. He bounded up and rapped sharply, then turned to survey the view. With the backdrop of the Hawkesbury River, the gardens could be magnificent. The colonial herd was so busy establishing its place in this strange society they paid little attention to matters of the soul.

"Come in, come in." A small man dressed in a rough jacket and dusty boots held the door open and ushered him through into a wide hallway.

"I'd like to speak with your master, Mr. Bishop. Is he available?"

A rumbling noise eased its way out of the man's mouth and he stuck out his hand. "At your service."

Stefan found his hand grasped in a firm, calloused handshake. "I beg your pardon, I . . ."

"Think nothing of it. What can I do for you?"

More what he could do for Bishop; the baron's promissory note glowed warm in his inside top pocket. The house, though solid, lacked any form of decoration; perhaps the rooms behind the doors were better equipped; however, he had a suspicion some additional money might not go astray. "My name is Stefan von Richter. May I come in and explain the reason for my visit?"

The man's woolly eyebrows took a leap up his forehead and a touch of color flushed his cheeks. "Come and sit down." He led the way into an equally sparse sitting room. Two high-backed chairs rested in front of an unlit fire. The saving grace was a set of floor-to-ceiling windows offering a spectacular view across the river to the sandstone cliffs.

Stefan settled himself into one of the chairs. "Baron von Hügel sends his greetings and thanks you for your kindness."

"Kindness?"

"I believe you have a metallurgical sample, sent to you by Professor Menge."

The stain on the man's cheeks deepened and he cleared his throat. "Yes. Yes. I did receive it."

"And I am here to collect it."

The high color then leached from the man's face. Perhaps Menge had offered something more than payment. Stefan stood up and reached into his inside pocket and withdrew the promissory note he'd tucked there for the very purpose.

Bishop shot to his feet as though affronted and stalked to the windows, hands clasped firmly behind his back, and stood rocking backward and forward on his heels. "I can't take money." He ground the words out. "The stone's not here."

"You have it in Sydney then." A wasted journey but not the end of the world. He placed the promissory note on the table.

Bishop swiveled on his heels and faced him, his face no longer red, more resembling blanched almonds. "I gave it away."

"Gave it away?" Menge was convinced it was a true opal, and of far better quality than any found in Europe in hundreds of years. Gave it away. "To whom? And why?"

"A man named Skeffington. Lives in Sydney. It was Primrose's last request." Bishop knuckled something suspiciously like tears from the corners of his eyes and sank once more into the chair. "She was right. Right all along and I didn't believe her."

There was more to this than he'd anticipated. Stefan perched on the opposite chair and waited while Bishop inhaled deeply in a vain attempt to compose himself.

"Mrs. Bishop, my darling wife, Primrose, was killed in an unexpected house fire."

As the governor had told him. What did it have to do with the opal? "My condolences."

"I am entirely responsible. When the package arrived from Professor Menge my curiosity was aroused. Unpardonable, but I opened it and what I saw took my breath away. The stone was not polished or presented in any way, but it glowed with a life of its own. I was captivated and, sadly, so was Primrose. She kept it on her person, fascinated by the way it changed color in the light. I hold the stone entirely responsible for her demise." Bishop pushed himself wearily to his feet and stood staring out the window into the meadow that led down to the river. Bert and the horses were nowhere in sight. "I brought her here, from Sydney, and buried her where the primroses bloom."

The poor man was distraught. But who was Skeffington and where would Stefan find him? And how could the stone be responsible for her death? Before Stefan could open his mouth to speak, Bishop continued in a sudden rush as though he wanted to get the matter out in the open air, dispel his misery. "Primrose was an avid reader, and once a story had captured her fascination it would never leave her."

What Primrose had read was irrelevant; he needed to know the whereabouts of the stone. It would be like searching for a needle in a haystack to find another, and with Menge dead he wouldn't even know where to begin.

"Primrose acquired a copy of Sir Walter Scott's novel *Anne of Geierstein*. The story tells of an enchanted princess who wore an opal that changed colors with her moods. Primrose became convinced Menge's stone was an opal. In the novel a few drops of holy water extinguish the stone's magic fire and the princess is reduced to ashes. As was my poor Primrose."

The hairs on Stefan's forearms stood to attention. How ridiculous! Bishop would have him believing this fictional nonsense before long. Only a year after the publication of Scott's book people began associating opals with bad luck until Queen Victoria became totally enamored with the gemstones and the demand rebounded to such an extent the Hungarian mines as good as dried up. But none of that was relevant. He wanted Menge's specimen, possibly the first opal to be found in this strange country. He'd made a promise to the baron.

"It is never easy to lose a loved one."

"After my wife's death I could no longer see any meaning to my life . . ."

Which would account for the barren nature of the house. The lack of comfort, both physical and emotional. He knew the ache of loneliness only too well. "And you gave the stone to this Skeffington fellow?"

"Robert Skeffington, yes. And not *gave* exactly, more used it in partial payment for this property. He resides in Sydney, is well known and thoroughly reputable. I am certain there will be no problem in reclaiming the stone." He handed back the promissory note. "In fact, I suspect he might be pleased. He has a very fine home in Potts Point, overlooking the harbor. Sladdin at the Berkeley can assist you if you are unable to track him down. He frequently attends the card games there." Bishop jumped to his feet, looking as though he'd shed a barrow load of concern. "Now, if you'll excuse me, I have work to do."

"Of course, thank you."

"I'm not able to offer you accommodation. It's very remiss of me. However, there is an excellent inn not far up the road in St. Albans. I apologize if you have had a wasted journey."

"No, not at all, and no wasted journey. I am expected at the Settlers Arms this evening and intend to spend some time familiarizing myself with the area."

"In that case . . ." With a relieved smile Bishop held out his hand. This time the calluses made sense. Despite the impressive house, the man was working his own property. Good luck to him. Stefan had nothing but admiration for these kinds of settlers, far removed from the toffee-nosed fools clustering around the false glow radiating from Government House.

Robert Skeffington. Potts Point. Surely the man couldn't be too difficult to find.

And nor was Bert. He'd come to no harm, sitting down by the river, back against the tree munching on an apple, the horses unsaddled and enjoying a graze on the verdant river flats. Bishop might think he'd been haunted by bad luck, but he'd snared himself a patch of paradise.

"D'you find what you were looking for?" Bert jumped to his feet, picking up his saddle.

"No. Not exactly. No matter. I can deal with it when we return to Sydney." If the beliefs about opals and bad luck had infiltrated the rest of Sydney society, it would be to his advantage. He had no doubt Skeffington would be more than happy to hand over the stone in exchange for the money Bishop owed to him.

"What is this opal biz, Capt'n? Only Opal I've ever 'eard of works down at the Rose and Crown at the Rocks and what she's got on offer ain't worth a pinch of salt, never mind that lot you got stashed in your top pocket."

"Do you know what an opal is, Bert?"

"Told you, only one I know is—"

"Yes, yes. An opal is a precious gemstone, a little like a diamond or a ruby."

"And these things, they're worth money?"

"There's quite a market for them. The Queen's very fond of them." Despite whatever ridiculous notions might be bandied around.

"Our Queen. The Queen in England?"

"Yes, your Queen. Victoria."

"Who's the Queen of Austria then?"

"We don't have a queen. Just princes and a profusion of minor aristocracy who spend their time squabbling."

"Don't hold much wiv all that politic stuff." Bert pulled off his hat, wiped his forehead, and wrinkled his freckled nose. "So why don't you forget about this 'ere opal and go and dig up some more and give 'em to the Queen. Wouldn't that make you 'specially important-like and you could set yourself up a treat?"

"It's not as simple as that. And I am going to have to ask you to keep this matter to yourself."

Bert puffed out his chest. "Secret-like?"

"Indeed. To the best of our knowledge this is the first opal to be found in Australia. It's important that it is tested and its quality and authenticity verified before the world gets to hear of it."

"And the man who knows first will have a head start. Be the first in the business and make himself a nice little pile." Bert spat on his palm and held it out. "Better shake on it then. Here's to sealed lips."

Without a second thought Stefan grasped Bert's hand, then clapped him on the shoulder. Educated or not, this lad had his head screwed on. He was a lucky find, and it was highly unlikely Stefan would regret his decision to give him a chance. "Sealed lips and secrecy."

"You sound like one of them posh blokes at Government House. Do they speak English in Austria? Don't they have something different—like the natives do here?"

Stefan let out a bark of laughter. Bert was going to be an entertaining traveling companion. *"Steh gerade! Sieh mich an!"*

"Sounds like you're throwing your weight around. What's it mean?"

No, he didn't miss a trick. "It means 'stand up straight and look me in the eyes.' The baron used to shout it at me all the time."

"So how come you speak proper-like? Like an English gent." Bert's mind skittered around like a rat on hot coals.

"My tutors were English."

"Chewters?"

"Teachers. Many years ago Professor Menge was one of the baron's tutors. That's how they knew each other."

"And he carked it before he could give the baron the opal."

"That he did, Bert. That he did."

Chapter 9

Sydney, NSW
1919

"Oh my dear!" Mrs. Lyttleton grasped both Fleur's hands. "It's a matter of acceptance. We all feel like that when we lose someone. It will come with time."

It wouldn't. She'd had all the time in the world. Weeks aboard ship with very little to do other than scan the face of every man, hoping against hope she'd see Hugh's blue eyes. "I didn't receive a telegram; there is no proof that Hugh is not coming home."

"There was no telegram, my dear, because after the death of his brothers, the army believed he had no next of kin, which is why Mr. Lyttleton was notified."

"What about his identity disc?" One of the soldiers on the ship had explained to her these were two tin discs worn around the neck. One green and the other red. Red for blood, to identify the dead soldier's personal belongings, and one grass green, to be buried with the body.

"I'm sorry, Fleur. I don't have his personal possessions yet, or his identity disc."

"Then you don't know he's dead." Her heart almost took flight.

Fleur tried to pull her fingers away from Mrs. Lyttleton's grasp but she held tight. "I'm sorry, there's no doubt. Hugh died in France. Give it time, my dear. Denial is often the first reaction to hearing such dreadful news."

Fleur dragged in a deep breath. First Mr. Waterstone and now Mrs. Lyttleton. "Are you sure there hasn't been a mistake?" How could she believe Hugh was dead? It would be a betrayal of their love, their dreams, his promises. "And how do you know what Hugh wanted?"

"Hugh was of sound body and mind when he gave Mr. Lyttleton his instructions. He visited the day he signed up and then sent further instructions after his brothers died." Finally, she dropped Fleur's hands and sat back in the chair, her arms folded.

"Exactly. That was before we'd even met, never mind married."

"Hugh then wrote and told Mr. Lyttleton of your marriage, named you as his next of kin."

"The only reason I'm here, Mrs. Lyttleton, is that when I spoke to Mr. Waterstone, he said if I didn't come the property would be sold and the monies deposited in my account."

Not quite the truth, because she hadn't even had an account at that stage, just the faded brown velvet handkerchief purse she kept under her mattress for her wages. Mr. Waterstone had taken matters into his own hands and opened an account with Barclays Bank in her name. She'd even been given a checkbook, though she couldn't bring herself to use it. Cashing the pound note for the cabbie was the first time she'd spent any of Hugh's money.

". . . properties."

"Hugh must have someone, a friend or relative he trusted who might know more." What had Mrs. Lyttleton just said? "Properties?"

"Yes. Properties."

"Where exactly?"

"I'm not sure precisely. The commercial premises are just up the road, that I do know. I believe there might also be assets both here and on the Continent, but that must be confirmed."

"Continent?" Good grief, she was squawking like a parrot. Fleur flapped her hands in front of her face. It was indescribably hot even with the window wide open. "Which continent?"

Mrs. Lyttleton's cheeks pinked and she ran her hand through her flyaway hair. "Europe, I believe. Until I find the paperwork I can't be entirely certain. As I said, Michael is currently involved with the repatriation of our troops. Over 165,000 of the poor boys. I have no idea how they'll manage. I was hoping to have the boxes unpacked before you arrived. I'm not sure of the exact details as I've had some difficulty locating the files. However, it falls upon me to advise you that you are a very wealthy woman, and as such have responsibilities."

There was that word again, *responsibilities* . . . Everyone kept banging on about her responsibilities. The only responsibility she had was to ensure that there hadn't been some ghastly mistake and Hugh was alive, injured somewhere. "Unless Hugh is alive."

"My dear, you must come to terms with this. What you need is time to settle in." Mrs. Lyttleton jumped to her feet. "Kip!"

The boy—no, he wasn't a boy, he was a man. She could see that now he had his shirtsleeves rolled down and a jacket on. Tall and lean with a raw, uneasy edge to him. Standing with his hands sunk deep into his pockets. Probably about the same age as she was except for his eyes. They seemed tired, as though he'd been awake for too long and couldn't think straight. Something she could sympathize with.

"Kip, would you please take Mrs. Richards to the Berkeley?" Mrs. Lyttleton turned back to her. "We'll discuss this when you've had a chance to settle. I realize it is a lot to take in."

Perhaps Mrs. Lyttleton was right. It was a lot to get her head around, a lot more than Mr. Waterstone had indicated. Maybe he was worried he'd frighten her off.

"I think the best thing is for me to track down the rest of the information and go through everything. Mr. Lyttleton is very thorough so I have no doubt once I find the papers, everything will become clear."

Kip cleared his throat, grasped her suitcase, and barged out the door.

"Don't go without your change." Mrs. Lyttleton scooped the handful of coins from the top of the desk and held it out. Fleur took the money and offered a wan smile—it was the best she could manage—before walking back out into the bright sunshine, her coat draped over her arm and her head whirling.

Throwing a quick look over his shoulder, Kip gestured down the street. "Shall I call a cab? It's not far."

"I'd like to walk. I need the fresh air. I feel a little as though I've landed on another planet."

Without a word he took off, her bag slung over his shoulder and his head down. She had to scamper a little to keep up with his long-legged strides. After a moment or two he stopped, took a deep breath, and lifted his head. "This is Hunter Street. Down here a pace or two is the Curio Shop."

She frowned up at him. "Curio Shop?"

"Yes, one of the Richards properties. Didn't Vera mention it?"

She shook her head, wondering if perhaps she'd missed something. *Assets here and on the Continent*—she could remember that. Her brain felt like day-old Yorkshire pudding, all soggy and flat, and the heat wasn't helping.

"The commercial property." Kip drew to a halt in front of a shuttered building, like the solicitor's offices although in a far worse state of repair. Large planks had been nailed crisscross across the door and the windows had been boarded. "The sign is still there. None of the tenants got around to repainting."

Fleur craned her neck to read the faded sign above the large front window: *The Curio Shop of Wonders*. "This belongs to Hugh?" It looked more like some dubious séance haunt in Soho.

"It's not leased at the moment. A lot of businesses closed. First the depression in the '90s and then the war."

"It looks as though it's been closed for a lot longer than that." Both the sign and the timbers across the door had faded to a chalky green color and in places the paint had disappeared altogether, revealing pale splotches of weather-beaten timber.

"I'm not sure of the details. You'll have to ask Vera for the ins and outs."

The door to the premises next door banged and Kip flinched, bringing the shuttered look back to his face. He picked up the pace again so she had to trot after him a little like a stray puppy. They crossed a couple of busy streets, then entered a shady park.

Once under the trees Kip's shoulders dropped and he slowed. "That's the Berkeley over there."

A grand three-story Georgian edifice dominated the road junction. "I can't stay there."

"Why not? I'd make the most of it if I were you." Without giving her a moment to reply he led the way up the wide sandstone steps, pushed open the glass doors, and she found herself in the tiled reception area with a long, polished desk almost the length of the wall. Kip marched up and hit the bell. The ping bounced off the high ceiling and a man dressed in a black frock coat, looking as though he'd escaped from a Dickens novel, scurried out.

"Good afternoon, Mrs. Richards. Mr. Sladdin, at your service."

Heavens above, did everyone in the entire country know who she was? A flush rose to her cheeks. How ridiculous. Obviously the clerk would know Kip; Mrs. Lyttleton had booked the room for her and asked Kip to ring ahead. She nodded.

"Just sign here, please." He turned the ledger and pushed it across the desktop to her. She scrawled her name, and after a cursory glance at her signature he pushed a room key toward her. "The baron's suite, up the stairs and on the right, nice view out toward the harbor. I'll have your bags sent up. Breakfast is served in the dining room until nine."

He pointed across to another double doorway. "Luncheon at your discretion and dinner from six o'clock."

Fleur turned to thank Kip but he was already disappearing through the door into the street.

The banister, worn smooth over the years, slid beneath the palm of her hand as she ascended the stairs. When she reached the top, she stopped and took in the long, sweeping corridor, then turned to her right and came to a halt in front of a shiny white-painted door. A brass sign, glinting like solid gold in a rogue sunbeam, proclaimed *The Baron's Suite*. For goodness' sake! She didn't need a suite of rooms, and certainly not one that belonged to a baron. In London she'd managed quite well in one room with a shared bathroom. Although she wouldn't miss that, or the cabbage stench.

The key turned smoothly and she pushed the door open. A curl of excitement twirled in her stomach as she took in the beautiful room. Wide floor-to-ceiling windows adorned with heavy olive-green velvet curtains caught back to allow the light to flood in and reflect from the highly polished surface of the small oval dining table. Between the two windows was a neat desk; headed notepaper and envelopes were lined up on a leather blotter next to a bottle of ink and an expensive-looking fountain pen.

Someone cleared their throat and she turned.

"Excuse me, miss. Your bags." A uniformed boy, hardly more than twelve, walked in and threw open a door on the other side of the room and placed her bag on a timber luggage rack at the end of a huge bed covered in snowy white linen. "Anything else, miss?" He stood hovering in the doorway.

"No, that's all, thank you." He still didn't move.

She tucked her hand into her coat pocket and pulled out a sixpence and held it out to him. His eyes lit up and she had the strangest feeling he was going to snatch it and bite down on it. "Thank you, miss. If you need anything else . . ." He let the rest of the sentence dangle and, when she didn't reply, closed the door quietly behind him.

Fleur slumped down into one of the soft leather armchairs, her head still spinning. The last time she'd taken stock she'd been the one receiving the tips; now she was dispensing them with hardly a second thought. When she next saw Mrs. Lyttleton she'd simply have to be more assertive. Hugh's family must have had dealings with the solicitors before, otherwise he wouldn't have asked them to draw up his will. They must know something about his family. They must help her find a definite answer. She didn't belong here in this life, in the baron's suite handing out tips.

Chapter 10

Sydney, NSW
1919

Despite the glorious weather outside the window, Fleur couldn't shake the feeling of lethargy. She sat stirring her cup of tea, throwing surreptitious glances around the dining room at the other hotel guests. Every single one of them looked as though they had an important position to uphold and a list of tasks that only they could complete. The besuited, starch-collared gentlemen and the women in pretty summer dresses gave no inkling of the deprivations London suffered. Truth was, she felt like a fraud. She ought to be serving the tea, not sitting here in this fancy dining room like Lady Muck. She had to do something.

Leaving the remains of her breakfast, she slipped out into the foyer and sneaked through the front door while Mr. Sladdin's back was turned.

Sydney's streets seemed different from London's. Wider and more organized. There was just as much traffic: cars, trams, horse-drawn carriages, and bicycles, so many bicycles. The buildings were impressive in their way, though nothing like Trafalgar Square, St. Paul's, or the Houses of Parliament with their ancient associations and oozing history.

It took her a moment or two to get her bearings, but once she saw the mass of sandstone buildings the cabbie had pointed out, she quickly found her way to Hunter Street and, thankful for the shade the shops provided, wandered along past a furniture business, a pharmacy, and a men's outfitters until she found the Curio Shop.

From the outside, it gave the impression of having been deserted. With a quick glance over her shoulder, she walked up to the front door. Heavy timber was nailed diagonally across the door, topped by a dilapidated *Keep Out* sign painted in rough letters that had faded over time. One large window, equally barred, fronted the street. With her nose pressed up to a tiny corner of glass she squinted inside.

Nothing.

She rubbed at the glass with the heel of her hand and then flattened her cheek against the small pane and stuck her fingers under the corner of the plank of wood. Taking another quick look over her shoulder, she tugged at the timber. The wet and rotten corner crumbled. She moved along a little and broke off another longer splinter, and another, until she'd cleared a small square about the size of her handkerchief.

A long, low-ceilinged room stretched the length of the building, a shimmer of light indicating a window at the back.

Pulling her cloche straight, she strolled past the buildings and down the hill to the end of the street, counting the buildings. Twelve by the time she reached the end of the road. Then she turned left. A little farther on she found an alleyway. Despite the warm sun she shivered as she entered the narrow laneway framed by well-maintained fences. It seemed so strange that the Curio Shop would be the only place locked and barred when all the others were in such a good state of repair.

The fence lines were broken by tall gates and small yards leading to the back of the buildings. When she reached the twelfth property she stood on tiptoe and peered over the fence. A bare patch of dirt led to the back of the building.

What she needed was a crate or a box or something to stand on.

With a sigh of frustration, she leaned her shoulder against the gate. It didn't budge. Rattling got her nowhere. Who had rented the shop last and why was it empty among all these thriving businesses? Next time she saw Mrs. Lyttleton she'd ask for the key and demand some answers, not sit there like a speechless fool. There could be something inside that would give her a clue about the Richards family.

She stuck her foot into a small hole in the gate and stretched up to have another look.

"What do you think you're doing?"

Her foot slipped from the toe hole and she slid down into the dirt in an unceremonious lump.

With her cheeks the color of a beacon she turned around to face a large blousy woman, her body cut in half by a lurid, flowery apron and her hair wrapped in curlers, half-heartedly covered in a scarf that had seen better days.

"I . . . um . . . I was just having a look over the fence." She bent down and rubbed at her throbbing shin. A large splinter stuck out at a right angle through her torn stocking. She gritted her teeth and reefed it out.

"Lucky that's all you've got to show for it."

Fleur spat on her finger and rubbed at the swelling bubble of blood, her heart racketing against her ribs and the blood rushing to her head. For one horrible moment the world darkened. Fighting her wavering vision, she concentrated on the woman's broken-down boots.

"Nasty." The boots receded and the woman bent down and peered at her leg. "Need something on that so as it don't get infected. Come with me." Not waiting for an answer, she disappeared through the gate next door.

Fleur peered up and down the laneway. Should she or shouldn't she? Maybe this woman would know how she could get a look inside now. For goodness' sake, it was a little too late to be worrying about taking chances; the mere fact she was in Australia was the biggest chance she'd ever taken in her life.

Straightening up, she took a deep breath, trying very hard to forget about the blood trickling down her leg and her ripped stocking, and followed the woman through the gate. Ducking under the flapping sheets on the washing line, she made her way to the back door.

"Sit yourself down there and I'll find some gentian violet."

"It's very kind of you." Fleur lowered herself onto the coal box, gingerly lifted the hem of her skirt, and eyed the nasty, throbbing mess.

"Now, this'll sting a bit." The woman scrubbed at her shin with a piece of toweling and some warm water. "Me old man got a load of sump oil and he did all the fences only last week. Don't want that muck rushing around in your blood. Don't know where it's been." She dried the gouge and then undid a small bottle of evil-looking purple liquid and painted it liberally onto Fleur's knee, shin, and stocking. "Keep this stuff handy all the time. Me three boys are terrors. Always doing something to themselves, they are."

Fleur let out a squeal as the liquid sank into her flesh. "Thank you," she muttered through gritted teeth.

"Now, are you going to tell me what you were up to?"

Color flushed her face. What was she going to say? She wasn't breaking into the property, but there was no way the woman was going to believe her story. "I was just having a look over the fence."

"English, are you?"

Fleur nodded. At least the subject had changed. "Yes, I arrived a week ago on one of the troop ships."

"Nurse? Nah. No nurse would react to a scratch like you did. I thought for a moment you were going to pass out on me."

True enough. She'd never been good with blood, especially not her own. "My family died in the zeppelin raids in London and I've come in search of some distant relatives."

"On 'Unter Street? I've lived here all me married life. Who are you looking for?"

For some reason she didn't want to mention Hugh's name, didn't want Mrs. Lyttleton to know she'd sneaked around the shop. "No one in particular. I was interested because from the street side it looks as though the houses are only two stories, but when I looked through the window . . ." No, that just made it worse. Now she was admitting to being a Peeping Tom.

"Well, I'm pleased to hear that. You wouldn't want to have anything to do with the Curio Shop."

"Whyever not?"

"Been empty as long as I can remember. My Fred's lived here all his life. Says it was leased a few times before the depression in the '90s but the businesses never thrived. A tailor, I think, and maybe a milliner. Been boarded up for donkey's years." She looked over her shoulder. "Some say the place is haunted." Her voice lowered to a throaty whisper.

The hair rose on Fleur's arms. "Haunted?"

"Well, not so much haunted, just full of bad luck. Last lot who rented it contracted some sort of family illness. They all got sick. Stomach problems. When the old man died the wife and kids packed up and left Sydney."

"What happened to them?"

"No idea."

"Have you ever been inside?"

"Me? No way."

None of this was getting her any closer to finding an answer and besides, it couldn't have had anything to do with Hugh's family, otherwise Mrs. Lyttleton would know. "Did it ever belong to people by the name of Richards?"

The woman shrugged her shoulders and ambled across to the

washing line to check her sheets. She started to pull them down. "Nope. Not that I know of."

"Thanks for your help, Mrs. . . ."

"Glad, just call me Glad. You all right now?"

"Much better." Fleur got to her feet and tested her leg. Stinging, but no harm done. She'd go back to the hotel and change her stockings and have a bit of a think. "Thanks for your help."

Glad bundled the sheets against her ample bosom and nodded her head. "Got to get these inside before the boys get home and start kicking that ball of theirs around and making them all mucky."

Taking one last look at the building, Fleur made her way along the lane back onto Hunter Street. Her heart as good as jumped into her mouth when she spotted Kip pacing up and down the street outside the Curio Shop, hands rammed deep into his pockets. He executed a very neat turn and their eyes met and all thoughts of avoiding him flew away.

"Mr. Sladdin thought I might find you here. Vera wants a word."

"It's very kind of you to come and find me. I don't want to be a nuisance."

"No trouble." His forehead creased into a frown and he stared down at her leg. "Have you hurt yourself?"

"It's nothing."

Seemingly satisfied with her answer he took off at a fast pace, looking neither left nor right.

When they arrived he took her straight into the front room where Mrs. Lyttleton was sitting at the desk. "I hope I haven't interrupted your morning, but I have managed to get hold of some more details. Do sit down." Two spots of color highlighted her cheeks and she seemed positively excited.

Fleur sank into the chair drawn up on the other side of the desk.

"I have some suggestions to make."

Suggestions? Perhaps that was what she needed, someone to take her in hand. Right now she felt rather like a piece of flotsam bumping along the Thames with the tide. No sense of purpose. "Mrs. Lyttleton . . ."

"Vera, please."

"Vera, I have to make myself clear. Hugh and I were married so quickly we hardly knew each other. We had only five days together. I didn't even know he had an inheritance." Heaven forbid the woman thought she was some kind of gold digger.

"But he expected that you would come to Australia after the war."

"Well, yes. We talked about it." Dreamed about it, made foolish plans about a large family and country living.

I'll teach you to ride. We'll camp under the stars and bathe in crystal-clear streams. We'll look at the Milky Way and make promises on shooting stars.

Promises. She didn't want promises. She wanted Hugh.

"I think it is very important that we make a plan and see if we can unravel the whole situation. Since Mr. Lyttleton isn't here and hasn't responded to my telegrams, we must do the best we can."

Vera's chair scraped on the floor as she stood up and walked around the desk. Her warm, reassuring hand squeezed her shoulder. "We'll sort this out. I applaud your courage in coming all the way to Australia. I'm not sure I would have had the strength." Vera glanced at the clock on the mantelpiece. "I have half an hour. Tea first, I think, and then we'll plan. Kip! You don't mind if I involve Kip, do you? As you can see I'm still at sixes and sevens with this move. He may seem a little taciturn, but his heart is in the right place."

"No, not at all."

Kip's head appeared around the door and he stood hovering, adjusting his braces, tucking in his shirt.

"Could you make a pot of tea and bring it in here, with three cups if you would, and some biscuits? We need your help."

His face broke into a tentative grin. Fleur couldn't help but smile in return, and pray that he wouldn't say he'd found her outside the Curio Shop that morning.

"Now let's start at the beginning. The envelope I have here contains very little: Hugh's original will made after he signed up, some information about two properties, and the letter telling Mr. Lyttleton of your marriage and naming you as his next of kin. Sadly, Hugh's two older brothers were killed in France."

"Yes. He told me. It was one of the things we had in common. My parents were killed in the first zeppelin raid in London at the beginning of the war."

Just the two of us against the world.

"Then you understand. As the only surviving brother, Hugh inherited the family fortune. And on his death it passes to his next of kin. And that, my dear, is you."

"But why didn't he tell me?"

"Perhaps there wasn't time. Or maybe he wanted you to love him for who he was and not what he had."

Kip reappeared with a tray bearing a pot of tea and cups and plonked it down on the table with a clatter. Mrs. Black would've had his guts for garters.

Vera tucked one of the many flyaway strands of hair behind her ear and looked down at a piece of paper.

"Now, there is the property a few doors down, the old Curio Shop. Kip tells me he took you past it on your way to the hotel. It's been boarded up, untenanted for as long as I can remember. I suggest we start there once I locate the key."

Fleur wrapped one leg around the other, attempting to hide the gash on her leg. The last thing she wanted to do was explain that she'd already taken matters into her own hands and been caught snooping.

"The only other thing I found in the envelope was a reference to an eighty-acre property in the Hawkesbury region just outside St. Albans, dated well before his brothers' deaths, which was to pass solely to Hugh."

St. Albans didn't sound very promising. It made her think of Roman soldiers and England, almost as disused as the old shop down the road. "Where is St. Albans?"

Mrs. Lyttleton rolled her eyes. "Oh, my dear, you sound as though you think I'm leading you on a wild-goose chase. The Hawkesbury region is in New South Wales. Right now I see no reason for you to go trailing out there. Since the war many of the properties have been abandoned."

"Hugh told me his father and brothers were miners. He didn't say very much more." He'd spoken about his dreams, that he wanted to be a farmer. Perhaps that's where the key to this mystery lay. "I think I'd like to go to the Hawkesbury and have a look." Whatever made her say that?

"Let's take one step at a time. I'll send another telegram to Mr. Lyttleton in the hope we can track down the keys to the Curio Shop and Hugh's belongings. I'm afraid I can't guarantee an instantaneous response. At least a week, I would imagine."

A week! What was she supposed to do for a week? "How far is it to St. Albans?"

"Please don't even consider it, Fleur. It's over sixty miles. The journey is a nightmare. First the train. Then an overnight stay and the choice between a river trip or a road, which could well be in disrepair. I believe the property is some way out of town, a place called Mogo Creek. Wait until we hear from Mr. Lyttleton."

Nothing will stop us. Nothing once this war is over. Mogo is the place of our dreams, where our life together will begin.

"Mogo Creek?"

"Yes, that's what it says here. Hardly suitable for a young girl in a new country to go traipsing into the middle of nowhere."

But she had to start somewhere, didn't she? And Hugh had mentioned Mogo. If he was anywhere, that's where he'd be. And besides, what was sixty miles when she'd traveled thousands?

Vera pushed herself to her feet. "I'm afraid Kip and I have to go now. Why don't you spend the next few days getting to know Sydney, and in the meantime I will try to find the keys to the Curio Shop."

"I really would . . ." Fleur's words dried on her lips as Vera held the door open.

"We'll speak in a couple of days. Let Kip know if there's anything you need. He's usually on the premises. He has rooms at the back."

Standing on the doorstep Fleur gazed up and down the street. It was almost as though she'd been dismissed, and if she was perfectly honest, she felt a little peeved. She'd traveled all this way and now that she was here, nothing was happening. It was beyond ridiculous. She'd give Vera one last chance and then she'd take matters into her own hands.

If Hugh was alive, the farm would be the place he would go.

Mogo is my safe haven. My place, my home.

Chapter 11

Hawkesbury, NSW
1853

"Careful with those boxes. That's important stuff, you know." Bert scowled at the young stable hand who rushed out to greet them when they arrived at the Settlers Arms.

"It's all right."

Stefan still couldn't believe his good fortune. Bert was a godsend. Stefan's botanizing box was far less fragile than Bert imagined, but he'd been fascinated from the outset by the compartments for the plants, flowers, and seeds and had adopted it as his own special responsibility.

Magnificent specimens had lined the track all the way to St. Albans, and the trip had taken far longer than he anticipated because of Bert's continual demands to stop and investigate some treasure beneath the wildly romantic canopy of bobbing yellow acacias and gum blossoms.

On entering the inn they were greeted by an old man with a long whiskery beard and bright eyes. He heaved himself to his feet and wandered around to the front of the desk. "I'll have to ask you to sign the register, sir. New rules and regulations. They're trying to keep up with all the coming and going. Just here, if you wouldn't mind."

"Just me or do you want my man as well?"

"Both would be good."

Stefan wrote his name and underneath Albert Peregrine Burless. That'd give the authorities something to think about. With a smile, he tucked the pen back in the inkwell and pushed the ledger across the table.

"Will you be wanting something to eat?"

"We would indeed."

"I'll let the missus know. Usually wait till after sundown just in case there's anyone else coming through. That suit?"

"Perfect. I'll take a walk. Stretch out the legs. We've been traveling all day. Bert, are you coming with me?"

"Nah! I've got the rest of the stuff to lug up to the rooms and those horses deserve a decent feed."

"Good lad."

"Will Mr. Burless be joining you for dinner?"

Bert's face turned a hilarious shade of puce and his mouth flapped like a fish. "Most certainly," Stefan replied.

"But I . . . we . . . Mr. Burless?"

"You go and see to those horses and we'll chat later."

"I ain't never eaten in no dining room." Bert hissed the words, his eyes wide with fear.

"You'll be fine. I'll see you in a while." He leaned forward. "And don't forget to scrub your face and hands. I'll take the compass and telescope."

"Yes, Capt'n." With a flurry of arms and legs Bert disappeared. Stefan wandered outside and stretched. Time in the saddle still caused him some discomfort; however, a gentle stroll would loosen his muscles. The sun was sinking toward the hills and strips of color highlighted the gathering clouds where an eagle hovered searching for prey. A creek meandered through a trail of Casuarinas, their long-fingered leaves rustling in the light breeze. A cockatoo screeched, another answered, starting an orchestra of frogs.

The track wound its way alongside the creek. Finding a series of stepping-stones, Stefan crossed to the other side and followed a narrow trail up over a small hill, picking his way through the thick undergrowth.

The trees thinned, revealing an open expanse of grass echoing with the strange haunting twilight cries of the birds. Good enough for a decent herd of cattle although there was no sign of any livestock. He breathed in the pristine air, letting it fill his lungs. A movement caught his attention. A flash of white, a dash of color, dusty red against the gray-green of the leaves. Dragon lizards skittered into hiding behind the rocks as he stepped out of the trees into the clearing.

A girl, hair dangling down her back in disarray, homespun skirt hitched up underneath a heavy leather apron, her brown feet bare, crouched beside a pool, hand outstretched to a pure white animal with large powerful hind legs and a long muscular tail.

He'd read about these strange quadrupeds in the baron's notes. Kangaroos, the New Hollanders called them, and they were plentiful, reds and browns and grays, but white? And the girl like some Valkyrie. Hair the color of warm chestnut settling around her sculptured face.

The sound of a gun cocking shattered his reverie. The hairs on the back of his neck bristled. "Stand clear!"

A colossal retort shattered the bucolic scene.

A musket ball whistled above his head and ricocheted off a tree trunk, splintering the timber not a foot from where the girl stood.

Della threw herself to the ground.

Gunshot.

She flattened her body against the rough grass and eased her head to one side. There was a gruff cry and the vibration of heavy steps reached her stomach.

A large man in a greatcoat erupted from the tree line. Before she could move, his long strides brought him into the clearing, and she stiffened, not daring to draw breath.

After a moment she raised her head to search for Tidda. She knew the shot was meant for the kangaroo, had known that one day this would happen.

Booted legs paused mere feet from her head. Red piping bright against the blue-clad legs. They paused for a moment and moved on.

She scuttled aside. If she could reach the creek she could make her way home without crossing his path . . .

An arm shot out from nowhere. Sent her sprawling on the damp earth. The shock of the physical contact made her body tremble. Whipping around, she sank her teeth into the hand grasping her shoulder.

He jerked his hand free and stood rooted to the spot glaring at her, even larger than she'd first imagined. His face was gaunt, high cheekbones accentuated by a sweep of pale hair falling across his brow. "What on earth do you think you are doing? You could have been shot." He lowered his gun.

She scrambled to her feet and planted her hands firmly on her hips. "What do you think you're doing? You could've killed her." Her voice caught on the last word and for one dreadful moment tears sprang to her eyes. She sucked in a steadying breath. "Your behavior is barbaric."

With a bright sapphire flash his eyes pinned her and a smile crept to the corners of his mouth as he slipped the gun into the pocket of his greatcoat. No, not a gun. A brass telescope.

How foolish she sounded. He couldn't kill anything with a brass telescope—deliver a nasty thump, but not much else. Unable to meet his eyes, she shrugged her shoulders and threw down the handful of grass still clasped in her damp palm. "What business have you here?"

Her voice melded with the pounding of her pulse. "You are trespassing. This is private property."

"Protecting you." He hung over her, his eyes roaming her body from the top of her disheveled head to her bare, muddy feet.

She stood motionless, nothing but their mingled breath and the blood pounding in her ears. "Me?" She glanced down; her thin blouse was damp and plastered to her body. Cheeks flushing, she hugged her arms across her chest.

He took a step closer and she backed away, her sense of dread growing. Who was he? And what was he doing here?

"The man had you in his sights. His gun was trained on you."

"I doubt it." More than likely it was Gus. He'd had his eye on Tidda for months, knew her pelt would fetch a tidy sum. The unwanted picture of her cherished friend lying on the workshop bench, skin peeled back, flashed before her eyes. She pushed away the image.

What was she doing standing here? The sun had fallen behind the ridge and the light was fading fast. There was nothing she could do for Tidda except pray she hadn't crossed Gus's path when she fled.

"Let me escort you home."

Filled with horror at the prospect, she lifted her skirts high above her knees and bolted down the path.

"Wait a moment! Come back."

The girl refused to stop, didn't even look back.

Stefan steadied himself, then traced the path back toward the creek, wondering if imagination had created the entire encounter. He hadn't dreamed the look of fury on her face nor the harsh words she'd spoken, not allowing him the opportunity to explain.

The picture of her simple beauty, loose-limbed grace, and blatant fury shimmered before him. So far removed from any other female he'd ever come across. The outrage rippling through her, so intense it radiated like heat from her body. Her eyes flashing, no sign of fear for herself. He hadn't wanted her to flee. He wanted to know more.

He rubbed at his hand where her teeth had broken the skin. Everything inside him compelled him to follow her but she'd vanished, taken no apparent track, and the light was fading rapidly.

With a sigh, he made his way back over the hill until the twinkling lights of the inn beckoned. Through the window he could see figures moving and the flicker of a fire. His stomach growled as he pushed open the door.

Bert sat tucked in the corner, his head sunk low and his feet shuffling in the dust and ash.

"What's upset you?"

The lad lifted his bloodshot eyes and jutted his chin in the direction of two men leaning against the fireplace. "Them."

One towered over the room, a goliath of a man tossing back a tankard of ale and bellowing with laughter. The other, rattier, thin and shrewd, leaned against the chimney breast, shaking his head. He glanced up and their eyes met.

"Captain von Richter?" He ambled across the room, tugging down a filthy vest. "I'm Gus. See you found the place."

Stefan wrinkled his nose at the cloud of gunpowder and something far less pleasant enveloping him. "*Guten Abend*. Mrs. Atterton's man, I presume."

"I'm nobody's man but me own. She said we'd find you here. Interested in a bit of trading, I hear."

"I was under the impression you had a meeting arranged with a group of New Hollanders. I'm interested in accompanying you."

A loud guffaw of laughter came from the big man over by the fireplace and Gus turned and glared at him. "It's all arranged. We'll be leaving at first light." He tossed his head in the direction of Bert, who still sat cowered in the corner. "Is he coming too?"

"Bert, come over here. Gus, this is my manservant, Bert Burless."

"So he tried to tell me." The flames hissed as Gus deposited a filthy ball of phlegm in the fire. "Tomorrow, first light then." He nodded his head and returned to the backslapping company of the giant.

"Ready for something to eat, Bert?"

"Not real sure. I'd rather 'ave mine in the stable."

"Rubbish. I'd like your company, and besides, I've got a story to tell you. It concerns an intriguing young woman and a white kangaroo." He threw an arm around the lad's shoulder and guided him into the dining room. He'd like to get to the bottom of Bert's sullen mood and if, as he suspected, the oaf by the fireplace had anything to do with it, he'd sort him out.

Chapter 12

Hawkesbury, NSW
1919

The last two days had dragged. Fleur had taken several walks around the city, unable to believe the beauty of the place. No gray skies, so much color, the beautiful Botanical Gardens, the sparkling harbor. Even the railway station looked like a palace.

It's the land of the future. Just wait until I show you. Even the city is beautiful.

Hugh hadn't lied.

She'd taken a ferry to Manly. Anything farther from the murky Thames she'd yet to see, and the beach was nothing like Brighton with its pebbles and slopping gray water.

Despite all the natural beauty, she couldn't settle. In a fit of impatience, she'd called at the Lyttletons' office but there was no answer, the doors locked tight and the curtains drawn. Not a person in sight. Not even Kip.

Surely it couldn't be that difficult to find a key. Weren't solicitors supposed to be organized? It wasn't as though they hadn't known she was coming, and even if Mr. Lyttleton was in London with his repatriation board, a telegram would have reached him by now. She kicked at a stray stone, then pushed open the door to the Berkeley Hotel.

At least Mr. Sladdin had stopped looking sideways at her. He'd become used to her incessant questions and constant requests for directions.

"And how was your day today, Mrs. Richards?" All long black legs and arms, he pulled a brochure from the desk drawer. "I thought you might be interested in attending the theater tomorrow. *Our Miss Gibbs* is playing at Her Majesty's. It's a musical comedy that might take your fancy. Alternatively, there is bound to be something on at the Crystal Palace. It's a very popular place for young people, all these modern films."

She took the brochure and tucked it into her pocket without a second glance. She'd only been to the picture theater once, in London with Hugh. Some film about falling in love with a gypsy. She'd been more interested in their love affair than Charlie Chaplin's.

"Thank you, Mr. Sladdin." She couldn't think of anything worse than sitting alone with her memories in a picture theater, although she knew the man was doing his best to keep her entertained. "Are there any letters for me?" Perhaps Vera had received word Hugh had been found alive and well and it was all a ghastly mistake.

Mr. Sladdin's dark eyes missed nothing. At least he had the grace to turn and check. The little wooden pigeonhole with *The Baron's Suite* neatly painted above it stared back at her as empty and hollow as the feeling in her stomach. A cry of frustration slipped out and she dropped her head into her hands.

"Mrs. Richards." Mr. Sladdin reached her side in two long-legged strides. "Are you all right? Can I get you anything? You look very pale."

"I'm fine. Thank you. Just a little overcome, and to be honest . . ." She clamped her lips together; she could hardly tell the hotel clerk her problems.

"Come this way, sit down in my office. I'll call for a cup of tea." Fleur let him lead her through a glass door into his small office off the foyer. He guided her onto a hard chair pushed up against the wall. "I'll be back in a moment. Take a minute or two to get your breath. A cup of tea is what you need."

She didn't need a cup of tea. What she needed was some concrete and solid information. Something that would tell her she hadn't wasted her time coming to Australia. She jumped to her feet and started pacing.

Short of breaking down the door to the Curio Shop, there was nothing she could do there. It still made her blush knowing that Kip had as good as caught her in the act. What about this St. Albans place? She had no idea where the Hawkesbury River was, and eighty acres sounded like an enormous amount of land . . . Come to think of it, she had no idea how big an acre was, never mind eighty of them.

"Here we are. A nice cup of tea." Mr. Sladdin set the tray down on his desk. "Shall I pour?"

"I'm sorry?"

"Shall I pour?"

"Oh yes." She'd drunk enough tea since she'd arrived to float a battleship. "Mr. Sladdin? Do you know where St. Albans is?"

He tucked his head on one side, rather like an enquiring blackbird. "North of Sydney, unless I'm very much mistaken. It was one of the very early settlements, in the Hawkesbury area. Let's have a look." He crossed the room and peered at a large framed map on the wall. Why in heaven's name hadn't she noticed it sooner? She moved closer. *The South-Eastern Portion of Australia compiled from the Colonial Survey and details published by exploratory expeditions*. "It's beautiful."

"And very rare. It belonged to my grandfather, and then my father. We have a very proud tradition of serving the Berkeley Hotel, and it seems only fitting that something of our heritage should remain here."

"Your grandfather was responsible for the survey maps?" She scanned the framed map, looking for the name *Sladdin*.

"Oh no. Not at all. He bought it from a man who owned a circus. Can you believe it?"

Mr. Sladdin pushed his glasses onto his balding head and squinted. "There we are." He traced his finger north from Sydney where a vast tract of water stretched inland. "The mighty Hawkesbury River. Now, it branches off here." His long nose almost touched the map, and the reflection of his head in the glass distorted his features. "Got it. Macdonald River and St. Albans would be about there." He stepped back, leaving his finger pressed against the glass. "May I ask why you are interested?"

"My husband owns property not far from there, at a place called Mogo Creek."

He hooked his wire-framed spectacles over his nose and squinted at the map. "Mogo Creek, you say? I don't seem to be able to locate it."

She eased in closer to the map. "It seems a very long way."

"In the old days, yes. Not anymore. The train meets the Hawkesbury River at a place called Brooklyn. Obviously not marked on this antiquarian treasure." He ran his hand over the glass in a caress. "I believe there's a ferry that runs upriver from Brooklyn." He stabbed at the map again. "Here. Wisemans Ferry. That's where the Macdonald River tributary runs off. Let me see." He stepped back, pulled off his spectacles and polished them, then hooked the wire arms back behind his large ears. "St. Albans. About ten miles, not much more."

A great bubble of excitement blossomed in her chest. The perfect solution. She'd take the train to Brooklyn while Vera sorted herself out. Have a look around and find out if she could get to Wisemans Ferry. There'd have to be someone going to St. Albans. She could beg a lift.

"Thank you, Mr. Sladdin. You might just have solved my problem." She flew out the door and into the street. It couldn't be more than half an hour to the railway station; she'd walked past the palatial edifice only the day before. She'd go and find out when the trains left. With a squeal of joy, she galloped off down the street.

It wasn't until she rounded the corner of the park near the station that she remembered poor Mr. Sladdin and his pot of tea! She'd have to apologize. Joining the throng of people crossing the road, she side-stepped a tram and worked her way between the horse cabs waiting in line and a row of motor taxis parked beneath two streetlamps. When she pushed open the imposing door into the ticket hall it was full of families and trolleys with clanking wheels. Easing her way through the crowd, she spotted a ticket office sporting a neatly lettered sign saying *Country Lines.*

She leaned toward the ticket window. "I'd like to buy a ticket to Brooklyn, please."

"Ain't no Brooklyn station."

No. Mr. Sladdin couldn't be wrong. "I beg your pardon." Not now, not when she was finally doing something constructive.

"No Brooklyn station. We've got one called Hawkesbury River. You can walk to Brooklyn from there."

"How far is it?"

"About 'arf a mile." He gave her a lopsided grin.

Oh, for goodness' sake! "In that case I'd like to purchase a ticket to travel tomorrow morning. What time does the train leave?"

The ticket clerk raised one hairy eyebrow and quirked a smile. "Been there before, have you?"

"What's that got to do with it? No."

"English, are you?"

Why did everyone keep asking her that? It wasn't as though she spoke a different language. She drummed her fingers on the counter. "I want to buy a ticket. I want to go to Brooklyn–Hawkesbury River Station." The man was driving her crazy.

"Visiting family, are you?"

"No, I'm not." She might be visiting family, if she could find them, and this man wasn't helping one iota. "I want to go to St. Albans, actually."

"Ah, right. Then I suggest you get back here at six o'clock tomorrow morning, get the first train. That'll get you into Brooklyn a little after eight, and with a bit of luck you can pick up the postman."

"The postman?"

"He'll take you upriver as far as Wisemans, then you're on your own."

Now it was beginning to make sense. "Thank you very much. I'll be back tomorrow."

"You do that, love, and good luck."

She might well need it, but what else was she going to do with herself while she waited for Mrs. Lyttleton to unpack her offices? At least she'd feel as though she was doing something. If she was going to go back to England with her tail between her legs, she may as well see a bit of the country first. And better to spend Hugh's money trying to find him than swanning around Sydney going to the theater.

On her way back to the hotel she took a quick diversion down Hunter Street. Lyttleton's premises were still locked up and so was the Curio Shop. She barreled through the door of the Berkeley, straight into the ever-attentive Mr. Sladdin.

"I'm so sorry I left before drinking the tea. I will be leaving tomorrow on the early train for Hawkesbury River. Thank you so much for your help. Will it be possible for you to keep my room? I'm only planning on being away for one or two nights."

"It'd be my pleasure, Mrs. Richards. The baron's suite is yours until you inform me otherwise. Dinner is being served in the dining room. I shall reserve a table for you while you go and get changed." He lifted his eyebrows as she shot up the stairs, her heart thumping nineteen to the dozen. At last something was happening. If she was lucky, by this time tomorrow she'd be in St. Albans.

After an almost sleepless night, Fleur stood clutching her satchel containing a change of clothes and her ticket, staring up at the huge indicator board trying to make sense of the clocks and lists of strange place names. Turramurra, Berowra, she could barely get her tongue around them. Finally, she found what she was looking for: Hawkesbury River. Platform three, 6.05. The ticket inspector flashed her a wink, and she climbed into the first carriage with only moments to spare before the train took off with a bellow and a hiss. It juddered over the lines of intersecting rails and threaded its way to the outskirts of the city, far dirtier and dustier than anything she had seen since she arrived, and so many stations . . . Ultimo, Surry Hills, Redfern, Waterloo—nothing like Waterloo station in London, the huge edifice where she'd said farewell to Hugh.

Goodbye, my darling. Next time we'll be together, heading to Australia . . .

And then the train picked up speed and the repeated sound of the wheels on the tracks replaced the wheeze of steam. The sun appeared from behind the clouds and the countryside opened up.

An hour or so later, a steep section of track dropped down and in front of her stretched the huge expanse of the river.

A mighty river bigger than the Thames, deeper and cleaner. Tall sandstone cliffs and secluded sandy coves. And fish . . . fish like you've never seen. Flathead too big for the pan.

The train shuddered to a halt and she stepped out onto the platform. Below her she could see the village and the wharves. By the time she'd reached the end of the platform the mailbags had been unloaded from the guard's wagon into a small trolley. She stuck right behind it, surely the easiest way to find the postman.

The porter wheeled the trolley down a slope and headed for the village. They crossed a narrow road and turned left, and her heart lifted when she saw ahead of her the neat timber vessel moored against a wharf proclaiming *The Postman's Boat*.

"You all right there, miss?" The porter turned to push the wagon toward the wharf.

"The man at Central Railway Station said I might be able to get a ride upriver with the postman," she called after his retreating back.

He stopped and turned around. "Ah, that makes sense. You'll need to have a word with Old Jimbo. Sure he wouldn't mind a bit of company on a lovely sunny morning. Follow me."

With a spring in her step she eased through the narrow gate and onto the wharf.

"You there, Jimbo?" the porter called.

A grizzly old man wearing a battered navy-blue cap and a frayed jumper minus the elbows appeared from the cabin. "Morning!"

"Got a passenger for you."

Chapter 13

Hawkesbury, NSW
1853

The clouds hung low over the hills, blocking any sign of the sun, and only the faint lightening of the sky behind the hills indicated the approaching dawn. Stefan tightened the remaining strap around his botanizing box and left Bert to saddle the other two horses. Gus and his overgrown companion hadn't made an appearance.

"P'rhaps they changed their mind."

Stefan didn't miss the hopeful note in Bert's voice. He'd refused to say anything over dinner against the two men; however, Stefan was in no doubt something the men had said had upset him.

Bert hefted his bag onto the packhorse and strapped it down. "I thought to leave the rest of the baggage here until we return."

"Not bloody likely. Wouldn't trust this bunch farther than I could throw 'em."

"Any particular reason for that?"

"Bunch of no hopers. The pair of them could do with a decent bath too."

His lips twitched. Since Bert had acquired his new set of clothes he'd become most scrupulous about his appearance, washing at every opportunity and polishing his boots within an inch of their life every night. And he appeared to have picked up a new vocabulary.

"Captain."

Stefan whipped around.

Gus and Dobbin sat on horses, muskets dangling and large, empty saddlebags hanging like elephant ears on the backs of their rough mounts. "Need to get a move on. We've got a fair few miles to cover."

"You have an agreed rendezvous time?"

"Nah. Blacks don't pay no heed to time. They'll be in camp until the sun gets high. Lazy buggers. Let's get a move on."

Without another word the two men led the way out of the courtyard. They followed a rough track alongside the creek, past the spot where he'd seen the beguiling girl and her albino kangaroo, and then up into the heavily wooded hills. After about half an hour they dropped down from the ridge onto a cleared plain, the remnants of burning still visible among the new grass shoots. "Has there been a fire through here recently?"

"It's the bloody blacks. They do it all the time. Set light to random patches. Make the place less than useless for any grazing."

Stefan studied the undergrowth as they made their way down the incline. Contrary to Gus's explanation, the land appeared to be abundant with bright new grasses. In some places small orchids and a wandering purple vine had broken through the charred leaves. After another hour or so a coil of rising smoke caught his attention, then the joyful shrieks of children playing, the murmur of voices, and the excited yap of a dog.

"Are we there?"

Gus turned in the saddle, acknowledging Bert for the first time. "Dunno. Difficult to tell. Move around too bloody much to keep track of 'em." He followed a narrow track into the trees, then brought his finger to his lips and signaled them to stop.

In the clearing he saw several small dwellings made from flattened sheets of bark, neatly placed branches, and foliage around a fireplace designated by rounded stones. The ground surrounding the fire pit was as scrupulously swept as any parlor floor. A pile of shells and bones was stacked on the outskirts of the clearing and a group of women sat in a circle around the fire, one nursing a small baby, another grinding something in a flat wooden bowl. Three young boys appeared, squealing and tumbling over each other as they chased a tan, wolf-like dog with a tapered muzzle. Their shrieks came to an abrupt halt as Gus approached them.

The women around the fire glanced up, called their children close. A white-haired older woman stared at them but made no attempt to move.

Dobbin leaped from his horse with an agility that belied his oversize body. He ran his gaze over the group as he swaggered toward them, his filthy smirk laced with disdain.

The women scrambled to their feet with a flurry of alarmed chatter and pushed the children behind them, huddling tightly together, trembling, waiting.

Dobbin slowly circled, his bullwhip rapping a tattoo against his booted leg while he considered them.

This was no trading venture.

One of the women stepped from the group toward Dobbin, shoulders thrown back, her dark eyes blazing.

Before she had time to speak, Dobbin raised the whip, brought it down hard, licking her skin, raising a welt. With a cry, a younger woman broke from the huddle and brought the injured woman in.

Dobbin raised his whip again, cutting her with a sharp crack across the cheek.

In Gottes Namen! Stefan leaped from his saddle. "Stop this! Stop this at once!"

Panic sent the women and children tangling together, tripping as Dobbin's whip cracks became a frenzied attack.

A young man, his lithe body rippling with wiry strength, appeared from the tree line, a long spear in one hand. He gave a guttural cry and stepped up.

Dobbin turned, took three steps, then spun the whip around his head. He brought it lashing down across the young man's arm.

For a moment no one moved, then, the young man's face contorting with effort, he tossed the tail of the whip aside and launched his spear.

It sailed through the air. And landed quivering in the dirt beside Dobbin.

The retort of a musket sounded.

The ball slammed into the young man's shoulder and his howl of pain erupted in the clearing.

Gus stood with a self-satisfied grin, a smoking musket in his hands. Stefan launched himself across the fire pit, his hands groping Gus's scrawny neck. "Murdering *Schwein*!"

Gus's eyes bulged and a pathetic dribble of saliva trickled down his chin. As he spluttered for air, the musket fell from his limp hand.

From the corner of his eye Stefan spotted Bert snatching Dobbin's musket from his saddle, his shocked expression bouncing between the men.

"Oi! That's mine, you miserable little bastard!" Dobbin stalked toward them, eyes pinned on Stefan.

"Got this one covered, Capt'n." Bert rammed the musket barrel into Gus's stomach and cocked it.

With a grunt Gus sank to his knees, just as Dobbin gave an outraged roar and charged, the bullwhip raised like a cudgel.

Stefan bent low and tackled the giant, sending them both sprawling to the ground in the struggle. A bolt of white-hot pain lanced through his thigh. The shock of it emptied the air from his lungs, momentarily sapping his strength. He had only a second to register the rock in Dobbin's hand before it crashed down toward his face.

He threw his head to one side. Heard the crack of rock against bone, the impact scoring his temple. A strange ringing in his ears had his head spinning as he desperately attempted to shift Dobbin's weight and ward off another blow.

It never came. The rock dropped harmlessly to the ground. A tentative glance showed Bert standing over him like an avenging angel, the musket pointed at Dobbin's head.

When Stefan came to, Bert was crouched by his side flapping his hands, loosening his shirt. He pushed him away and struggled to his feet, the trees swimming, merging with the patches of blue sky in a kaleidoscope of nausea.

"They've gone."

He whipped around. And regretted it. The area around the fireplace was deserted, only the New Hollanders' dwellings sitting in silent witness to Dobbin's outrageous attack. Stefan shook his head, trying to clear the ringing in his ears.

"You've got a lump the size of an emu's egg on your 'ead."

He raised his hand and gingerly felt the throbbing mass, slick with blood. Wiping his hand down his trousers he staggered to regain his balance.

"You're bleedin' something rotten."

Like a persistent fly Bert hovered about him. Stefan pushed his way through the dizziness and batted him away. If it was the last thing he did he'd make certain Gus and Dobbin were brought to justice, made to pay for their crime.

"I had visions of you 'anging like a slab of meat in a butcher's shop, the way that Dobbin was chucking 'is weight around."

Stefan took another look around the camp. No sign of the laughing children or the gossiping women with their gentle brown eyes. The camp was stripped bare. And worst of all there was no sign of the courageous young man save a blood-soaked patch of dirt and the broken shaft of his spear.

"I told you they were no bloody good. The women scarpered while Dobbin was havin' a go at you. Then he and Gus gathered up all the stuff they could find—dishes, blankets, them digging sticks and that bark string—and took off."

"And what about the young man?"

Bert spun around on his heel. "Dunno." He gestured to the bloody patch of dirt. "Reckon he did a runner."

"And you let Gus and Dobbin go."

Bert's face fell. "I thought you'd copped one too. But I got the muskets. Hid 'em in the bush when I went looking for the young fella."

"Guter Mann." Stefan rubbed at his head and bit back a groan. Bert couldn't have done anything. Not against those two, not alone. It was lucky he'd had the sense to take Dobbin's musket when his back was turned. The fault was Stefan's. He'd willingly followed Gus and Dobbin, too interested in what he might find to wonder about the way they might treat the New Hollanders. What an arrogant fool. He'd chosen to ignore the signs that Bert had so clearly seen.

"Better get you back to the inn. Bump like that on your head ain't good."

It was his judgment, not his head, he regretted. "I'll be all right. I have every intention of bringing this matter to the governor's attention as soon as possible. This unprovoked attack is an outrage." And if Gus and Dobbin were acting on Mrs. Atterton's instructions, she would be answering to the governor as well. "We'll take a more direct route, skirt the inn, and head straight for Sydney." He was in no fit state to take on Gus and Dobbin.

"Think you can find the way?"

Stefan slipped his hand into his pocket and closed it around his compass. "That's what this is for." The glass had cracked across the face, but when he held it flat the needle spun and, if the sun was any indication, gave an accurate reading. "We'll go up over the ridge and drop down into the valley, then cross the river. How long was I out?"

Bert threw him a rueful grin. "Long enough to scare me."

"Right then. We'll scout around and see if we can find the young man and then head off. I want to get back to Sydney as soon as possible."

Stefan and Bert searched around the camp, but there was no sign of the young man and thankfully nothing to indicate he was badly injured. The sky darkened and a low rumbling issued from the burgeoning clouds. They fought their way over a succession of ridges until the light turned to a sulfurous yellow and large drops of rain began to fall.

"I'm so hungry I could eat the arse-end of a wombat. Does that compass tell you 'ow much farther?"

"Sadly, no." Stefan wiped a hand over his face and tried to ignore the throbbing in his temple and his blurred vision. Either he'd gotten them well and truly lost or it was a lot farther to the Great North Road than he'd imagined. "We might have to call it quits, find somewhere to shelter for the night." As if to prove his point, a large slash of lightning spooked the horses and sent them skittering sideways.

Bert pulled up sharp as the answering thunder echoed back from the sandstone rock face. "There's a cave up there." He pointed into the fading light. "Saw it in the lightning."

"Think you can see a path?"

"Yep." Bert eased his horse back off the track and Stefan followed. "There it is." He pointed to a small depression in the rock face, hardly a cave but enough to give them some protection from the rain.

The lad lay fast asleep, snoring gently, tucked under his oilskin coat, as comfortable as in a feather bed. Stefan groaned. He was getting soft, too much sitting around in comfortable surroundings poring over the baron's notebooks. On the upside, the throbbing in his head had settled overnight. He rubbed at his thigh, getting the blood to circulate; nothing out of the ordinary there.

As the first thin fingers of dawn touched the treetops, he tilted the compass to get a decent reading. He might be useless in a fight, but at least he could still use a compass. They needed to return to Sydney as fast as possible—he had no intention of letting Gus and Dobbin get away with this or any other raids; it was unconscionable. Amoral, unethical. The words filled his mind, viler than any swear words. The governor would hear of it, and so would Mrs. Atterton. *Schwein!* A man didn't treat another human that way.

"Wake up." He shook the boy's shoulder none too gently. Bert's eyes snapped open and he shot to his feet. "What's wrong?"

He searched the area, alert, on the balls of his feet.

"Saddle the horses. It's time we left." He turned back to his compass.

Despite the improved weather, the wind had sprung up and made the horses restless and jittery; they turned and twisted, giving Bert hell's own trouble.

"Here, give me the reins." Stefan yanked on his horse's head and sprang up into the saddle, reaching down for the lead rope of the packhorse. "Sort yourself out and hurry up."

"All right, all right. Give me a minute."

"Do as you're told and hurry up. We've got no time to waste."

"I'm hungry." Bert's stomach gave a resounding rumble to prove his point.

"We'll worry about food later."

With a disgruntled sigh, Bert clambered atop his horse and they made their way through the tightly packed trees until they crested the ridge and the frail morning sun warmed their faces.

Below lay an area of cleared land bounded by stands of ancient eucalypts, a natural and obvious grassed route, and in the hollow a curl of smoke drifting upward.

Chapter 14

Hawkesbury River, NSW
1919

The old man took his pipe from his mouth and peered at Fleur. "Where do you want to go, love?"

"Wisemans Ferry if that's possible."

"That might be a bit tricky. I'm only going as far as Spencer."

"The man at the railway station said you went to Wisemans Ferry." Her stomach gave a lurch. It had all seemed so simple when Mr. Sladdin's long skinny finger had pointed out the route on the old map.

"Not anymore."

"I was hoping to get a lift to St. Albans." She should have planned better, asked some more questions. What was happening to her? Ever since the first meeting with Mr. Waterstone she'd been jumping in, boots and all.

"What would you be doing that for?"

"I'm looking for a place called Mogo Creek. It's off the Macdonald River." She couldn't mask the slight quiver in her voice.

"Well, Spencer will do you. You can get a lift from there. Just let us load these mailbags and you can come aboard."

"There you go. Have a good trip." The railway porter stepped down from the gangplank and picked up the handles of his trolley. "Lovely day for it."

He was right, and a trip up the river was nowhere near as impulsive as her trip to Australia. Thankful for her sensible boots, she stepped onto the narrow plank and in a few quick strides found herself on the deck.

"Sit yourself down there and stay out of the way. Got a few more bits and pieces to take aboard and then we'll be off."

She leaned back, inhaling the clear smell of the river, and felt her lungs expand. Flashing darts of light lit up the placid surface of the water. A couple of men sat on the bank, fishing lines dangling, and to her right a series of boats swayed on their moorings, anchor chains clanking.

"Looks like you're me only passenger this morning. Better get to know each other. Call me Jimbo, everyone does."

Fleur took the calloused hand he offered. "My name's Fleur. Pleased to meet you, Jimbo."

A man with a crate of beer perched on his shoulders walked onto the wharf and brought it aboard, then he returned with a barrow full of building supplies, which he loaded before releasing the ropes. In a matter of moments the little steamer eased its way out into the river.

"First stop Dangar Island. The old boy died a while back and his son's sold the property."

Fleur followed his scarred finger and picked out a large wooden house.

"And that there, that's the Pavilion, where the gentlemen retired after dinner to smoke their cigars. Bet there were some hijinks there back in the old days." He eased the boat alongside the wharf and threw out a mailbag, then turned for the railway bridge. "Rumor has it they're going to open the island up to the rest of us before long. I can see meself with a nice little shack there, maybe even a cigar or two."

As they rounded the bend in the river, the banks on either side rose steeply forming great bluffs, sometimes bare, but more often timbered to the water's edge. Elsewhere, outcrops of brown sandstone caught the rays of the sun and shone like beaten gold.

Farther downriver the rough sandstone mountains threw deep shadows, making Fleur shiver. In the cry of the birds Hugh's laugh echoed across the water, and in the breeze she felt the warmth of his breath on her cheek. In the past she'd never felt him so close, but in the daylight under this bright sun on the river she heard him, his gentle drawl, the lilt of his voice patiently reminding her of his promises.

As quickly as the cliffs appeared they retreated, and the boat passed farms nestling beside quiet waters, quaint little shacks where women and children stood on the banks waving and shouting their greetings before flocking to the wharf to receive their supplies and load their own cases of oranges and lemons and other choice fruits to be taken to market.

Jimbo greeted everyone by name and promised he'd be back with their invoices. "Be nice and fresh when they get to Sydney tomorrow morning. That way the Hawkesbury farmers get a decent quid."

From the trees fringing the shores came the caroling of magpies and peewees, and the strange sound of what might have been laughter.

Fleur spun around and squinted at the trees. "What's that?"

"Jackass. Laughing jackass. They keep you on your toes, I can tell you. Call them kookaburras these days. The old name suits them better."

"How long have these people lived here? It seems so isolated." Nothing could be further removed from the hustle and bustle of London, or Sydney for that matter. "What would they do without you?"

"I'm not the only transport. There's been steamships in these waters for a long time now. All started with an old pioneering family up St. Albans way."

Fleur pricked up her ears. Maybe Jimbo would know something of Hugh. "What was the family's name?"

"Jurd. Archie was the mover and shaker. As a young man he joined the service of the old Hawkesbury Steam Navigation Company, was appointed captain of the steamer *Hawkesbury*, and worked his way up. He's got the big steamer these days. You would have picked it up yesterday if you'd come then. Only runs two days a week, Tuesdays and Fridays. I do the run on the other days. Don't usually have many passengers. Makes a nice change having a pretty young lass to keep me company. Spencer's the next stop. Usually have a cuppa and a word or two. One of the best fishing spots on the river."

So many fish they jump into the boat. Everything a man could ever want—except for you.

"We'll pull into Spencer in about ten minutes and I'll hunt out Skipper. What you need is a lift from here up the Macdonald River. Too shallow for my little darling." He gave the wheel a gentle caress. "He'll know what's what, and if that doesn't work then you're no worse off. I'll take you back to Brooklyn. Mind you, Wisemans is a lovely old place. Built by a bloke called Solomon. Convict he was, but made good with a vengeance. Once he had a bit of money behind him he never looked back. In those days once a convict always a convict. All those new settlers came out here from England with more money than sense, reckoning they could be all upper crust and buy their way into a position in society. These days some think convict heritage is a badge of honor, but it wasn't back then."

She stood gazing at the rocky headlands, inlets, and creeks, chewing her lip, wondering if she'd done the right thing.

"Don't look so worried. Leave it with me. Jimbo will see you right. Keep an eye out over to the east and let me know when you see the curve in the river and the sandbank. That's where the channel into the wharf starts."

"I can do left and right, but throw a compass point at me and I'm lost. Besides, isn't everything upside down here?"

Jimbo gave a bellow of laughter. "Wouldn't know about that. Born and bred here. Both me great-grandfathers came out here courtesy of His Majesty's government. They were lucky enough to hook up with that Flinders bloke, circumnavigated Australia he did in a boat about half the size of this one, called it *Tom Thumb*. That's why I call this one *Thumbelina*, bit of a nod to the past.

"It's easy, real easy, love. Port's your left. Starboard's your right. Not too hard, right? Once we get this far up the river there's a fair bit of silting so I have to stick to the channel."

And that brought Jimbo's reminiscing to an end as he spun the wheel down hard and they rounded the bend.

With her arms hugged tight around her body, as if Hugh were holding her close, the river brought her memories alive, made her even more determined to find the truth.

There's only us now. Just you and me. We'll make it, you'll see.

"Spencer up ahead. Can't see anyone on the wharf. Reckon you could throw the rope out, then jump ashore?" He shot her a look from under his shaggy brows. "Good to see you're dressed for it."

And she was thankful too. It was windy on the river and she'd only put on trousers as a second thought. One of the best things that had happened because of the war. All this nonsense about women dressing as ladies had been left far behind.

The boat edged sideways across the current and slid neatly against the wharf with a bump. She grabbed the end of the rope and stood on the seat, then closed her eyes and jumped. For a moment she seemed suspended in the air, then her feet hit the timber boards with a whack.

"Good on yer. Make a sailor out of you yet. Now tie that rope tight around the bollard."

She wrapped it around two or three times and yanked down hard. "Do I tie a knot?"

"Nope. Just hold her steady." He cut the engine and clambered out onto the front of the boat and grabbed another rope. With a surprisingly agile jump he landed on the other end of the wharf and tethered the rope with a couple of neat flicks of his wrist. "Right. Now this is what we do. Three times around the bollard, then loop this end over there and pull."

With a sigh the timbers strained and the boat came to rest. "Got a few letters here for Skipper." He pushed his hand into his inside pocket and pulled out some envelopes. "Come with me. If we're lucky, he'll have the kettle on and we can ask him if he knows of anyone heading up St. Albans way."

They crossed the track running parallel to the river. "See up there. That's Skipper's house."

Fleur lifted her head and gazed up at the neat little white house tucked into the hillside with a commanding view of the river. It had a wraparound veranda with chairs facing out and a telescope on sentry duty.

"What a beautiful spot." She and Hugh could be happy here in this secluded place.

"I brought every one of those timbers up here. Skipper spends most of his time here now. He's got a good few ships on the seas but he prefers the river. Says the place gave him his start and that's where he intends to finish it. Phew!" He bent almost double and took several deep breaths. "Lungs ain't what they used to be."

"Would you like me to take the letters up?"

"What, and miss me cuppa? No chance." He straightened up, his face bright red and shiny. "Not much farther now."

"Ahoy there."

Fleur looked up at the veranda where a small man stood waving his hand. "Kettle's on. Get a move on." He bounced off the veranda and came trotting down the path to greet them. "Welcome. Welcome. And who's this lovely young lass?"

"Name's Fleur." Jimbo heaved, resting his hand on the gate post.

"Welcome, Fleur. Just call me Skipper, everyone does." He took her hand and bent low over it, his beard tickling her skin. She laughed, resisting the temptation to pull away. "The wife'll be pleased to have some female company."

He jangled the bell at the bottom of the veranda and then stood back to allow them to climb the steps.

Jimbo flopped down into the first seat he came to, some wooden box stowed against the wall. "Swear those get steeper every time."

"Rubbish. It's that pipe of yours and that rotgut you insist on drinking. Nice cup of tea'll see you right. Ah! Marianne, me darling. Come and say hello." Skipper wrapped his arm around the waist of the petite figure encased in French silk, lace, and whalebone stays, her blonde hair piled high on her head. "This is Fleur."

Marianne eased past her husband, balancing an overloaded tray with a teapot, cups, and a plate piled high with something that smelled delicious. Fleur had given no thought to breakfast in her excitement that morning, making do with a glass of water.

"Come and sit down next to me, Fleur." Marianne patted the bench seat by the table. "We'll leave those two old fools to chat." She picked up the teapot and strainer and poured two cups of tea, added milk and several teaspoons of sugar, and carried them over to the men, then sat down. "How do you like your tea, dear?"

"Milk with one sugar, please." How many people in England would give their eyeteeth for a cup of tea with sugar and milk?

"And have one of these. Just out of the oven." She lifted the napkin and revealed a plate of steaming scones, a pat of golden butter, and a pot of strawberry jam.

Fleur's stomach gave an embarrassing rumble. "I'm sorry."

"Don't be. It's the river air, always makes you hungry." She offered the plate of scones and Fleur loaded up her plate.

"Now, what brings you to Spencer? You've got the look of the city about you." She ran a critical eye over Fleur's trousers.

"I'm on my way to St. Albans."

"And you'd be looking for a ride, would you?"

Fleur's cheeks grew hot. She'd rather hoped Jimbo would do the talking. She nodded her head and bit down on the scone, almost groaning with pleasure.

"And I suppose Jimbo here told you I couldn't resist a damsel in distress?" Skipper winked.

"The lass thought to take a trip with me as far as Wisemans, then see if she could find a ride with someone to St. Albans tomorrow. I'd take her meself if I could but I got the postal contract to consider. Thought maybe you could help 'er out so she'd be at the Settlers Arms before dark."

"Come along now, you know you like any excuse to take that little sailing boat of yours out for a run."

Fleur sat and let the conversation wash over her as the scone and tea settled. Right at this moment she'd be happy sitting here in the sunshine for the rest of the day, savoring her memories of Hugh. She let out a long sigh and put the plate back on the table. "I really don't want to cause any trouble."

"No trouble at all." The little man bounded to his feet. "Marianne's right. Nothing better than a sail on a lovely day like this. I can have you in St. Albans in time for tea. Come on, Jimbo, finish that tea and on your feet. You can give me a hand and then I'll return the favor so you're not late back to Brooklyn."

"That's very kind of you." Fleur pushed to her feet.

"You stay right where you are." Marianne patted her arm. "Have another cup of tea and let the men do the heavy work. I'll make you some sandwiches for the trip, and you and Skipper will be off before you know it."

Fleur looked from one face to the other, warmed by their hospitality. Everyone seemed to be so keen to help a stranger, not like London with its shuttered faces and gray misery.

It's another world out there. Right again, Hugh.

Chapter 15

Mogo Creek, Hawkesbury, NSW
1853

Sunlight spread across the home paddock where the kangaroos grazed, drawn from the early-morning shadows to the warmth. Walking across the yard, Della inhaled the fresh after-rain scent and listened to the creek rushing and twisting. Later she'd go down there and see if she could find Tidda.

She swung open the big barn door and the smell of damp skins flooded out to greet her. She hadn't set foot in the workshop since Gus and Dobbin left.

The embers from their fire still littered the fireplace, and the empty pot of mutton stew stood on the hearth surrounded by crumbs and the last remaining piece of bread tossed to one side. Filthy pigs. Thank goodness they'd gone. They didn't usually stay the night, just dumped the supplies and hightailed it to the one of the local inns, which was the way she preferred it. She didn't want their company. Dobbin made her flesh creep and Gus's sly eyes carried more than a hint of warning.

A muted sound made her stop. She cocked her head to one side. The last skin from the table slithered down to the floor, which was odd, because she remembered stacking them all on the table in case the rain leaked in under the door.

Bush rats! It had to be. She took two steps forward, spotted another heel of bread under the table. Damn Gus and Dobbin for their foul habits. She and Charity worked long and hard to keep down the infestation. When they'd first arrived the place was totally overrun and she'd used more than half the white arsenic intended for curing the skins just to get rid of the pests. They chewed anything and everything. Last night they must have had a feast.

She shuffled forward and squatted down to retrieve the heel of bread. A whelp of pain issued from under the stack of skins and a dark head appeared.

"Jarro!"

Uttering a mournful groan, he rolled himself into a ball and curled back into the pile of skins.

"What are you doing here?" She lifted the top skins and dumped them back on the table. "Come on. Get up. You can't stay here, Charity will have a fit."

She reached out, and his skin almost seared her hand. "You're burning up." Now she was closer the beads of sweat on his neck were clearly visible and his hair was damp, plastered down to his skull. Not smallpox. *Please don't let it be the dreaded pox.* It had as good as decimated the local tribes over the years, and only a handful of the Darkinjung people now survived in the area.

He struggled upright and thrust his shoulder forward. Even in the dim light, the entry of the musket ball was clear to see. "Who did this?" Her mind flew back to her meeting with the women and their talk of hunters. "Have you been up Wollombi way?"

It had to be a settler; none of the local tribes had muskets, at least not as far as she knew, and she was certain they wouldn't take them up to Yengo. The site was a sacred meeting place, not a place for violence.

"Hunters come. Hurt the women." His face crumpled.

She ran her hand over his shoulder and turned him gently to the light. "We have to report these attacks before anyone else is killed." He might well die. There was no exit wound. None that she could see.

Jarro groaned again and shrugged her off. "You fix?"

"I don't know. It's gone deep."

"Fever go."

"No, Jarro, it won't. The fever is from the musket ball under your skin. In your muscle. It needs to come out. Maybe your medicine is better." But only if the musket ball was removed.

Jarro struggled upright and frowned at her, then waved his hand in the direction of the leather pouch on the table. "You fix."

Della looked at her tools on the table, her heart sinking. It was one thing stitching and sewing an animal hide, but a living man . . .

Jarro let out another groan and stumbled to his feet, swaying in the strengthening patch of sunlight streaking through the shutters. His swollen and bloodshot eyes pleaded with her. She couldn't send him away. He was in pain.

She could imagine the musket ball lodged in the muscle of his arm, the dirt and poison working its way into his blood. She let out a long puff of breath. "I'll give it a try, but first I have to prepare some things and make sure Charity doesn't disturb us. You stay here out of the way. And drink some water." She picked up the enamel jug and popped it on the table.

Once she'd stoked the fire and settled Jarro in the corner away from prying eyes, she pulled the door of the workroom closed. How was she going to make sure Charity didn't come looking?

"And what're you up to, miss?"

Della jumped and turned around, guilt making her cheeks flush. "I'm just getting a bit of fresh air before I attack the mess Gus and Dobbin left in the workroom."

"I'll give you a hand when I've finished with the chooks and the 'orses." Charity swung the bucket of weeds from the vegetable garden around in a circle. "You've got a lot of work to get done, especially if Gus and Dobbin want to take some of those skins back." She let out an irritated huff.

"I can manage, Charity. You finish with the stores for the house. The workroom's my responsibility. It's wet and smelly in there after the rain. It won't do that cough of yours any good."

"Sing out if you need my help. Can't have you working your fingers to the bone. All that stitching and cutting's hard on the hands."

Della's cheeks flushed again. She'd certainly be cutting and stitching, only not the way Charity had in mind. She shuddered and scooted into the house for clean cloths, a basin for boiling water, and some tea. She collected everything together and then as a final thought rummaged in the back of the cupboard where Charity kept her secret stash of rum. She pulled the small flagon out and hid it under the cloths. It might give poor Jarro a bit of relief.

Charity's out-of-tune lullaby curled over the chook shed and drifted across the yard, some song from her past about losing her true love to a redheaded witch. Della slid back inside the workroom and closed the door behind her. The sound of Jarro's teeth rattling turned her attention, and she pulled another of the skins around his shoulders to keep him warm while she heated the water and cleaned her tools.

Once she'd added a tot of rum to the tea, she handed it to Jarro. "Tell me about the men."

He shrugged his shoulders. "Three men, one boy, musket and whip."

"Why did they shoot?" He hung his head. "It's not your fault. You can't be expected to protect the women from three grown men. Drink some more rum."

He sniffed it and pulled a face. "No good for us fellas."

"I know, but this time it might help. This is going to hurt."

He grunted as though she'd made some affront to his masculinity and made a frail attempt to puff out his chest. He looked dreadful; if it hadn't been for his dark skin she was certain he'd have that ghastly chalky look. "Drink it. You must trust me. I'm going to need you to keep still and you can't yell out." She handed him a rolled cloth. "Put this between your teeth in case you scream. We can't have Charity in here."

He tossed back the tea and rum, then stuffed the cloth into his mouth, his feverish eyes sparkling at her while she scrubbed her hands.

"Ready?"

He nodded and she lifted the scalpel and separated the skin. There was a big difference between live flesh and dead flesh, and the thought of having to delve deep for the musket ball scared her to death. What if she slipped and he bled to death? She'd be no better than one of the hunters.

The blood swelled, making it impossible to see what she was doing. She dabbed at it, then drew the blade across his skin a good three inches from the entry wound, taking note of the direction the musket ball had entered.

How long she'd prodded and poked she had no idea, but when the door to the workshop flew open, she dropped the scalpel and turned, expecting to find Charity, arms akimbo, ranting and raving.

Instead, the silhouette of a man. A tall man.

Chapter 16

Hawkesbury River, NSW
1919

Fleur sat in the small wooden boat in the middle of the river trying to keep her arms and legs out of the way while Skipper ran up a brilliant white sheet of canvas and tethered the ropes. "A bit of tacking and bending until we round the bluff, then the wind evens out and we'll have a clear run."

The sail billowed and the wind caught the little craft, sending it and her hat skimming toward the opposite bank. She grabbed her hair and held it tight against her neck and gave a shiver. Despite the warm sun, the wind had a chill to it, and every so often they'd hit a patch of shade where the tall trees skimmed the water's edge. Skipper sat with his pipe clamped between his teeth. Short stubby legs stretched out and his arm looped around the tiller.

"Done much sailing?"

"No, none. A wherry across the Thames. The trip from Brooklyn was the first time I've ever been on a riverboat."

"From England. Thought as much. Here for good?"

"My husband was from the area."

"Came to grief, did he?"

She shook her head. "He's missing and I'm trying to find his family. They own a property at a place called Mogo Creek."

Skipper's head came up. "Mogo Creek? That'd be the old Atterton place, would it?" His voice held an edge, and for a moment Fleur wished she hadn't mentioned it.

"No, not Atterton, Richards." Something made the color rise to her cheeks.

"Nah, that don't ring no bell. Three brothers, if I remember rightly. The older two had their sights set on the mining business. Not interested in farming, that's why the place is a bit worse for wear. The youngest always wanted to make something of it. Said he'd be back after the war and turn it on its toes."

The air whooshed out of her lungs in relief. "Yes. Hugh Richards. We married in London, before the Armistice was declared." The familiar sob caught at her throat and she swallowed it down.

"Early days yet. It'll take them a while to get all the boys home. Nice young chap."

For the first time her spirits lifted as the old man spoke of the Hugh she knew. "Yes, yes, he is."

"Chin up. We'll have one of those sandwiches Marianne packed. Fresh home-cured ham and her mustard unless I'm mistaken."

Fleur lifted the napkin from the wicker basket under the seat and pulled out the packet of sandwiches, neatly wrapped in waxed paper and tied with a piece of string. She balanced them on her knee.

"Fingers'll do."

She handed one of the chunky doorsteps across to him.

"Fresh air always gives me an appetite. If I know Marianne, there'll be a couple of bottles of ginger beer in there too. Likes to keep me away from anything stronger when I'm on the river. Help yourself."

Fleur upended the bottle and washed the whole lot down with a gulp.

Skipper took out his pipe and banged it over the side of the boat, then carefully packed it with tobacco. After much poking and prodding he held the match to it and puffed contentedly for a few moments. The scent of the tobacco, faintly flavored with apple, curled around. "And so you're here to sort things out." It wasn't a question. Just a statement of fact.

"I hope so. Do you know any more about the place?"

Skipper drew his craggy eyebrows together and snapped the bowline. "Not really. Know it was one of the first grants around here. Never been sold. Never been farmed much either. Shame because it's good land. Some call it the Forgotten Valley, though that's not just the Mogo holding, the whole area. The road to Wollombi runs past the property, not that it's used much these days. Mogo's a bit off the track. Creek frontage, good soil. House set well back so no problems with flooding. We get a fair few floods. Last was before war broke out. Not as bad as the '89, thank God. Covered the bridge. Police quarters got washed away, though that's no great loss." He let out a bellow of laughter. "We river people ain't keen on the law. Like to look after things ourselves."

A man can be himself. Follow his dreams. Will you share my dream?

Before she could respond to Skipper the wind gushed down from the ancient sandstone cliffs, making the boat almost topple over.

"Mind your head. Changing tack." Skipper scurried across to the other side, and she ducked as the boom flew across and the wind filled the sails again. They picked up speed; she felt like one of the seabirds skimming the waters behind the ship as they'd come into Sydney Harbor.

"That was quite some flood, that '89 one. Left a seven-foot hole in front of the hotel, water right up to the first-floor veranda. Make more sense when you see the place. It's not much farther now."

True to his word, they rounded a bend and a cluster of buildings came into view.

"There you go. St. Albans. If you'd stuck with old Jimbo you'd just be stepping ashore back in Brooklyn." He pulled down the sail and bundled it under the seat, then let the boat run up onto a small sandy stretch in front of a double-story stone building with a veranda running along the front. There were a couple of old men lounging on a bench outside, legs stretched out, tankards clasped in their hands and their faces turned to the sun.

The sun always shines or it pisses with rain. None of this halfway English mizzle drizzle.

Feeling very much the seasoned sailor, Fleur jumped ashore, taking the rope with her and hanging on tight while Skipper grabbed her satchel in his rough sailor's hands and clambered ashore. He exchanged the rope for her satchel, which she slung across her body, then she grasped the bow and helped him pull the boat clear of the water.

"There's a few people I know who could do with a deckhand like you. Let me know if you need a job."

"Thank you. I enjoyed every moment." She held out her hand. He clasped it in both of his and squeezed.

"I'll sort the boat out. Go up and have a word with Pete; tell him I sent you and that you'll be needing a room for the night. I doubt they'll be full in the middle of the week. And good luck."

The path led directly to the hotel, and as she walked up she could feel the eyes of the two men following her. She lifted her hand in salute, and they both responded with a grin. She hadn't felt as comfortable in Sydney. She drew in a breath of air, as fresh as any she'd ever breathed, and her shoulders dropped. She could be at home here.

Ducking her head, she walked through the door and stood for a moment, waiting for her eyes to adjust to the darkness. She could make out a bar with some wooden stools drawn up, and to the right and left tables and chairs, all empty. Once she could see clearly, she crossed the wooden floor to the bar where a man leaned on his elbows waiting for her.

"Afternoon."

"Good afternoon. I was wondering if you had a room for the night."

He looked over her shoulder at the door, probably to see if she was alone.

"I came from Spencer with Skipper. He said to mention his name."

"That'd account for it. Wasn't expecting anyone else through today. Quiet in the middle of the week. Staying long?"

"No, just for one or two nights, I think. I was hoping to go out to Mogo Creek either this afternoon or tomorrow."

"Bit too late now. It's a good two-hour hike, maybe more." He leaned over the bar and raised an eye at her trousers. "I see you're dressed for a walk. I'd leave it until the morning. Dinner?"

She was still quite full from Marianne's scones and ham sandwiches, but she had to pass the time somehow. "Yes, thank you."

"Right. I'll let the kitchen know. Chicken pies tonight. If you go through that door to your right, I'll meet you at the bottom of the stairs and show you your room."

Fleur woke in the big lumpy bed before the sun had risen, her neck stiff, shoulders aching, and with absolutely no idea where she was. She lay very still for a moment inhaling the faint smell of mildew and mothballs while the room came into focus, then rolled over and peered out the small window at the pinprick stars.

The sky's as soft as velvet and studded with stars as bright as your eyes. Hugh's voice whispered in her ear. Promising this. Not the searchlights of London slashing their ominous arcs across the sky, bouncing off the cloud cover. Clouds that carried fear, destruction, and zeppelins.

When the first inkling of dawn shimmered above the trees, she rose, splashed cold water from the jug on her face, and scrubbed, removing the remaining traces of yesterday from her skin.

The clanking of pots and pans from downstairs told her she wasn't the only one awake, so she dressed and laced her boots tightly before making her way down the stairs and out into the courtyard. The warmth from the kitchen drew her, and she stuck her head around the door.

"You're up early." Pete sat at the table, a mug of steaming tea in his hand, his hair standing on end like one of the cockatoos Hugh had talked about. "Can't do breakfast yet, bread's still in the oven. Like a cuppa?"

"Yes, please." She sat down in the chair opposite him and the woman standing at the stove plonked a mug of tea in front of her.

"Want milk and sugar?"

"Thank you." She wrapped her hands around the mug and inhaled the steam.

"So you're off to Mogo today. The old Atterton place, Skipper said."

There was that name again. "Who were the Attertons?"

"Not real sure. Could ask around when you get back."

She might very well do that. "Is it an easy walk?"

"Pretty much flat all the way. Just follow the road over the common. You can't get lost. If you hang around there might be someone going through and you could beg a ride."

"That's all right, I'd like to walk."

"From England, aren't you?"

"How did you know?"

He raised one eyebrow and his forefinger. "First your accent. Sounds like you've got a plum in your mouth."

Her accent? She didn't have a posh accent. Far from it. "Really?"

"Yes, really, and two"—he held up another finger—"your clothes."

"My clothes?"

"Yep. Don't have no problem with women wearin' trousers. Been happenin' around here since long before I was born, practical-like, but I ain't never seen a woman wearin' a pair of trousers that look like her own."

"Oh." The color started to rise to her cheeks and she sipped at her tea to cover her confusion. "Lots of women wear trousers now. It was the war, you see."

"Good for you." He pushed the chair back from the table. "Dot'll give you some bread and honey if you want to leave before breakfast." He nodded to the woman pulling two golden cobs from the oven. "Make sure you take somethin' to drink. It'll be hot later in the day, and the cattle foul the water on the common."

"I will. Thank you."

Dot slapped the loaf down onto the table along with more of the same delicious-looking butter Marianne had provided, and honey this time. No rations in this part of the world. She spread the butter thinly, not wanting to appear greedy.

"Give it here." Dot grabbed the knife from her and spread the butter about half an inch thick. "We don't stand on ceremony." Then she put a dollop of honey in the middle and tipped the bread until it drizzled to the very edge. "Can't have you dying of starvation in the middle of the common."

Highly unlikely that would happen. She wouldn't fit into any of her clothes if she kept eating this way.

"More tea?"

She swallowed the last mouthful of bread and honey. "No, that's fine, thank you. It looks like the sun's up. I'll be on my way."

"Sensible girl. It'll be hot in the middle of the day. Got a hat?"

"No, I haven't. I lost it on the river."

"Take one of these then." She pulled a battered felt hat from the peg by the door and handed it over. "That'll keep the worst off. Don't want to end up spoiling them English peaches and cream."

Nodding her thanks, Fleur rammed the hat down on her head, threaded her arm through her satchel strap, pulled the bag around so it sat comfortably on her hip, and set off.

The cliffs across the river flickered with golden light and long shadows ran across the track into the hills. It was still cool so she strode out containing the curl of excitement spreading inside her. She could feel Hugh beside her, the weight of his arm around her shoulders, his warm breath brushing her cheek, the sound of his laugh in the kookaburras' morning greeting.

The track weaved around a few bends past an old church and a graveyard. Substantial two- and three-story houses dotted the hillside on both sides of the track, and she could see another property on the other side of the river. The area looked as though it had been populated for a long time, yet Skipper had told her Mogo was one of the first land grants, so it must be older than those she was passing.

The land flattened and ahead rich grazing land spread, littered with stretches of water, too big to be called ponds. A collection of long-legged birds tiptoed through the shallows, their narrow, pointed beaks darting down into the water every few seconds in search of food. She turned to the left and her breath caught. Drifting in the middle of a large patch of water were several swans.

Everything is different. The swans are black and their beaks are red.

Everything Hugh had told her, truer than she'd dared believe.

There's room to breathe. The sky is higher.

Walking along in this place Hugh loved with the limitless blue sky above and his country around her, she felt closer to him than ever. Surely she'd find him, walking down the road toward her, hands pushed deep in his pockets, his wide smile ready to greet her.

Large sleek brown cows, healthier than any she'd seen before, lifted their heads and threw her laconic glances before turning back to their chewing.

A large boulder by the side of the track offered a comfortable seat, so she sat, pulled the bottle of water out of her satchel, and took several long gulps while wriggling her toes in her boots.

It couldn't be much farther. She must have covered more than half of the distance. With a grunt of determination, she stood up and set off again, past a sign marking the boundary of the common where the track turned into more of a road in places paved with crushed sandstone. It made the going easier and she picked up her pace.

On either side, scrubby stands of trees crowded down overhanging the road, and if she craned her head upward she could see caves lining the rock face.

Hugh had told her about the early days when the area had been populated by natives and many of the rocks and caves had carvings and handprints. Resisting the temptation to veer off the road and take a look, she continued to climb, the muscles in her legs complaining as the road made a sharp turn and crested the hill.

With her hands on her knees and her head down, she fought to regain her breath. Straightening up, she shaded her eyes. The track widened and disappeared up yet another rise, pulling away from the creek. Not a sign of any buildings, nothing to show that the land was farmed. No fences, no chimney pots, no dwellings, no neatly tilled fields.

She pushed on up the hill and came to a halt on the curve of a bend, the suspicion that she might have embarked on a wild-goose chase eating at the edges of her mind. Through the trees the creek rambled, a series of pools linked like a string of pearls twinkling in the sunshine. She leaned out over the edge of the cliff and looked down.

A slow smile curved her lips.

Nestled on a teardrop-shaped piece of land sat a series of small buildings hemmed in by the creek and the high rise of the ridge. Fluffy daisy-like flowers with gray leaves carpeted the ground, and high in the spreading branches of the long-fingered trees, huge red-tailed blackbirds, a perfect match for the swans, shrieked as they cracked and spat rounded nuts onto the grass below.

Without a moment's hesitation, she clambered off the track and slid down the steep incline, loose rocks chasing her path. Down and down, until finally she came to rest in the small green valley. With a whoop of excitement, she leaped through the long tufty grass and headed toward the outcrop of buildings. Ahead a dilapidated gate swung from one hinge, and when she untwisted the wire that tied it to the post and pushed it wide, it collapsed with a groan at her feet.

And there on the ground she found what she was looking for. Faded letters burnt into the crossbar, *Mogo Creek*. A mixture of emotions swirled in her stomach as she surveyed the tumbledown buildings. Somewhere in her mind she'd had a vision of a cozy Cotswold cottage and green fields neatly encircled by stone walls. The sort of picture they put on Christmas cards and sent to the boys in the trenches: *Greetings from home and hearth*.

This was nothing she'd expected.

Mogo's as far from England as you can imagine.

And yet she felt closer to Hugh than she had since she'd arrived in Australia.

Once level with the buildings, she could see the layout. To one side a large timber shed, joined to the house by a walkway, marked by pink trumpet flowers, their faces turned to the sun, revealing their vermilion throats. A winding track led through the grass from the gate to the shed.

She hesitated. The last thing she wanted to do was to be accused of trespassing. For all she knew the property could be leased. Her stomach plummeted and the wisdom of her plan withered.

"Hello!" Her voice bounced off the ridge and echoed back at her. "Hello . . . Hellooo!" She waited to see if anyone appeared and then, with a shrug, headed for the shed.

Outside there was a water butt and next to it a tree stump with a rusty ax embedded in the crumbling wood. Two huge timber doors held closed by a crossbeam barred her way. No sign of any padlocks or chains. She wriggled the timber and lifted one end; it slipped easily aside and the door swung open, letting a shaft of light onto the hard-packed dirt floor. With a quick glance over her shoulder she stepped inside.

A strange smell caught at the back of her throat. Rats and something else that made her stomach churn, earthy and pungent, reminding her of the liver and onions swimming in coagulated gravy Mrs. Black served every Thursday.

A huge table dominated the center of the room. She ran her hands over the smooth timber, not polished but worn smooth and bleached as though it had been scrubbed daily within an inch of its life. And silence, such a deep, peaceful silence.

Stepping farther into the room she found a long workbench running the length of one wall and above it narrow shelves lined with glass jars and tins, their labels peeling, the writing faded. She reached up and pulled a large square tin down. It was heavy. She pried off the lid and peered inside at the fine powder—sugar, or was it salt, or maybe flour? She licked her finger and stuck it in, then brought it to her lips.

"Not a real bright idea."

The lid of the tin clattered to the benchtop and her hand froze in front of her face.

Chapter 17

Mogo Creek, Hawkesbury, NSW
1853

"Ugh, it smells like a bloody butcher's shop in there."

Stefan inhaled; the lad was right. "Get outside." Rotting carrion, undigested food, battlefield detritus. His gorge rose as he peered inside the darkened outbuilding, blinded, while he waited for his vision to adjust and his stomach to forget the memories he'd hoped he'd left behind.

"Who are you and what are you doing here?"

Ah! The dulcet tones sounded familiar. A figure stepped forward into the light and a grin tugged the corner of his lips. The girl with the kangaroo. What was *she* doing here? "Good morning."

Her hand flew to her mouth. "It's you! And I suppose you're involved in this too. First my kangaroo and now a harmless young man." Her face was flushed and she waved a very thin and very lethal scalpel in front of her. He took a step closer and the pungent odor of blood and animal hides intensified.

He raised a hand, palm up. "I mean no harm, and I was not in any way accountable for the shot at the kangaroo." Surely she must have noticed he wasn't carrying a gun. "I'm heading back to Sydney. Could you give me directions?" His compass had already answered this question, but Bert's incessant whining about food had got the better of him. The blade lowered an inch or two.

"The road's that way." She pointed over her shoulder. "Less than an hour's ride to St. Albans."

"I wondered if you could provide some food. We've been traveling since yesterday and were forced to spend the night on the ridge."

"The ridge? What were you doing there?" Her hands slammed onto her hips, and thankfully the blade disappeared into the pocket of her apron. "What about the attack on the camp?" She let out an irritated huff and her dark eyes flashed.

"Steady on, steady on." He raised his hands.

"What a stink!" Bert reappeared in the doorway, grabbed at his nose, and pinched his nostrils tight. "Are we staying? Do you want me to unsaddle the 'orses? They're starving and so am . . ."

The scalpel reappeared and wavered in Bert's direction, leaving his eyes wide and his mouth gaping like a landed fish.

"I told you to wait outside. Get out."

The girl toyed with the stiletto and glared, blood ringing her fingernails, and she kept turning her head, darting a glance over her shoulder. Stefan took a couple of steps farther into the room. A jumble of feathers and fur covered the workbench, pelts hung from the rafters, and bird's nests crammed the spaces between the bottles and jars. Whatever was she up to?

She swiveled around and placed herself in front of the fire.

A long-drawn-out groan answered his question. He ducked around and stopped dead. A New Hollander wrapped in some sort of filthy animal skin sat on a small stool in front of the fire. Stefan took a step closer and peered at the young man. One shoulder was uncovered, revealing a gaping wound, fresh blood trickling down his muscled arm. He'd put money on the fact that the ball came from Gus's musket. "What in the world are you doing?"

"What does it look like? I'm trying to get the musket ball out. It'll fester if I don't."

"No, it won't, not from the musket ball, only from the treatment you're dispensing. Let me have a look."

The man's eyes widened in pain as she dabbed at the blood oozing from the ragged hole.

"It's the lubricant on the wadding that causes the problem. Let the body heal itself. Have you got any alcohol?"

"I've given him some already. It hasn't lessened the pain."

"I'm not surprised if you've been poking around in there. Is there an exit wound?" He peered over the man's shoulder.

"No, it's lodged in the muscle. I'm trying to dig it out."

"You're wasting your time. Better off leaving it there." He'd seen men die all too often from the interference of well-meaning quacks, come close himself. All the prodding and poking was worse than any musket ball, then gangrene struck and the limb had to be amputated. "Better clean it and bind it up." He pulled the lid off the flagon sitting on the table and sniffed. Rotgut, but alcohol all the same. "Is this all you've got?"

She nodded. "It's rum."

"Of sorts." He drew the cloth out of the man's hand and dabbed at the seeping blood on his skin. "This'll sting." To give the fellow his due he hardly moved; only his jaw clenched as Stefan tipped a healthy slug into the gaping wound. "Right now you need some clean soft cloths. Petticoat or shirt for bandaging. Have you got that?"

She produced what looked remarkably like a pair of cotton bloomers from a box under the table and ripped them into strips, color dancing on her pretty cheeks.

"It'd be better if we stitched it up." Her words brought him up short.

"It would, if you had a strong needle and some stout cotton."

She didn't answer, instead reached over to the workbench and retrieved a leather pouch. Above on the shelves stood bottles of preserving solution, bell jars, piles of cotton and tow, large rolls of wire, and trays of sharp stilettos. With a degree of reverence, she pulled a curved needle from the pouch and skillfully threaded the cotton through the eye.

"You seem well prepared."

She tilted her chin in challenge. "I'm a taxidermist by trade." Which would account for her lack of the vapors and the contents of the shelves. His lips twitched. If he'd been aware of the range of knives and stilettos at her fingertips he might have taken more care. There was no doubt she could defend herself quite adequately.

"I can stitch up his skin. I seemed to be inflicting more pain on Jarro than necessary."

She knew the boy's name. "Jarro?"

Without answering, she dunked the needle and cotton in the cup of rum, then began to pull the sides of the wound together with neat stitches. A hell of a lot neater than the cobbling that ran from his thigh to ankle. Providing the young man's fever didn't worsen, it was unlikely he would suffer from more than the occasional bout of stiffness in cold weather.

After each small stitch, she tied the thread off and continued patiently. Once she'd secured the last knot she raised her head. "This wasn't the first raid on their camp . . ."

The statement hung in the air, her implication clear. "I am not responsible, miss. I did everything in my power to stop the attack."

"Why should I believe you?"

"Ask your patient."

"Jarro, did this man hurt you?"

When the New Hollander shook his head, her face softened and her shoulders relaxed.

"I intend to pursue this appalling outrage and bring it to the governor's notice. I know the men responsible."

Now he had her attention. She folded the cotton around the

needle and slipped it back into the pouch, her dark eyes never leaving his face.

"Their names are Gus and Dobbin. They are in the employ of one Mrs. Cordelia Atterton who runs a shop in Sydney called the Curio Shop of Wonders."

Her brows came together in a tight frown and he fancied the color drained from her cheeks. "Mrs. Cordelia Atterton of Hunter Street?"

"The very one. You know of the establishment?"

"I do. Yes."

"Let me assure you the matter will be raised with the authorities."

She jumped to her feet, his words clearly offering little assurance. "The Curio Shop of Wonders, you say. Not the Taxidermy Shop?"

"No, I am not mistaken. I met Mrs. Atterton and she gave me a tour of her premises. She was particularly proud of the collection of native curios and implements and invited me to join her collectors. Something I admit I did with great enthusiasm, not knowing what evil they would perpetrate."

"*Her* shop. Native *curios*. *Mrs*. Atterton." She let out a sigh and sank down on the three-legged stool and dropped her head into her hands.

When the poor girl lifted her head, she gazed at the boy who had pulled the dirty skin over his shoulders. "I'm sorry, Jarro. So very sorry." Tears pooled in the corners of her eyes.

"Get away from me!" The raucous shout sliced the quietness.

"Charity!" She leaped to her feet. "Jarro! Go now. Out the window."

The boy shot to his feet and vaulted through the open shutter at the back of the room, appearing none the worse for his suffering.

"Get away from me!" Bert's indignant shriek echoed, followed by a solid thud and a scream.

Stefan belted through the door and slid to a halt, unable to curb his laughter at the sight of Bert dancing around the puddles trying to avoid a thrashing from a black-haired harridan brandishing a soggy mop.

"Madam!" His voice cut the air and the wretched woman stopped in her tracks.

"Oh! Am I glad to see you, Capt'n." Bert sidled over and stood in his shadow.

"Captain? What captain? I don't see no captain." The red-faced woman blustered and threatened Bert with a slightly less vicious swipe.

"Captain Stefan von Richter of the court of Vienna, aide-de-camp to Baron von Hügel, at your service, madam." He executed an exaggerated bow and clicked his heels, which brought the woman to a standstill and a grin wider than her bucket to Bert's face.

She sank into some sort of fumbled curtsy, displaying her hobnail boots and a fair amount of pudgy calf. "Beggin' your pardon, Captain. We wasn't expecting no visitors."

"I require refreshments for myself and my man."

Encouraged by his words, Bert stepped out from behind him, straightened his shoulders, and puffed out his bony chest.

"And for my horses. I have funds I feel certain will suffice."

"There will be no need for that." The girl appeared at the door of the workshop sporting clean hands and tamed hair, nothing to indicate that five minutes ago she'd been up to her elbows in blood. "Charity, please go and set the table. There's plenty of mutton stew left over from last night. Make some bread and put the kettle on the hob."

The woman edged her way back into the cottage. As soon as she was out of sight, the girl lifted her skirts and rushed to the back of the workshop building.

Curiosity aroused, he followed. When he rounded the corner, she stood a good fifty feet away staring down the narrow pathway that disappeared into the tree line.

She turned and walked back toward him. "He's gone." With a loud sigh she straightened her skirt and shoved her hands into her pockets. "Charity is terrified of the Darkinjung and is a liability with a musket in her hands. Jarro would be worse off than he is now. She's a crack shot. Are you sure he'll heal? I really think I should have taken the musket ball out."

"Providing he fights off the fever he'll recover quickly."

"The women will see to that. Some of their medicines are far more effective than anything I can offer."

This was just the sort of thing he wanted to learn about the New Hollanders. What he'd hoped to discover on the trip with Gus and Dobbin. A fine mess he'd made of that. He'd make certain the two men got their comeuppance when he returned to Sydney.

"Come back to the house. Charity will have food ready. I'm afraid I can only offer you tea to drink. I used up all the rum." She bestowed a radiant smile on him, her eyes sparkling with merriment. What a mass of contradictions. He resisted the temptation to take her arm and instead walked by her side, watching the play of emotions on her face.

"Who is Baron von Hügel?"

"It's a long story. He holds positions of power in the Austrian government and I have the privilege to serve him."

She frowned. "Aren't you English? You sound like an Englishman."

"Brought about by a string of English tutors and many years traveling. Enough of me. What is your name?"

"Della . . . Della Atterton. Oh!" Her hand covered her mouth and her big brandy-colored eyes widened.

Atterton. That would explain her interest in the Curio Shop. What was her relationship to Cordelia Atterton?

"I hadn't intended to tell you that until I found out a little more." They'd reached the yard where Bert, obviously recovered from his mop lashing, had found water for the horses and was busy wiping them down.

"There's plenty of feed in the stable." Miss Atterton pointed to another building that formed a side of the yard. "Help yourself, then you can either leave the horses in there or let them out in the paddock behind the vegetable garden. They won't come to any harm, and the creek runs through there so you won't have to cart water."

Bert tipped his hat and winked, then raised an eyebrow in question.

"Yes, Bert, go ahead. We will avail ourselves of Miss Atterton's hospitality."

"Atterton, that's—"

"Thank you, Bert. Off you go." The boy was far too sharp for his own good. Fortunately, he was learning to keep his mouth shut. He threw a puzzled frown and led the three horses toward the stable.

"Come and sit down. We'll eat on the veranda if you don't mind. The sun is such a pleasure after the storm. I'll arrange some tea."

The sun was indeed a pleasure. It picked up the highlights in Miss Atterton's glorious hair, the color of roasted chestnuts, and that's where her physical resemblance to Cordelia Atterton ended. Cordelia was all jutting bones and sharp angles, whereas Della was delightfully rounded. However, now was not the time to be sideswiped by her charms. He wanted to find out what lay behind this fortuitous coincidence.

He lowered himself onto the bench and stretched out his leg, his thigh screaming after Dobbin's attentions and the extended time in the saddle. A wonderful vista spread before him. The creek meandering through the fields, the wind whispering in the Casuarina trees still jeweled with the morning's dew. Hills ringed the entire property, giving it a safety and seclusion he envied.

Miss Atterton reappeared armed with three cups of steaming tea. "The bread will be a few more moments, but I thought you might like a drink now."

"Thank you. I would. And I expect Bert would too. We've had nothing but water since the evening before last at the Settlers Arms. I rather expected to return there last night, but nothing progressed as intended."

She leaned back against the veranda rail, both hands clasped around the cup. "I'd very much like to know more. The Darkinjung people have been suffering these raids for some time. It shouldn't be happening. How are you involved?"

"Let me start at the beginning. I arrived in the country only a week ago and had business in this area. When I met Mrs. Atterton at Government House, she suggested a trip with her collectors."

"Collectors! Gus and Dobbin are not collectors. They are hunters. They supply the skins I use for my taxidermy. The specimens are sold in the Sydney shop. The *Taxidermy Shop*. It belonged to my father and I am now the owner. I had no idea my aunt Cordelia had changed the name or the nature of the business, or that she attended functions at the governor's as *Mrs.* Atterton. She's not married."

And now he had the answer to another of his questions. Those beautiful displays of the birds and the water mole were her work. But what of the artifacts and women's clothing?

Miss Atterton pushed off the veranda rail and started to stride up and down. "And I certainly wouldn't condone the raids on the Darkinjung. They are my friends. What on earth does Cordelia think she is doing?"

Chapter 18

Mogo Creek, Hawkesbury, NSW
1919

Fleur spun around, the sound of her pounding blood filling her ears. A figure, stooped, rounded shoulders, hat shading the face. The sunlight streamed in from behind, robbing him of any features.

"Oh!" She wiped her fingers on the seat of her trousers and took a step closer. He didn't look too intimidating, old and leaning heavily on a cane.

"I called but no one answered." She sounded pathetic, her voice laced with guilt. She should feel guilty; she was trespassing. No doubt about it. "My name is Fleur. Fleur Richards. My husband, Hugh Richards, owns this property."

"Where is he?" The man's voice was gruff, rusty, as though it hadn't been used for a long time. He cleared his throat.

"I don't know." Grief seeped in, made her words wobble. Every one of Hugh's promises crowded her heart now she'd finally arrived at Mogo.

She turned away, taking in the rows of tools, the neat line of jars and tins on the thin shelf. The practicality of it all gave her a sense of order; perhaps not everything in the world was upside down or topsy-turvy.

Once she'd regained her composure, she turned back to the old man. He'd perched on a stool and had pulled off his hat, revealing a head of closely cropped steel-gray hair. His face was like old leather, covered in fine wrinkles and large freckled age spots. When he lifted his head his eyes swam with tears.

"Do you know Hugh?"

His eyes narrowed and raked her with a calculating gaze. "Your husband, you say?"

"Yes, we married in London. That's why I'm here. I'm hoping to find his family." Hoping to find Hugh, if the truth were known.

He gave a start and sat up straight, one hand held out in front of him, his wrinkled palm turned. "You've got something for me, have you?"

She took several steps back, her spine bumping against a set of freestanding shelves and sending a series of rolled leather packets down onto the floor with a thud. "No, no, I haven't. I'm sorry." Goodness, what did he want? Then she remembered the young boy waiting at the door of her hotel room. She rummaged in her pocket and pulled out one of Mr. Waterstone's pound notes.

"I don't want your money." His shoulders slumped and he propped his head on his hands. "So he hasn't come back?"

"No, not yet." Should she tell him? Tell him they thought Hugh was dead? "I'm sorry. You startled me. Do you know Hugh? Are you related to him?"

"Always thought he'd be the one to sort it all out." He levered himself to his feet with a sigh. "Well, that's it then. Where is it?"

"I'm sorry. I have no idea—"

"The family heirloom. You'll know when you find it. And get it to me fast, before it's too late." He gave an annoyed grunt and stomped off on legs bowed from years in the saddle.

The air rushed out of her mouth and she sank down on the stool. Her hands were shaking and her heart beating a thunderous tattoo. What was he talking about?

She couldn't leave now. Not when she'd come so far. "Wait. Wait." She jumped up and followed the old man outside. He was standing, staring out across the ridge, hat pushed well back, showing his freckled forehead.

"Excuse me. I'm sorry, I should have explained."

"Nothing to be sorry about. Not your fault. How did he die?"

"I don't know if he's dead. I haven't received a telegram."

His mouth was set in a grim line, belying the laughter lines about his eyes. It made her feel guilty. "Could you spare me a few moments? I'd like to explain why I'm here."

The corner of his lips twitched. "Persistent little thing, aren't you?"

"I have a reason for that."

He sniffed and pulled his hat down, covering his eyes. She couldn't tell whether he was angry, amused, or simply fed up with her. "Come on. We'll have a cuppa."

He led the way back inside the workshop, stooping to pick up the rolled pouches from the floor where they'd fallen.

"Let me do that." Fleur picked up the first. It fell open in her hands, revealing a series of knives and sharp, shiny instruments that looked more as though they belonged in a hospital than in this old shed. "What are these?"

"Tools of the trade. Taxidermy."

She paused for a moment, running her finger along the ivory handle of a particularly evil-looking blade, and shuddered. "Taxidermy. Stuffed animals and the like?"

"That'd be it. And that white powder you were about to help yourself to might've made you into a rare specimen."

"What was it?"

"Arsenic."

"Arsenic—that's poisonous. Deadly." She had some vague memory of Mum buying it to kill the rats that made a trip to the outhouse a life-threatening experience.

"Good rat poison. Good for lots of things. Preserving skins. Killing more than rats." He stopped with his hand resting on a pile of moth-eaten animal hides. "See, if you want your specimen to survive, you've gotta give it a going-over with arsenic. Used to make a soap with it, wash the skins, then dust the specimens off with the powder. Nasty stuff if you swallow it. Knock you over in no time."

"So this is a taxidermy workshop."

"Once. Long time ago now."

"And everything's still here?"

"Place hasn't been lived in for years."

"How well did you know Hugh?"

The sadness clouded his eyes again. "Let's find a cuppa."

Fleur followed the old man under the covered walkway. The overgrown creeper swiped at her face and shoulders, the scent of the flowers mingling with the fragrance of the trees. It reminded her of the soldier on the ship. She picked up a eucalyptus leaf and crushed it between her fingers. "Do all gum trees smell the same?"

"What? Nah, thousands of different smells. It's the oil. On hot days it gives off a haze you can see for miles. That's how the Blue Mountains got their name, from the haze, from the oil in the air."

The gloom of the interior contrasted with the bright sun outside, failing to mask the sense of neglect and the smell of mildew; however, the pot hanging over the fireplace was already boiling. Blackened and dented, it dangled from a tripod affair over a small fire, steam billowing. It was almost as though he'd expected her.

"Did you know I was coming?"

He threw his hat down on the chair next to the fire and winked at her, creasing the deep laughter lines around his eyes. "Been watching you for a while. Wasn't sure you were coming here, but there's not much else along this track unless you fancy another three-hour walk." He lifted the lid on the pot, threw in a handful of tea leaves from a tin on the hearth, snatched the gum leaf from her fingers, and threw that in for good measure.

"Do you live here?"

"Some and some. You wanted to tell me about Hugh."

Not exactly. She wanted to *ask* him about Hugh, but maybe this was the best way to go about it. "Hugh and I married in London some months ago. He promised me we'd come and live in Australia when the war was over. He told me all about Mogo Creek. I think he saw it as some sort of haven and the memory of it helped him get through the war." She picked up the cup he'd placed in front of her, an oddly out-of-place china cup with a faded floral pattern, and sipped at the scalding black brew, steadying herself. "I received a letter from the Ministry of Information in London; they told me he'd died and left everything to me. But I don't believe he's dead."

His head came up and he stared at her. His curiously unnerving glare seemed to drill right inside her, as though he could read her every thought. "Yeah, well, it might not be as fortunate as you might think."

"They said they'd sell everything and deposit the money in my account if I didn't come. I'm not entitled to it. I came to see if I could find out who might be." It was too foolish to add that she believed she might find Hugh. She stared out through the sunlit window; a parrot flashed by, vivid red and blue, bright against the dark leaves.

"You came here from London. To sort out Hugh's estate?" He put down his cup and rocked back in the chair. Arms folded, head nodding. He made her feel as though she'd gone up in his estimation, encouraged her to go on.

"The solicitor's wife in Sydney is having difficulty tracking down the paperwork. I was tired of waiting . . ."

"So you took matters into your own hands."

"Something like that."

He shook his head. "Did they give you his papers, his tag, his personal belongings?"

"No. At least not yet. You see, Mr. Lyttleton, the solicitor, is involved with the repatriation of the troops and his wife is holding the fort. They've just moved offices and she doesn't seem . . ." She didn't want to be rude about Vera. She was the nicest woman, but it was driving her mad that she'd managed to come all the way from London only to reach this stalemate.

"To have her wits about her."

"Yes, that's it. That's it exactly."

"Well, there's not much anyone can do then, is there, until they sort it out." He picked up his tea and the light went from his eyes as he stared at the wall, hands clasped around his tin mug. "Right then, that's that. Drink up. You've got a long walk back to St. Albans."

No! She didn't want to go. She had hundreds of questions she wanted to ask. "Are you related to Hugh? Do you know of anyone I should try and contact? There must be someone."

"Nope. There's no one. Come back and see me when you get all his things. Check his personal belongings carefully, very carefully. You're looking for a family heirloom. And don't waste any time bringing it to me. You're a kind girl. Well-meaning. Wouldn't want anything to happen." He pushed out of the chair and held the door open, dismissing her.

With her mouth still gaping and the flurry of questions circling in her head, she made her way back to the road. Flocks of white cockatoos took flight at her approach, their screeching cries adding to her sense of unease.

It was only when she was a good mile down the road back to St. Albans she realized she hadn't asked his name.

Chapter 19

Mogo Creek, Hawkesbury, NSW
1853

Della's heart pounded like an anvil. Cordelia had sanctioned the raids. She was responsible for the trouble Jarro's family had suffered—the stolen spears and dilly bags, the injuries and the disruption. The killings up Wollombi way. Cordelia was behind it!

Unaware of her thoughts, the captain sat there, legs stretched out, his back resting against the wall of the building, his eyes half closed and the sun highlighting the golden stubble on his chin, looking for all the world as if he were attending a picnic. How could she be certain he was telling the truth? What was a foreigner, with boots as expensive as his, doing cavorting around the countryside with one loudmouthed stable boy and Gus and Dobbin?

On cue Charity appeared, all of a lather, carrying a piping hot bread and a pat of butter as though they were the crown jewels. She'd dug out Ma's best china, dumped her mob cap, and braided her favorite red ribbon through her hair.

She placed the platter on the table, then produced a tablecloth and cutlery from under her arm and proceeded to lay the table. Lay the table! Since when . . . She then executed some sort of a curtsy and sashayed into the house, almost sending the poor boy toppling off the veranda.

"Bert, come and sit down." The captain moved along the bench and reached for the teacup, which looked ridiculously small and dainty in his large, long-fingered hands. "Drink this."

"Thanks." The boy, Bert, took the cup, leaving the saucer in his hand, and tossed the tea back in one gulp, then sighed loudly and wiped the back of his hand across his mouth. "Me stomach thinks me throat's been cut." He eyed the bread and licked his lips.

"Would you like a piece now while we wait for the stew?" Della broke a chunk off the warm bread, put it on a plate, and passed it and the butter to the boy. "Captain von Richter?"

"I'll wait until we're all sitting down."

"Sorry, Capt'n." Bert dropped the bread and sat on his hands, his eyes never leaving the plate.

Whatever was Cordelia up to? She had to find out more. She'd been so busy feeling sorry for herself, wallowing in her misery, that she hadn't given a second thought to Cordelia and Sydney. She'd presumed that life, the shop, Pa's work would continue as it always had. It sounded as though Cordelia had made big changes she knew nothing about.

"Will you return to Sydney immediately, Captain von Richter?"

"If we may impose on your hospitality, I'd very much like to remain in this place tonight." His English was just short of perfect; it carried the slightest lilt that she couldn't place, practiced rather than natural. "The horses need to rest. I intend to travel back to Sydney via the Simpson Pass and then stop at Wisemans, and there's the matter of the weapons." His eyes snapped with anger, revealing a strange contained energy.

Bert shot to his feet. "I've left them in the stable." He took off down the steps three at a time and disappeared across the yard.

"The weapons?"

"Bert had the foresight to remove the men's weapons. I intend to take them to Sydney to show the governor, as some form of proof of the attack."

So he'd taken on Gus and Dobbin and got their muskets. She couldn't imagine either of them giving up without a fight, which might well account for the gash on his temple.

"You've a wound on your temple." She reached out her fingers to lift the fall of hair, then pulled back in a flurry of embarrassment, color flooding her face.

"It's nothing." When he raised his hand to brush back his hair, his sleeve rose, revealing a neat bite mark near his wrist.

The imprint of her teeth. "I am so sorry. I jumped to a very incorrect conclusion. I held you responsible when I should have known Gus and Dobbin were behind the raid and the pot shot at Tidda."

Her words were met with a dazzling smile, which turned his eyes to the brightest blue. He rubbed his thumb across the mark her teeth had made. "I consider this a reminder of our serendipitous meeting."

Della swallowed the lump in her throat. She had no idea how to respond; instead, she turned to look out across the paddocks and down to the creek, unable to shake the thought that Gus and Dobbin might appear.

"Where do you want these, Capt'n?" Bert held out the two muskets. There was no doubt about it, she'd recognize them anywhere. Dobbin's had an irregular row of notches carved in the butt. She shuddered. Notches representing what?

"Can I see them, please?" She took one of the muskets from Bert. This one was definitely Gus's—he'd taught her to shoot with it when they'd first come from Sydney. Said she and Charity needed to be able to protect themselves from the *savages*. The irony made her want to scream.

"You said there had been other attacks."

She put the musket down against the bench and choked back the sour taste coating her mouth.

"Yes. In the Wollombi and Yarramalong districts. Not only Jarro's family, other camps, other people. There is so much misunderstanding about the Darkinjung, and with the growing number of land grants they find life increasingly difficult. For thousands of years they've managed the land. They have their own beliefs—the Dreaming. Stories that explain the creation of life, of all the animals."

"I wasn't aware they had a religion."

"They have no priests, no idols, no symbols, but they have a very structured system; everyone has a role to play. The trouble is the settlers have no respect for their way of life. We have replaced their traditional hunting and farming grounds with cultivated fields and paddocks full of cows and sheep, and when they kill an animal for food, because their hunting grounds have been taken away, they are rounded up like dogs, accused of stealing, and shot."

Della ran her hand over the butt of Dobbin's musket, feeling the notches. What Gus and Dobbin were doing was far worse than stealing food. They deserved to be punished.

Charity plonked the camp oven down in the middle of the table. "What're you doing with Gus and Dobbin's muskets?" That sealed it. Even she recognized the firearms.

Della shot a look at the captain. What would he say? Charity would be all in favor of killing the Darkinjung. She reckoned they were vermin.

"I'm taking them back to Sydney for repairs." He swallowed and his eyes shot to one side. She'd imagined he'd be a smoother liar; he was probably worried Bert would say something.

"Are we going to eat that stew?" Bert's mind was on other matters; he ran his tongue around his mouth and groaned.

The captain gave a relieved laugh at the change in subject while Charity lifted the lid of the pot and ladled a serving onto everyone's plate before sitting herself down next to Bert. She'd even seasoned the stew with herbs that the night before she hadn't bothered to pick.

It was a bit early for lunch; however, the plate of steaming stew made Della's mouth water. It had been an unusual morning: she'd sewed up a man's shoulder and a handsome captain had landed on her doorstep. She dashed a look at him from beneath her eyelashes and a heady warmth washed her cheeks as he met her gaze. "I'm sure there has been some mistake," he murmured. "The shop appeared to be very successful. I doubt Mrs. Atterton is aware of Gus and Dobbin's activities."

She wasn't so sure. Something didn't ring true. The meat turned to paste in her mouth. Pa had made her promise she'd keep the shop running, said it was her inheritance and asked her to look after Cordelia. What nonsense. Cordelia was obviously doing a very good job of that on her own. How had she managed to snaffle an invitation to the governor's? Everyone knew Sir Charles's views on emancipists. The days of sponsorship and support vanished with Governor Macquarie; now it was all about rich English settlers and what they could bring to the country. Pa had brought the family to Australia to make Cordelia's sentence easier, not to have her take over the shop. That hadn't been his plan.

She pushed her plate to one side. She couldn't eat. All she could see was the gaping great hole in Jarro's shoulder and the anguished faces of the women and children. The crack of the long bullwhip Dobbin always carried echoed in her mind. He would have ridden in and rounded them up like animals.

Except that Captain von Richter had stalled them. She had to talk to him alone, away from Charity and Bert, and quiz him about Cordelia.

She lifted her head and found his eyes still on her face, as though he could read her thoughts.

He placed his knife and fork down on the plate. "Thank you, Charity. That was the most delicious mutton stew I have ever tasted." Della doubted mutton appeared on this man's menu very often.

She certainly couldn't imagine it on the governor's table; that would be all about oyster patties and pigeon in aspic.

Charity beamed like an overblown sunflower and lifted the lid, and her eyebrows.

"No more for me, really, but thank you."

Bert, however, had other ideas. He simply held his plate out while Charity filled it full to overflowing.

Della couldn't sit still a moment longer. "Would anyone like more tea?" Without waiting for a reply, she leaped to her feet.

Once off the veranda her breathing settled and she stood for a moment gazing up at the ridge, letting the fresh air blow away her terrible thoughts. How she hoped Gus and Dobbin hadn't tracked the women.

"I thought perhaps you'd need the teapot." The captain appeared at her shoulder and headed for the kitchen.

He could read her mind, she was certain of it. She scampered after him.

"I felt there was something you wished to ask me. Some more information about the attack perhaps? To the best of my knowledge none of the women and children were seriously injured. There was only one shot, and they disappeared into the scrub. Gus didn't have time to reload before Bert got the muskets."

She liked him for that. He'd called them women and children, not savages or blacks. She drew her hair back from her face. "Yes, yes, I would. I do. Oh, for goodness' sake, I don't know where to begin." She wiped her damp palms down her skirt and filled the kettle. "What you have said disturbs me deeply. Cordelia must know Gus and Dobbin are behind the raids on the camps. Surely she didn't think the Darkinjung would hand over their weapons and tools in a gesture of friendship."

"There is a possibility she thought they were trading. That's what she told me."

That was true enough, and maybe she was jumping to conclusions, but coupled with the changes in the shop, something felt wrong. It wasn't what Pa had intended, and why hadn't Cordelia mentioned the native curios in her letters?

She should have paid more attention. Too busy feeling sorry for herself. The time for mourning was over. She owed it to Pa and Ma, to Jarro, to the Darkinjung people. "I need to return to Sydney." But how? She and Charity had traveled with Gus and Dobbin in the wagon. "But I don't know how I can organize it."

"I would be more than happy to escort you." He offered a sharp bow and clicked the heels of his boots, which she found almost as attractive as his broad shoulders and handsome face.

"I can't leave Charity here alone."

"Could she perhaps stay at the inn at St. Albans?"

Della's mind spun in circles. That would work, but she had no money to pay for a room for Charity, and besides, she'd never agree. Charity wanted to go back to Sydney too.

The captain pressed the tips of his fingers together and peered over the top of them at her as though deep in thought. "Allow me to assist you. We have three horses. I would happily escort you to Sydney. I have a room booked at the inn. Perhaps Charity could wait there for your return, and take the coach if you're delayed."

Not only was the man handsome, he had an answer for everything.

"As I said, I must call in and see the Wiseman family, but that is simply one night's stop. We could easily make the trip in a few days."

The kettle sent out a billow of steam in appreciation. It was the perfect solution. She could be in Sydney before she knew it and Charity would hardly turn down a night or two at the Settlers Arms.

"I would very much appreciate your corroboration when I speak to the governor. He must be made aware of these appalling attacks," Stefan added.

And she had to find out how Cordelia was involved. She couldn't believe it. It couldn't be something Gus and Dobbin had dreamed up. Truth be told, she'd delight in seeing them get their just deserts.

"There is of course one small problem . . ."

There was? Not one she could think of. "And that is?"

"I don't have a suitable saddle for you. For any lady."

Warmth rose to her cheeks again and she swallowed the desire to giggle. Something she couldn't remember doing for a long time. "First, Captain von Richter, I hardly think I classify as a lady. I was four years old when I arrived in Australia. And when my father secured this land grant, he insisted that I should learn to manage a horse."

Chapter 20

Hawkesbury, NSW
1853

The last time Della had traveled this road she could think of nothing and no one other than poor Ma and Pa. The furtiveness of the journey had weighed heavily, as though they'd been running. They had been, in a way, running from the memories. When Cordelia had insisted she and Charity should leave Sydney, she hadn't had the strength to argue. She'd believed Cordelia was acting in her best interests, as Pa would have wished. She was his sister, for heaven's sake.

The thought of Cordelia and Pa's shop, his life's work, being somehow involved in the ghastly attacks had firmed her resolve. She had to help Jarro and his family. They may have moved on, but they would return because the pathways along Mogo Creek led to their special places.

She'd locked up the house and the workshop as best she could, and Charity couldn't leave the place fast enough. She'd insisted she was quite capable of getting herself to St. Albans in the cart.

Della led the way, showing the captain the Darkinjung pathway along the ridge to the Simpson Pass. It made her feel a little less of a nuisance and saved hours of backtracking.

The road spread out before her, the ground a blaze of color after the rain, sheer pleasure under the brilliant blue sky. For the first time since Ma and Pa's death she had a sense of freedom and the ability to breathe. The captain insisted she ride Bert's horse and he had quite happily taken the pack animal. Their mounts managed the terrain with the greatest of ease. Strong and wide-boned, gentlemen's horses, nothing like the rattle-boned heaps of misery they kept at Mogo.

Clustered everywhere were low-growing bushes covered in dazzling pink flowers and above them the yellow of the wattle.

"*Boronia ledifolia*."

How personable and attentive he was, with his ruffled hair and a half smile of amusement hovering on his lips. "I'm sorry?"

"The pink bushes, and above us *Acacia*, and those big red flowers over there."

She turned and gazed at the densely packed red flowers bright as Indian rubies against the bush.

"*Waratah Telopea*."

Was there anything this man didn't know? "You know so much."

"Not really. I can read." He leaned across in the saddle, his scent clean, woodsy, and masculine. Soap with a hint of perspiration and musk. He produced a well-worn, leather-bound notebook, then reined in the horses and thumbed through the pages. "This is what I was looking for." He held the page open and showed her a rough-drawn map. "We have to make a turn west before long."

"I've only been this way once before." Her tears had mingled with the rain back then as she'd clutched a blanket tight around her shoulders, unable to see anything but the piles of dirt they'd shoveled over Ma and Pa in the cemetery. "I'm sure we stay on the road."

"It says here that the road runs along the ridge and opens up at Simpson Pass."

"So you have been this way before?"

"It's the baron, 'e has. Baron von Hügel." Bert bowed low over his horse's neck and performed some sort of clicking action with his heels against the flanks. "The captain's writin' up his notes so they can make them into a book."

Della looked sharply at the captain's chiseled features as he scanned the pages. He'd mentioned being the baron's aide-de-camp, but she hadn't paid an awful lot of attention to what he'd said, her mind fixed on Cordelia and the raids. "Who is this baron?"

"My mentor, my savior, my surrogate father."

"And he's visited Australia?"

"Almost twenty years ago, in the early 1830s. I owe my life to him in more ways than one. He dragged me out of the gutter, saved me from a life on the streets."

"He wot?" Bert's jaw went loose, causing his mouth to fall open. "You weren't always a proper gentleman then?"

"You see, Bert, people aren't always what you expect them to be. Just because I wear a uniform doesn't tell you the man I am underneath, the boy I was."

"Well, tell us then."

The captain turned to her and raised an eyebrow in question, asking her permission.

"I'd love to hear your story. I know so little of anything beyond my sheltered life." She smiled into his eyes. The irises were the most unexpected color, the blue of the freckles on a kookaburra's wing feathers, with flecks of green radiating from the dark pupil. The corner of his mouth quirked as he caught her studying him, sending her heart into the most unusual rhythm.

"I didn't know my father. My mother died and I was left to fend for myself on the streets of Vienna. Winter can be very cold, snow and ice and biting winds."

"Bloody freezing in Sydney too."

"Bert! There is a lady present."

"Beggin' your pardon, miss."

She threw Bert a wink, not wanting to slow the captain's story. She'd never seen snow, only in a storybook. A magical castle with turrets and tiny windows, the flickering light reflecting on the pristine pure white carpet. Ma and Pa used to talk of English winters and roasted chestnuts, but she suspected he was remembering something far less enticing.

"Colder than Sydney, I'd imagine. Several feet of snow and icicles longer than a man's arm hanging from every window."

"And the baron found you huddled in a doorway and took you home?"

"Not quite. I tried to pick his pocket."

"You wot?"

"I tried to steal from him. He grasped my wrist. I remember his hand, big like a cuff, fingers cutting into my skin. I thought he'd cart me off to the authorities. He didn't. He took me back to his gardens. Had me fed and scrubbed within an inch of my life and then asked me what I was going to do to atone for my sins."

Bert's eyes shone bigger than pennies. "A-tone? What's a-tone?"

"Make up for. I said I'd do anything he wanted. So I stayed, did all sorts of odd jobs around the gardens until one day he called me into his study. He said he wanted to teach me a game." Stefan paused.

"Go on. Don't stop now." The words fell out of Bert's mouth, saving Della from uttering the very same. "What's the game?"

"Chess."

"I seen that. Those little knights and castles. They got one in one of the inns in the Rocks."

"In Vienna they play it in the squares. Great big sets."

"And you'd played before so you won." Della clamped her hand over her mouth. "I'm sorry, I shouldn't have interrupted."

"But you should. You see, you're right."

"And so he thought you were real smart and he got you them chewters and then you joined the army."

"That's about it, Bert."

"Go on. Then what happened?"

He tightened the reins and nudged his horse forward. "Another time. I don't want to fall behind." He pointed to the baron's notebook. "A few more miles and then we should crest the ridge."

Impressive stands of flowers, bigger than anything she had ever seen, lined the track. Red as blood and clustered around a stem taller than even the captain astride his fine horse. "What are they?"

"The flame lily. *Doryanthes excelsa*. It derives from two Greek words—*dory*, meaning spear, and *anthos*, meaning flower." He pored over the notebook again. "A truly iconic plant, indigenous to the Sydney area. The botanic name, *Doryanthes*, refers to the beacon-like flower heads that stand out in the bush."

Della stared at the massive clumps of shoots as thick as a man's arm and twice the height. "And these were here when the baron came this way."

"I presume so. He mentions them."

"They must survive with barely any water or soil. It's so dry up here."

"And so am I. We'll stop for some refreshments shortly."

They continued for several more miles along the ridgeline, then crossed two small bridges and dropped down onto a well-constructed road.

"Such an amazing feat of engineering. Look at the culverts and the carefully laid stonework. The baron maintained that he could employ every one of the convicts who built this road and make free men of them. I think this would be the perfect place to stop."

"Should we light a fire? It's very dry."

"We'll make a fireplace. There are plenty of rocks." He reached up his hands and swept her from the saddle and drew her close before easing her gently to the ground. "Come, sit down and rest."

Rest? It was highly unlikely she'd ever be able to rest in this man's company. The very nearness of him set her heart racing.

The warm pressure of his hand on the small of her back guided her to a seat on one of the rocks overlooking the distant folds of hills and valleys that merged into the blue haze of the mountains. She had expected the journey to Sydney would be tedious. How wrong she had been. She wanted it to last forever.

"I have something to ask of you."

She tilted her head up, searching for the flecks of green in his eyes. "Yes?"

"I would like to use your name, the name you were born with. Della. It is a beautiful name. I believe it means 'noble.' William the Conqueror named one of his daughters Della."

Her stomach swooped and her mouth dried. She'd never asked why she'd been named Della or where it had come from. Just taken it for granted. Noble!

"And, Della, I would like you to call me Stefan."

She lowered her head and stared at her interlaced fingers, not knowing how she should respond. No one had ever asked permission to use her name before.

"Ask me a question, Della. Allow me the pleasure of hearing my name on your lips."

Her mind went blank. Every thought, every piece of information wiped clean like her tools after a day's work. She gazed around, trying to force something, anything into the vacant space where her brain once lodged.

"Why are you here?" No, that wasn't right. "What made you come to the Hawkesbury, Stefan?"

He beamed down at her. "There, that wasn't too difficult, was it, Della? I had some business to conduct in the area, and I intended to traverse the same route the baron took in the 1830s. And thanks to your knowledge of the area, we have succeeded. You've saved us numerous wrong turns and at least half a day."

Before long Bert presented her with a mug of tea and a lump of bread and treacle, which she suspected Charity had provided as a token of thanks for her room at the Settlers Arms. Della rested back against a tree trunk and savored the sweet smell of the bush and the quiet company of the man sprawled beside her.

Once he'd finished his tea Stefan pulled his compass from his pocket and studied it. "Bert and I were provided with first-class accommodation at Wisemans on our journey to the Hawkesbury. We will avail ourselves once more. Until then I'm afraid tea and bread will have to suffice. Once we crest the next ridge we will see the Hawkesbury River and the Wisemans' properties. Old man Wiseman died not long after the baron visited him. His family continues to manage the property."

As Stefan promised, they crested the ridge and below them lay the river, like some majestic inland sea cradled between tall mountains, turned to a dark mirror by the afternoon shadows. They dropped down into the valley cradling farms that made Mogo look as ragged and moth-eaten as her early attempts at taxidermy. Sleek brown cows grazed on the river flats, full-fleeced sheep ambled in neatly fenced paddocks, and everywhere there were women tending the flourishing crops.

"Down there."

Della tracked the path of his hand to the opposite bank where extensive fields and gardens spread.

"We'll go down and take the ferry." He raised his hands to his mouth, let out a long coo-ee. After a minute the two men on the other side raised their heads and clambered aboard a strange-looking craft.

"Do you know the story of Old Wiseman?" Stefan opened the baron's notebook. "He sounds like a fascinating character."

Della shook her head. So strange to have this man from another land, another life, telling her about the country she called her own.

"He was sentenced to transportation back in the early days for dealing in contraband. He had an extensive knowledge of the sea and earned his pardon by rescuing the crew of a wrecked ship and was granted one hundred acres. This is what he selected. The baron believed it was one of the most beautiful spots in the colony."

As they waited for the ferry to take them across the wide river, Della had no reason to disbelieve the captain's baron.

Chapter 21

St. Albans, NSW
1919

Fleur pushed open the door to the Settlers Arms and ducked her head under the lintel. Although it was still light outside, the lamps were lit. Pete sat propping up the bar, deep in conversation with Skipper. Both men raised their eyebrows when they saw her, questions written all over their faces.

"Come and sit down, love. Looks like you've had a long day." Pete handed her a glass of lemonade.

"Thank you. I'll take it into the dining room."

"Nah! Stay here in the bar. No one around to complain. It's early yet."

She stretched up onto the rickety stool and with a sigh sipped the cool lemonade. She had very little memory of the walk, her mind fixed on Hugh and the old man and his strange insistence about Hugh's personal belongings. She couldn't remember, in the brief time they'd spent together, Hugh having any special possession, and the old man had said a *family* heirloom.

What did people have as heirlooms? Silver teapots, jewelry, photographs? The Browns, who'd lived next door before the zeppelin had taken out their house, had a family Bible. It weighed a ton, and every time another baby came along the name and date got written down. She couldn't imagine Hugh carting something like that around France.

"Find what you were looking for?" Skipper's face crinkled in a concerned smile and she had a sudden yearning for Marianne, in her cozy house full of sunshine and the homely scent of freshly made scones.

"I found the property. What's the name of the man who lives there?"

"No one lives there. Been empty for years. Empty when I was a boy. Never been farmed. Some of the paddocks along the creek have been leased over the years. Good grazing land. Attertons had the first grant, then the boy used to come up here when he was on holiday from that fancy school in Sydney."

"I thought the old man might live there. The fire was alight and he made me a cup of tea."

She didn't miss the glance Skipper and Pete exchanged, the raised eyebrows and a bit of a frown, but she couldn't do anything about it. She'd been trespassing as much as he had. Maybe Vera would have some idea about him.

"Will you be wanting your room for another night?"

She hadn't given a thought to what she intended to do next, and she was tired, very tired. "I . . . I don't honestly know. I suppose so. Then I have to get back to Sydney." Even if it meant camping on Lyttleton's doorstep she intended to find some answers. The old man at Mogo had told her to come back when she had more information, and Lyttleton's was the only place she was going to get it.

"Why don't you come back with me? Marianne would love the company and then you could pick up the steamer at Spencer tomorrow morning. You'd be back in Sydney by afternoon tea tomorrow."

That sounded like a dream come true. "I don't want to be a nuisance."

"Not at all. I wasn't expecting to be here today, otherwise I would have offered yesterday, but things got in the way."

"A hand of cards got in the way, you mean. How're you going to explain that one to Marianne?"

"That's my business. Now, Miss Fleur, what would you like to do?"

"If you're sure it would be no trouble, I'd very much like to do that. I need to get back to Sydney as quickly as I can."

"Given the hour I suggest we get a move on. I'll meet you down at the boat."

Dredging up the last skerrick of energy from deep within, Fleur took off up the stairs to pack up her few belongings and pay her bill.

Despite the sunshine, a stiff breeze buffeted the small boat as Skipper pushed off from the little beach below the bridge. She turned up the collar of her gabardine coat, thankful it was sufficiently waterproof to deal with the spray, thrust her hands deep in her pockets, and propped her feet on the seat.

"You look comfortable there."

"I am, thank you. I really didn't want to spend another night at St. Albans. I don't feel as though I achieved anything." She shrugged deeper into her coat. "I don't understand why no one knows the old man. I can't believe I was foolish enough not to ask his name."

"I wouldn't worry too much about it. Sounds to me as though your hands are tied until this solicitor gets matters sorted."

"He knew Hugh. He asked me if I'd got anything for him. I thought at first he was some sort of tramp and he wanted money. I think I offended him. He said I'd know what he was talking about when I got Hugh's belongings."

"You haven't got those yet?"

"No. It's all so complicated. Everyone seems far too busy sorting out the living to worry about someone they believe dead. I'm beginning to think I should have stayed in London and waited."

"You're here now. And that's what matters."

"I'm sorry." She let out a huge sigh.

"What you need is a drop of Marianne's home cooking and a comfortable bed for the night. You've had a busy few days. A nice lazy morning and we'll have you on the big steamer before midday and back in Sydney in time for afternoon tea."

She couldn't think of anything better.

Arriving back in Sydney was almost like coming home. Fleur pushed open the doors to the Berkeley Hotel and Mr. Sladdin greeted her like a long-lost relative, ushering her upstairs, arranging for hot water and dinner to be sent to her room. Money made life so much easier—one of the few things she'd learned since she left London.

Except that it wasn't *her* money. She emptied out her satchel and burrowed through her purse. She still had most of the fifty pounds Mr. Waterstone had given her, although the hotel bill would make a serious hole in that.

First thing tomorrow she'd go around to see Mrs. Lyttleton, hammer on the door and demand some answers, and if she wasn't there she'd find out where she lived and track her down.

At nine o'clock sharp the next morning Fleur stood outside the Lyttletons' offices, gazing up at a sign that read *Open Monday to Friday 9 a.m.–5 p.m.*, which was a load of rubbish because they hadn't been open for days.

Clenching her fist, she hammered on the door and stood back, tapping her foot impatiently. After a few moments, the door opened a fraction to reveal a very disheveled-looking Kip, his hair standing up on end and his cheeks flushed as though he'd been doing some heavy work. "We weren't expecting you." He hovered half in and half out of the partially open door.

"Well, I'm here now." And she had no intention of being put off a moment longer. She stepped over the threshold, forcing him to swing the door wide. "I'm sorry to disturb you, but I really need to speak to Vera. Is she about?"

He ran his fingers through his hair, releasing a shower of dust. "Um, yes. Yes, she is. We're, um . . ."

"Who is it, Kip? I told you we didn't want to be disturbed. I have to find these wretched papers."

"It's me, Fleur Richards." She stepped past Kip and headed down the hallway past the office where she'd first sat, to a door standing ajar.

"Oh dear." Vera Lyttleton appeared from behind a large stack of boxes dressed in a pair of overlarge men's trousers hitched around her waist with what looked like an old tie, a smudge of dirt marking the end of her nose. The cyclamen pink scarf wrapped like a bandage around her head only emphasized her distress.

"I'm sorry to disturb you, Mrs. Lyttleton. It's imperative I find out more about Hugh. I've been out to the Hawkesbury and all that has done is confuse the issue."

"Whatever made you do that? Come in. I apologize for the mess. Kip and I have been trying to make sense of Mr. Lyttleton's filing system. I still haven't had word from him."

Fleur resisted the temptation to groan and eased between the chaotic mess of tea chests, stacked files, and open-drawered cabinets. She unbuttoned her jacket and set it on the back of the chair. "Perhaps I can help."

Wringing her hands, Vera sighed. "I don't think it would be appropriate. Some of these files are confidential and Mr. Lyttleton would be—"

This was ridiculous. "Mr. Lyttleton need know nothing about it, and besides, I have no idea who any of the people are. Surely another pair of hands would make matters easier."

She turned to Kip, hoping for some support. He flicked her a wry grin but remained standing in the doorway, scratching his head, looking as confused as poor Vera.

"Is there some sort of a system?" She'd always been good at sorting things out; even Mrs. Black had remarked upon it when she'd attacked the store cupboard, making lists to record their supplies, keeping the rationed goods, like the coffee Hugh had loved so much, and the sugar, up high where it couldn't be knocked over and wasted. And she could balance books and read a ledger. Not that she imagined she'd be doing anything as complicated as that. The chaos had to be righted first.

"I'm thoroughly embarrassed by the whole matter. When Michael left I had just a few days to pack the remaining paperwork. Everything was such a shambles, tea chests everywhere. He was called away the very day we signed the new lease and since then . . ." She lifted her shoulders and let them fall, heaving another sigh.

Fleur rolled up her sleeves and peered at the first of the tea chests, surprised to find they were neatly labeled with a grouping of letters and a span of two dates. "Didn't you say Hugh came to see Mr. Lyttleton right after he enlisted?"

"Yes, that's what he told me."

"And I know he was in France in 1916 so anything after that we can ignore. You told me he'd written notifying Mr. Lyttleton of our marriage. I'm certain the file would be under the original date, so we can disregard all of these." She moved around the room looking at the alphabetical listing and dates. "We only want those tea chests marked R–T and with dates before 1916."

"Oh, of course, how very clever of you. I only looked in Michael's desk drawers because it was a current matter."

This time Fleur got a wider smile from Kip and he started moving all the tea chests labeled otherwise to the back wall.

"The dates on the filing cabinet are more recent, so we can ignore those for the time being. Have you got a hammer or a screwdriver?"

"A hammer?"

"To wrench the lids off."

Kip delved into his pocket and produced a penknife attached to a lanyard. "This'll do it." He flicked open an evil-looking spike and proceeded to lever the lid from the first of the chests.

Bundles of files were neatly stacked and bound with string. She lifted the first out: *Rathwell*. "No, this isn't the right one."

The next four boxes were dated after 1916 so those were moved to the back of the room, as were all those with letters other than the letter *R*. Finally, they were left with three tea chests. "My dear, you are so clever. I felt as though I was hunting for the proverbial needle in a haystack."

Kip removed the lids of the remaining boxes and pulled out the files, stacking them on the desktop while Fleur flicked through the names and checked the dates. Vera might be thoroughly disorganized, but Mr. Lyttleton was nothing of the sort. She could well imagine him arranging something as complicated as repatriation of the troops if he had this kind of mind.

Having taken the next bundle out of the box she flicked through the files. *Richards*, bold as brass. "I think I've found it." Fleur handed the file over to Mrs. Lyttleton, her hands shaking. "Why don't I go and make a cup of tea and then I'll check to see if it is the right one." Whatever had made her say that? All she wanted to do was rip the neatly tied black ribbon off the file immediately.

"Kip will do that."

He grunted his agreement with a look of disappointment and eased through the muddle of boxes to the door while Mrs. Lyttleton took forever to clear a space on the desk, sit down, and untie the ribbon.

Fleur's mouth dried. At long last some answers. Resisting the temptation to peer over the woman's shoulder, she stared out the window at the buildings across the road, wondering if the keys to the Curio Shop might be inside the folder.

"Right. I see." Mrs. Lyttleton straightened up and pulled the scarf from her head. Fleur was at her side in a moment.

"Here's Hugh's letter with his instructions. 'Following the death of my brothers, please accept this letter as my last will and testament. In the event of my death the family legacy should pass to my next of kin.'"

Fleur shot a look at the date at the top of the letter. December 1916. "But we hadn't met then. I wasn't Hugh's next of kin."

Vera reached out and patted her hand. "That's what it says." She passed another sheet of paper to Fleur.

It contained a list of properties. Mogo Creek she recognized and the old Curio Shop, but Wilcannia and White Cliffs made absolutely no sense at all and Gauermanngasse 2–4 1010 Wien made even less. It sounded like a string of swear words.

"There's also reference to several bank accounts."

Fleur suddenly remembered the words of the old man. "Do you know if Hugh's belongings have been returned yet? Mr. Waterstone said they would be forwarded to you."

"Oh dear. One step forward and two back. No, I don't know. And we haven't found the keys for the old Curio Shop either." Fleur propped herself on the corner of the desk, her fingers lifting and dropping the handle to the drawer. There was something soothing about the rhythmical clatter as it fell, like a metronome.

Kip appeared with a tray and Mrs. Lyttleton closed the file and moved it aside. "Milk and sugar, I seem to remember."

Fleur stood, her fingers still hooked through the handle on the drawer. It pulled open. "Oh, I beg your pardon." She moved around the desk and went to push the drawer shut when her eyes lit on a large bunch of keys, each neatly labeled with a beige cardboard tag. She lifted them out. They were heavy, putting her in mind of a medieval lady of the castle walking down the ramparts with clanking keys dangling at her waist. "Do you think one of these might belong to the Curio Shop?"

Mrs. Lyttleton peered over the rim of her cup. "Where did you find those?"

"In the drawer. They're labeled."

"I had no idea. Have a look."

Each key had a tag tied to it, with the same neat handwriting. Names and more names. None with Richards on it. Her shoulders slumped. For one glorious moment she'd thought she might have stumbled upon something useful. She turned over the last tag: *Atterton 84 Hunter Street.*

"I think I may have found it." She fingered the ornate key, the top fashioned into the shape of a raven, then clasped it in the palm of her hand, hefting the unexpected weight. The idea of the lock it would open set her pulse racing. Someone's teacup clattered into the saucer.

"What number in Hunter Street is the Curio Shop?"

"Number 84."

She was right! "Do you know anyone by the name of Atterton?"

Mrs. Lyttleton's mouth twitched and her brow creased. "No. No, it doesn't ring a bell."

Atterton rang the loudest bell for her. *The old Atterton place*. That's what Skipper had said.

"Let me see." Vera turned the label this way and that. "Eighty-four is definitely the number of the Curio Shop." She pulled at the long ribbon and dangled the intricate key tantalizingly between her fingers.

Fleur couldn't contain herself a moment longer. She snatched the key from Vera's fingers. "I'm going to go and try it. Can you see if you can find any record for the Attertons? The man at the Settlers Arms called Mogo the old Atterton place."

"That shouldn't be too hard. There's only one box for the *A* files."

"I'll go with you." Kip was on his feet, grabbing his cloth cap from the hat stand in the corner, hardly able to contain his excitement. "Just wait a minute and I'll go and find some tools. We'll need to pry the boards off to open the door."

"I'm not sure—"

"Vera, you told me I was Hugh's beneficiary and number 84 Hunter Street is part of that estate. We have it in writing." She slapped her shaking hand down on the manila folder. She would not be stopped. Not now. Not after all the waiting. And what harm could it do? They might find something that would lead her to Hugh, or at least make sense of the old man's words.

"Very well. If Kip goes with you. I couldn't countenance anything happening to you. I would feel personally responsible."

"I doubt anything will happen. I shall simply see if the key opens the door and have a look inside."

"Be careful. The place has something of a reputation."

The memory of Glad's words made her nerve endings tingle.

"Are you ready?" Kip appeared at the door, his face flushed, clutching a canvas tool bag in one hand.

"Come straight back here and tell me . . ."

Kip closed the door on Vera's words and took off up the road at a gallop, leaving Fleur wondering what she might find. He must have sensed her hesitancy, because he cast a glance back at her and gave a wide smile and stretched out his hand. It firmed her resolve to go and unlock the Curio Shop of Wonders.

Chapter 22

Sydney, NSW
1853

Nobody spoke as they reined their horses to a stop on Windmill Hill. Della gazed down at the sprawling vista of Sydney. The new hospital, the big Catholic church, and the prison stood out, their sandstone façades bright in the afternoon sun, and beyond were the park known as the Domain and Government House with wide stretches of lawn, groups of trees, and well-laid-out flower beds. So different from Mogo, where the she-oaks whispered in the wind and the fluffy gray flannel flowers carpeted the ground.

Stefan gave her hand a reassuring squeeze. "It's very like some of the larger European towns, somewhat confused in the older parts, as though the buildings were built pell-mell with neither plan nor direction. The newer areas not so."

"But it's 'ome and I'm happy to be here." Bert sat astride the huge bay, his legs not long enough to encompass its wide girth but his eyes shining. It hadn't occurred to Della in the last few days to wonder about Bert's origins or how he came to be traveling with the captain. They seemed to have such a natural understanding. He treated Bert with an amused tolerance that belied his status.

"Were you born in Sydney, Bert?"

"Dunno. First I remember is the orphanage out Parramatta way.

Dumped, left with nowt but a name as long as me arm." His mouth turned down at the corners and her heart clamped. She couldn't imagine her childhood without Ma and Pa. "Did a runner wiv some other boys 'bout seven years ago."

"Seven years!" He was hardly more than twelve now, too young to have hair on his face. "How old were you?"

"Dunno much about the kid I was. Only know what I know about Sydney. Grew up down there. Always found a way to earn a shilling or two." He squared his shoulders. "Then I got me barrow and things looked up."

"How did you do that?"

He sniffed and stuck out his jaw. "I didn't nick it."

"Nobody said you did, Bert." Stefan ruffled the boy's hair and shook his head, his eyes full of compassion for Bert's sudden outburst.

And she knew why. Stefan's story of his childhood explained that, and the reason he treated Bert with such respect. He'd worn the same boots, walked a similar road, and was repaying as only he would.

"There's a few more ships in port since I arrived." Stefan neatly changed the subject, saving poor Bert from his memories.

Thirty or so three-masters lay moored with their flags flying and the usual number of small boats skimmed the surface of the water, criss-crossing in all directions, and at the various wharves and quays of the major merchants, ships were unloading. A boy with a barrow could do well for himself, even better if he had a patron like Stefan.

"Let's make our way into the town. I'm sure you're keen to see Mrs. Atterton."

Now that the moment had come, Della wasn't too sure if that was the case. "Cordelia can be very determined."

"I'm sure there will be a simple explanation." Stefan's eyes narrowed, his expression belying his platitude. "I shall accompany you."

This was something she had to do alone, not hiding behind the greatcoat of this man, no matter how safe and secure he made her feel. "I would rather arrive alone. Thank you for the thought, but it is my responsibility." She sounded so pompous. Would he insist? A mixture of emotions flickered across his face and then he gave a disgruntled sigh.

"Very well. We will leave you at the end of Hunter Street and wait while you go into the shop. Bert has the horses to return to the stables and I shall be at the Berkeley Hotel. Should you require any assistance, send a message."

"I won't be far away, Miss Della. You just shout."

She could imagine that. Bert lurking in the street waiting to see if she needed any help. She wouldn't. She had every intention of getting to the bottom of Cordelia's involvement. During the journey to Sydney she'd tried to convince herself she'd jumped to conclusions and Cordelia knew nothing of Gus and Dobbin's actions, that it would all prove to be a misunderstanding. Now she wasn't so sure.

The crush of people grew as they reached the more built-up areas and the last few miles into the town seemed to drag. Then they arrived at the end of Hunter Street and the time had come to face Cordelia.

Stefan leaped down from his horse and held out his arms to her. She slid down into the comforting warmth of his embrace. Over the past few days she'd come to admire him more than any man she'd ever met. Not only for the stand he was taking against Gus and Dobbin but also for the compassionate way he treated Bert. "Thank you for the escort, the use of your horse, and the company. I have enjoyed the last days more than any I can remember."

His warm hand encompassed hers. "Don't hesitate to call upon me if you have any concerns. I shall make an appointment to speak to the governor about the attacks and drop you a note to let you know when I am to see him. As I said, I would appreciate it if you would accompany me. Your knowledge of the local tribes and the indignities they have suffered would be of great assistance when I put my case."

Bert passed her small carpetbag down to her. "Take care of yourself, Miss Della."

"Thank you, Bert. I'll see you soon, I hope." She hefted the bag onto her arm and with more confidence than she felt strode off down Hunter Street.

Nothing had changed. She passed the grocer, the saddler, and the stationers and nodded to the woman sitting outside the drapers knitting in a small patch of sunlight before coming to a halt outside number 84.

The black cockatoos had pride of place on the right of the window and on the other side the water mole. She stepped back and looked up. Ma and Pa's room. She swallowed down the sudden surge of remorse. She'd neglected them, too caught up in her own misery. She hoped they'd understand. Tomorrow she'd go to the Devonshire Street cemetery with flowers.

Then her eyes lit on the painted sign stretching the width of the building and her heart stopped. The word *Taxidermy* had been painted over and in its place *Curio* and beneath it *of Wonders*. She took two steps back: *The Curio Shop of Wonders*. She'd thought Stefan had been mistaken when he'd first mentioned the name. A slow-burning anger flushed through her. What right had Cordelia to change the name of Pa's shop and take Ma's name. *Mrs.* Atterton. What rot! She pushed open the door and marched inside.

A crowd of women stood in the center of the shop, presumably in front of Pa's desk, but she couldn't see for the excited crowd gesticulating wildly, examining a series of muffs and stoles. One woman extracted herself from the crowd, clasping a feather headpiece as though she'd snatched a prize. She stood before a mirror, removed her hat, and pinned it in place, preening like an overexcited wagtail.

What in heaven's name was going on? Della dropped her bag onto the floor and nudged it away from the door with her foot.

The wooden display cabinet that had housed Pa's butterfly

collection had vanished and in its place stood a table piled high with tanned skins. She ran her fingers through the top skin, recognizing the pelt of a wallaby, so like Tidda's soft fur it made her heart wrench. Below it a series of possum skins had been stitched together to form a patchwork blanket. Wherever had Cordelia got hold of these? She'd seen one of the Darkinjung elders wearing a possum cloak but nothing as fancy as this one. She turned it over, admiring the fine stitching. Not something Cordelia had worked; she had neither the patience nor the skill.

A hoot of laughter brought her head up with a snap. The woman at the mirror was now parading about wearing a ridiculous crown-like affair of yellow feathers resembling the plumage of an irate cockatoo.

The crowd parted and there was Cordelia. On her feet, staring at her with eyes as sharp as a paring knife and twice as deadly. "What are you doing here?" She delivered the words in a flat matter-of-fact manner, the high color on her usually pale cheekbones confirming her surprise.

"Good afternoon, Aunt Cordelia."

The women stopped their twittering and examined her with as much curiosity as they had the collection of furs and feathers.

Cordelia swept forward. "The shop is now closed, ladies. I shall reopen tomorrow at nine o'clock."

She gestured to the door and all but one of the women filed out without a word. The remaining woman stayed planted by the desk. "The tonic. I want the tonic now." She thrust a small package wrapped in black cloth onto Pa's desk and leaned closer. Cordelia flashed her a quick look and lowered herself in the chair. She pulled open the desk drawer and extracted a bottle of Ma's tonic and scooped up the package.

"You said I would need three bottles."

"I have the others here, marked with your name. I'll deliver them." Cordelia slammed the drawer shut and stood again, her eyes glued to the woman as she tucked the bottle into her voluminous muff and scuttled out the door.

Cordelia looked nothing like the person Della remembered. With her hair piled fashionably on the top of her head and several strategically placed ringlets framing her thin face, she could have graced any of Sydney's upper-class functions. She was dressed in a virulent green satin dress, more suited to the ballroom than a taxidermy shop, and draped across her shoulders lay a shawl of the finest silk with long, knotted tassels.

Only her complexion remained the same. The two spots of color on her cheekbones had faded, leaving her skin white and almost translucent, and her eyes, framed by carefully arched brows, appeared luminous.

The two of them stood facing each other, the silence stretched as taut as an overdried possum skin. Eventually Cordelia moved from behind the desk. Of similar height, they stared into each other's eyes. She'd never seen such a look on her aunt's face: murderous was the only way to describe it.

Cordelia's long fingernail jabbed at her collarbone, then she turned to the window, running her fingers through the silken tassels on her shawl. "This is unexpected. Where is Charity?"

"Charity is staying at the Settlers Arms."

"And who's paying for that?"

"The captain was kind enough to offer her his room. I said I would repay him."

"Which captain? I hope you haven't made a fool of yourself." Cordelia's eyes roamed her body, as if she could sense the change in her demeanor, pick the bloom in her cheeks.

"Captain von Richter escorted me to Sydney."

"Captain von Richter?"

Della couldn't put it off a moment longer. She'd discuss her trip later. Right now she had to bring up the matter closest to her heart. The longer she left it, the more difficult it would become. "Why have you changed the name of Pa's shop? Why are you using Ma's name? Calling yourself *Mrs.* Atterton? What are all these furs?" Della picked up a brown muff and slid her fingers inside, feeling the smooth silk lining. "This is wombat fur. Who made it?"

"I have employed a little additional help. The shop is going from strength to strength. You should be well pleased. We're catering to high society. And now that you're here you're going to have to dress more appropriately, do something about the way you look. I can't have all my hard work going to waste."

Della ran her hand down her mud-splattered skirt. "Why didn't you tell me?"

"You weren't here."

"But you could have told me in one of your letters." She turned in a full circle, searching for some of the specimens she had given Gus and Dobbin on their earlier trip. Her eyes lit on a display illuminated by a shaft of afternoon sunlight. Her heart stuttered as she stumbled toward the back of the room, her boots clattering on the timber floor.

In the center stood a large grasstree and against it a range of hunting spears, throwers, clubs, and axes. Pa's cedar display cabinet now housed a series of woven baskets and bags, fiber nets and fishing traps, the bush string and grass stalks meticulously coiled, twined, and looped; a slab of sandstone with a collection of handprints, so like the ones on the cave walls dotting the Darkinjung pathways, alongside a pair of grinding stones and a beautiful carved coolamon lined with paperbark, just like the one Yalana used to carry her newly born children. Della swallowed the surge of bile rising in her mouth. "This is why I am here." She stabbed her finger against the glass cabinet. "Where did all of this come from?"

Cordelia's laugh pealed. "You know as well as I do. Gus and Dobbin have been trading. Antipodean curios are the height of fashion—these artifacts, and of course the native furs and feathers. Why, the governor himself remarked upon—"

"Cordelia, stop!" The blood pounded through Della's temples and she rubbed at her eyes, trying to still the vision of the gaping hole in Jarro's shoulder and the memory of Dobbin's musket hanging from the captain's saddle, every notch a tear in her heart. "Trading. Trading what, with whom?"

Cordelia gave a dismissive wave of her hand. "Gus arranges it all. The natives have a liking for rum, I believe, and flour and sugar. I pay Gus when he delivers. The rest is up to him."

"And you sell these?" She lifted the lid to the display cabinet and took out a painted coolamon, holding it to her nose, inhaling the scent of grease and smoke. Imagining the women sharing the ripe apple-berries. "Do you know how Gus is getting these things? What he is doing?"

Cordelia shrugged and rearranged her shawl as it slipped down from one bony shoulder.

"He is murdering the Darkinjung." There, she had said it. Not a moment's hesitation in believing it was true. "Attacking their camps and shooting them, stealing their possessions."

"What a load of nonsense. And anyway, why should I concern myself? I haven't seen you expressing any great angst over the animals and birds you see fit to disembowel. How are the natives different?"

"Cordelia, the Darkinjung are not animals, they are people. Flesh and blood like you and me. Gus and Dobbin are running them down and killing them."

"Nonsense. Why would they do that? They have no need. I shall discuss it with them as soon as they return. You're tired and overwrought after your trip. Come upstairs."

She wasn't tired. If anything she felt rejuvenated, determined. "I'm not letting the matter rest. Captain von Richter witnessed one of the attacks. He intends to take the matter up with the governor. And I will be supporting his evidence."

In an instant Cordelia's disposition changed; the defensive glint vanished from her eyes and she smiled. "You're not thinking clearly. Come and rest. We'll talk later. A nice glass of lemonade is what you need." Her voice was as sickly sweet as bush honey.

Chapter 23

Sydney, NSW
1853

"Ah! Captain von Richter. I thought you had forsaken us." Sladdin flapped from behind the desk, wringing his hands. "Allow me to take your greatcoat. You are just in time for our evening game."

Stefan's mouth framed the word *no* and then he swallowed it. He'd almost forgotten over the last days Bishop and his original reason for visiting the Hawkesbury. "Thank you. Yes. I would very much like a seat. Is there anyone attending I might know?"

"Mr. Philpott—you may have met him the other evening, the governor's physician—and his friends Mr. Robins and Mr. Thompson."

"And Mr. Skeffington perhaps?" That would be too convenient for words.

"Mr. Skeffington?" Sladdin tipped his crow-like head to one side and frowned as though he couldn't understand how he'd missed such a tasty morsel.

"I believe he has interests in the Hawkesbury region. I was hoping to speak with him."

"Ah, very good, very good. I shall make some inquiries. I have a recollection of hearing that he had been unwell. Leave everything to me."

Why did the man make a great mystery of everything? Couldn't he speak plainly? He shook his head and reached for the door. Sladdin beat him to it and flung it open with a flourish.

Green lamplight flickered against the wall and several tables were arranged around the room.

"Captain Stefan von Richter." He gave a short, formal bow and slid into an empty chair at the table in the corner where three men sat, the deck of cards in front of them and a bottle of brandy and glasses arranged in the center of the table. The men half rose to introduce themselves.

"Mr. Robins." The bespectacled man glanced up, then dealt four hands of cards.

"Mr. Thompson." The second man threw him a half-hearted smile.

The remaining man, long and lanky, stood and offered his hand. "Philpott. Physician."

Perhaps one or all of them remembered Bishop, or knew of Skeffington.

"Good evening, gentlemen." He reached for the bottle of brandy. "Can I interest anyone in a drink?"

"Yes, yes, indeed." Philpott picked up a glass and the other men followed suit. "To Lady Luck." They raised their glasses and drank.

Lady Luck indeed, but not on the cards. "Before we begin, gentlemen, I have to admit to an ulterior motive in my attendance."

All three of them placed their cards facedown on the green baize tabletop and lifted their gaze.

He had nothing to lose; they may as well know. "It's a long story and the reason for my visit to your fair shores."

"I believe Baron von Hügel has commissioned you to act as his amanuensis." Philpott rearranged his cards, ensuring they were aligned.

Was nothing a secret in this town? "Indeed he has." He paused, waiting to see if any mention would be made of the opal. When nothing was said he continued. "I was also hoping to collect some specimens for the baron, from a Mr. Bishop. I visited him in the Hawkesbury. It seems a Mr. Skeffington now has them in his safekeeping." He picked up his hand and cast an eye over the cards.

"You have traveled all this way simply to collect some specimens. They must be most valuable if they couldn't be shipped." When he didn't reply, the bespectacled man, Robins, lost interest and laid out his first bet.

"That is not my sole reason. As Mr. Philpott said I am also transcribing the baron's journals for publication."

The man on his right topped up his glass and shot him a quizzical look. "And you had no luck with Bishop? Sad business. Wife killed not a mile from here. A kitchen fire that consumed the house. Lost all will to live, then upped and moved to the Hawkesbury. Rumor has it he's sunk all his money in a mansion outside St. Albans. Primrose Hill, if I remember rightly. Named for his wife. Acquired the land with Robert Skeffington's assistance."

Stefan sat back and sipped at his drink. No need to ask questions, the brandy had loosened the men's tongues.

"Skeffington resides in Sydney." A large balding man brought his chair over to the table. "He doesn't appear to be here this evening."

"No, he's not." Philpott leaned forward and spoke in a lowered tone. "I am not at liberty to discuss a patient; however, he is somewhat indisposed."

Stefan's heart sank. "But he is presently in Sydney?"

"Oh yes indeed. He is at home."

"And what a home it is." The balding man tossed back his brandy. "Lovely spot, one of the new residences at Potts Point."

"May I ask the nature of this specimen Skeffington has?" Philpott peered from under his shaggy eyebrows with an intelligent gaze.

Stefan cast a cursory glance at his cards then laid them down: an ace, ten, king, queen, and jack. "A winning hand, I believe, gentlemen. *Guten Abend*."

Stefan finished his favored breakfast and peered down into the street looking for Bert. He could do with the rascal's company, but he had other matters to attend to. First and foremost, to secure a meeting with the governor and then a trip to Potts Point to see if he could track down Skeffington. He pulled on his jacket and took the stairs two at a time.

The obsequious Sladdin met him, wringing his hands in the ridiculous manner he had. "How can I help you this morning?"

"In no way at all, thank you, Herr Sladdin. I am out for a walk."

The weather was delightful. A fine breeze and a clear blue sky. The country did have a lot to recommend it. Not least the beautiful women. He now regretted not arranging a further meeting with Della. Already he missed her lively conversation and pleasing company, never mind her glorious smile and sparkling eyes. The sooner he secured an appointment with the governor, the sooner he would have an excuse to seek her out. He had no doubt she would corroborate his evidence. He picked up his pace. Yes, he would call at Government House and then he would go to the Curio Shop and visit the lovely Della. Perhaps suggest an afternoon walk.

Hearing footsteps, he glanced over his shoulder and grinned. Bert had taken slightly longer than he'd anticipated. A good three minutes. He'd almost reached the Domain.

"Morning, Capt'n." Bert bounced alongside him.

"No barrow today, Bert?" He ruffled the lad's orange hair, which was sticking out at all angles, putting him in mind of one of the great apes of the Malay Archipelago.

"Nope. Got a job later this afternoon. Thought you'd want to know about Miss Della."

"Is something the matter?"

"Seems she had a bit of a run-in with her aunt when she arrived, but things have settled down. That shop certainly does some business. Not sure what all those women want with them furs and feathers though."

"It's called fashion. Something mere mortals like us have no understanding of."

"Some men do. That creep Sladdin called in this morning. Had a word with Cordelia, he did, then slithered away."

Stefan's lips twitched. He would have described Sladdin more as a discontented raven, but the reptilian analogy fitted well. "I'm sure I shall find out. I intend to call on the governor's secretary and make an appointment to see Sir Charles, then visit Miss Della and suggest a walk."

Bert gave a couple of skips and caught up. "I'm looking forward to seeing her again. I kind of got used to havin' her around."

"Sorry, Bert. That wasn't an invitation." Whatever made him say that? There was no reason why Bert shouldn't come along.

Bert's face fell to his highly polished boots. "You got nothing for me, then?"

"Not this morning. Why don't you drop by tomorrow morning and we'll have a chat?"

"Right you are, Capt'n. See yer tomorrow." He scuffed off, shoulders drooping.

Sometimes a man had to put matters of the heart before a young boy's sensibilities.

He strode through the gates into the gardens of Government House. Curiosity got the better of him and he followed the paved footpath down some steps to the water. A goodly number of trees had been planted but their spindly shape gave no pleasure, the sandstone soil not deep enough for them to prosper. There was not a sign of any of the delightful native trees that flourished across the water. The entire garden had the look of neglect, although it had been laid out with some taste. What he wouldn't give for the opportunity to make some suggestions—a walkway framed by the giant lilies would make a remarkable Antipodean statement. So foolish of these settlers not to embrace the beauty nature had bestowed upon them. The baron was right. They would never recreate an English park here no matter how many deciduous trees they planted.

Leaving his thoughts behind, he ran up the steps and arrived at the main door invigorated and full of promise. Once the governor heard of the enormous injustice that had been perpetrated on the New Hollanders he would undoubtedly send out the redcoats and bring Gus and Dobbin to justice. With their muskets as evidence and Della's additional testimony, the matter would be resolved in an instant. He gave one short, sharp rap on the door.

It swung open and a butler who would have done Victoria proud stood in front of him. "May I help you, sir?"

"I would like to speak with the governor."

"I'm afraid that's not possible. Who may I ask is calling?"

"Captain Stefan von Richter."

"I beg your pardon. I didn't recognize you, Captain."

Obviously a hint that he should have paid more attention to his dress, but surely on a sunny morning he couldn't be expected to be in full military regalia. Ridiculously pompous, these imported Englishmen.

"The governor is at his Parramatta residence. I can refer you to his secretary, who will have a clearer idea of his movements. Please follow me."

The butler led the way into a wide paneled entry hall and gestured to a wooden bench. "Perhaps you'd be good enough to wait here for a moment." He beetled off into the dark depths of the hallway behind the stairs and a few moments later a wizened man with flyaway hair and spots of something vaguely unsavory attached to his cravat appeared.

"Captain von Richter, good morning. Unfortunately, the governor is in Parramatta and will be for the next few days. I am Sir Charles's secretary. May I be so bold as to inquire the reason for your request?"

"It is of the utmost importance and, without wishing to exaggerate, a matter of life and death."

"Good heavens, that sounds very dire."

"I have recently returned from the Hawkesbury region where I witnessed an appalling and unprovoked attack on a group of New Hollanders. I know the men responsible and managed to remove their weapons, but unfortunately they disappeared into the scrub before I could apprehend them. I witnessed the shooting of one of the New Hollanders, and I am led to believe they are responsible for many such attacks." He could feel the outrage building once more, the appalling manner in which Dobbin had rounded up the defenseless women and children, the crack of the whip as it cut into their flesh. "Women and children have been beaten and treated no better than animals. I have a witness who can corroborate my evidence and testify that this is not a singular occurrence."

"These attacks are unfortunate; however, the settlers have a right to defend their land."

"It was not a question of settlers defending their land—this was an out-and-out attack on a group of defenseless people who were doing no harm. If anything, the boot was on the other foot."

"Oh, come now, Captain, we all know these natives don't have fixed habitation. They wander. Nomadic."

"They were in no way encroaching on any settlers' land grants. They have every right to be on their own land."

"Their own land. Please, please. The concept of *Terra Nullius* was established over twenty years ago by Sir Richard Bourke. We simply do not recognize the natives' right to occupy the land. Just let the matter drop, Captain. There is no more harm in shooting a native than one of the wild dogs."

"This is ridiculous." A pulse began to throb in his temple. "I insist that I speak with Sir Charles."

"As I said, Captain, the governor is not in Sydney at present. He is in Parramatta on urgent business."

"Then I will ride to Parramatta."

"He cannot be disturbed."

"We'll see about that!" He took a step forward, his temper bristling, then pulled up short. It would do his case no good to cause a disturbance.

The despicable little man held out his filthy hand and gestured to the door.

The walk across the Domain and the fresh air helped his frustration cool. He would need to speak to the governor. Parramatta was hardly more than a couple of hours' ride and he had a raft of invitations to stay in the district should it be necessary. He might take Bert with him.

There were, however, several things he must do before he left. First, speak with Mrs. Atterton; perhaps she could throw some light on the situation. The men must be brought to justice, otherwise the atrocities would continue. Surely she wasn't aware of the way Gus and Dobbin were acquiring the artifacts. Why else would she have invited him to go along? And if she was not forthcoming, he could possibly exert some leverage by refusing to purchase any of Della's wonderful specimens. Besides, it would give him the perfect opportunity to call. Then he would attend the card game again and ask a few pertinent questions. Everyone seemed to know everyone's business in this town.

Within moments he was standing outside the Curio Shop. The door was open and a large group of women crowded the interior. He inhaled the now-familiar odor and slipped inside. Cordelia sat at her desk in deep discussion with two women; however, there was no sign of the lovely Della.

Had he made a mistake allowing Della to return unaccompanied? Bert had said they had exchanged words. He shook the thought away—he was jumping to conclusions. It was highly unlikely Della's aunt would be responsible for Gus and Dobbin's appalling actions, and now that he had their guns as evidence, he doubted they'd dare show their faces.

"Mrs. Atterton, good morning." His voice carried over the tittle-tattling of the women who all turned their faces to him and presented him with simpering smiles. If their appraising looks were anything to judge by, the marriage market was alive and well in this corner of the world, as it was everywhere else.

"Captain, good morning." Cordelia rose from the desk, dressed again in the brilliant green she favored. "I must thank you for escorting Della back to Sydney." She held out her hand to him. He took it, ignoring the bemused whispers of their audience. "Have you come to discuss your purchases?"

"Yes, yes, I have." However, he had no intention of discussing anything in front of these gawking women. "I also thought I might suggest a short walk to Miss Atterton. It's a beautiful afternoon, and I have it on very good authority there are strawberry ices to be had in George Street."

"I'm sure Della would be delighted to see you. You'll find her upstairs in the back room. She's resting. She found the trip to Sydney quite tiring."

How very strange. He hadn't imagined for one moment she would have suffered any side effects. She'd been as bright as sunshine, and although they had made the journey quickly, they'd hardly broken any records.

"If you can find your own way." She indicated the stairs. "I shall finish up this little piece of business and be right up to join you."

There was a communal intake of breath at Cordelia's suggestion, and he masked the grin on his face by offering a sweeping bow to the gaggle of women in the shop. Emancipists like Cordelia were perhaps not quite so concerned about propriety as the newly arrived, affluent English matrons.

Reaching the top of the stairs, he stopped and waited for his eyes to adjust to the dim light on the small landing. Two firmly closed doors greeted him. Cordelia had said the back room so he knocked gently on the door and, receiving no response, eased it open.

In the semidarkness, it took him a moment to see Della. She sat in a chair by the curtained window overlooking the backyard, her hands in her lap and her head bowed as though deep in thought. When he cleared his throat, she lifted her head. "Stefan." She offered a wan smile and attempted to struggle to her feet.

He reached her side in two paces. "Please sit down. Don't tire yourself." He helped her back into the chair.

"I'm sorry, it's so silly of me." She groaned and settled into the cushions like an old woman. "I'm perfectly all right, just a little tired. Could you open the curtains? Some light will cheer me up."

It didn't cheer him one iota. It only served to emphasize her appalling pallor. Her glorious hair hung limp around her face, and the light in her eyes had dimmed to such an extent he could hardly believe she was the same person he'd left only twenty-four hours earlier.

"If I had known you were unwell I would have come sooner. Why didn't you send a message?"

She tried in vain to straighten her shoulders, her face ashen. "I'm simply suffering from a headache, a little queasiness."

"Let me call a doctor. Mr. Philpott, the governor's physician, frequents the Berkeley. I met him last evening."

"It's nothing. I'm sure it will soon pass. Cordelia has been looking after me. Now tell me what you have been doing. It'll cheer me up."

"Can I get you anything? A drink. A cup of tea."

"I should be offering you refreshments."

"I think we are long past such niceties."

His words brought the slightest smile to her bloodless lips. "A glass of lemonade would be lovely. There's some in the bottle on the table. Cordelia made it up especially for me. I've been so very thirsty."

He poured the lemonade and carried the glass back to her, then drew up a chair and brought it to the window.

"When did the illness commence?"

"I'm not very sure. The hours seem to have merged. How long have we been back?" She rubbed her hand over her eyes and slumped back in the chair.

He opened his mouth to answer, but her eyes were closed. Reaching for her small hand, he held it in both of his. Her mouth quivered with a smile and he rubbed his thumbs gently over her fingers. Such small hands, yet so capable. The vision of her drawing the needle through Jarro's skin with such skill and precision flashed through his mind. In the few days since he'd known her, he'd come to hold her in such high regard.

After a few moments, her eyes flickered open. "I'm sorry. I seem to be drowsy. I'm sure it's just the change of air. I'll be fine by tomorrow. Have you spoken to Cordelia?"

"Only briefly. She said she would be up in a moment. The shop appeared to be very busy."

"All the women. I was angry at first when I saw the changes she had made, but it seems to be very successful and I'm certain Pa would be pleased to know she has done so well. I just wish she'd told me. She doesn't seem to think there is anything untoward about Gus and Dobbin's activities, and they haven't returned."

As he suspected. He wished now that he'd put musket balls through the pair of them. Once he spoke with Sir Charles, the matter would be resolved. "I've called on the governor . . ."

"And?" The light came back to her eyes and she sat a little straighter.

"Unfortunately he is in Parramatta on business. I intend to ride out. I was going to ask you if you would like to accompany me."

"I'm not sure I'm well enough. Is it possible to delay it for a day or two? I'll be better soon."

He didn't want to delay a moment, but his case would have much more credibility if Della accompanied him; she knew so much more about the New Hollanders and their way of life. "It can wait a day or two. His secretary said he'd be there for a week." And besides, he might have a better solution.

As if on cue Cordelia swept into the room. "Ah! That's better, Della. There's more color in your face and I see you have been drinking the lemonade. Captain, can I get you anything? A glass of brandy perhaps. I have a keg of very good French brandy. And we have business to discuss."

They did. He inclined his head and Cordelia swept from the room.

"Business?"

"Yes. I told Cordelia that I would like to purchase some of your work. The black cockatoos and the water mole particularly. They are delightful."

Her pinked cheeks were almost reward enough, but he had a better plan. He just had to phrase it correctly.

Cordelia reappeared with two glasses of brandy. "I have closed the shop. Would you like to continue this discussion downstairs?" she asked, her expression bland as milk, her back ramrod straight.

"I'm sure Della would be interested in our proposed transaction; after all, she is the owner of the shop, is she not?"

Cordelia's eyes narrowed, stripping the warmth from her smile. "She is. However, I've become used to managing alone." She threw Della a sideways glance and moved to sit on the window seat. "Now. A transaction, you said . . ."

"I'm interested in purchasing a quantity of specimens for my Antipodean collection."

Her gaze seemed to lose focus and her expression darkened. Then a spark of animation returned to Cordelia's eyes. "I can sell you any number of specimens and artifacts. The shop is now following a different path, leaning more toward ladies' fashions."

"I do, however, have serious concerns about the native artifacts and the methods of acquiring them." He folded his arms and pinned the woman with his most ferocious stare.

"I can assure you that the merchandise in *my* shop . . ." She cleared her throat and shot a glance at Della. "*The* shop is entirely reputable. This nonsense about my men harming the natives is just that . . . nonsense. Some simple mistake."

"I assure you it is not. I witnessed the incident myself. Della treated one of the injured men."

"In that case both Gus and Dobbin will be severely reprimanded the moment they return." She wiped her hands together as though washing away any impropriety. "If you'd like to come downstairs we can discuss the pieces you wish to purchase."

"Until the matter of the raids is resolved I am not prepared to commit. I intend to bring the issue to the governor's attention."

Her eyes clouded momentarily and then the corner of her lip lifted in triumph. "I doubt very strongly the governor will be the slightest bit interested. I believe the authorities sanctioned a raid on the Hawkesbury natives only a matter of weeks ago. They have been making life hell for the settlers in the area."

There was no point in arguing with the woman; she appeared

so self-assured and as unconcerned as the governor's secretary. The treatment of the New Hollanders was, as Della said, nothing less than barbaric.

"I will leave you to consider my offer." He turned away from her to Della, who was staring out the window, an absent look on her face. "Della, I must go. I'm expected at the Berkeley." The poor girl was certainly in no condition to take a walk. "Are you sure you wouldn't like me to call a physician?"

She lifted her head and pulled her shawl tighter around her shoulders. "I will be better in a day or two."

"In that case I beg your permission to call tomorrow."

His words brought a fragile smile back to her lips. "I'd like that very much." She made some attempt to rise from her chair but he restrained her. "Stay here and rest. I'm certain Mrs. Atterton will show me out."

"I'd be delighted. After you."

Once they'd reached the bottom of the stairs he turned to Cordelia, his mind made up. "Mrs. Atterton, I am determined the New Hollanders should not be subjected to this gratuitous violence. Ensure your men leave the Hawkesbury district and I am prepared to purchase a large amount of your stock."

"Blackmail, Captain?" She raised one eyebrow. The wretched woman was enjoying the jousting.

"No, Mrs. Atterton. Fact." Without another word, he walked from the shop and strode down Hunter Street, his cane banging against the flagstone path. The woman was outrageous. He no longer doubted she was behind the raids and if, as she said, the matter was of no consequence to the authorities, then he would have an uphill battle.

Chapter 24

Sydney, NSW
1919

Fleur's fingers fumbled as she tried to fit the heavy key into the lock. "It's no good. The boards are in the way."

Kip stepped in front of her. "Stand back and let me see what I can do." He pulled a claw hammer and crowbar from his tool bag. "I'm going to see if I can lever these off, then we should be able to get to the lock."

Against her will she stepped away from the door and stood on the edge of the footpath, jiggling from one foot to the other, unable to keep still.

Kip hefted the hammer, then rolled his shoulders and inserted the claw under the corner of the plank of wood. Nothing moved. He flashed her a sympathetic smile. "Patience." He repeated the process all the way down the length of timber and then returned to the corner closest to the lock. "Ready?"

She nodded, her heart pounding like a drum, the raven on the top of the key cutting into her palm.

He threw all his weight against the hammer and levered it up. With a splintering groan and a screech the nails gave. "Here, take this." He passed the hammer to her and dug his fingers under the wood. "One, two, three."

An earsplitting crack sounded and the plank lifted. "Hammer, please." She passed it to him and he worked his way along the length of the next piece of wood, then handed it back. "I think I've got it now." He gave a huge yank and the plank lifted.

Dying of impatience, Fleur stepped up to the door. "Not yet. The other one is across the hinges."

Biting back her frustration, Fleur stepped back again and waited while he repeated the entire process all over again.

The splintered wood fell away in chunks. "They're rotten. Rain must've collected underneath. Give me a hand."

Together they peeled back the damp timber, their hands scrabbling faster as each piece came away, revealing the remains of some black paint. Kip flashed her another grin, his eyes dancing.

With a final groan the last piece came free and they both dusted the splinters from their hands and surveyed the peeling door.

Now that the moment had come, a stab of fear sliced Fleur's stomach. Not so Kip. His wide mouth took on a skeptical tilt. "Come on. Put the key in, or do you want me to do it?"

Her heart pricked in her chest. "No, no. I want to." The only sound was the rattle of the key as she inserted it into the lock, then the door swung open with hardly a sound.

She stepped over the threshold into the dim interior and sucked in a breath of the cold, damp, melancholy air of a place long abandoned. Despite the heat outside a chill crept around her ankles and snaked up her calves.

She took a couple of measured steps into the long room running the length of the building.

Dust quivered and swirled in the strange light, as if the past were rising to meet her. The uncanny atmosphere reminded her of the crypt at St. Paul's, ghosts stirring the air with their whispering.

And then the smell hit her, dark and musty, the air redolent with the odor of vermin and, strangely, an overtone of something oniony.

"It's so dingy."

"That's because all the windows are boarded up."

She took a few steps farther into the room. "There are windows at the back."

Kip's hand came down on her arm. "How do you know?"

Her cheeks flushed. "I looked over the back gate. I had to give up when I grazed my shin. Glad, the woman next door, patched me up."

He huffed out a laugh. "Hadn't picked you for such an adventurer. That and your trip to Mogo."

A trip that had proved worthwhile. "Come on, then. I can see a glimmer of light at the end of the hall. Are you game?"

The timber boards creaked in complaint as they walked the length of the room. A short flight of stairs led them down to the back door.

"This one's boarded up, same as the front."

"And these back windows have shutters." She ran her hands down the timber until she found a clasp and unhooked it. Sunlight streamed in, disturbing the shaft of hovering dust motes, and revealed a long timber desk pushed against one wall and a cracked and faded leather sofa. She turned slowly and her heart jumped into her mouth. Her scream erupted in the silence.

"Oh my!"

A striking, pure white kangaroo stood in one corner surveying her with a haughty look, a tuft of dried grass clasped in its front paws.

"It's okay, it's not alive." Kip ambled up to it and ran his hands down the fur on its nose. "At least not anymore. I expect someone shot it as a trophy."

She would swear the animal's eyes followed her as she approached. She stood in front of it, nose to nose. "It's been stuffed."

"Taxidermied, yes."

She stuck her nose closer and inhaled. The same oniony smell of the workshop at Mogo, the smell she'd noticed when she first entered the building. "Can you smell it?"

"What?"

"Come closer and smell."

Kip inhaled and his cheeks pouched, then he let out a breath. "Pouf! It's bloody disgusting, worse than a French dunny."

"Did you fight in France?" She sounded surprised, but why should she be? Probably most of the able-bodied Australians went and fought, so why should she think that Kip wouldn't have? He didn't answer her, just took a few steps back into the shadows, a closed look on his face.

A few moments later he reappeared and paced the length of the room, his forehead creased in a frown. "I can't get the hang of the layout of this place. It looks like two levels from the front but it's three at the back."

"I noticed that too."

"When you fell off the gate?" His lips twitched and the frown slipped away, giving her the distinct impression he was teasing. He kicked at the battered leather sofa and ran his hand along the old desk. "There's a veranda at the back; that's why the steps go down over there. Let's see if we can get the back door open; apart from anything else it'll give us some more light." He took the steps in two strides and shot the bolts on the back door, then put his shoulder to the door. It didn't budge. "Must be barred from the other side. Or else we need another key."

Fleur stepped up alongside him and ran her hands over the timber of the door. "Even if it was, it shouldn't stop it from opening. It opens inward." She grabbed hold of the doorknob.

Kip covered her hands with his. "Ready." He almost had his arms around her and for a split second she had to resist the temptation to lean back. The thought sent a bolt of surprise through her and she shot away, yanking on the door. It flew open, sending them both toppling.

She disentangled herself and took a good look at the light streaming in from the outside. The doorway was barred as the front door had been, but the timbers were narrower and shafts of light slanted in, patterning the floorboards.

Kip jumped to his feet and offered his hand to help her up. "Sorry about that. I didn't hurt you, did I?"

She brushed the dust from her skirt. "No harm done."

"Turn around, you've got something stuck in your hair." She rotated away from him and peered into the darkness, trying to ignore the touch of his fingers in her hair.

"Got it." He held a long timber splinter of wood over her shoulder, but she hardly noticed. In front of her a steep flight of steps descended into the gloom and at the bottom another door, closed tight.

"Look." With her arms outstretched and her palms flat against the walls on either side, she edged into the gloom. She smoothed her hands over the door until she found the doorknob and above it the indentation of a lock. She tugged at the handle. "It's locked as well."

Kip was by her side in a moment. "Is it bolted like the other one?"

He stretched above her, arms held high. "Yes, there's a bolt here. Hang on a moment." She stepped back up one of the steps to give him more room. He rattled and shook it for a moment, then there was a satisfying grate as it slid back. "There's probably one at the bottom." He crouched down and slid the other bolt. "Now let's see if it's locked as well."

The handle turned with barely a whisper and the heavy door opened with a groan of rusty hinges into a pitch-dark space full of stale air, dust, and a bitter and pungent smell laced with damp, reminding her of the cellar where Ma kept the root vegetables in winter.

"I can't see a thing. Why didn't we bring a torch, or at least some candles?"

"I might be able to help there." Kip produced a box of safety matches from his trouser pocket. With a crack the flame ignited, and in the sudden blaze of light Fleur snatched a glimpse of row after row of shelves wreathed in cobwebs before the flame guttered and died.

He lit another. Not four feet in front of her were piles of stacked furniture, chairs on top of a table, crates, a metal bedhead, boxes, all manner of odds and ends cluttered to the point of confusion. She stepped closer and froze. A giant spider, all hairy legs and bulging eyes, glared at her. Her scream filled the air and Kip grabbed her arm. The match spluttered and died.

"Oh, I'm sorry. Spiders! I can't bear spiders."

"He won't hurt you. Just a huntsman."

"A huntsman?" Her voice quavered. A huntsman waiting to trap her.

"It's the redbacks you've got to take notice of. Much smaller, shiny black with a red stripe, or a funnel-web, now they're real nasty."

"Stop it!" She pulled away and headed for the steps.

He gave a laugh. "We need to go back and get a lantern or some candles—this isn't only dangerous, it's foolish. Never mind the spiders. One false move with a match and everything would ignite in a second. My trench lantern's back at the Lyttletons'. I didn't think, because we left in such a hurry. We'll need candles, lots of them. Come on."

She bolted the back door and made her way to the front of the building, stopping to try to get some understanding of the layout. "There must be rooms upstairs too because from the street there's two sets of windows."

"Makes sense." He slammed the front door and took the key from her and locked it tight. "Two stories on this level and three at the back because of the slope of the land. We'll find out when we come back.

We need to take the timbers off all the windows, let in as much natural light as possible. Is it easy to get in from the back?"

"There's a locked gate. I couldn't get over. We could ask Glad about the layout. The two places are probably similar." On second thought, she didn't want to share their adventure with anyone else. "Let's go back and get some candles."

They bolted back to the Lyttletons', falling through the door and straight into Vera, who grabbed Fleur by the arm and dragged her into the front office.

"Fleur! Thank goodness you're back. I was about to come and get you. I've found another file."

Chapter 25

Sydney, NSW
1853

Della threw back the bedcovers and stretched. She felt so much better after an entire night's sleep, untroubled by the dreams that had haunted her since her arrival in Sydney.

Cordelia's changes had made the shop much more popular. A constant stream of ladies visited, and it was hardly surprising Cordelia had changed the name, because they were in no way interested in the specimens Della had labored over so meticulously. It was the cozy slippers made from kangaroo skins; the lizard- and goanna-skin purses, theater bags, and slippers; and all the other paraphernalia that held their attention.

At first she thought Cordelia had been responsible for the bulk of the creations, but after a flick through the accounts ledgers she had come to realize that the work was entirely outsourced. She splashed her face with some cold water and drew the brush through her hair, fastening it behind her ears with a feathered comb she had found in the shop, and went downstairs.

She hadn't seen Cordelia since the night before when she'd appeared dressed to the nines because it was Wednesday night and she had to attend the parlor games at the Berkeley.

Hunter Street was already busy and two women waited outside the shop. Della flipped the sign on the door to Open and unlocked the door. "Good morning." She stood back to let them into the shop.

They stood in the middle of the room beneath a sign that read *Furs cleaned and renovated* and gazed around the room. "May I help you?"

"It's Mrs. Atterton we wish to see."

"I'm afraid *Mrs.* Atterton is unavailable at present. Can I help you? I'm her niece, Della Atterton."

The older of the two women stared down at a piece of paper in her hand. "I am to speak with Mrs. Cordelia Atterton and no one else."

"Then in that case I'm afraid I can't be of assistance. Perhaps you could call back tomorrow."

With a toss of her head and some mutterings, the woman swept out of the shop along with her companion, the jangling bell marking their displeasure.

Della shrugged off their rudeness. Nothing was going to spoil her day. The sun was shining and the lethargy that had plagued her had vanished. Without a doubt, the trip had exhausted her. She simply hadn't realized it. She picked up the feather duster sitting in the corner by the desk and flicked it across the surface, releasing a cloud of dust. Fresh air! The shop needed fresh air. She propped open the door, then returned to her dusting.

The back corner of the room was in relative darkness. She gave the collection a cursory swipe with the feather duster, then ran her hand down the length of the spear propped on the dried grasstree. She couldn't imagine any of the men parting with their hunting spears, or the women their coolamons for that matter. It made her blood boil. She lifted the lid of the display cabinet and took one out, running her hands over the smooth timber. Hours of work had gone into the painted designs and the intricate carving. If she had her way she'd return every single item to its rightful owner.

As she placed the wooden bowl back in the case her knuckle rasped. A jagged lump of rock rolled across the inside of the case and came to rest in one corner. She picked it up and carried it to the window.

It was the strangest thing. Rough against her fingers until she turned it over. Where the outside coating had chipped away, a blinding flash of color shone. She twisted it in the sunlight, producing a play of color more startling than any rainbow. Whatever was it? Nothing she'd ever seen before. It certainly didn't belong with the Darkinjung pieces.

When the bell rang, she slipped the rock back into the cabinet and turned.

"G'day, Miss Della."

"Bert! What are you doing here?"

"On the capt'n's business, and come to see you, of course," he added with a twisted grin. "Fact is, he thought you might like a bit of fresh air. Said you'd been peaky."

"I'm well. Just a bit tired after the trip. I'm looking after the shop."

"Doesn't look like you've got much business." He wandered around running his fingers over a pile of carriage rugs. "It's soft, isn't it? What's that made of?"

"I believe it's native bear." She smoothed her hand across the pale gray fur. "Can I interest you in a carriage rug, sir?"

His spontaneous laugh made her realize how much she enjoyed his lively chatter.

"Nope. But I might be able to interest you in something. Come and have a look." He grabbed her hand and towed her to the window. Drawn up outside the shop sat a magnificent carriage and pair. A dusty urchin who might well have been Bert in a former life stood jiggling from one bare foot to the other, overawed by the responsibility.

"Capt'n's taking a trip to Potts Point. Said I should hire a carriage, thought you might like a spin in the fresh air."

His words sent a series of sparks through her veins and her cheeks and brow began to glow. It was exactly what she'd like. She cast a quick look around the shop. "How long will we be?"

"An hour. Two at most. Capt'n's going to call on some Skeffington bloke, said it'd only be for a few minutes and if you didn't mind waiting in the carriage while he did that we could come back through the Botanic Gardens and stop at Mrs. Macquarie's Chair and take the air."

She couldn't think of anything she'd rather do and there was no one waiting to come into the shop. Cordelia would be back soon and besides, if the two rude women were anything to go by, there was little she could do. "I'll be right there. I just need to get something warm. I won't be long." Lifting her skirt she bolted up the stairs.

What did one wear for a carriage ride with a man like Stefan? Gloves and a cloak perhaps. Nothing she had would be appropriate. She opened the cupboard where Cordelia kept her clothes. Surely she'd have a cloak that would do. And she could hardly mind if she didn't know. A cloud of musty dust billowed out as she opened the door, making her nose prickle.

She slid the clothes along until she found a dark-blue cloak, the hood trimmed with brownish-gray fur. It might look a little like evening wear, but it wasn't inappropriate for a ride in a carriage as smart as the one Bert had waiting outside.

She slipped the cloak over her shoulders, pulled up the hood and pushed her hands inside the matching muff, and ran back down the stairs. Bert had vanished from the shop so she locked the door, slipped the key into its hidey-hole, and stepped out onto the footpath.

Bert handed her up into the open carriage, flicked a coin to the urchin, then picked up the reins. They took off at a smart pace down the road and rounded the corner into Bent Street.

Standing outside the Berkeley Hotel was Captain Stefan von Richter, his long boots gleaming and the shiny buttons on his jacket accentuating the golden shimmer in his hair. Blood surged beneath her skin, sending her heart into a frantic patter.

It wasn't until they drew up that she noticed he was pacing up and down restlessly, totally out of character. She'd never seen him anything but self-assured. He stopped his agitated striding to pull out his pocket watch and snap it shut again.

"Here we are, Capt'n."

At the sound of Bert's voice he turned. A smile leaped to his face. "Della, I was afraid you might still be unwell."

"No, I'm much better this morning. I had an excellent night's sleep. I wasn't sure where we were going and how I should dress." Her breathless laugh sounded ridiculous.

"I can't imagine any situation in which you would not look beautiful. Astride a horse, digging musket balls from young men's shoulders, or here in Sydney taking a carriage ride." With a grin that showed his teeth, a bright contrast to his sun-browned skin, he stepped up into the carriage and sat down next to her. She caught his scent, a mixture of leather and earthy smells and something she thought might be ambergris.

"We're heading for Potts Point. I have some business to attend to . . ."

"Bert told me."

"And your aunt can do without you for an hour or two?"

"I haven't seen her today. She left last night, said she had appointments."

"Why didn't you call for me? You shouldn't be left alone."

"You seem to forget that I have lived on Hunter Street almost all my life. Ma and Pa came here when I was still a babe in arms. And besides, Cordelia has employed a woman to come every morning to keep the place tidy. If I had a problem I could call on her."

He grunted some sort of acknowledgment and leaned forward to give Bert directions.

They skirted the Botanic Gardens and took the road along the wharves, slowing to a walk to accommodate the hustle and bustle. Once they were out of the chaos, the buildings diminished and the road widened. She might have lived all her life in Sydney, but she'd never taken a carriage ride or even visited this part of town. The wind tugged at her hair and she inhaled the fresh air blowing in from the ocean, free of any of the Tank Stream odors. It was almost like being back in the Hawkesbury.

A driveway led to an impressive stone house overlooking the ocean. Bert slowed the carriage and eased to a halt.

"Good chap. I'll walk the rest of the way. You entertain Miss Della with stories of your misspent youth." With a laugh, Stefan jumped down from the carriage and strode down the drive; despite favoring one leg, his long, lean frame covered the distance in no time.

"Wanna walk or just sit here?"

"I'm quite happy here, thank you, Bert. Why don't you come and join me? There's a wonderful view." Out across the harbor the ships were under full sail as they left Sydney for all parts of the world.

"Whole world out there waiting to be discovered." Bert echoed her thoughts. "Don't fancy it meself. Enough country here to keep me happy. What about you?"

"I've never considered it, but now, when I see those ships and think of all the places the captain must have seen, I sometimes wonder . . ."

"He seems determined to track this man down. But then he's like that. Honorable. Wants to do the right thing."

What on earth was Bert talking about? "I'm sorry. I don't understand what you mean."

"This Skeffington bloke. 'Fore we met up with Gus and Dobbin we called in on this other bloke. Bishop his name was. Apparently some professor had sent him a specimen he'd found. The capt'n was to collect it, but Bishop got rid of it to this Skeffington. Not sure why anyone would get so excited about a lump of rock, mind you. Gold maybe."

"So who has this specimen? I'm not following you."

Bert let out a long-suffering sigh as though she were somehow lacking. "Bishop had it. He gave it to Skeffington in part payment for his land. That's why the capt'n's in Australia. Wants to get it back so he can make good his promise to the baron."

She could imagine a promise being important to a man like Stefan; he was possibly the most honest and trustworthy person she'd ever come across. His outrage at the treatment the Darkinjung had suffered and his determination to see Gus and Dobbin brought to justice only made her respect him more. To think when she'd first seen him standing in the doorway of her workroom she'd feared for her life and Jarro's. How wrong could a person be?

"'Ere he is. That didn't take long."

And from the look of it, things hadn't gone the way Stefan hoped. With his head down and his hands thrust deep into his pockets, he meandered back to the carriage scuffing his boots in the dirt. Bert shrugged his shoulders and scampered back onto the box.

"Is everything all right?" She moved over to make room for him on the seat.

"No, not really. I wasn't able to speak with Mr. Skeffington. He is indisposed. His wife spared me a moment."

"What now, Capt'n?"

"I'm sorry, Bert?"

"Where'd you want to go?"

"I'll leave that to you. We'll take a bit of a ride, then back to town in time for lunch."

The carriage pulled away and Stefan sat in silence staring out at the passing landscape, a frown creasing his brow. When she couldn't stand it any longer, Della threw prudence, and good manners, over the cliff. "Is there no other way you can fulfill your promise to the baron?"

His head came up with a snap and his blue eyes pinned her. "I beg your pardon."

"Bert told me."

"Ah, Bert, of course. You're going to have to learn to keep your mouth shut, young man."

Bert turned with a rueful smile. "It's Miss Della. Didn't fink you'd mind."

"You're right, and a problem shared . . ." He took her hand in his. "I could do with a friendly ear. May I bore you with my problems?"

"Of course you can." She could think of nothing she'd rather do, and with her hand clasped in his warm palm, she would happily sit and listen to his problems until the sun set in the east.

"A man named Johann Menge was exploring on behalf of the South Australian Mining Company, a great friend of the baron. Professor Menge found what he believed to be a valuable gemstone, an opal. He had no way of confirming his beliefs so he wrote to the baron, who arranged for him to send it to a man he'd met in Sydney to await collection. It is the main reason for my trip here."

She'd heard of diamonds and rubies, but an opal? "I'm sorry, but I'm afraid I have no idea what an opal is."

"They have been mined throughout Europe for centuries, were prized by the Romans, and are still valued today. Professor Menge discovered what he believed to be the first in Australia and wanted to have it authenticated. The Hungarian mines are exhausted and supply is short. Both Queen Victoria and Prince Albert are very taken with the stones and they are much in demand."

"And this opal is lost?"

"Not lost exactly."

Goodness gracious, this was a world she never could imagine. "The baron asked me to reclaim it for him."

He had traveled thousands of miles at the bequest of this baron in search of a gemstone. He sounded like a chivalrous knight in an ancient fairy story, setting out on a magic quest. "Why is this particular opal so important? What happened to Professor Menge? Did he find any more opals?"

"The professor died in the Victorian gold fields, a place near Bendigo. He knew he was unwell, and one of his last acts was to send the stone to Bishop for safekeeping until it could be retrieved and examined. The baron counted the professor as his friend and wanted to fulfill Menge's last request, to prove his friend correct. A fitting tribute to a great man. Without the opal he can't do that."

"Does an opal look like a diamond?"

"The opals I have seen come in many shapes, sizes, and colors. Some like fire—when you hold them up to the light their colors flash like flames; others are milky white and pale."

The skin on her arms prickled. "I'm sure other people would have found them. What about the Darkinjung? Surely they'd know about them."

"What makes you say that?"

"They have lived here for thousands of years. They know things about this country we can't comprehend. I believe Cordelia has something that reminds me of your description in the Curio Shop with the other artifacts."

Silence descended like a wet rag until Stefan snapped to attention and grasped Bert's shoulder. "Back to Hunter Street, fast as you can."

Della grasped at the hood on her cloak, holding it tight as they bolted back along the wide road.

"Where are you going, man?" Stefan yelled at Bert.

"There's a better route. Quicker. We'll miss the quay and the fort and all the ruckus."

As usual, Bert was right and before long they pulled up outside the shop. A crowd of women clustered around the window. Stefan handed her down onto the footpath and Della reached into the hidey-hole and took out the key. "Cordelia can't be back yet."

"Is that a concern?"

"No. Not really." She wasn't sure why she was pleased Cordelia hadn't returned, maybe because she found his company so enticing, with his tales of faraway places and mysterious treasures, and she didn't want it to end. She slipped the key into the lock and opened the door.

As if on cue Cordelia, swathed from head to foot in green silk, erupted from the back of the shop and slammed the door behind her.

"Where have you been, might I ask?" Cordelia's voice, icy and calm—a sure sign that she was seething inside—sent a spike of dread down Della's spine. She met her cold-eyed stare.

"I've been taking the air with Captain von Richter."

"Have you indeed?"

"Mrs. Atterton." Stefan exhaled slowly as if he was trying to calm himself. "I invited Della to accompany me. I felt it would be beneficial to her health, and I'm sure you can see that she is greatly improved."

Cordelia glared at her, then shrugged her shoulders. "Change the sign on the door, Della. We have customers waiting." It was as though her anger had evaporated with Stefan's presence.

A swarm of women entered the shop cackling like Charity's chickens and started wandering around touching and trying things on. No one seemed to require any help so Della drifted to the back of the shop and opened Pa's glass cabinet. The stone lay tucked back in the corner where she had left it.

"Get that guttersnipe out of my shop."

Della swung around in time to see Cordelia twisting Bert's wrist until his palm was facing upward over the desk. "I thought as much." She gave his hand a violent shake and half a dozen bright green lozenges fell to the desktop with a clatter. "Not for the likes of you."

"What in heaven's name do you think you're doing?" Stefan's red face glared at the poor boy.

"Sorry, Capt'n. I just wanted one. Never had one of them before. They were just sitting there-like. I thought they were to eat."

"Wait for me outside." Stefan gave him a hearty shove and, throwing Della a rueful grimace, Bert skedaddled through the crowd of gaping women.

"I apologize. I don't know what came over him. Not once in our entire time together has he done anything to indicate he was light-fingered."

He took Della's arm and edged her away from the women crowding around Cordelia. "I'd very much like to have a closer look at the stone."

"It might be better not to disturb Cordelia at the moment. She's busy with all the customers."

"If you have the opportunity, perhaps you could bring it to the hotel?"

"Are you suggesting, Captain, you would like me to be light-fingered?" She couldn't resist throwing him a wink.

"As owner of the Curio Shop I wouldn't have thought that would be an issue."

"I'll see what I can do."

"I must impress the importance of this. The baron believes that Menge's opal is the first sample to be found in Australia. If there are others it puts a completely different view on matters. Particularly if it came from the Hawkesbury along with the other artifacts. I would ask you not to discuss the matter with anyone."

"What exactly did Mrs. Skeffington say about the opal?"

"She said she had no idea what I was talking about and no time nor inclination to discuss it."

"Della!" Cordelia's cold voice made her jump. "I require your assistance."

"Perhaps I could bring it to the Berkley tomorrow. I must go. I'm in enough trouble for leaving the shop unattended."

"Then I owe you my apologies. I should not have detained you." He brought her hand so close to his lips his breath warmed her skin, then he clicked his heels in that very special manner he had, turning her thoughts back to gallant princes and fairy-tale castles.

Stefan closed the door on the clamoring women and stepped out into the street in two minds whether to leave Della or not. Cordelia seemed to exert some sort of strange control over her, something more than the respect due to her because she was her aunt, particularly as Della owned the shop—a fact Cordelia didn't dispute.

He found Bert kicking up the dust looking as though he were heading for the gallows.

"Come on, Bert. Let's get this carriage back to the stables and you can explain to me what possessed you to steal. I didn't expect it of you."

Bert hung his head. "Sorry, Capt'n." He picked up the reins and one of the lozenges fell from his pocket. Stefan scooped it up into his hand and turned it over. The silvered green paper glinted in the sun.

"I wouldn't bother if I were you. They taste worse than dog droppings."

"Serves you right. I hope it teaches you a lesson."

"Nah, I spat it out." Bert shuddered. "Bloody awful. Real sickly sweet, then when you suck on it, it's like you've taken a bite out of the butt of a gun."

"Make a habit of sucking on guns, do you?"

Stefan handed the offending item back and Bert stuffed it into his pocket. "Drop me off here and take the carriage back. I'll let you know when I need you again."

"You ain't giving me the push, are you?"

"Keep stealing and I will."

Chapter 26

Sydney, NSW
1853

Della had done her best to keep out of Cordelia's way. She'd been dancing around all morning like a scalded cat pulling open drawers, flicking through ledgers, casting them aside, then taking others upstairs. She'd told her that if anyone asked specifically for her, she was to tell them to come back tomorrow as she had important business to attend to, and with that she'd left.

Since then Della had sold four evening bags, three muffs, and two carriage blankets and entered the transactions neatly in the ledgers as always. One man had come in wanting to purchase a native toy for his son. The kind that came back when thrown away. She hadn't been able to resist telling him a boomerang wasn't a toy and it could fell a fully grown kangaroo, as heavy as a man. Hardly a suitable gift for a child. He'd hummed and hawed and then finally stomped out muttering. And now, thankfully, the shop was quiet.

Lifting the lid of Pa's display cabinet, she stretched to the back and pulled out the stone. When she turned it over it flared in the shaft of sunlight from the window, myriad colors twinkling. She licked her finger and wiped across the smooth surface and her breath caught. It was beautiful. If Cordelia hadn't returned by nightfall she'd take it to Stefan.

Her heart almost stopped when the doorbell tinkled. She shoved the stone into her pocket and braced herself, expecting Cordelia. "Charity! What are you doing here?"

"Sick to death 'anging around like last week's laundry so I traded me last few days at the Settlers for a ride on the coach."

And a new dress, unless she was very much mistaken; she'd never seen Charity look so pretty. "You used Stefan's money?"

"And what's wrong with that? Stefan, huh? That'd be the fine captain, would it?" Charity threw her the biggest wink, which sent her cheeks the most despicable red. "He said the room was mine for as long as I wanted it. Didn't say nought about giving him any money. Besides, that black fella was 'anging around, scared me to death, he did, creeping around like a ghost."

"Black fella? Do you mean Jarro?"

Charity picked up one of the feathered combs, wrinkled her nose, and tossed it aside. "The one you used to hang about with down at the creek."

"Was he all right?"

"Well, how would I know? Didn't pass the time of day with him, did I? Took off at a fair old gallop once I told him you'd gone to Sydney. And how's my girl?"

Della huffed out a sigh of relief. Jarro didn't sound as though he was suffering any ill effects from the musket ball. "I'm better, thank you, Charity."

"Better? Was you not right?"

"I was just a little tired after the trip. Headaches and a bit queasy, and strange pins and needles in my hands. I'm much improved."

"Where's Cordelia?" She narrowed her eyes and squinted into the back of the shop.

"She went out early, said she had some business to do."

A frown flittered across Charity's forehead and she tossed back her long black braid. "What kind of business?"

"I don't know. She asked me to look after the shop."

Charity smoothed down her ruffled skirt and made a slow lap around the room. "And she's been making a few changes in our absence, I see."

"I know. I was quite angry at first. All I could think of was all Pa's hard work going to waste, but the shop's very prosperous. Mostly ladies, though there was a man who came in wanting to purchase a boomerang. I still haven't got to the bottom of the raids . . ." She let her words fade.

Charity was so busy walking slowly around lifting bundles of fur mittens, delving into the evening headwear, poking her nose into cupboards, and scanning shelves that she thankfully took no notice. Della left her alone, not wanting to get into an argument with her, not when she'd just returned, and anyway, she and Cordelia weren't going to be of any help as far as the Darkinjung were concerned. Until they had spoken to the governor she would have to hope Gus and Dobbin stayed away. She stuck her hand into her pocket and hefted the stone. It sat warm in her palm, felt almost as if it were breathing, as though it had a life of its own.

"So is me bed still me bed or has she changed that too?"

Della pushed the stone deep into her pocket. "No. Cordelia's using Ma and Pa's room now, so we won't have to share." Perhaps she could get Charity to keep an eye on the shop while she popped around to the Berkeley to see Stefan.

"What are these? They're new." Charity dug her hand into the carved wooden bowl and let the lozenges trickle through her fingers. She turned one over and started to unwrap the paper. "Look like toffees to me."

"They are, I think. Cordelia likes to call them bonbons. She's pandering to all the highfalutin ladies."

"Sounds French." Charity unwrapped one and brought it to her nose. "Doesn't tickle my fancy." She twisted the paper and threw it back in the bowl. "Right, well, I'm going to get meself sorted and then I might take a bit of a walk before it gets dark. Reacquaint myself with the town. It's been too long. I've missed the old place."

Charity would be doing her reacquainting down at one of the pubs in the Rocks more than like. Catching up with old friends, showing off her new dress, and making sure she had a supply of rum. She wore her ex-convict status like a badge of honor, unlike Cordelia, who went to great lengths to forget she was the reason Pa had upped sticks and moved halfway around the world. Just to keep his little sister safe.

After an evening at the gaming table and the most appalling night's sleep he'd had since he set foot in Australia, Stefan spent the morning working on the baron's journals, trying to prevent himself from racing back to the Curio Shop. Della would bring the stone to him as soon as she was able, and he didn't want to alert Cordelia to the possibility that she had something of value tucked in her display cabinet.

He'd ended up flicking through the pages of the journal, searching for references to the New Hollanders. There were very few—just a comparison between those who lived miserable lives in the towns addicted to alcohol and tobacco and those who lived more traditional lives, their skills as trackers, and their apparent health and fitness. Nothing that suggested any trading relationship with businesses in Sydney.

With a sigh he pulled on his jacket, intent on clearing his head with a quick walk around the Botanical Gardens.

Bert spotted him as he rounded the drinking fountain and slid alongside him. "Might be a good time to go and have a chat with Miss Della about that there opal."

"And why would that be?" Until now he'd managed to resist the inexplicable lure of Della and the stone and now Bert was sending all his good intentions awry.

"Because the green witch ain't there."

He tried his very best to curtail his grin and failed. "I take it you are referring to Mrs. Atterton."

"Yep!"

"And how would you know that?"

Bert tapped the side of his nose. "On me way over here I learned something interesting."

"Eavesdropping again, Bert?"

"Do you want to know or don't you?"

The boy was far too canny for his own good. "Go ahead."

"She and Sladdin were havin' a right to-do."

"Mrs. Atterton and Sladdin?"

"Told you they were mates. She was jumping up and down about me nickin' those lozenge fings and something about that Skeffington chap you was lookin' for."

Stefan stopped in his tracks and grasped Bert's arm, none too gently. "Is there somewhere we can go and talk?"

"You mean somewhere no one will get wind of what I got to say?"

"Lead the way."

Within ten minutes Stefan and Bert were parked in the darkest corner of a seedy-looking harbor-side pub. Bearing in mind the state of the premises, Stefan declined Bert's suggestion of ale and settled on a glass of rum.

"Right. Let's have it."

Bert cast another look over his shoulder and slid up close. "Mrs. Atterton, she was in a right fuss. Told Sladdin Mrs. Skeffington was all of a to-do and that the doctor chap was coming back to talk to her."

"Is that so?"

"Said she had business out of town and he needed to clear everything out."

"What kind of everything?"

Bert shrugged his shoulders. "Dunno. She gave him the key to the Curio Shop."

"How do you know it was the key to the Curio Shop?"

"You can't mistake it. It's got that bloody great raven on the top of it. Gives me the shivers every time I see it. They 'ave ravens at the Tower of London, you know. They peck the eyes out of the poor blokes that 'ang." Bert shuddered and pulled a face that would have sat well on one of the Tower's gargoyles.

"I'm not sure that's true."

"Well, that's what me mate says and he should know, 'is old man hanged there." Bert sat back with an injured look. "I ain't lying. I thought you'd want to know, seeing as how Miss Della is at the shop alone. I wouldn't like to see her get into no trouble with that Sladdin fellow. He's as bad as one of them ravens."

And if Cordelia was away from the shop, then it was the perfect opportunity to have a look at the stone. He dug into his pocket and pulled out a sixpence.

"I don't want your money. You've given me enough. I just wanna see Miss Della safe."

"Right you are, Bert." He pocketed the sixpence. "You better come with me. It's always good to have a right-hand man."

With his chest puffed out like a bantam cockerel, Bert shot to his feet, swallowed the rest of his ale in one gulp, and made for the door. "Bloody hell!" He swung around and grabbed hold of Stefan's sleeve, dragging him back down onto the seat in the corner, then dropped his head into his arms. "Keep your 'ead down. That Charity just walked in."

Stefan propped his head onto his hand and studied the pitted tabletop.

"What's she doin' here?"

"I've no idea. I thought she'd still be in St. Albans, staying at the inn."

"Well, she ain't."

"Are you sure it's her?"

"'Course I am. Looks good all scrubbed up, 'specially with that ribbon in her hair."

Stefan lifted his head. Charity's long hair hung down her back to her waist and she'd threaded a bright red ribbon into the braid.

She hoicked herself up on the bar and leaned over. The bloke behind the bar planted a large, loud kiss on her cheek, which she returned with relish, then he rewarded her with an equally large glass of rum.

"Reckon we could slide out now if we're quick." Bert slithered under the table and reappeared at the door, tipping his head to one side.

Stefan had no intention of following suit. He wasn't expecting to see Charity back in Sydney, and her presence reminded him that he'd given no further thought to Gus and Dobbin's whereabouts. Perhaps they had traveled from St. Albans together. It might well be a good thing if they were here and he could get them in front of the governor. But right now he was more concerned about Della. He slipped through the door and out into the street, sidestepping a couple of argumentative drunks. "I'm not sure why it matters if we bump into Charity. I presume she'll go straight to the Curio Shop to see Della."

"Maybe, maybe not. She might have other people she wants to see."

"I'm sure she has friends in Sydney."

"For a gent that had chewters you can be real thick sometimes. She and Sladdin were old mates, before Cordelia had her carted off to that Mogo place."

"And how was I supposed to know that?" Stefan straightened his shoulders. Bert was becoming far too familiar. "And I am not so thick that I can't see that this would be the ideal time to have a look at Della's stone." And assure himself she had come to no harm. Bert's reference to Charity's and Cordelia's friendship with Sladdin had, for some reason he couldn't explain, made him uneasy.

All Stefan's concerns vanished the moment he opened the door to the Curio Shop and Della's radiant smile greeted him.

"Hello, Stefan, Bert. You'll never guess who's here!"

"Tell me."

"Charity! She got a ride in a coach from St. Albans. Oh!" Her hand covered her mouth as though she'd said something she shouldn't.

He swallowed the temptation to mention the fact that he and Bert had seen Charity. "And?"

"She traded the remaining days at the inn for a seat on the coach, and a new dress." Della opened the drawer of the desk. "How much do I owe you?"

"Nothing. Nothing at all."

"Oh, but I do." Then she smiled again. "You might like to take a closer look at this. I'm sorry I wasn't able to bring it to you as I promised." She buried her hand in her skirt pocket and with a great deal of care deposited a rough, uncut stone onto the table.

He carried it to the window and put it down while he removed his gloves, then held it up to the light, turning it over in his hands. "If I have understood the description, this may well be an opal. I wonder how it came to be here."

"I haven't had the opportunity to ask Cordelia where she got it. She left early this morning and I've been busy. I didn't want to close the shop again."

"Can I touch it?" Bert's hand hovered over the stone. "It's real pretty, but how can it be a jewel? It's just a lump of rock."

"Cutting and polishing an opal is a great skill. The outer casing has to be removed with a diamond saw and then it is shaped. The Romans mastered the art thousands of years ago."

Della ran her finger over the stone. "Where did the name *opal* come from?"

"From the Sanskrit meaning 'precious stone,' and later the Greek derivative *opallios*, meaning 'a change of color.'"

"You can certainly see that." She twisted the stone in the light and let out a small sigh.

"So you have no idea how Cordelia acquired it?"

"No, nor when. I'll ask her when she gets back."

"I'd rather you didn't do that." He took the stone from Della's hand and turned it in the light. He was no mineralogist, but the stone could well be an opal; whether it was the one Menge had sent to Bishop was another matter. "Pardon my inquisitiveness, but I wonder if perhaps Cordelia keeps records of the transactions."

"Of course. Why didn't I think of that?" Della walked around the desk and sat down and opened the drawer.

The image of Cordelia on his second visit to the shop with her head bent over the ledgers flashed through his mind. There'd be a record, of that he was certain. Cordelia was not the kind of woman who would leave much to chance.

The pages of the ledger flicked as Della ran her finger up and down the list of figures; it was all he could do not to snatch the book from her. Bert had wandered off and stood weighing a boomerang in his hand. "Put that down. I don't want a repeat of the lozenge nonsense."

Bert threw him an evil look, replaced the boomerang with the other artifacts, and clasped his hands behind his back as if to prove he had his light fingers under control.

"I think I've found it." Della lifted her head and stabbed at the center of the page. "Just a few days ago. 'Mrs. Skeffington. Account settled. Colored rock—seek evaluation.'"

"Skeffington?" He couldn't help himself. He snatched the book away. Mrs. Skeffington had lied when she said she had no knowledge of any stone.

"I have Bishop's word that he gave the stone to Skeffington and the ledgers confirm that it was used to pay Skeffington's account."

"So we traipsed all the way to the Hawkesbury and the thing was sittin' right here under our nose."

"Hardly a wasted journey, Bert." Much to his delight, Della's cheeks pinked. "I would appreciate it if you would keep our discussion private until I have had the opportunity to look at it under my magnifier. May I take it with me?"

"That probably ain't a real good idea, Capt'n."

"I beg your pardon." A few lessons in manners wouldn't come amiss. "Explain yourself."

Bert strolled up to the desk, hands in his pockets, chewing his lip. "Look at it this way. If Cordelia finds out the stone's gone she's going to wonder why, and Miss Della might get blamed."

"Then in that case I shall purchase it." He delved in his pocket and produced the baron's promissory note.

"Says in that there ledger 'seek evaluation.' It sounds like she thinks it might be worth something and if—"

"I take your point, Bert." Nobody's fool, this boy. Nobody's fool. The last thing he wanted to do was jeopardize Della's safety. "Very well." He pocketed the promissory note and handed the stone back.

"I shall leave it in your care until I can return with my magnifier and examine it more closely."

"When Cordelia ain't here."

"Thank you, Bert. That will be all." It was a conversation Stefan didn't want to continue. Bert had a nose for anything underhanded, and he had no intention of discussing Cordelia and her meeting with Sladdin until he understood the implications.

"Yeah, right. That's just what I think. I'll be seeing you tomorrow then." Bert threw Della a nod and took off, sporting a petulant pout.

"Do you know if Gus and Dobbin returned with Charity?" Stefan asked in an attempt to change the subject.

"I presume not, because she came on the coach. I expect they'll be back soon."

That he doubted very strongly. Gus would be lying low. "Would you care to take a walk, Della? We haven't sampled one of those strawberry ices yet."

She uttered a wistful sigh and shook her pretty head. "I'd love to, but until Cordelia returns I must stay here. I have to keep the shop open."

"I shall call tomorrow morning." He brought her hand to his lips, wished he could pull her into his arms, then clicked his heels, bowed, and left.

Chapter 27

SYDNEY, NSW
1919

Vera pulled Fleur into the room at the front of the house where they'd met on the first day and fussed about puffing up cushions and bringing a small table between the two chairs. The petals had fallen from the roses and littered the floor in front of the empty fireplace, giving the room a desolate look.

Fleur sat, her breath still rasping and her mind crowded with unanswered questions. She didn't want to be here; she wanted to be back at the Curio Shop, back with Kip, some candles, and his tool bag. The whole idea of the place had grasped her imagination. She was certain the answers to the Richards lay there.

Clearing her throat, Vera lowered herself into the chair. While they'd been away she'd run a brush through her hair and slapped on some lipstick. In her hurry she'd missed and a little bit had smudged across her teeth. She placed a very large, fat folder fastened with a ribbon on the table between them.

"Now, my dear. I think I've found everything we need to put your mind at rest. I am so sorry it has taken so much time." She lifted her hands in the air, palms up. "I have no doubt you will be thrilled when I explain."

For goodness' sake, would the wretched woman just spit it out?

"You see, the papers had been filed under *V*."

Why would the papers be filed under *V*?

With her face wreathed in smiles, Vera patted the folder between them. "Lyttleton & Sons was established back in the late 1850s by Mr. Lyttleton's grandfather. It's been a family business ever since."

She didn't want a history lesson. She wanted to know what was inside the file. Her hand drifted to the table.

Vera beat her to it and snatched up the file. "You see, von Richter." She traced the name printed on the front of the large buff-colored envelope with the kind of look a grandmother gave a recalcitrant grandchild.

Von Richter? "I'm sorry, I don't understand what this has to do with me."

"My dear. Your husband's birth name was Hugo von Richter."

Hugo von Richter? "It's a mistake. I'm Fleur Richards, not Fleur von Richter." Von Richter sounded German, brought to mind Manfred von Richthofen, the Red Baron, and those bloody planes. Worse than the zeppelin that had taken out half of Islington.

She'd married Hugh Richards. An Australian. How else would he have acquired that cute accent and the singsong way he had of making everything sound like a question?

I love you, Fleur?

A cold tremor seeped its way through her body, worked its way across her skin, stealing her breath, turning her blood to ice. "Hugh was a German?"

"In fact, I believe the family was Austrian. It's nothing to be concerned about."

A dizzying wave of faintness washed over her and all the remaining warmth drained from her body. She hardly had the strength to draw breath and was colder than she'd been since she'd left London. She rested her head in her hands, leaning forward trying to settle her breathing.

Vera touched her elbow, her words lost in the buzzing in her ears. How could Hugh be German? He was Australian through and through, and proud of it, with his slouch hat and rising-sun badge proclaiming him a member of the Australian military forces.

It's the best place in the world. Come home with me.

Bile filled her mouth and she closed her eyes, forcing her will to overcome the shock.

"There must be some mistake." Hugo von Richter? Not Hugh Richards. He wouldn't have lied to her.

"No mistake. Hugo was of Austrian-Australian descent. His grandfather was Austrian, his grandmother Australian. His father and mother were born in Australia, as were Hugh and his brothers."

The hairs on the back of her neck prickled, and for a moment she could see nothing but the devastation the zeppelins had wrought on London, Mum and Dad, the wounded men on the ship, the horror of those long black days. She gasped and a wrangled sob slipped between her lips.

"Breathe, my dear. Take deep breaths."

Fleur inhaled, and again and again.

"That's enough, otherwise you'll become dizzy."

Fleur lurched to her feet and stumbled to the window, gazing at the passing parade. Motorized vans, a horse and cart, a woman with a basket overflowing with brightly colored flowers. Such a far cry from the gray drabness of London with its bombed buildings like gaping holes in an old man's teeth, the rationing and suffering. Sydney didn't look as though it had suffered a moment's hardship. Maybe that was why this woman could sit there with a benign smile on her face and tell her the man she'd married wasn't who she believed him to be.

"Let me explain." Mrs. Lyttleton walked around the desk and rested her hands on Fleur's shivering shoulders. "When the war broke out, there were thousands of Germans and Austrians living in Australia, a well-established and much-admired community. Many of the sons and grandsons of those original migrants wanted to join up to fight for the country they'd made their home. As you can imagine, anti-German feeling erupted and they became scapegoats.

"So many of them chose to use an anglicized version of their names to prevent harassment from the government and war-mad community, as did Hugo, when he enlisted. He is as Australian as anyone else. We all came here from another country. By the way, Hugo's belongings have arrived."

"I'm sorry?"

"Hugo's possessions."

"I don't want them." She wanted Hugh, the man she'd married. Not some other man's things. "I don't want Hugo von Richter's possessions. I have no right to them, no right to his inheritance." She reached out for the doorknob and stilled. If Vera had Hugo's belongings, and Hugh *was* Hugo von Richter, then he was dead. There'd definitely been a mistake. "I married Hugh Richards. An Australian soldier. I am Fleur Richards, not Fleur von Richter."

"Oh, tosh and nonsense! Hugh saw himself as an Australian. I think you should take his belongings, my dear. One day, maybe not today, but one day you'll cherish them. We can talk about the other matters tomorrow or later in the week." Vera held out a package wrapped in brown paper and tied with string. "Take it. I won't hear otherwise."

"No!"

Fleur couldn't remember leaving, or walking anywhere. All she could see was Hugh's face, the sparkle in those robin's egg–blue eyes, the shock of blond hair that he swept back from his forehead so he could see her better, the smile on his face as they raced across Westminster Bridge and along the Embankment in the pouring rain.

He'd picked her up and twirled her around and around until

she became dizzy, dizzy with love for her handsome soldier, Hugh Richards—not Hugo von Richter.

She dragged her eyes from the horizon, felt the warmth of someone's body next to her, and turned her head. "What are you doing here?"

Kip rammed his hands into his pockets. "Vera's worried about you. Asked me to keep an eye out."

"I'm perfectly all right." She made to stand, but his hand came down on her arm. "I don't need any company." She wanted peace and quiet. No, what she wanted to do was jump on the ship she could see steaming out of the harbor and go home. Back to England. Back to where she belonged. As far away from this ridiculous country and its stinking hot weather and relentless sunshine as she could get.

If Mr. Waterstone had told her the truth from the outset, she wouldn't be sitting here thousands of miles from home, the one golden memory of her life lying at her feet in a puddle of blinding sunshine. Didn't it ever rain in this wretched country? She reefed off her hat and wiped her face and found tears slipping out of her eyes—useless tears.

A crumpled blue handkerchief was pressed into her hands. She scrubbed at her face, then balled the sodden mess. "Thank you," she mumbled. She couldn't hand the disgusting thing back. Picking at the embroidered initials in the corner, she turned her head and offered Kip a half-hearted smile—more of a grimace.

"That's better. Vera wasn't trying to interfere, just thought maybe I could help."

How could he help? She ran her fingers over the embroidery on the corner, *ABC*; the sort of thing a child would have in the corner of his handkerchief, except it belonged to a man, the man sitting next to her. "I can't believe Hugh lied to me. I can't believe the man I married wasn't who he said he was." She sniffed loudly, disgustingly. Surely she hadn't any more tears. "I loved him."

"Nothing wrong with that."

"He wasn't who he said he was!"

"Doesn't make him any less of a man or change the person he was."

She pushed his soggy handkerchief into her pocket and her fingers brushed the package Kip had placed on her lap.

"So he is dead. I didn't need a telegram." For a moment the pain was so sharp she had to fight back a wave of nausea. She turned the brown paper parcel over and over and toyed with the idea of throwing it into the harbor.

"Why don't you open it?"

"I think I'm frightened."

"Why? Because you might find something else you didn't know about him?"

"Maybe." She worried the knot with her fingers and it slipped free.

"Careful. You don't want to lose anything."

Didn't she? What if there were more lies?

Chapter 28

Sydney, NSW
1853

Stefan pushed open the doors to the Berkeley deep in thought. He had no idea how to approach Mrs. Skeffington. He'd already made the mistake of calling at the most inappropriate of times. He could hardly repeat his faux pas, yet it was essential that he confirmed the records from the Curio Shop. He simply needed Mrs. Skeffington to admit she had used the stone to pay for purchases at the Curio Shop. Unusually, the foyer was empty. The place had a deserted air.

No sign of Sladdin and no sign of any card game in progress. "Captain von Richter." Philpott appeared from the card room with a large glass clasped in his hand. "I was hoping I would find you. I was wondering if you could spare me a few moments." The man looked dreadful, his eyes bloodshot and huge in his pale face.

Why would Philpott want to speak to him? He'd only met him once over a game of cards. Stefan forced a smile. "Certainly."

"To be honest, I have a matter I'd like to discuss with a man of science."

"I'm not sure I fit that description."

"I'd appreciate an educated opinion. I was hoping to catch you, but it seems card games are not on the agenda today."

"No. It's very quiet. How may I help you?"

"It is a private matter . . ."

"In that case, may I suggest my sitting room?" Stefan gestured toward the stairs.

"Thank you." Philpott's step was heavy as they made their way to his suite. "I hate to impose, but I have nowhere else to turn."

"Can I offer you another drink?" He gestured to the decanter of brandy. "Or some tea perhaps."

"The brandy is working its magic." He held out his glass. "Mr. Skeffington died early this morning. I am at my wits' end."

Stefan concentrated on pouring the brandy into the tumblers. Mrs. Skeffington had given the distinct impression there was little hope of her husband recovering, so why was Philpott so distressed? He took the offered glass and with a nod tossed most of it back. "I'll get straight to the point. I fear my original diagnosis may have been incorrect."

"May I ask why?" Stefan lowered himself into the chair.

"I believe Mr. Skeffington was poisoned."

"Poisoned?"

"There has been an outbreak of what we believed to be cholera, a wasting disease we usually see confined to the poorer areas of the town where sanitation is still, despite our best efforts, appalling and clean drinking water impossible to come by. However, with Skeffington's death I have come to realize that his case does not fit within the usual parameters. And he is not the only one. Several have died. All the victims have been men, well-to-do men. Their immediate families have not contracted the disease, not even those nursing them, so I doubt they suffered from cholera, which is highly contagious."

Stefan put down his glass and fixed his gaze firmly on the man in front of him. "Have you contacted the authorities?"

"As yet, no. I would like to ensure the governor is aware of the matter, but he is at Parramatta. It is only with Skeffington's death I made the connection. I am disappointed with myself for not picking up on the inconsistencies."

"Poisoned with what?"

"Arsenic would be my guess."

"*La poudre inheritance.*"

"Indeed."

"And can you not test for this?"

"It is possible, yes. The Marsh test. James Marsh first published his results some fifteen, twenty years ago, but it has been less than well received and of course it requires permission of the next of kin. A difficult thing to ask a wife who has just lost her husband."

"Providing she is innocent. What are the symptoms of arsenic poisoning?"

"Initially headaches, drowsiness, confusion, sometimes muscle cramps, tingling in the extremities, and severe stomach pains. Internally the arsenic is producing an inflammation of the internal lining of the stomach and bowels. This causes the most violent spasms and intense agony, which leads to chronic retching and vomiting and other exhausting distresses."

"Is there nothing that can be done to police its use?"

"Arsenic is readily available through pharmacies as a rat poison, although we do now have a register to monitor purchases. Besides, it's all around us." He gestured to the green wallpaper. "This green that is currently so fashionable contains a degree of arsenic to hold the intensity of color. Those pretty young ladies at the governor's in their green dresses—there's a reason they're called drop-dead gorgeous. They are dancing in a cloud of arsenic powder. Women also use it in their cosmetics. A powder will keep the skin pale and a paste will remove unwanted hair."

"Then why aren't there more deaths?"

"Long-term ingestion of small amounts can produce a tolerance, but even that catches up eventually. In the final stages, dark and foul-smelling urine, diarrhea, even nerve defects and then the breakdown of internal organs occurs."

"Yet a large dose will kill instantly."

"Within two to five days, a measured regular dose can mask the symptoms and present as an illness; cholera is most frequently diagnosed, as I said."

No wonder the poor man was at his wits' end.

"Forgive me, I have burdened you with my incoherent ramblings."

"There is nothing to forgive. Often in talking aloud we find an answer to our questions. Do you think Mrs. Skeffington could be responsible for her husband's demise?"

"Wittingly or unwittingly. That is the difficulty. Someone is, unless I have become totally inept. I cannot see that she has much to gain. My problem is that if she refuses to allow an autopsy I will not be able to prove poisoning. Forensic toxicology is a very new science, Captain. And to perform an accurate test I would need a sample of body tissue."

"And you believe Mrs. Skeffington may refuse that imposition?"

Philpott nodded, his forehead creased, then he delved into his pocket and brought out a small brochure: "'Tonic. For the improvement of all ailments,'" he read aloud, then held out the paper to Stefan.

The print looked familiar, and when Stefan turned the brochure over his blood cooled. "Just one moment." He hadn't thrown it away. He knew he hadn't. He rushed into his bedchamber and rummaged through the pocket of his greatcoat. Nothing. Then his riding jacket still muddy from his trip. He must get Sladdin to see to it. Sladdin! Sladdin had given him the original flyer about the Curio Shop on the very day he had arrived. Where was it?

"Can I be of any assistance?" Philpott's figure loomed in the doorway.

"I shan't be a moment." Then his eyes lit on his dress uniform. He shoved his hand into his pocket and brought out the flyer. He was right!

VISITORS TO SYDNEY SHOULD NOT LEAVE WITHOUT CALLING UPON THE CURIO SHOP OF WONDERS AT 84 HUNTER STREET. SKINS OF NATIVE BIRDS, BEASTS, AND REPTILES WELL-PRESERVED AND READY FOR SETTING UP. FUR AND FEATHER RUGS . . .

Without a word he handed Philpott the piece of paper. "Interesting. Very interesting. But hardly proof."

"Do you have a sample of this tonic Skeffington was taking?"

"No, none at all."

"And there is no residue in a glass or anything in the sickroom?"

"Impossible to discern without testing everything in the house. Arsenic has no flavor and is easily mixed into any drink, or food for that matter."

"How much does it take to kill a man?"

"It varies. The body is strange. As I said, a person can build up a resistance, and in many cases arsenic may be beneficial. It is used in the treatment of syphilis for example."

"Then I suspect your suspicions may be difficult to prove."

"Without a tissue sample, yes."

Stefan picked up the bottle and studied the label. "Do you know how Mrs. Skeffington came to have the tonic? Was it recommended?"

"That is where the situation becomes interesting. I'm not sure whether you are aware of the fact, but when the card games are being held many of the members' wives also meet. I believe they play parlor games."

Stefan's mind skipped from stone to stone and the path got slipperier by the moment. "And more than one of these wives have lost their husbands?" It was an outrageous suggestion.

"Suffice to say that many of the victims of this 'cholera' have connections with the Berkeley."

"But you can't prove they died of arsenic poisoning?"

"Without exhuming the bodies and performing the Marsh test, no."

"How long has this been going on? Surely someone has noticed a pattern."

"The first case was possibly five years ago."

"Five years! And you haven't brought it to the notice of the authorities?"

"I'm basing that on my uncle's records. I arrived in Australia two years ago and took over his patients. He passed on last year. A heart attack. He was seventy-one." Philpott offered him a wry grin. "It was only when I was reviewing his records that the pattern emerged."

"And these women who have lost their husbands, they are healthy?"

"Indeed. They have gone from strength to strength. Some have remarried; others have chosen to remain single and manage their deceased husbands' business affairs. Did you know that more women own businesses in Sydney than men?"

"No. I didn't." And that brought his mind back to the Curio Shop.

Chapter 29

Sydney, NSW
1919

Despite everything Kip said, Fleur couldn't bring herself to open the package containing Hugh's possessions, nor could she throw it away. It rested, still neatly wrapped, on her bedside table along with Kip's carefully washed blue handkerchief.

She'd thrashed about all night trying to make up her mind what to do. She should just accept the truth. It had taken long enough to ferret it out. Go back to England and pick up where she'd left off. Put the whole horrible set of circumstances behind her. Mrs. Black would take her back and she'd find a room to rent, maybe not as close to work, but there had to be one available somewhere. She was as much of an imposter as Hugh. Would she have married him if she'd known the truth? The only thing that made her feel halfway sensible was the fact that she'd spent very little of his money—the hotel bill and the fares to Mogo, a few meals here and there. All in all, she couldn't have made much of a dent in the bloody von Richter fortune.

Surely she could find a job on a ship returning to England; they must have a need for kitchen staff. Ships of all sorts, full of returned servicemen, just like Kip, arrived every day, then turned around to collect their next cargo of wounded soldiers.

She slipped Kip's handkerchief into her pocket; she would return it the next time she saw him. Hugh's package was another matter. What if it was another parcel of lies? If only she knew a little more about his life and his family. She'd never forget Hugh, *Hugo von Richter*, she corrected, or come to terms with the foolish mistake she had made in believing everything he'd said. She had to find out the truth for herself.

Out the window the view of the bustling docks contrasted with the serenity of the harbor. The prospect of gray, damp, drizzle-ridden London held nothing for her anymore. Going home, giving up and crawling away, wouldn't solve her problem. She'd spend the rest of her life wondering. What she needed was some sort of a compromise, something to help her understand why Hugh had seen fit to leave her the von Richter fortune.

Snatching up the package, she bolted down the stairs. "Mr. Sladdin."

The clerk lifted his beady gaze from the ledger, his head tortoise-like on his long neck, and put down his fountain pen.

"I was wondering if the hotel has a strongbox."

"Indeed we do." He straightened up, rubbing his hands together and making the dry skin crackle, as though he relished the ability to be of service.

With a surprising degree of difficulty, she lowered the package to the desk. "Could I place this in your safekeeping?"

He picked it up, running his long, sinewy fingers over the paper, reminding her of a child at Christmas trying to guess the contents of a present. His brow furrowed, his curiosity getting the better of him. "Corporal Hugh Richards." He traced a nail across the writing on the front. "Of course, I quite understand. Will there be anything else?"

Surely he would take it and lock it up immediately. She had the most ghastly feeling he might open it and discover everything she was too much of a coward to face. She clenched her fingers, resisting the temptation to snatch it back. "Should I have some sort of receipt?"

"Ah yes, of course, of course." He rummaged in the desk drawer and produced a small booklet, made a play of organizing the sheet of carbon paper, then scribbled the date and wrote *Personal Possessions Corporal Hugh Richards* on the top and slid it across the desktop. "If you'd just sign here please, Mrs. Richards."

She picked up the fountain pen and scribbled her signature, then, with mumbled thanks, pocketed the receipt and left, determined to discover for herself the truth about the man she married.

The key, with its ornate bird perched on the top, sat comfortably in the palm of her hand, almost as though it belonged. She couldn't wait to get back into the shop. Before anything else, the boards had to be removed from the windows to get some light and air into the place and dispel the smell of dust and decay. Then she'd approach the whole conundrum in an organized manner. She was good at that; she always found comfort in her ability to create order from chaos. After all, it had worked when Vera couldn't face the piles of files and folders. Not that the result was anything she'd boast about. She swung the key in a high arc from its piece of faded ribbon and came to a halt in front of the shop.

Someone had moved the remnants of the timber boarding from the step. She unlocked the door, swung it open, and stood rooted to the spot. Sunlight flooded the honey-colored floorboards and a warm gust of wind drifted through the building; the shutters at the back were open, the boarding gone.

From the back came the sound of a hammer, then a crash and a crunch. She ran to the back door, shot the bolts, and threw it open.

There was Kip, the biggest grin on his face, some sort of apron full of tools around his waist, his sleeves rolled up and a pair of filthy trousers suspended from braces that had seen better days.

"Ah! You beat me to it. I was hoping I'd have this lot cleared up before you got here." His voice, his face, everything about him radiated pleasure.

She stepped out into the yard to better appreciate his handiwork. Not only were the downstairs windows open, so were those above. "You've done so much." A lump rose to her throat.

"Makes a lot of difference once you can see what you're looking at. Come and have a gander." He reached for her hand, and without a second thought she took it. He led her up the stairs and into a small room overlooking the yard.

In one corner there was a sheet draped over what looked like a pile of furniture.

"Go on. Take the sheet off. Carefully."

She tugged at the corner; it snagged then released, bringing with it a cloud of dust.

A small falcon, a stormy petrel with an amazing sheen, stood perched on a branch eyeing her with beady eyes. Next to it an owl-like bird, the likes of which she'd never seen. Its speckled brown plumage blended into obscurity with the bark of a tree. "What's this?"

"A tawny frogmouth."

"And look at this. A giant hedgehog."

"No!" Kip's eyes danced as he smothered a laugh. "It's a spiny anteater, better known as an echidna. I've decided the downstairs room was used for display. I reckon they left the kangaroo down there because it was too heavy to move. Glad next door said it was a tailor's shop for a while. I can just see that white kangaroo in top hat and tails, wouldn't need a shirt." He struck a pose, his thumbs hooked through his braces, one toe raised as though he were about to launch into a jig.

"Oh, but wait, you're missing one thing." She reached into her pocket and pulled out his handkerchief, folded it into a neat triangle, and tucked it into the top pocket of his shirt, patting it into place with the palm of her hand. "Thank you, thank you for everything."

For a fleeting moment he held her gaze, then he gave a curt nod and pushed up his sleeves. "What's next? The cellar? I haven't been down there. I've brought my lantern and some spare candles in case you want a closer look. Thought I ought to wait for you."

She gave him a wide smile. "Let's finish here first. What can I do?"

"There's a bucket and some old rags in the scullery. I thought you might want to give the windows a bit of a clean. Get as much light in as we can. The pump's in the yard." He pointed out the window to a rickety lever lurching against the small outhouse.

He seemed to know exactly what she needed, had made her laugh and hadn't asked any difficult questions or pressured her about Hugh's package. He was just there to help. Fleur rolled up her sleeves and followed his lead.

Once the bucket was filled she set to washing away the grime of goodness knows how many years. The front window would be a challenge; apart from the fact that it was bigger, it was made up of lots and lots of small leadlight panes.

"Most people I know wouldn't go to all this trouble. They'd just take the money, get on and enjoy themselves, and forget about the past." Kip's voice floated down the stairs, echoing in the empty room.

"I can't. I just can't." No matter how hard she tried she couldn't shake the feeling that she'd missed something. She'd had that dream again the night before—Hugh standing on the hill bathed in sunlight, holding out his hand to her, or was he waving goodbye?

Kip's face flushed red. "They keep telling me to forget about the past." With a thundering clap, the last of the planks fell to the ground.

"Were you in France?"

"Yeah. Don't like to talk about it." He jumped down and started collecting the fallen timber.

So he had been in the army; she'd thought as much from the way he carried himself. He didn't appear to have any lasting injuries. Maybe he was one of the lucky ones and had come home early. She scampered up the steps and stood in the middle of the room, the kangaroo in the corner viewing her with a quizzical look.

"The room is huge," she called, spreading her arms wide and twirling slowly around. "I wonder what the old Curio Shop sold."

"Australian curios, among them taxidermied specimens from the look of this chap and the stuff upstairs." He gave the kangaroo another pat. "Never seen a white one before. Have you got the key there?"

She handed it over.

"I wonder who Atterton was." He fingered the faded letters on the tag still attached to the key.

"Must have been the owners of the shop, and when Skipper told me about the Mogo property he called it 'the old Atterton place.' He said it was one of the first grants in the district. He said he remembered Hugh." She sank down on the bottom step.

Home is Mogo Creek. It'll be our place, our special place.

"Hugh told me it was home."

"St. Albans was settled really early. If that's not proof enough that his family had lived in Australia for a long time, then what is? And this place was built years ago. Look at the walls. They don't use blocks like this anymore." He ran his hand over the sandstone. "You can see the convict marks. That's how they kept tally of how many they'd cut."

"I don't know. Maybe Atterton was his grandmother's name. Vera said she was Australian, maybe English originally. I don't understand any of it. When will Mr. Lyttleton be back? I don't mean to be unkind, but it seems as though Vera is at a total loss."

"I've no idea. Repatriation could take months. We'll have to see what we can sort out." He turned around and picked up a small lantern. "Come with me." He held out his hand. "Let's go and have another look at the stuff in the cellar. My guess is that this room was cleared when the place was leased and all the contents stored downstairs."

It made perfect sense. "Come on, then." She swung around the banister and followed Kip down the stairs, her heart in her mouth.

Once lit, the lantern threw a circle of light onto the irregular sandstone walls. The cellar appeared to stretch the length of the entire house. Alongside the steps there was a narrow cubbyhole crammed with boxes. After every few paces, Fleur stopped, praying she wouldn't encounter one of Kip's goggle-eyed huntsmen.

Under her feet the floor sloped up to the street, forcing her to crouch as she moved forward. A solid bank of tea chests lined the front wall. Against the side wall stood a glass-topped cedar display case and on top of it were more teetering boxes speckled with dust and rodent droppings.

Without thinking she pushed her hand onto the top of the pile. An uncontrolled scream ripped out of her mouth. The rank, musty odor of rats coated her nostrils. "Argh!" Fiddling her fingers in the air she tried to contain the wave of panic crawling across her skin. "It's a rat."

"Here, let me." Kip tipped the box and shone the lantern inside. He laughed and pulled out a fat roll of soft fur dangling from a silken cord.

She took it from him and gingerly slipped her fingers inside. "It's a muff." The soft satin fabric was smooth to the touch.

"A what?"

"A muff. They were very popular in the last century. Ladies wore them around their necks and kept their hands inside." She delved deeper and found a small pocket. "There's a pocket in here. A lady's pistol would fit very nicely in there."

"Maybe just her loose change. I don't like the idea of my lady carrying a pistol."

"A lady wouldn't be seen dead carrying money in those days." She laid it down on the glass top. "What else is in the box?" She tipped it over and spread out the contents. "Look. Gloves and stoles, and evening bags, purses, and these. A pair of leather slippers. I wonder what they're made of." She ran her fingers over the soft skin, shook out fur coats, stoles, and three painstakingly stitched patchwork blankets. The pile in front of her grew.

"Looks like possum. Kangaroo, wombat maybe? Leather could be emu."

"Do they use Australian animals for clothing and blankets?" And did all of them have this strange earthy, oniony smell?

"Dunno. Not that I've heard of. I thought rich folk went for mink and ermine and maybe fox." He cracked a laugh. "I've seen old pictures of natives wearing cloaks a bit like these. Can't imagine them at Government House though." It was as though Kip had come alive in the drab and dusty building full of strange smells and unexplored corners. Like a child in a museum, his eyes stretched wide with wonder. He ran his long fingers over each item, dusting them with care with his big blue handkerchief.

They continued to work their way through the top boxes; a lot more of the same, and then feathers. Headdresses, fascinators, little hats with netting attached. "Look at these." She picked up a hair comb with a spray of pale, curved feathers and stuck it into her hair, pulling it back behind her ear.

Kip shone the lantern directly onto them. "Lyrebird by the look of it."

"A what bird?"

"Lyrebird. They're the best mimics. The male bird fans out his tail, bit like a peacock, to attract the female."

The atmosphere in the cellar shifted ever so slightly and she pulled the comb from her hair and stuffed it back into the box. A puff of dust rose and then settled, filling the space with the pungent smell again. "Have you any idea what that smell is?"

Kip scratched his head, making his dark hair stand out at oddly endearing angles. "It reminds me of tripe. France." He shuddered and lifted the lantern. A closed look masked his face. "Sheep stomach. They cook it with garlic in this foul white sauce. Coats your mouth like plaster."

And then she remembered. "It's the smell at Mogo. In the workshop."

A grunt came from Kip and then the sound of something shifting. She edged along the wall into the lantern beam. "What have you found?" The shelves were stacked, the contents threatening to spill onto the floor: scrolled maps and manuscripts, books and leather-covered ledgers, piles of documents, numerous scrolls and quills.

"Here, hold this." He thrust the lantern into her hand and heaved himself up, his arms crammed with a stack of long, thin leather-bound volumes. "I'll take them upstairs."

Fleur blew out the lantern, left it on the table next to the matches, and followed him.

By the time she got upstairs Kip had dumped the ledgers on the desk and stood surveying them with his arms folded and a satisfied grin on his face. "These should tell us something."

A strange knot formed in her throat when her hands rested on the first of the faded green ledgers. She opened it, releasing the scent of the past: leather, parchment, and ink.

The Curio Shop of Wonders
84 Hunter Street, Sydney
1853

Rows and rows of neat columns of figures for each day of the week, carefully listed and marked. Names and amounts and quantities. Quantities of what? It didn't say. And then items. *Feathered accessories.*

Fur accessories. Tonic. Native artifacts. Specimens. Specimens of what? A shudder ran down her spine and she closed the book and picked up a bigger one that had fallen to the floor.

The Taxidermy Shop
93 Islington High Street, Islington, London
1835

"Look at this." She lay the open book flat on the table. "This one isn't from the Curio Shop, it's from Islington in London. What a coincidence. I lived there before the zeppelin raid."

His eyebrows disappeared under the shock of brown hair hanging over his forehead. "Zeppelin raid?"

"Mum and Dad were caught in it. Our house went too."

Kip gave a grunt of sympathy and Fleur turned back to the flyleaf. *Thaddeus Atterton*. "Atterton. See." She stabbed at the faded script.

"At least that makes sense of something. Same name as on the key."

"Same name as Mogo. I wonder who Thaddeus Atterton was. Did Vera find anything in the records?"

He gave a noncommittal shrug. "Let's not wonder. Let's see what we can find."

As they worked their way through the pile of ledgers, the pages flicked past, one after another, the breath of the past stippling the back of her neck, making her eyes blur. Finally she had four separate piles.

"Right. We have the ledgers from the Taxidermy Shop in London owned by Thaddeus Atterton."

"You don't know he owned it."

"True. I'm hazarding a guess. Then ledgers from the Taxidermy Shop at 84 Hunter Street, also owned by Thaddeus Atterton. And others from the Curio Shop of Wonders, at the same premises and owned by Cordelia Atterton."

"Thaddeus's wife?"

"Maybe."

"I'd say definitely."

"And finally these. 'Noble Opals. Della von Richter.'"

"Let me have a look."

Fleur's mind was whirling in ever-decreasing circles. If nothing else it proved a link between the Attertons and von Richters, but Noble Opals? And then her heart skipped a beat.

Dad was a miner. That's why they put me on tunneling duty.

"What do you know about opals?"

"Not a lot. A gemstone. You find them all over the place—Lightning Ridge, Broken Hill, and somewhere in South Australia too, I think. Not sure. Don't have much call for stuff like that."

"But where do you get them? Do you mine them?"

"Not real deep. I think you just dig for them with a pick and shovel. Maybe blast. I've got some memory of them being fragile. Sorry, not much help."

"But people call themselves opal miners."

"Reckon so."

She ran her finger down the list. "There's reference to Hugh's brothers, Clemens and Carl, in the ledgers. Otto and Della von Richter and someone called Burless."

Kip hunched over her shoulder and peered down at the ledger. "Burless?"

"How did an Austrian opal miner end up owning a shop in Sydney? Maybe he didn't. Maybe the opals were only sold from here." That made more sense. "What do you think, Kip?"

Receiving no answer, she closed the ledger with a snap. Kip's pacing drove her mad, his feet echoing on the timber floor as he strode up and down. Almost marching, from the window at the front to the back, a neat parade-ground turn, then back again. "Stand still."

He came to a neat halt and a tense edginess swept over his face.

"What's the matter?"

He raked his hair back from his forehead. She noticed a few spots of sweat beading his forehead. "I've had enough, sick to death of it."

"Don't be ridiculous. We—"

Before she had the opportunity to finish her sentence, he grabbed his cloth cap and barged out of the building.

Chapter 30

Sydney, NSW
1853

The baron's journals held no interest for Stefan. Instead of editing the notes he'd made during the trip back to Sydney, he spent the entire night mulling over Philpott's words. Arsenic poisoning was nothing new. It had been the poison of preference for centuries; even the Romans had a partiality for it. Why would Mrs. Skeffington want to dispose of her husband? What had she to gain? If the rumors were to be believed, the man's interests were property-heavy and he had a penchant for the gaming tables; the brief glimpse of the house in Potts Point proved they were in no way impoverished.

He peered out the window. Below, in the street, Philpott strode across the road in a most determined manner carrying his doctor's bag. He didn't make it to the door.

Stefan bit back a grin as Bert fell into step alongside the tall man and grasped his bag. He had to take five steps for every two of Philpott's and listed dangerously to port due to the weight.

Pulling on his jacket, Stefan ran down the stairs to fend off Sladdin's morning greetings.

"Ah! Captain. The very man." Philpott tipped his head in the direction of the stairs and raised his eyebrows in question. "A moment of your time, if you'd be so kind."

Abandoning Bert to Sladdin, they took the stairs two at a time. It wasn't until the door was firmly closed that Philpott said, "I called in to see Mrs. Skeffington this morning."

"And she agreed."

His face fell. "No. As I expected she refused outright to allow any interference, as she called it, with her husband's body. The undertaker had already called and was preparing the embalming. The funeral is tomorrow."

A resounding bang interrupted his words, and Bert fell through the door, Philpott's bag clutched in one hand and the other rubbing his backside.

"Bert!"

"Sorry, Capt'n, but that Sladdin. I reckon he's got lead caps on his boots." He dumped the bag on the floor and rubbed his backside again.

Stefan ignored Bert's tirade and turned back to Philpott, who hefted his bag onto the table and fiddled with a series of clips and locks. "I was wondering if you could help me, Bert. I need to procure a bottle of tonic from the Curio Shop. Mrs. Skeffington admitted to buying the tonic and some lozenges that were recommended by Mrs. Atterton at one of their parlor-games parties. I thought if I gave Bert some money he could go and—"

"You'd be meaning one of these, would you, Guv?" Bert slipped between the two men, his hand outstretched.

Philpott lifted the green-wrapped lozenge from Bert's hand. "How did you come by this, boy?"

Bert's face flushed the color of borscht. "I, um. I, er—"

"Payment for services rendered." Stefan tousled his hair and winked. "It would seem we have solved your problem. Can the tests be carried out on this?"

"Yes, of course. I have the necessary equipment in my bag. I will also have to confirm the tonic contained arsenic, but this is indeed a start. A very good start." He carefully removed a burner, a metal stand, and a selection of glass tubes from his bag.

"Arsenic. That's poison, ain't it?" Bert edged his way closer. "How's all that clobber going to 'elp?"

"We place the lozenge in here and some of this zinc powder, and if there is arsenic present it will react and form a gas. We then heat the gas and it will leave a film of metallic arsenic on the glass—we call that the 'arsenic mirror.'"

Bert stared openmouthed as Philpott arranged the equipment and lit the burners.

"The test is so sensitive it can be used to detect minute amounts of arsenic in foods or in stomach contents. I'll pop the lozenge in and add the zinc. Now wait a moment while it heats."

Stefan held his breath, hardly able to contain his impatience as the shiny black powder formed.

"And there we have it. An arsenic mirror." Philpott straightened up, a glow of triumph on his face. "Conclusive. Arsenic is definitely present."

A knock prevented Stefan from responding. Before he had a chance to reach the door, it swung open. The scent of freshly brewed coffee preceded Sladdin pushing a trolley. "There's a letter for you from the governor, Captain von Richter, and I have taken the liberty of bringing you some refreshments."

Stefan felt the color rise to his cheeks. Sladdin's timing couldn't have been worse. "Leave it outside, thank you." Wretched man sticking his nose into everyone's business. How he wished Philpott would restrain himself until Sladdin left the room. Bert would have the sense to keep his mouth closed, but Philpott didn't know that Sladdin and Cordelia appeared to be acquainted.

"I think that is sufficient evidence to prove the presence of arsenic. Now to confirm my suspicions and get hold of a bottle of tonic."

"Would you be referring to the tonic from the Curio Shop?"

Philpott's head came up with a snap and his eyes drilled Sladdin.

"I recognize the green paper."

He picked up the paper from the lozenge that had fallen to the floor. "Most efficacious in the case of minor irritations of the throat." Sladdin held out a cup and saucer to Stefan. For some incomprehensible reason Stefan took them. He wanted to bundle the man out of the room and slam the door in his face, not have him serve coffee.

Philpott had no such concern. "What do you know of this tonic?" His words echoed like gunfire in the confines of the room, and a slight smile tipped Sladdin's thin lips as he shrugged his shoulders. "I know the lozenges are available from the Curio Shop and as I said are most efficacious."

"And poisonous. Deadly in sufficient quantities. Manufacture of such items could be construed as . . ."

Sladdin gave a simpering smile. "I doubt the arsenic was incorporated during their manufacture. If they come from the Curio Shop, they are bound to contain traces of arsenic. I expect every item on the premises does."

Whatever was the man talking about?

"The shop was originally a taxidermist. They still sell many specimens. You've seen them yourself, Captain. Intend to purchase some, I believe. Arsenic is used to preserve the skins of the specimens, otherwise they'd be disintegrating before your very eyes, eaten away by moths and insects. And besides, anyone can purchase arsenic. It's hardly a crime. Just go down to the pharmacy on the corner and sign the poison register. I use it myself to keep the rats at bay in the cellars."

Stefan couldn't stand it a moment longer. Sladdin was the last person he wanted involved. "That'll be all. *Danke*."

Sladdin handed Philpott a cup of coffee and then busied himself cleaning up the trolley and wheeled it, squeaking, from the room.

"Remind me of the initial symptoms of arsenic poisoning, Philpott."

"Headaches, sore joints, dizziness, lethargy."

A tugging at Stefan's jacket sleeve caught his attention. "Sounds like the way Miss Della felt. Maybe Sladdin's right. The whole shop's full of the stuff. Won't catch me going in there again." Bert gave a dramatic shudder and closed the door behind Sladdin.

Stefan's heart gave a lurch. The symptoms were identical to those suffered by Della when they first returned to Sydney. Thank heavens she had recovered. "Do I remember you saying that in small doses a tolerance can develop?"

"That's right. A fatal dose varies. It is in the range of one grain per pound of body weight per day."

"What do you intend to do next, Philpott?"

"Unfortunately there is a possibility that Sladdin is correct and the presence of arsenic could simply be coincidental. It rather depends on the quantity. We really do need a bottle of that tonic."

"Well, let's go and get one." Bert reefed open the door.

"Not so fast, Bert. Not so fast." Stefan's eyes lit on the folded piece of paper lying on the table where Sladdin had left it. He picked it up and turned it over, revealing the governor's crest. He unfolded it and grunted in satisfaction. "Excellent."

"Wot's excellent?"

"The governor has returned from Parramatta and requests my attendance at eleven o'clock." He glanced at the clock on the mantelpiece. "If I leave now I shall have time. Philpott, can you manage here? Bert will give you a hand. I might be able to procure you a bottle of tonic on my way to Government House."

"How're you goin' to do that?"

"I'll worry about that. You stay here and help Mr. Philpott pack up and I'll let you know if I need anything else."

Chapter 31

Sydney, NSW
1919

Fleur picked up the final opal ledger and took it over to the light and ran her finger down the list of names: *Otto von Richter*, *Carl von Richter*, and *Clemens von Richter*. A family business, except for Bert Burless, and there was no mention of Hugh, or Hugo. Quantities, weights, and what might be a description: *Black*, *Boulder*, *Crystal*, *White*. Halfway through the book in July 1914 the records stopped, just before the outbreak of war.

The ledgers did little more than link the Attertons and the von Richters, something she already knew.

The hairs on the back of her neck prickled to attention. Glad said the shop had been closed for donkey's years before the depression in the '90s, yet the last date in the Noble Opals ledger said July 1914. Someone must have put it there. Someone must have been inside the Curio Shop long after it was boarded up. How had they gotten in there? She was missing something, something important.

Turning back the pages, she traced her finger across the list of place names Kip had mentioned—*Lightning Ridge* and *Broken Hill*—as well as *Coober Pedy* and *Andamooka*. Where were they? They sounded like names in a storybook. And what was it in the ledger that had made Kip storm off? She simply didn't understand what had happened. It had been two days since he'd marched out of the shop, and she missed his companionship.

Locking the Curio Shop, she pocketed the key and walked down the road toward Lyttleton & Sons.

"Vera, I've got a few questions to ask you. I wonder if you'd mind."

"I am a little busy. As you can see I'm beginning to make headway. I must do something. It seems unlikely Mr. Lyttleton will be back for another three or four months."

Fleur's stomach sank. So much for her idea about waiting until Mr. Lyttleton arrived home to ask questions. She had to decide what she was going to do; in the meantime maybe she could find out how she had upset Kip. "I won't take very much of your time. It's about Kip. He worried me."

Vera's head came up with a snap and her eyes narrowed. She let out a long sigh. "I'm so sorry. He's perfectly all right most of the time. I really thought he had gotten past the worst, and this sudden interest in the Curio Shop has been so good for him."

"I don't understand."

"Shell shock, my dear." Vera lowered her voice and leaned in conspiratorially. "So many of our boys suffer from it. They look right as rain on the outside, then for no reason they go off like a rocket. He had such a bad war."

"What do you mean 'go off like a rocket'?"

"The most random event can spark the symptoms."

"What are these symptoms?"

"Loss of memory, insomnia, terrifying dreams, attacks of unconsciousness, convulsive movements resembling an epileptic fit, obsessive thoughts, usually of the gloomiest and most painful kind, even in some cases hallucinations and delusions . . ." She rattled off the list like some kind of medical specialist.

None of them seemed to apply to the Kip Fleur knew. It was only when they'd found the opal ledgers he'd become upset.

"We've been doing all we can for the poor boys. Mr. Lyttleton has something of a soft spot for Kip. He'd worked for us on and off before the war. He was such a happy-go-lucky boy, always keen to please, full of love and laughter. We took him in when he came home, but he's different now. It's as though he left a part of himself behind."

"He wasn't physically injured?"

"No, nothing you can see. He worshiped the ground his brother walked on and is convinced he took the bullet intended for him. Simply fell apart right there and then. He was shipped back to England; they did that to all our boys. Gave them a few days off, then sent them back to the trenches. Archer Waterstone and Michael have been friends for years. Back to the African War. They got Kip an early discharge and we offered him a place to stay. He uses the spare room out back; he's been acting as a sort of night watchman while we moved into the premises. He can't face his mother, you see. Convinced she would never forgive him for letting his brother die."

How could Fleur be so blind, so inconsiderate? No wonder he'd rushed off. Her ranting and raving about the von Richters must have been too much for him to bear and brought back all kinds of terrible memories. If only she'd realized. "Then he's been here since he left the Curio Shop?"

"Now you mention it, I haven't seen him. He very much comes and goes as he pleases. I don't like to be too demanding if he's going through a bad patch."

"Actually, there was something else I wanted to ask. I hope you don't think I'm being too intrusive. We—Kip and I—found some old ledgers in the Curio Shop. They go way back to London in the early nineteenth century, but also there's a more recent one. I don't understand—both you and Glad said the shop had been boarded up for years."

"Glad?" Vera's eyebrows raised, making Fleur's face flush beet red. Now she might have to explain her failed attempt to climb over the fence.

"The woman who lives next door to the Curio Shop. She said the place had been boarded up for as long as she could remember, well before the war. The last date in the opal ledger I found is July 1914. That means someone must have been in the shop relatively recently."

"I don't see how anyone could have been in the shop. Opals, did you say? They've never attracted me very much, milky, soft-looking things. Some of those miners made a fortune though. Sold their pickings to the German traders." Her hand covered her mouth. "Is that what set Kip off?"

"There's no doubt about the connection between the Attertons and the von Richters. However, there's one other thing, the only thing I can think of that might have upset him: the name Bert Burless. I wondered if it rang any bells."

"Oh!" There was that silly high-pitched girlish sound Vera made. However did Mr. Lyttleton put up with it? Vera shook her head and pulled down the corners of her mouth. "I have no idea, my dear, no idea."

"As soon as he saw the name he started pacing around, then slammed out of the shop and disappeared. I feel dreadfully guilty, but I have no idea what I have done."

"Oh, my dear. That's Kip, and so many others like him. So touchy. You might never know what it was that set him off. If you want to set your mind at rest, why don't you go around and have a word with Kip's mother, Mrs. Cassidy? I usually pop in once a week to let her know how he's getting on, and to be truthful I have been negligent." She gestured at the pile of boxes and files spread on every surface, such a stark contrast to the neatly piled ledgers in the Curio Shop. "Maybe Kip's found the courage to face his mother."

"I might just do that." She couldn't help but feel responsible for what had happened. Kip had spent so much time with her, helping her, it was the least she could do. "And I have one more question. Do you know the name of the tailor who leased the shop?"

"I have no idea. Maybe somewhere in this . . ." She gestured to the floor.

"Never mind. I'll take your suggestion and go and see Mrs. Cassidy. Do you have an address?"

"Twenty-six Argyle Place, Millers Point."

"I'm not sure . . ."

"I'm sorry, I keep forgetting you don't know Sydney. You seem to have settled in so well, as though you belong. Down to the end of Hunter Street, turn right onto George Street, immediately left onto Margaret Street, then into Kent and right again at the Lord Nelson. It's not too far."

"Are you sure it will be all right? I don't want to make matters worse."

"No, no." Vera buried her head in the nearest box, mumbling about files and legal ramifications, none of which seemed to have anything to do with Kip.

Fleur straightened her hat, pulled down her sleeves, and set off down the street.

Less than half an hour later, with the overwhelming stench of beer and tobacco choking her, she gazed up at the three-story sandstone façade of the Lord Nelson Hotel. The last thing she wanted to do was go inside and ask for directions, so she ducked across the road behind a large Clydesdale pulling a dray packed with barrels and spotted a street sign saying Argyle Place.

The crowded street was a far cry from the Berkeley Hotel and the buildings in Macquarie Street, more like the back alleys of Islington. A group of grubby children clustered around one of the doorways while two older girls battled it out on a hopscotch grid marked out on the pavement, their cheerful cries belying their drab, colorless clothes and pinched faces.

"What'd you want?" A boy with a cloth cap four times too large for him sidled up to her.

"I'm looking for 26 Argyle Place."

He flicked his thumb over his shoulder. "Down there a piece."

"Thank you."

A little girl nudged the boy in his ribs. "She ain't home."

"Any idea where I might find her?"

"That's her there." She pointed across the road where three women stood nattering, propping up a dilapidated front fence.

Fleur crossed the road, plastering a bright smile on her face, aware of the women's eyes following her every move. "Good afternoon. I wonder if you can help me. I'm looking for Mrs. Cassidy."

"And who might you be?"

"My name's Fleur, Fleur Richards." She held out her hand, which they all ignored. "Vera Lyttleton said I might find her here."

Vera's name worked a treat. A thin woman in a faded paisley apron straightened up. "What can I do for you?"

"Mrs. Cassidy? I wondered if I could have a chat with you. It's about your son, Kip."

"What's he done now?" All three of the women ran their eyes over her midriff, making her realize her mistake.

"Nothing. Nothing at all. He's been helping me and I . . ." Her voice petered out. She didn't want to discuss Kip in front of all these women. She had no idea who they were, if it would be some sort of betrayal.

It seemed Mrs. Cassidy was of the same mind. "Come with me." She took off across the road and pushed open the door of a small house that smelled of sweat and stale bodies. The plaintive cry of a hungry baby and the sound of children squabbling drifted down the stairs. "I rent out the top. It brings in a little bit. Now, what's all this about Kip?"

Still standing in the hallway, Fleur dropped her voice. "I'm worried about him. He took off and I don't know where he's gone."

"He's a grown man, even though he mightn't act like one."

"The thing is, he's been helping me with some old records and I think we found something that may have upset him." She swallowed; she didn't want to appear intrusive. "I thought it might have brought back memories of the war."

A shuttered look crossed Kip's mother's face. "I don't want to hear anything about the war. Those Germans have done enough damage to last a lifetime." She held the door open. "Get out."

"Not all Germans are responsible for the war. Some of them simply got caught . . ." The words dried in Fleur's mouth. What was she saying? This woman was just repeating everything she believed and here Fleur was defending the von Richters.

"Responsible in my mind. Killed my eldest son and sent the youngest back a raving lunatic. Turned family against family. They never should have let them set foot in the country in the first place. Even the internment camps were too good for them."

Internment camps? Mrs. Lyttleton hadn't mentioned those when she was talking about the von Richters. Fleur hovered on the doorstep. "I don't wish to cause you any further grief. I'm concerned for Kip." Surely the woman must care about her only living son. "I'm worried he saw something that upset him and I feel responsible."

Mrs. Cassidy's shoulders dropped and she dragged a breath in through her pale lips. "What did he see this time?" She sank down on a rickety chair pushed against the wall in the hallway.

"Can we go and sit down somewhere more comfortable? Perhaps I could make you a cup of tea?"

The silence stretched out and Fleur was about to leave when Mrs. Cassidy dragged herself to her feet and shuffled down the hallway.

"The war's bad enough. I lost both my boys. Kip might as well be dead for all the good he is to me now." She glanced up at a well-worn photograph on the mantelpiece above the stove. Two boys, grins as wide as their shoulders, sat in some sort of homemade wooden cart, a man with an overlarge mustache behind them, arms folded, eyes staring into the distance. She got the distinct impression he'd rather be somewhere else.

"If it wasn't for the Germans I'd still have a family."

"I'm so sorry."

At a loss for words, Fleur busied herself filling the kettle and lighting the range.

When the kettle whistled Mrs. Cassidy shrugged. "There isn't a family around here who hasn't lost someone, and now we've got influenza on our doorstep." She gave a long, slow shake of her head. "What's Kip done now?"

"He's been helping me go through some old family records." Where had that come from? Family? "In the Curio Shop," she added, determined not to let herself be sidetracked. "I was wondering if any of these names mean anything to you."

"Names?"

"Otto, Clemens, and Carl von Richter, Bert Burless . . ."

If Mrs. Cassidy had paled before, she now looked like a milksop. Not a vestige of color in her face and her eyes wide and staring. "Burless, you say."

"Yes, that's right. It's quite unusual. Not a name I've heard before."

"It's my maiden name, Kip's middle name too. Albert Burless Cassidy. Named for his grandfather. Not that it did him much good. His mates all call him Kip." With a shaking hand Mrs. Cassidy reached up to the mantelpiece and brought down a small round tin. The photograph fluttered to the floor and she made no move to pick it up.

She opened the tin and offered Fleur a cigarette. "No, thank you."

Mrs. Cassidy's hand shook as she cupped it around the flame of the match and brought it to her mouth. She inhaled deeply, the tobacco smoke circling up to the ceiling, filling the small kitchen with a blue haze.

After several more drags the tip of her cigarette glowed as she sucked the smoke deep into her lungs; in just a few moments it would be ash and Fleur's time would be up.

Sitting at the table, Mrs. Cassidy fiddled with the edge of a chipped saucer full of butts. "Those von Richters should have been sent back where they came from. They always thought they were a cut above the rest with their airs and graces and clicking heels. My father always cared more about them than Mother and me, chasing around the world after them, leaving us to fend for ourselves."

Fleur didn't know whether to agree with her or not. Her feelings regarding Hugh and his family seemed to swing like a pendulum.

"My parents died in the zeppelin raids in London."

Mrs. Cassidy stubbed her cigarette out and stood, chewing the edge of her finger as if she couldn't make up her mind whether she'd said too much. "They've all got blood on their hands."

Fleur sat quietly waiting, hoping that eventually it would all make sense.

"It's not my story to tell. I just live with the consequences." Mrs. Cassidy gave a shuddering sigh. "See yourself out."

Chapter 32

Sydney, NSW
1853

Della wrapped the green paper around the muff and placed it onto the table. "That will be six shillings and sixpence, Mrs. Thompson. Thank you."

"Will you be getting some more of those possum blankets? I believe they are deliciously warm and with winter closing in . . ."

"I'm not sure." She certainly hoped not. She'd taken the last three and put them on a back shelf in the cellar, harboring some forsaken hope that she might take them back to Mogo next time she went. There was still no sign of Gus and Dobbin, nor of Cordelia for that matter. "Perhaps if you'd like to call back in a week or so."

She walked to the door and opened it, careful not to let it slam, because she still couldn't find the key. The last time she remembered having it was when she had returned from the carriage ride with Stefan.

"Good morning, Mrs. Thompson."

The overblown woman swept out in a waft of attar of roses and Della stood relishing the patch of frail sunlight, imagining herself down by the creek feeding Tidda a handful of sweetgrass while she listened to the Darkinjung women tell their stories. On days like this she found the town claustrophobic. What she needed was another ride in one of those lovely carriages. She grinned at her foolishness and turned to look down the street.

As if in answer to her unspoken wish, Stefan's tall figure appeared striding down the road. No uniform today; instead he looked like a profitable squatter in a worsted jacket, matching cravat, and long boots.

She lifted her hand in greeting and he picked up his pace, as good as ran, a broad grin on his face.

"Good morning, Stefan." She inhaled his scent of ambergris and musk.

"Della, good morning. You look a picture of health and happiness."

Health, yes. Every trace of the lethargy and dizziness that had plagued her had vanished in the past days, and with Captain von Richter holding both her hands and smiling down at her, she felt exceptionally happy.

"I was wondering if I could ask for your assistance. Sir Charles is back and has requested my attendance at eleven. In just half an hour."

"That would be . . . Oh no, I can't. Cordelia's not back yet and I can't find the key." The night before she'd locked both the front and back doors with the inside bolts, but she could hardly leave the shop open in broad daylight.

"I would very much like you to accompany me. Your testimony would add weight to my story. Could Charity not keep an eye on the shop?"

The thought hadn't crossed her mind. Charity never looked after the shop. She helped with the dusting, cleaned the windows, did most of the cooking, but even when Ma and Pa were alive, she'd never had responsibility for the shop. "I'm not sure." Oh, but she so wanted to go with Stefan. Not only for the pleasure of spending some time in his company. This was for Jarro and all his family. And not just for his family. For all the others who'd suffered Gus and Dobbin's awful raids. It was time she stood up for what she believed in. "I'll ask her. I won't be long."

Much to her surprise Charity jumped at the idea, assuring her she was more than capable of attending to the customers. Cordelia simply didn't appreciate her skills.

With that problem solved Della ran upstairs, repinned her hair, pinched her cheeks, and unearthed Cordelia's blue cloak. When she returned downstairs Charity sat ensconced behind the desk looking quite the lady of business while Stefan waited impatiently outside drumming his cane against the edge of the footpath.

"I'm sorry I kept you."

"No matter. Charity appears to be pleased with her responsibility."

"She's keen to stay in Sydney and wants to prove her worth. She hated being out at the farm with me."

"And what about you? Do you miss the freedom or are you happier here in Sydney?"

"Truthfully I miss it. Charity said Jarro was asking after me."

"And was there any sign of Gus and Dobbin?"

"No, none."

He reached for her hand and tucked it in the crook of his arm. "Now let's put our mind to what we are going to say to Sir Charles. I have no intention of letting Gus and Dobbin continue their unconscionable behavior."

By the time they'd reached Government House Stefan had convinced her Sir Charles would use Gus and Dobbin as examples and prevent any further attacks. He spoke so persuasively and with such intelligence she doubted she could add anything to the argument.

"Thank you for your time, Sir Charles."

"It's my pleasure, Captain von Richter. Miss Atterton, good morning."

Stefan tucked Della's arm into his own and led her down the road. "You're very quiet."

"I had no idea so many had suffered so greatly."

"There is no reason you should have known. The massacre Sir Charles mentioned took place a long time ago."

"Twenty-eight men, women, and children. Where did it happen?"

"A place in northern New South Wales, Myall Creek."

"And to think that so many people share Cordelia's lack of concern for the Aboriginal people. I never thought I would say it, but I am pleased those killers were brought to justice and hung."

"The fact that it has established a precedent is in our favor, although as Sir Charles said, nothing can be done until Gus and Dobbin are found and brought before the courts."

"Oh yes, something can be done. I intend to make sure every one of those stolen possessions at the shop are returned to Jarro and his family, and just as soon as Cordelia returns I will find out the full story. It's appalling to think that the shop, Pa's shop, should be involved in such . . . in such atrocities."

And that brought him back with a crash. He'd been in such a hurry to get to Government House he hadn't mentioned Philpott's findings to Della and in truth had no idea how to approach the matter. The last thing he wanted was for her to be implicated. "Where has Cordelia gone?"

"I'm not certain. She simply said she had business to attend to." Della lifted her pretty shoulders and shook her head.

"There's something I need to tell you. It concerns Skeffington."

"And the stone?"

"It can wait. At the moment this is rather more important." He drew in a deep breath, suddenly unsure how she would take the news, the accusation. After all, he was about to implicate her aunt yet again. "Let's sit for a moment." He drew her down onto a bench overlooking the harbor. "I think I mentioned Mr. Philpott, a doctor I met at the Berkeley."

"Yes, you did. When I was unwell."

"Philpott conducted a test on the lozenges Cordelia has for sale in the Curio Shop and he discovered that they contain arsenic."

"Arsenic? How could that happen? We're always very careful with the supplies both here and at the farm. It's dreadfully poisonous. That's why it's used to kill rats."

"So you know there is arsenic on the premises?"

"Of course. I use arsenical soap to preserve the skins, otherwise my displays would disintegrate in a matter of months, eaten by moths and larvae."

Sladdin was quite correct then. "Where do you purchase this arsenical soap?"

She threw him a quizzical glance. "I don't. Charity and I make it." Which would account for a tolerance, as Philpott suggested, but why had she suddenly become ill when they'd returned to Sydney?

"It is a mixture of white arsenic, around two pounds, soap, camphor, powdered chalk, and salts of tartar. I sometimes add some thyme leaves to improve the scent."

"And you never suffer any ill effects?"

"No. None at all. Pa taught me. It must be treated with a great deal of respect. We keep it in labeled tins. It can easily be mistaken for sugar or flour. Perhaps that's how it got into the lozenges."

"And you've made the lozenges?"

"No. I'd never seen them before. Cordelia must have introduced them while I was away. In fact, until Bert picked up that handful I hadn't even noticed them."

"And what about the tonic?"

"We've sold the tonic for as long as I can remember. It's an herbal mixture. A health and strength restorer. From a recipe Ma's mother gave her."

Providing the recipe hadn't changed. That would be up to Philpott to determine with his Marsh test. "Would it be possible to test the contents?"

"Yes, of course, but why?"

And here was the crunch. "Philpott believes that Skeffington died of arsenic poisoning caused by the ingestion of tonic and lozenges from the Curio Shop."

"Oh, how ridiculous." Della shot to her feet, eyes blazing. "What are you suggesting, that we are running some sort of arsenic racket as well as murdering the Darkinjung?" She didn't wait for a response, simply strode off down the path, shoulders tense, head held high. He was suddenly reminded of the first time he'd met her down by the creek.

Cursing the remnants of the musket ball in his thigh, he raced after her. It wasn't until she turned into Hunter Street that he caught up. "Della, wait, please."

She took no notice and came to a halt in front of the Curio Shop. The door was wide open and Charity's strident tones echoed into the street. "Get your hands off me. You can't do that."

Without further thought Stefan barged past her into the shop but stopped abruptly. There was a resounding crash and a display cabinet toppled, depositing Bert onto the floor in a nest of furs and feathers.

"In Gottes Namen . . ."

Philpott stood at the back of the shop facing off an irate Charity, arms akimbo, face flushed, hair falling around her face like some harridan.

"Would someone please explain what's happening?" Della stepped past him and held out a hand to Bert, who pulled himself to his feet.

"This man 'ere says he's a doctor and he wants some of our tonic. I told 'im we ain't got none." Charity adjusted her dress and dragged her hair back from her face.

Swallowing his groan, Stefan glared at Philpott. Why couldn't he have waited as he'd suggested instead of barging in demanding the tonic?

"Charity, give the man a bottle of Ma's Health Tonic, please."

Charity's face flushed. "There ain't none."

"Was the other day." Bert pointed to the shelf above the display he'd ruined. "Was up there. Rows of the stuff."

"Well, we sold out. It's all gone. Mind your own beeswax, boy."

"What's this then?" Bert unclenched his fist to reveal a bottle, neatly labeled.

"Give it to me." Philpott reached out and took it. With a cry Charity sprang forward. He raised it above his head, out of her reach, and turned to the light, squinting at the label.

"I think it would be a good idea if we sat down and talked about this sensibly." Della walked back to the door and pulled the key from the lock, then placed it in the palm of her hand, a frown marring her face. "You found the key?"

Charity's face flushed. "Sladdin found it and brought it over."

Della pocketed the big brass key and sat down at the desk. "Mr. Philpott, I don't think we've met."

"I beg your pardon." Philpott straightened his jacket, ran his fingers through his hair, then sketched some vague bow. "Philpott, surgeon and physician, Miss Atterton."

"Please take a seat."

This was a side of Della Stefan hadn't seen. Gone was the young girl in the leather apron and in her place was a businesswoman in command of the situation. He pulled up another chair and pointed Bert to a spot over near the door.

"Now, Mr. Philpott. How can we help you?" She folded her hands in her lap and tucked her feet neatly to one side.

"As I said, Miss Atterton, I wish to purchase a bottle of the tonic."

"I'm sure we can arrange that. Charity?"

"Told you. We ain't got none. It's all sold."

"Then Mr. Philpott can have the last bottle."

"That's already been paid for."

Philpott cleared his throat. "This is interesting." He pointed to a scrawled name across the label. "It says Skeffington." Stefan didn't miss the frown that flickered across Della's face, nor her sideways glance at the shelf.

"I believe it may be contaminated, contain traces of arsenic. One of my patients recently passed away, and I suspect the tonic might be responsible. If that is the case, the authorities must be informed."

All color leached from Charity's face and she dropped down into the chair. "I'm sick to death of all this malarkey." She buried her face in her arms. "I don't want nothing to do with the authorities. It's nothing to do with me. I ain't been here. Ask Della. It's bloody Cordelia again."

Della didn't move, but the atmosphere in the room shifted, and even Bert kept his mouth closed. A picture of Della standing in the dock flashed before Stefan's eyes. As the owner of the shop she would undoubtedly be held responsible. "Charity, is there something we need to know? Where is Cordelia?"

"No bloody idea. Up to her old tricks again, I'll be bound. It's time she got her comeuppance. I ain't going to see Della 'eld to account."

"Old tricks?" Stefan encouraged.

Charity sucked in a deep breath, then straightened her shoulders.

"Time the truth came out. Della don't know nothing, she was just a babe in arms. Started before she was born, in London. Cordelia had a nice little racket going skimming off the arsenic from the taxidermy shop Della's pa, Thaddeus, owned and selling it. Even had a list of instructions on the amount, make it seem like they died natural-like."

Philpott cleared his throat again and raised his eyebrows.

"It was all fine until they caught up with her. She managed to convince Della's pa she was selling the arsenic to shore up the business because they'd hit hard times. He spoke for her. Said it had all been a mistake. They gave her seven years. He couldn't bear the thought of his little sister being shipped away when she'd been doing it all for him."

Della's face had turned the color of chalk and she sat still, so very still.

"Thought she'd turned over a new leaf, Thaddeus did, but she 'adn't, had she?"

"Ma's tonic?" Della's voice barely rose above a whisper.

"That's right." Charity's nose wrinkled in distaste. "Cordelia knows how to get rid of an unwanted husband or child. She's had enough practice. Then it's a simple matter to inherit."

Chapter 33

Sydney, NSW
1853

Della's blood turned to ice. "What do you mean, Charity?"

"She laced it and sold it here, just the same as in England, with the instructions. Get it right and you can't pick up the symptoms. Makes it look like a wasting disease or the Asiatic cholera."

Della pressed her hands tightly against her waist in a vain attempt to hold herself together, frightened she might crumble. Unable to control the agonizing howl, she leaped to her feet and fled up the stairs. No! It couldn't be. It simply couldn't be true. Charity must have something wrong. Her brain too addled by the rum she loved to drink. Getting her own back, angry with Cordelia for banishing her to the farm.

She stumbled into the big bedroom. Ma and Pa's room. The room where she'd nursed them through the last horrid weeks of their lives. Watched them waste away, wracked by pain, their bodies shriveling to nothing more than bones and stretched yellowed skin while she fed them spoonful after spoonful of Ma's tonic in the vain hope it would offer some respite.

Another scream ripped from her throat.

She'd killed Ma and Pa, as surely as if she'd twisted a knife in their hearts.

"Della, Della, where are you?"

She burrowed under the quilt, blocking out the light, blocking out the world. How could she face Stefan? How could she face anyone? She'd killed her parents.

Her body rolled to the edge of the bed and the familiar scent of ambergris and musk surrounded her.

"Please sit up." Stefan pushed back the quilt and stroked the hair from her face with his warm hand. "I am so sorry. This must have come as a horrible shock. Perhaps Charity has made a mistake."

"She hasn't." She'd known the moment Charity mentioned Ma's tonic, understood what Cordelia had done and why. She'd wanted the shop for herself, the life she'd been denied when she'd been transported to Australia. And Della hadn't seen it, so blinded by her grief she'd given Cordelia free rein. "I'm the one who has made a mistake. A huge, irreparable mistake."

"You couldn't have known what Cordelia was up to. Let Philpott test the tonic and confirm the presence of arsenic. If the test proves positive, he will contact the authorities and they will question Cordelia. I'm sure we can resolve the situation."

Ma and Pa's faces rose in her mind, the realization of Cordelia's duplicity making the pain as raw and real as the day they'd died. The same day, within an hour of each other, bound in death as in life. Another howl ripped out of her. "You don't understand. I gave them the tonic every morning and every night."

How long she lay there she had no idea, but when her weeping settled to hiccuppy sobs, she lifted her head to the gloom of the evening. Stefan still sat on the bed, one hand cupping her head, the other gently rubbing her shoulder. "I thought the tonic would help. Ma sold it for years. She always gave it to me when I was sick."

His eyes, wide with grief, reflected her pain. "Do you know what was in it?"

Of course she did. She'd helped make it more times than she could remember, continued to make it at the farm. "Gentian root, ginger, hops seeped in lemon balm tea sweetened with honey." Her chest ached as she recalled the familiar ingredients. "I can't believe Cordelia would have let me give the tonic to Ma and Pa if she'd known it was contaminated." Unable to stop the tears streaming down her face, she buried her face in the pillow.

Stefan's strong arms wrapped around her and he pulled her close against his warmth. "It's not your fault." His whispered words grazed her cheek as he rocked her backward and forward. "When Cordelia returns . . ."

"I don't understand where the bottles have gone," she murmured against the soft wool of his jacket. "They were in the shop yesterday."

"Are you sure they weren't sold?"

She nodded her head and gave a disgusting sniff. "And I don't understand what Sladdin was doing with the key."

"We'll worry about all of that tomorrow. You need to sleep."

She didn't want to sleep, didn't want Stefan to leave. She wanted to stay safely wrapped in his warm arms, where everything seemed so much simpler. "There's so much that doesn't make sense."

"Let me get you some tea, or maybe some of that lemonade Cordelia . . ." His words dried and so did her throat. Cold fingers tiptoed down her spine.

Stefan pushed her from him, stared deep into her eyes. "Della, where is the lemonade?"

"In the back room, beside the chair at the window, I think. Cordelia made me another batch but I've been so busy I haven't had a moment to myself to drink any."

Before she had time to gather her wits, Stefan was out the door. She heard him push open the door and enter the room, then leave, his irregular tread clattering down the stairs. Pushing back the quilt, she slipped off the bed.

Her legs wobbled as though they were jelly as she made her way down the stairs, one step at a time. Much to her surprise the shop was tidy, the cabinet back where it belonged, against the wall, beneath the empty shelf. But for the missing bottles of tonic the entire debacle might all have been a dreadful dream.

Stefan stood by the window, deep in conversation with Philpott, the lemonade clasped in his hand. Next to them on the table a strange assortment of bottles and tubes balanced on wooden stands; a metallic smell hung in the air.

"There's no doubt about it. Both the lemonade and the tonic contain significant quantities of arsenic. The concentration is too great to be contamination from the items in the shop."

"See, I told you." Charity folded her arms across her ample chest. "Up to 'er old tricks."

"We can't jump to any conclusions. I'm going to have a chat with Mrs. Skeffington." Philpott began to pack up his strange assortment of tubes and bottles. "And in the meantime, the authorities must be informed. They'll want to talk to all of you."

Charity's face turned puce. "I ain't done nothing. I weren't here and neither was Della. Cordelia bundled us off to the farm, got us out of the way."

Philpott wrapped a black cloth around one of the glass tubes, then lifted his head, a quizzical look on his face, as though he'd forgotten who she was. "Miss Atterton, do you know exactly when your aunt left the premises?"

"The day before yesterday. I remember because that's when the key went missing, after we got back from the Skeffingtons'. She was angry because Bert had taken a handful of lozenges and—" She broke off, trying to stifle the rising sob.

"And you've no idea when she'll be back?"

"She said she had business to attend to. I thought she'd be meeting . . . Oh!"

Gus and Dobbin, where were they? "Charity, did Gus and Dobbin return to the Settlers Arms?"

"Nah, just the young Darkinjung fella. Didn't see hide nor hair of 'em. That's why I got the coach. Anyone like a cup of tea, something stronger?"

Della swayed, her head suddenly dizzy. Stefan was at her side in a moment supporting her, such sorrow in his soulful gaze.

"I'm certain Cordelia sanctioned the raids on the camps." She lowered her voice, not wanting Philpott to overhear her words. "If she's responsible for this, the lemonade and the tonic, then what would she care about Dobbin and Gus's hunting trips? I don't understand why. Any of it."

"That's easy."

Della whipped around. She'd almost forgotten Bert was in the room.

"She got your ma and pa out of the picture. Packed you off. Had a nice little sideline going. Then you come back to Sydney and stuff up her plans. And while we're at it, what are you going to do about this?" Bert opened his hand. The peculiar rock sat in the center of his grubby hand catching the light from the lamp.

"Where did you get that?"

Bert flushed to the roots of his carrot hair. "Found it on the floor. It must've been in the cabinet."

"Give it to me." A strange look of intensity flickered in Stefan's eyes as Bert put the stone into his palm. "I hope you have everything you need, Philpott. If I can be of any further assistance let me know."

He held open the door; but for his good manners Della was certain he would have pushed Philpott out into the street.

With his packed bag in one hand and the bottle of lemonade in the other, Philpott made his way to the door. "I'll go immediately and report my findings to the authorities. I have no doubt they'll want to talk to Miss Atterton and Charity, but nothing to worry about. When Cordelia returns—"

"If Cordelia returns."

"I beg your pardon, Charity."

"I said *if* Cordelia returns. Reckon she's upped and gone." With a flounce of her new skirt Charity spun on her heel and disappeared upstairs.

Once Stefan had firmly locked the door behind Philpott, he turned the sign to Closed and delved in his pocket. He brought out a small box and unscrewed the lid.

"What's that?" Bert asked the question, saving Della the need.

"Coddington's invention—a magnifier. I told you I need to examine the stone and see if it conforms to Menge's description." He brought out a white cylindrical-shaped tube with glass at either end. "Two plano-convex lenses with a V-shaped groove ground in the center. Painted black to block light from the edges."

"Don't understand." Bert scratched at his hair, his head tipped to one side and a frown of concentration on his face.

"It magnifies objects, about ten times."

Della couldn't keep silent a moment longer. "And you'll be able to tell whether or not this is an opal?"

"According to the baron's instructions, it should have a transparent or white body tone, then we must look at the background color, a slight tinge of color, like a spark of fire." Stefan gave a satisfied grunt and held it up to the light. "It has a wonderful luster and play of color."

Della peered over his shoulder. "Where do they come from? How are they made?"

"Mother Nature at her best. Unique conditions first. Heavy seasonal rains in parched desert regions where the ground is rich in silica."

"What's sillyka?"

"A colorless chemical compound, one of the most common elements on earth after oxygen."

"Then what makes this so special? You'd think we'd trip over them all over the place. I ain't never seen one."

"Because the conditions must be just right. Rainwater trickles down into the earth and carries silica-rich solutions into the cavities between the rocks. Then hot summers dry the earth, and as the water evaporates the silica stays in place, and over millions of years the opals form. The purity, intensity, and brilliance of color increases the deeper the rock is penetrated."

"Before it just looked like a dirty white pebble."

"You're right. The actual color is a pearl gray; sometimes you see a little pale-red or yellow tint, but with reflected light it presents all the colors of the rainbow."

"So this is the baron's opal?" Della held out her hand and Stefan dropped it into her palm, then handed her the magnifier. Her breath caught as she stared down at the thousands of gorgeous tints playing through the opal, flashing and sparkling as she turned it this way and that.

"Professor Menge's opal, in fact."

"Can't be his, he's dead."

"Sadly that's true, Bert. I am convinced this is the stone Professor Menge found and I believe his assessment is correct. This is the first opal to be found in Australia."

A curl of excitement wound its way through Della's insides. She could see why men and women through the ages had become besotted with opals. It was as though an almighty hand had scooped a palmful of emeralds, rubies, sapphires, diamonds, and pearls and mixed their radiant hues. Fit for a queen. Such a noble stone. "And where there is one there will be more?"

"I think we can safely assume more will be found in Australia. But first I must fulfill my obligations and deliver it to the baron as I promised. It is for him to decide what becomes of it."

Bert nudged against her shoulder, his eyes wide as he squinted through the magnifier. "How much are these things worth?"

"It depends very much on their quality. Fine opals are of great value, second only to diamonds."

"And you know where we can dig some of these up?"

"Yes, Bert. Yes, I think I do." Stefan's lips twitched. "Menge gave the baron that information."

"It's an opal, no doubt about it." Bert took the stone from Della's hand and twisted it this way and that. "Look at that luster and play of colors."

"He's a quick learner, this boy." Della ruffled Bert's hair. "Shall we go opal hunting, Bert?" She meant it as a joke, but as the words left her lips Della knew that it was not only the opal that had captured her heart and her imagination.

"What do you think, Capt'n?"

"It's a tempting proposition, Bert. A tempting proposition, once I've fulfilled my duties. Now, off you go and see what Mr. Philpott needs of you."

"What a brilliant day!" Bert bolted out onto the street, performed an extraordinary leap, and took off down the road.

The door slammed, leaving Della alone with Stefan and a thousand words she couldn't frame.

Stefan lifted his gaze to her face; their eyes locked and the true meaning of his words slashed a path of misery across her heart. To fulfill his duties Stefan would leave, return to Vienna or Tuscany or whatever far-flung destination the baron chose for his aide-de-camp. "When will you be leaving?" Her voice caught and she turned to stare at the passing parade beyond the window, thankful neither Bert nor, heaven forbid, Charity would witness her misery.

He stepped closer. "Not for a week or so. I must seek passage."

"I see." But did she? She could see nothing but an indeterminable future stretching before her. A future without Stefan.

"I'm sorry, Della. I should have been more thoughtful." His eyes, crystal clear as a winter sky at Mogo, held such a look of despondency.

"Don't apologize. I know you must leave. Will you take Bert with you?"

"I hadn't thought of it. Why do you ask?"

"I will need his help." As she spoke the idea came to her fully formed, something Ma and Pa would thoroughly approve of. "A covered wagon, food supplies, new blankets. I'm going to take all the artifacts back to Mogo. Ensure they are returned to their rightful owners. If the governor can't act until Gus and Dobbin are found, I can at least do my part to rectify the situation."

"And the shop?"

Right at this moment she couldn't give a hoot about the shop. Cordelia had tainted her memories, and she'd rather be at Mogo. "I'll leave Charity here. She's quite capable of managing until Cordelia comes back. I think she'd like that."

"And when I return?"

"Will you?" She lifted her hand to still the wishful pitter-pattering of her heart.

His warm hand covered hers and he drew her close, cradling her against his broad chest. "Do you need me to answer that question?"

She wouldn't want to spend her life living on a promise. She would hold the memory of the time they spent together close. Treasure it and let it strengthen her while she waited for his return, because he would return, of that she was certain. Above all else he was a man of honor, a man of his word.

Chapter 34

Sydney, NSW
1919

Fleur rubbed her eyes. Row after row of meaningless numbers jostled for space on the closely packed pages. The figures meant nothing. She hated them. All they did was emphasize the size of the von Richter fortune. A fortune she hadn't known Hugh possessed and one she wasn't entitled to. She drummed her fingers against the desk and contemplated her next move.

Three laps of the room did nothing to ease her frustration. If only Kip would come back and together they could investigate the rest of the boxes in the cellar, maybe find something other than old ledgers that would help her unravel the mystery of Hugh's bequest. But what were the chances of that happening? Kip had vanished and she'd made matters worse by interfering and going to see Mrs. Cassidy, although Vera didn't seem to be the slightest bit concerned when she'd told her what happened, just shrugged her shoulders and buried her head in a jumble of papers and files. There had to be something she'd missed.

One more circuit of the room brought her to the top of the cellar stairs. With the back door wide open and the windows unshuttered, light filled the building, tempting her to brave the claustrophobic darkness and the spiders alone.

She hesitated for only a moment or two longer, then pushed aside the fluttering in her stomach and eased the door open. Dark, musty air billowed up to meet her.

All she had to do was get down the stairs and light Kip's lantern. It was on the tabletop; she'd blown the candle out and left it with the box of matches when Kip carried the ledgers upstairs.

Puffing out a series of short breaths, she took the steps to the cellar one at a time, hands outstretched to ward off the nasty inhabitants. What she wouldn't give for Kip's solid presence and no-nonsense approach.

When she reached the bottom step, she paused and wiped her clammy palms against her skirt while she picked out the shadowy outline of the lantern only a few paces ahead.

A gust of wind billowed, whipped around her ankles. The door slammed closed, stranding her in an all-encompassing blackness.

She choked back the scream in her throat. The lantern. She had to find the lantern, otherwise she'd never be able to wrestle the rusty door open.

One pace, then another, and another until her hands met the timber of the tabletop. Snaking her fingers forward she groped for the matches. Where was Kip? She'd take him in any mood, good or bad. She didn't care. She just needed his comforting presence.

A crack and a snatch of sulfur. She reached for the lantern, held the match to the wick. The seconds stretched and the flame singed her fingertips before a faint glimmer flickered and steadied. She lifted the lantern, scanning the walls, imagining the hairy huntsmen, redbacks, and funnel-webs, their beady eyes watching and waiting, just beyond the lantern's glow.

It wasn't until she'd reached the top of the stairs and shouldered the door open that her breathing settled and her heartbeat returned to normal. Refusing to give in and go back to the ledgers, she propped the door wide and edged back down the stairs.

Beyond the table, in the wavering pool of candlelight, the line of tea chests formed a solid head-height wall, the roof above dripping with lacy cobwebs. Unable to control her trembling, she balanced the lantern to one side, clamped her teeth, and tugged at the top tea chest. She could do it. She had to. She couldn't spend her life waiting for someone to come and help.

One tremendous heave and the chest toppled into her arms, releasing the solid, pungent odor she'd come to associate with the shop, full of the cloying sweetness of decay. Staggering back, she dumped the tea chest on the tabletop and shone the lantern into the cavity.

A hidey-hole, not much wider than her shoulders, ran the length of the building. It made no sense. Why block off the extra space? She shoved the lower tea chest aside, dropped to her hands and knees, and crawled forward, lantern in hand.

A wooden box, about half the size of one of the tea chests, neatly stenciled with the words *Coffee—Kangaroo Point*, sat pushed against the wall. But for the name it might have come straight from Mrs. Black's storeroom. Grasping the rope handles she tugged it forward. It couldn't be coffee; it weighed more than the tea chest she'd lifted. She squatted on her haunches and ran her fingers around the lid, her nails snatching at the soft timber. It opened with little complaint, releasing a putrid stench.

Hundreds of pieces of disintegrating green paper and neatly packed brown bottles filled the box.

Pulling one out, she held it up to the beam of lantern light and peered at the label.

TONIC

THE GREAT HEALTH AND STRENGTH RESTORER.

CURES ALL MANNER OF AILMENTS

BY RESTORING THE BLOOD.

ARE YOU WEARY OF BRAIN AND BODY?

RELY ON ATTERTON'S TONIC. AVAILABLE ONLY FROM THE CURIO SHOP OF WONDERS.

She wrenched a cork free and sniffed. The strange metallic odor filled her nostrils, clogging her mouth, making her gag. Blowing out her cheeks she corked the bottle and rocked back on her heels. Taxidermied specimens, fashionable furs and feathers, opals, and now medicinal tonics. What else had the Curio Shop offered? By waving the lantern from side to side, Fleur began to make sense of the narrow cavity; not much farther and she would reach the front wall of the house.

The knees of her stockings snagged and small stones bit into her hand as she crawled forward until the rough surface of the sandstone blocks confirmed she'd reached the farthest wall. Careful to guard the flame of the candle, she sat up, flinching as her head brushed the sloped roof.

The musty odor of the undisturbed air coated her nostrils and she gulped down a short breath before brushing aside a film of cobwebs. A large rectangular trunk with a curved lid filled the shadowed corner.

Easing onto her knees, she ran her fingers along the edge. A small bolt sunk into the wood surrounded by a flat circular pull held the lid shut. She slipped her fingers around the metal and tugged.

The lid sprang open.

Air, thick and heavy, billowed out. Bile rose in her throat, the acid making her gag. With her mouth covered against the fetid stink, she lifted the lantern high and peered inside.

An obscene splash of emerald green.

She leaned closer, a cold sensation seeping from under her breastbone. A dusty cloak cradled the remains of a body. Copper-colored hair spread from beneath the hood. Gnarled hands lay crossed and bound with a red satin ribbon tied with the utmost care. Patches of yellow mold spotted the green material, but the woman's facial features were still discernible. High forehead, sharp cheekbones, an arrogant nose. All remarkably preserved.

Unable to control the sense of panicked suffocation, she slammed the lid closed and fled, the sound of her pulse hammering in her ears.

When she reached the top of the stairs she couldn't contain the scream building in her chest. It ripped from her, shattering the stillness of the Curio Shop. She brought her hand up to her face, found it damp with tears.

The stench lingered at the back of her throat, making her gag.

Her stomach heaved.

Gasping to steady her breathing, time skewed. She stood rooted to the spot. Was her mind playing tricks? Was it some crazy dream brought about by the confusion swirling in her head, her shattered dreams, her longing for Hugh?

A knock sounded and the front door opened, bringing a flood of sunshine, but she couldn't move.

Dear God, let it be Kip.

A discreet cough and the tap of a stick on the timber floor pierced her stupor and she turned.

"I hope I'm not intruding."

In front of her stood the old man from Mogo Creek, his face flushed, holding out a large white handkerchief.

She took it and scrubbed at her face. "Yes. No. Well, maybe." For goodness' sake, what was she supposed to say? Admit to the fact that she'd found a disintegrating corpse in the cellar? She slammed her lips closed.

"Why don't you sit down and take a minute?" He nodded to the old leather sofa against the wall and lowered himself into the swivel chair, then propped his walking stick against the desk. With a sense of familiarity, his fingers smoothed the timber on the armrests and he peered down at the ledgers.

She wasn't sure what to do. Pull them away and slam them closed? She slumped onto the sofa. He took matters into his own hands and, with a look of regret, slowly closed them. "It was a good business while it lasted. Made us all a tidy sum."

Us? "Who are you? I didn't ask at Mogo."

"No, you didn't, and I didn't tell you. Have you found it yet?"

Heavens above! Each and every one of the hairs at the base of her skull prickled. Did he know what was in the cellar?

"I don't know what you're talking about. Perhaps you should start by telling me your name." Her words came out sounding as though she was in control. She wasn't sure how she managed it, because the inside of her head was a mixture of soggy cotton wool, scraps of green velvet, and strange fizzing flashes.

"The name's Burless. Just call me Bert."

"Kip's grandfather?"

"Not that he or my daughter are overkeen on publicizing the association."

The ledgers! She jumped to her feet and opened the top one. She blinked twice to bring the names into focus, confirm she wasn't mistaken. *1914 Burless, seven thousand pounds.* "This Burless?" She stabbed at the first column.

"That'd be the one."

Fleur picked up one of the earlier ledgers, 1885. "And this one?"

"Yep."

"So you do know Hugh's family."

He lifted his head and stared into her eyes. A cold finger trickled down her spine and snatched her breath away. More to the point, he might know who was downstairs in the trunk.

"Better than I knew meself."

"And the shop?" She shuddered, her eyes drifting to the cellar stairs.

His eyebrows almost met as he peered at her. "You all right, love?"

She licked her dry lips, tried for a yes, but couldn't force out the word.

"Your face is bone white."

Fleur pushed the image of the withered fingers to the back of her mind. She didn't know why or how, but the kindly look on his face broke her resolve. "I've found something. Someone in the cellar." Who else could she turn to? Not Kip, he'd vanished. Certainly not Vera. She'd throw her hands up in horror and give that nasty little screech, then call the police. She wasn't ready to do that yet.

"You better show me."

Every muscle in her body told her not to step down into the cellar again, but she led the way, arms wrapped tightly around her body, steeling herself for the sight and the stench of the woman in the green dress.

Chapter 35

Sydney, NSW
1919

Fleur hadn't expected to sleep, but she drank the glass of brandy Sladdin had thrust into her shaking hand and crawled to her room. She'd drifted into an empty black space where there were no dreams, no memories, and no feelings. And now it was morning and she had to face Bert, the police, and all that the entire debacle entailed.

By the time she'd dressed and made her way downstairs, Bert was settled in the dining room surrounded by a silver coffee service and the biggest plate of food she'd ever seen, something that involved black bread, hard cheese, and strange sausage. It didn't look, or smell, very appetizing. "Good morning, Bert."

He swallowed his mouthful, half rose, and poured her a cup of strong black coffee.

She turned and looked over her shoulder for the waitress. "I'd rather have tea if you don't mind."

"Try the coffee. *Wurst* and *Käse*—best breakfast in the world. Want some?"

She slid the cup closer and took a sip. "Bert? Are you going to tell me?"

He shot her a sudden bright-eyed glance, so like Kip it snatched her breath away.

"What's to tell?"

"The woman in the trunk. You know who she is, don't you?"

"Wait and see what the police say. Can't be sure."

"Yes, you can. And you know how she got there. Why won't you tell me?"

"Better let the past rest." He huffed out a sigh and concentrated on the cheese, cutting it into the finest slices.

"I need to know, and you're the only one who can tell me. How can I unravel the tangle of Hugh's inheritance if I don't know where it came from?"

"It all came from Noble Opals. The biggest opal business in the world at the time. Went looking in South Australia first, then Queensland, but it wasn't until we found the White Cliffs fields in New South Wales that things took off proper. Sold the stuff all over the world. Never thought I'd find myself in London, Paris, and New York. Whole thing went down the drain once the war broke out though."

"But what's all this got to do with the woman in the trunk?"

"Ah. That depends on whether you believe in fairy stories."

"Fairy stories?" Fleur took a sip of the strong black coffee. It did nothing to cure the swirling confusion in her mind. "Who is she?"

"Her name's Cordelia, Cordelia Atterton."

The owner of the Curio Shop. Fleur took a bigger sip of coffee and her heart began to hammer.

"First trip the capt'n and me took, he told me about this opal. He'd been asked to collect it."

"Just a minute. Stop. Who is this captain?"

Bert rolled his eyes and rested his chin in his hand. "Stefan. Captain Stefan von Richter. Hugh's grandfather."

Hugh's grandfather! She'd found a Della von Richter in the ledgers, and Hugh's brothers, and someone called Otto, but no Stefan.

"He told me people believed opals were unlucky. Some story about a princess who strayed from the straight and narrow and paid the price. Went up in a puff of smoke. I always thought there was some truth in it. Every time we thought we'd tracked down Menge's opal, the owner had met an untimely death and it had passed to someone else."

"Cordelia owned the opal?"

"For a while, she did. Then she disappeared."

"But she didn't disappear. Someone must have murdered her. She wouldn't lock herself in a trunk and tie her hands with a red ribbon." The wretched hairs on the back of her neck began to prickle again. "Was it the captain?"

Bert gave a rough bark of laughter, then caught his breath.

She thumped him on the back and waited impatiently for his breathing to settle. "You know what happened to her, don't you?"

"I don't *know*, but I can make an educated guess." He gave another splutter. "Never thought I'd use that word in a sentence talking about meself. I didn't have an education. Not one you'd call legitimate. The capt'n gave me an education. Great bloke. A true gentleman. He took a punt on a dirty little guttersnipe. Without him I wouldn't be where I am now."

"I still don't understand." A shudder shook her. "If it wasn't the captain, then who was it?" She studied his weathered face. "Who killed Cordelia?"

"Doubt we'd ever prove it. Better to let sleeping dogs dream." He stretched back in the seat and rummaged in his jacket pocket. "But this as good as tells me who it was." He pulled out a long red ribbon and laid it on the table with a degree of reverence.

Her stomach gave a lurch, threatening to bring the coffee back. "That's the ribbon that was tied around Cordelia's hands. What will the police say? I told them no one had touched the body."

"What the cops don't know won't worry them. Nothing they can do about it now. Let her sleep, I reckon."

She reached out and took the slippery satin ribbon and ran it through her fingers. "Who does it belong to?"

"Charity. After Cordelia vanished, Charity ran the Curio Shop for Cordelia's niece, Della, who owned the place, though it didn't last long. She upped and married, and before long the shop was boarded up."

"And you think this woman, Charity, killed Cordelia? Why would she do that?"

"No thinking about it. I know she did. It all makes sense now."

Not to Fleur it didn't.

"Tell me about her."

"Not much to tell really. She and Cordelia knew each other from London, came out here on the same transport."

"They were convicts?"

"The pair of them. See, Cordelia had everything Charity wanted. *Coveted* is the word, I reckon."

"How can you be sure the ribbon belongs to her? Anyone could have tied Cordelia's hands with a ribbon."

"Not this one. You see here? The little row of pearls sewn onto the ends?"

She peered at the hemline on the ribbon. Tiny pearls used to stop the fraying.

"Me memory's not too hot now, except for the past. I can remember that day clear as the sound of Della's laughter. We'd had a run-in with a couple of no 'opers. The capt'n had taken a fall and the rain was bucketing down. Ended up sleeping in a cave. When the sun came up we took off again, came across the farm."

"*The* farm? At Mogo Creek?"

"Want to hear this or not?" Bert scowled across the table at her. "I was so hungry I thought me throat had been cut. Charity flounced along the veranda with this plate of piping hot bread and golden-yellow butter. Think I would've been interested in the food, but I couldn't take me eyes off the long braid of her hair, black as night and shiny as a raven's wing, straight as a die down her spine, the ribbon threaded through her hair, these pearls dancing in the sunlight. Bloody near fell flat on me face." His cheeks colored a little and he gazed past her into the distance. "A man never forgets the first time his body stirs. The first awakening."

Fleur let the silence lie for a while. She didn't know what to say.

He rolled up the ribbon and stuffed it back in his top pocket and patted it.

"You loved her?"

"No. Lust, not love. The memory's just an old man's foolishness."

"What happened to her?"

"She married. She'd only had eyes for—Sladdin. Though I can't understand why. Nasty little lickspittle he was. Had Cordelia and Charity wrapped around his bony finger."

"Mr. Sladdin? That's the name of the clerk here at the hotel."

"One and the same."

He'd told her his grandfather and his father had both been clerks at the hotel and it was a family tradition. "His father?"

"Nope, grandfather."

"So he and Charity . . ." She couldn't bring herself to say *murdered*. "Put Cordelia in the trunk?"

"Nah. I don't reckon Sladdin had anything to do with it. He was Cordelia's fancy man. Those were the very words Charity used. He wouldn't have done it. Had too much to lose. What Charity didn't let on was that she was as jealous as all get-out. Wanted Sladdin for herself, always had."

"I think you should tell the police."

"Why?" He lifted his shoulders. "What good is it going to do?

Leave it be, I say. Can't make a man pay for the sins of his grandparents. Whole country would grind to a halt. More to the point, what are you going to do?"

"Me?" She knew she'd have to answer this question eventually. All the searching and still she didn't know what to do about Hugh's inheritance. All she'd found was a maze of mystery and intrigue. "I think you deserve Hugh's legacy more than I do. You've been with the family from the very beginning."

"No good to me, love. I ain't going to be around much longer."

"What about your daughter? What about Kip?"

"They'll be taken care of. Always have been, though they didn't know it. I didn't spend me time hanging around the opal business letting the daisies grow. Hugh wanted you to inherit. He wouldn't have notified Lyttleton of your marriage otherwise."

"That first time we met, at Mogo . . ."

"Wondered if you'd get around to that."

"You asked me if I had something for you. You said 'a family heirloom.'"

"I did."

"What is it?"

"You'll know when you find it. You have to hand it over, of your own free will and all that."

"I really don't know what you're talking about. There are the investments, deeds to the shop and the property at Mogo, properties on the Continent, at Broken Hill and Wilcannia . . ." Her mind still spiraled out of control every time she thought about it.

"Della always loved the place at Wilcannia, beautiful house on the river. That's where the boys were born. Hugh and his brothers."

More money than she could spend in a lifetime. And Bert had already said it wasn't money he was after. "I have Hugh's personal belongings. I couldn't bring myself to open them until I had more answers." Maybe what Bert wanted was there. "I asked Mr. Sladdin to put everything in the strong box." Perhaps the time had come. "Bert, will you stay while I open them?"

"Nope. That's your business. Yours and Hugh's. Besides, someone's got to have a word with the police. They want to know about the arsenic. Reckon it's preserved the body. I'll meet you by the steps in Macquarie Street, the ones that run down to the quay, say four o'clock?" With little more than a nod, he crossed the dining room and disappeared through the doors into the foyer.

Fleur poured herself another cup of coffee, savoring the aroma. She'd turned her nose up at it when Hugh had ordered it from the coffee stands along the Embankment. Said she'd take tea any day. Now she wasn't so sure. It seemed to clear her head, make it easier to face the inevitable. She left the table and went in search of Mr. Sladdin.

As always he stood waiting, as though in some telepathic way he knew when he'd be needed. Bred into him, no doubt, through generations of service. She could see nothing in his face to indicate the police had questioned him. Why would they? Unless Bert changed his mind and told them about Charity, and she doubted that. "Good morning, Mr. Sladdin. I was wondering if I could have my items from the strongbox."

"Indeed, indeed." He bustled into the office behind the desk.

When he reappeared, he handed the small package over with a degree of hesitancy. As she studied his face, she couldn't get over the thought that his grandmother might have had a hand in Cordelia's death.

"Thank you, Mr. Sladdin." She restrained herself from snatching the package, just held out her hand. With a long-drawn-out sigh, he relinquished it. Throwing him a brief smile, she made her way up the stairs trying to convince herself it was the two cups of black coffee that had caused her pounding heartbeat and not the prospect of finally confirming Hugh's death.

Once she'd sat down on the bed she made a table with her knees and ran her hands over the package. It felt flexible beneath her fingers so she carefully unfolded the brown paper. A small box sat balanced on the top of a pocketbook.

She gave the box a quick shake. It rattled in response; doubtless it would be his identity tag or maybe the commendation Vera had mentioned. She put it to one side and turned to the pocketbook.

The stained and dusty leather cover carried no name. She held it to her nose and inhaled, hoping against hope there'd be some trace of Hugh. Nothing, just worn leather and maybe boot polish. Her fingers shook as she opened the cover.

Pressed between the first page and the flyleaf was a small disc threaded onto a frayed piece of string and a photograph. She turned the disc over.

Richards, Hugh. Corporal 1st Australian Tunneling Company AIF 5158.

His identity disc. The final, irrefutable proof.

Through her tears, Hugh's face stared up at her from the photograph tucked inside the pocketbook, his arm wrapped snugly around her shoulders.

Her heart clenched. No matter what name he chose, he hadn't changed. Hugh, as she remembered him. Laughing eyes and that big broad smile, while she had the most ridiculous grin on her face, her head tucked into his shoulder, just where it fitted so perfectly.

Searching his face for some sign of duplicity, she came up wanting. She'd never met a more honest person.

The sound of his laugh came to her and goose bumps stippled her skin, her body recalling the feel of his arms around her, the warmth of his breath on her cheek, and his gentle drawl, the lilt of his voice.

We'll be together. I promise. It's my Armistice Promise.

How long she sat with Hugh's pocketbook resting in her lap, her hand loosely covering it as though she might find some heartbeat beneath the ink-stained cover, she had no idea. When she snapped her eyes open, the day had turned cloudy.

She put aside the photograph and the disc and turned the closely packed pages one by one. The date, the fine writing with looping tails to the letters bounding across the page. How could handwriting contain the essence of the man?

She flicked through, not reading, just absorbing his spirit from the paper, the paper he'd touched, the place his arm may have rested.

When she reached the final page she was ready.

November 3, 1918
France

I love you, Fleur. You are my heart and soul, my past and my future. You are with me always. You will have blue skies and freedom—everything I wished for us. Live for me, my love.

Live and enjoy everything I dreamed would be—but for a random piece of misfortune. If I could change anything it would be to hold you in my arms once more.

Find Bert Burless—he will show you the way. Don't be tempted, as we all have, to outrun the inevitable or think you can win. You can't.

I pray to God you take my words and act upon them and then, and only then, will my promise be realized. You are the one to heal the past. There is not a bone of greed in your body.

Farewell, my love.

She fanned the rest of the pages, all blank—no, not all.

On the final page, at the very back of the book, there was a list.

Frowning, she moved closer to the window. The ink on the first entries had faded, the later still bold and bright, added over time.

Johann Menge 1852
Primrose Bishop 1852
Richard Skeffington 1853
Baron von Hügel 1870
Stefan von Richter 1876
Otto von Richter 1898
Carl von Richter 1916
Clemens von Richter 1917
Hugo von Richter 1918

Hugo von Richter—Hugh Richards. Her Hugh. How had he known he would die?

Chapter 36

Sydney, NSW
1919

A sharp rap on the door made Fleur lift her head. Beyond the window the cloud cover made it hard to know how much time had passed. She closed Hugh's pocketbook with a sigh and gave the small leather box a rattle, then eased off the lid. A heavy gold chain lay on a faded bed of satin. She eased it from the box. The swivel fob twisted and the stone flared, myriad colors blazing as the light angled in.

Find Bert Burless—he will show you the way. Don't be tempted, as we all have, to outrun the inevitable or think you can win.

She had to talk to Bert. Ask him to explain.

With one last look at Hugh's smiling eyes and lopsided grin, she pushed the fob and chain back into the box, shoved it deep in her pocket, grabbed Hugh's pocketbook, and rammed her hat on her head.

Hugh was asking her to complete some unfinished business. "I'm coming."

By the time she'd opened the door no one was there. She peered over the banister, down into the hallway, and caught sight of Kip's cloth cap rounding the bottom of the stairs. "Kip, wait. Please. I want to talk to you." She clattered down the stairs and found him leaning against Mr. Sladdin's desk, his face pale and dark circles scoring the skin beneath his eyes. "I'm so pleased you're here." She beamed up at him, making no comment about his disheveled state.

Slipping her hand into the crook of his arm, she led him through the door. Much to her surprise he didn't shake her off, just walked along scuffing at the stones on the pavement, head down and hands in his pockets.

What did she have to lose? She couldn't make him any angrier. "Why didn't you say anything when you saw Bert's name in the ledger? Why did you storm off?"

"Not my business."

"What do you mean it's not your business? He's your grandfather." How she wished she had a family. He had a mother and a grandfather, more than she had, and he didn't seem to want to have anything to do with them.

"Why did you have to interfere, stir up the past? It's too late to fix anything."

What was he talking about? Bert or her gruesome discovery in the cellar? "Did Vera tell you about the trunk?"

"I was there when the cops called round to question her." He pushed his hands farther down into his pockets and hunched his shoulders.

"I'm sorry, Kip, I would have told you myself, but I didn't know where to find you."

"You didn't need to go and see my mother behind my back either."

A guilty flush blossomed on her cheeks. She had no idea what had possessed her. "Because I was worried about you."

A scowl darkened Kip's face. "I don't want anything more to do with the blasted Curio Shop. All it's done is stir up problems."

"It's over. They came and took the trunk, said they may have more questions later." She had questions too, and there was only one person who could answer them. "I'm going to meet your grandfather. Will you come with me?"

Taking Kip's grunt as some form of agreement, she turned into Macquarie Street and headed toward the tram terminal. "I told him

I'd meet him at the top of the steps at the quay, the ones leading down from Macquarie Street. He says that's where he first met the captain so it's a suitable place."

Kip shrugged. "Don't know much about him and his mates."

"Didn't he tell you stories when you were little? I thought that was the kind of thing grandfathers did." Not that she had any idea. She hadn't known her grandparents on either side; they were long gone before she was born. Bert was more than alive.

"Mum hates him. Says he's a toffee-nosed old fool who gave himself airs and graces. Sent her off to some posh school. She loathed it so much she ran away. Met me dad and next thing she knew she'd had two kids and a husband who liked the 'orses. We never knew where the next meal was coming from."

It was probably the longest sentence Kip had ever uttered. She didn't want to stop him or interrupt. His description didn't sound like the Bert she'd come to know. And besides, Kip's mother said she owned the house in Argyle Street—true, it wasn't much compared to Hugh's estate, but the money for that must have come from somewhere.

As if he could read her thoughts, Kip turned to her. "Once Dad shot through, things got better. Mum found out she owned the house. She rented out the top and got herself a job at the bakery. Leastways we always had something to eat."

"She must have loved your grandfather, otherwise she wouldn't have named you after him."

He shot her a sideways glance. "How do you know that? Don't tell me—Mum. Let's get this over and done with."

True to his word, Bert was at the top of the steps, leaning against the sandstone base that supported the streetlamp. A mixture of emotions flickered across his face when he saw Kip, but neither of them spoke so Fleur kept her mouth closed.

"Used to climb up there. Can't do it anymore, but let me tell you it's the best place to keep an eye on things. Bit of extra height gives a man an advantage." He attempted to straighten up, leaning heavily on his walking stick. "Come on. Follow me." He took off at a fair gallop toward the tram station. "Always liked this place. Macquarie's Fort, it used to be. The capt'n reckoned it looked like a kid's cardboard castle. I thought it had a touch of style until I saw some of those castles in Bavaria."

They rounded the corner and reached a sandstone wall at the edge of the harbor where the path to the Botanic Gardens led up the hill. There were steps and a bench built into the rock.

Standing on the point with the fresh wind blowing across the harbor made Fleur shiver. She pulled the package out of her pocket. The wind whipped at the brown paper and blew it out across the water. She clamped her hand tight around Hugh's pocketbook. She couldn't lose it now. His words were waiting for her. She wanted to read the rest.

"You loved him." Bert's statement, not question, broke her reverie and she slipped the book into the safety of her pocket.

"Yes, yes, I did." She didn't falter, not as she'd done in the past, not when she'd hidden behind Mr. Waterstone and Vera Lyttleton, blaming them, and Hugh, for her own misery. She straightened her shoulders, firming her resolve.

"Then what does it matter what his name was, where his family came from? Hugh was Australian born and bred, and he'd have knocked anyone who suggested otherwise from here to kingdom come. He was Australian through and through."

"Then why change his name? Why pretend to be someone he wasn't?"

"Pull yourself together, girl. Because it was the only way he could fight for the country he loved, Australia. The alternative was an internment camp."

Heat rose to her face. She'd behaved like a fool. All that mattered was his heart. He'd fought for his dreams and his beliefs, for their future. There was, however, one thing she didn't understand. "Why did Hugh think he was going to die?"

"What makes you think that?"

She foraged in her pocket and brought out Hugh's pocketbook and flicked to the back page. "Because of this." She ran her finger down the list of names until she reached Hugh's name and the date . . . 1918.

"Ah!" Bert squinted at the list. "Always thought he'd worked it out."

"Are you saying Hugh really did know he would die?" It was ridiculous.

"Took him a while." Bert shuffled along the stone bench. He didn't acknowledge Kip when he sat next to him, their thighs touching, but she caught the smile ghost across his face. "This here—the professor." He pointed to the name at the top of the list. "He found the opal. Wasn't sure at that stage what it was so told the baron—"

"The baron?"

"Baron von Hügel, top bloke." He stabbed at the fourth name on the list. "Pulled the capt'n up by his bootstraps, made a man of him. Always thought that was why he gave me a go. Paying his debts like."

"Tell me more about Stefan von Richter? His name is on the list too."

"Will you give a man a chance?"

Kip smothered a laugh as Fleur cupped her fingers across her lips and nodded her head.

"Right. Where was I?"

"The professor told the baron." Kip leaned across his grandfather and pointed to the list of names.

"And the baron told him to send it to a mate of his, Thomas Bishop, which he did just before he died."

"That was lucky."

"Oi!" Bert glared at her. "Not so lucky for poor old Primrose. See, Bishop thought the light shone out of his wife's . . ." He cleared his throat. "Beggin' your pardon. Bishop let his wife have it and she died. He blamed Menge's opal, used it to pay off some debts to a man named Skeffington to get rid of it. Skeffington's wife used it to buy some tonic to kill her husband."

"From the Curio Shop, the bottles in the coffee box?"

"They're the ones. She used Menge's opal to pay Cordelia. Couldn't figure that one out. We thought she'd done a runner, but looks like she hadn't."

It all seemed a bit far-fetched. "Are you saying that whoever owned Menge's opal died?"

"That's what I reckon."

A slight breeze blew in across the water, stirring Fleur's hair and bringing the touch of Hugh's fingers on her cheek.

Find Bert Burless—he will show you the way.

She shrugged away a shiver. It couldn't be true. Omens like that were for the weak-minded, yet there was nothing weak about this craggy old man who sat beside her, his eyes almost black in their intensity.

"Then how did this baron manage to stay alive until 1870?"

"Interesting chap. He became a swanky ambassador in Tuscany and then in Brussels. After the capt'n took Menge's opal to Europe and had it assessed, it stayed in Vienna. Then the capt'n resigned his commission and just as he promised came back for Della. That's when the fun started. Best years of me life, they were. Reckon we covered more miles than any man had a right to. Right across South Australia, in terrible heat, then through New South Wales, up to Queensland."

"What happened to Della?"

"She came too. Weren't no way she was going to be left behind.

Young Otto, he was born in Queensland, and not long after that we found the biggest and the best opal anyone had ever seen. Sparkled and danced it did in the sunlight, every color known to man."

"This Otto?" She pointed to the list of names in Hugh's journal.

"That's the one. Della and Stefan's son, Hugh's father. We packed the traveling in after he was born. Took what we had to London. To the Grand Exhibition." Bert pulled out his big white handkerchief, gave a derogatory snort. "Half of them couldn't believe their eyes, thought it was a con job, quality was too good. No one had seen anything like our Australian opals before, but we found a jeweler in Hatton Gardens prepared to give it a go. When we got to London I finally got to see those ravens."

"Ravens?" For a horrible moment, the possibility that Bert was spinning some fairy tale hovered. She could imagine him rocking back and slapping his thighs, telling her it was all a load of rubbish and she'd been well and truly hoodwinked.

"At the Tower. Always been fascinated. Mate told me about them. Then there was one perched on the top of the key to the Curio Shop. Seemed like fate."

"You met the baron in London . . . ," Fleur prompted. She had to keep Bert on track, could see him getting lost in his memories.

"Nah. The baron had decided to leave Brussels and go back to Vienna. He'd had Menge's opal set, wore it all the time. He didn't make it to Vienna, died on the way to Brussels. Not good for Stefan."

"He must have been like a father to him."

"True. But that's not the point. He left Stefan Menge's opal."

"And six years later Stefan was dead." It was all beginning to make sense—if you believed in fairy tales. "How did Stefan die?"

"Alfred Nobel's blasted powder."

"Dynamite?" Kip leaned forward, his eyes wide as he listened to his grandfather's story.

"Thought it would be a great way to get at the opals. Otto inherited Menge's opal when he was twenty-one. Managed to last a few years, long enough to sire the three boys."

"Hugh and his brothers."

"Yep. Della brought them up in Wilcannia in the house by the river after their mother died. She ran the opal business from there. I kept the records. Became a bit of a habit. Didn't know what to do with the ledgers after Della went so I lodged them at the shop."

"How did you get in? The place was boarded up."

Bert tapped the side of his nose. "Coal box, round the back. Leads into the basement. Surprised you didn't find it."

Fleur swallowed her groan. How had she missed it? "Tell me about Hugh and his brothers."

"Clem and Carl were born with opal in their blood, I reckon. All they wanted was to mine. They worked at White Cliffs until the war broke out. Hugh, he was different. Hated it. Went to school in Sydney and every holiday I'd take him to Mogo. Even as a little boy all he wanted to do was run the farm. Didn't want anything changed."

The sun broke through the clouds, warming her face.

Will you come with me? Marry me and be a farmer's wife?

All those words of love. All those promises for the future cut short. Hugh hadn't believed he would die. They'd made plans and promises, dreamed of their future.

"Never understood how he ended up a tunneler. He hated being underground. Question is—are you going to take the inheritance?"

"If I could think of something worthwhile to do with it I would. I can't take it just for myself."

"Good lad, that Hugh. Knew what he was doing when he chose you."

You are the one to heal the past.

Bert stretched out his hand. "There's something you have to give me first."

What was he talking about? She wouldn't part with Hugh's pocketbook, not now, not ever. "What?"

"That there box. The little one you have tucked in your pocket."

"How do you know?" Fleur delved into her pocket and dropped the box into his wrinkled palm as the sun bathed the water in a golden glow.

Bert lifted the lid slowly, his hand shaking, and pulled out the thick watch chain. He dangled it in front of his eyes, the sunlight catching the flashes of color in the gemstone embedded in the fob. The look of anger on his face stopped her breath.

He lifted his arm and flicked his wrist.

The fob and chain arced through the air, out over the water, hesitated for a moment, then dived below the surface with barely a ripple.

It was all Fleur could do to stop herself jumping in after it. She turned on Bert. "What did you do that for? You've no right—"

"For you, for Kip, for me daughter, for anyone who comes after. Bad luck, that thing is. Only thing the capt'n and I disagreed about. Should've buried it with the baron. There's a long line of people whose lives were cut short. Capt'n thought he could outrun it. He was wrong." He brushed his hands together. "Right, that's that sorted. I tried to tell 'em, but they wouldn't listen. Family heirloom, family curse. Rubbish. Good riddance."

Epilogue

Sydney, NSW
January 1920

Fleur stepped inside the Curio Shop into a shaft of sunlight and inhaled the intoxicating scent of the future.

She had every intention of leaving the baron's suite at the hotel and moving in. Vera thought she was insane, but the place held no fear for her anymore. They'd taken Cordelia away and she'd been buried alongside her brother, Thaddeus Atterton, and his wife.

Bert was the first to arrive, in a dark suit and a pin-striped waistcoat, his boots shining. "All sorted then?"

"I've just got one more question to ask." Fleur moved to the corner of the room and placed her hand on the head of the white kangaroo.

His lips twitched. "Just one? I reckon there'll be more."

Maybe there would be, but the kangaroo had fascinated her since she and Kip first found it. "Do you know anything about this fellow?"

"That ain't no fella. She's Tidda."

She didn't take the bait; she'd learned Bert's ways. She waited while he came and stood next to her.

"Della's pet she was, out at Mogo. Near broke her heart when we found her. An albino kangaroo would be worth a bit to hunters, but she didn't have a mark on her. I wanted to bury her, but Della wouldn't have hear of it. Locked herself up in the workshop with those tools of hers and didn't come out until the job was done. We brought Tidda back here to keep an eye on the shop." He gave the kangaroo a pat, then settled himself on the sofa.

So many stories and so much history. The Curio Shop, with its sparkling clean windows and the furniture from the cellar, felt like the home she'd never truly had.

Moments later Kip and the Lyttletons arrived, Michael carrying a large buff-colored folder and Vera a vase of roses that she placed on the desk.

Thanks to Hugh's legacy, his promise, so many people would benefit. Death had cast its shadow over this family—more than that, over all the owners of the opal. Bert was right. It had to go. But she wouldn't be saying goodbye to Hugh. His memory would be with her forever. He'd given her more than his love. He'd given her, and so many people, a future.

"Are you ready, Fleur?" Michael Lyttleton stood behind the desk, his hands resting on the back of the chair. "Come and sit here. It seems appropriate."

With her heart thumping, in fact her whole body vibrating, Fleur settled at the desk and reached out her shaking hand for the fountain pen.

"Just sign here." Michael bent over and flicked through a few more pages. "And initial here and here, and one more signature at the end. Are you sure you're certain?"

"Yes. I am. Bert, Kip. Are you sure you want to do this?"

"Bloody sure. Can't think of a better use for Hugh's money."

Kip wrinkled his nose. His relationship with Bert was still new and fresh, but since his mother had admitted her part in their estrangement he had gradually come to appreciate Bert. It made her laugh because they were so alike as to be ridiculous. "There'll be a lot of families who'll thank you for this. Especially after the mess that influenza's caused. Mum's got it all under control. Soon as we can, we'll get the work done on the warehouse."

Kip had changed so much. Gone were the sullen scowls and the irrational sparks of anger now that he had meaning in his life. The Noble Opal Trust would provide support for returned soldiers and war widows and fill the gaping great hole the government seemed unable to plug, and it was the perfect solution to her long-held belief that others were more entitled to Hugh's family fortune.

It was only then, with the people she'd come to know and love grouped around, she understood Hugh's promise. He had brought her home.

In the slash of sunlight Bert's mouth curved in a satisfied smile.

She signed the paperwork with a flourish.

Fleur von Richter

Historical Note

The Woman in the Green Dress is a work of fiction; however, in some cases fact has fed fiction.

Fact: Baron Charles von Hügel (1795–1870), Austrian noble, army officer, botanist, and explorer, visited New Holland between November 1833 and October 1834 in an attempt to recover from a broken heart. (Truly!) In 1848, he aided Prince Metternich in escaping Vienna during the March Revolution and went on to become a diplomat. His New Holland notebooks were acquired by the Mitchell Library in Australia in 1932 for the princely sum of nine pounds. In 1994, they were translated into English and edited by Dymphna Clark. (Baron Charles von Hügel, *New Holland Journal*, translated and edited by Dymphna Clark, MUP, 1990.)

Johann Menge (1788–1852), a linguist and geologist, was born in Germany and employed by the South Australian Mining Company. Various sources credit him with the discovery of the first opal in Australia in 1850, but what became of it is not known. It wasn't until the International Exhibition in London in 1873 that the world became aware of the quality of Australian opals.

Wollombi Road, in the Hunter Valley, New South Wales, runs parallel with Mogo Creek from St. Albans, over the Common, to Bucketty. This area is part of the traditional country of the Darkinjung people, who are the custodians of Mount Yengo. Their land is bounded by the Hawkesbury and Hunter Rivers, the Pacific Ocean at Wyong, and the Wollemi peaks in the west. It has been estimated that in 1788 there was a population of five thousand Darkinjung people, but they were severely impacted by smallpox epidemics, and settlement and settler killings. By the 1850s, few survived, and Mogo Creek was one of the last places the Darkinjung people lived before they were taken from their traditional lands to a reserve near Lower Portland on the Colo River.

The Settlers Arms in St. Albans is still open for business (I can recommend their chicken pies!), and an inn certainly operated there in 1853; however, there seems to be some confusion as to when the name was first adopted. For consistency, I have used the name Settlers Arms in both timelines.

In the latter part of the nineteenth century, two women, Tost and Rohu, opened a shop in George Street. An advertisement claims they sold "all kinds of taxidermical work" and held "the largest stock of genuine native implements and curiosities and possum, native bear, kangaroo, and wallaby skins made up into carriage and travelling rugs."

The rest is fiction.

Stefan and Della, Bert, Fleur, and Kip are all figments of my imagination. They did not exist, nor did the Curio Shop of Wonders or Cordelia Atterton. A line in the introduction to Dymphna Clark's book sparked this story. She stated that von Hügel's New Holland notebook was written in the hand of an amanuensis. In a flight of fancy, I dreamed up Stefan von Richter, Baron von Hügel's (fictional) amanuensis, and the story of *The Woman in the Green Dress*.

Acknowledgments

I would like to acknowledge the Darkinjung and Eora people as the Traditional Owners of the land on which I live, work, play, and have set this story, and pay my respects to Elders both past and present.

Thanks are due, as always, to so many people: my publisher, Jo Mackay, and the fabulous HQ team, Annabel Blay and Alex Craig, for your never-ending patience and insightful editing, and Natika Palka and the wonderful HarperCollins sales team who take my stories into the world. And in the US my thanks to Amanda Bostic, Julie Monroe, and everyone on the Thomas Nelson Fiction team. It is a pleasure and privilege to work with you all.

As always my love and thanks to my long-suffering friends who walk every step of the way with me, especially Carl Hoipo, historian extraordinaire, for introducing me to Baron von Hügel, to Bert for the loan of his glorious name, and to Chief Researcher #1, Charles, who continues to hold the title of the Best Plot Wrangler in the business.

And finally, my loyal and enthusiastic readers. Thank you. Without you my stories are nothing. I hope you enjoyed *The Woman in the Green Dress*.

About the Author

Tea Cooper is an established Australian author of historical fiction. In a past life she was a teacher, a journalist, and a farmer. These days she haunts museums and indulges her passion for storytelling. She is the bestselling author of several novels, including *The Horse Thief*, *The Cedar Cutter*, *The Currency Lass*, and *The Naturalist's Daughter*.

www.teacooperauthor.com